Foxy Roxy

ALSO BY NANCY MARTIN

Foxy Roxy

Nancy Martin

Minotaur Books ≈ New York

FOXY ROXY. Copyright © 2010 by Nancy Martin.
All rights reserved. Printed in the United States of America.
For information, address St. Martin's Press,
175 Fifth Avenue, New York, N.Y. 10010.

www.minotaurbooks.com

Design by Kathryn Parise

THE LIBRARY OF CONGRESS HAS CATALOGED THE HARDCOVER EDITION AS FOLLOWS:

Martin, Nancy, 1953–
    Our lady of immaculate deception / Nancy Martin.—1st ed.
       p. cm.
    ISBN 978-0-312-57372-0
    1. Single mothers—Fiction. 2. Mafia—Fiction. 3. Salvage (waste, etc.)—Fiction.
4. Billionaires—Crimes against—Fiction. 5. Rich people—Fiction. 6. Art thefts—
Fiction. 7. Pittsburgh (Pa.)—Fiction. I. Title.
    PS3563.A7267O87 2010
    813'.54—dc22

                                                                      2009041127

ISBN 978-0-312-67318-5 (trade paperback)

Previously published under the title *Our Lady of Immaculate Deception*

First Minotaur Books Paperback Edition: January 2011

10 9 8 7 6 5 4 3 2 1

Dedicated to Robert Jeffrey Christopher

❧ Acknowledgments ❧

The author wishes to express appreciation and much affection to:

My blog sisters Kathy Sweeney, Sarah Strohmeyer, Harley Jane Kozak, Elaine Viets, Michele Martinez, and Lisa Daily. Come see us at www. thelipstickchronicles.typepad.com.

Mary Alice Gorman and Richard Goldman of the Mystery Lovers Bookshop, who are championship booksellers, but Mary Alice really helped me out in a pinch this time.

Nancie Hays, the Gun Tart. Watch out for the rattlesnakes, babycakes.

The rest of the Six get a special shout-out:
    Kathleen George
    Heather Terrell

✳ Acknowledgments ✳

Kathryn Miller-Haines
Rebecca Drake
Lila Shaara

Kelly Harms, where are you now? You found Roxy first!

Heidi Lawrence, who provided inspiration as well as a beautiful new kitchen.

Meg Ruley and the team at the Jane Rotrosen are the best, no kidding, and they're plenty fizzy, too.

I'm new to Team Minotaur, but everybody has made me feel so welcome. Thank you Kelley Ragland, Matt Martz, Sarah Melnyk, Matthew Shear, Tara Cibelli, and cousin Andy Martin.

And many thanks to many more who read, offered expert info or otherwise held my hand, including: Sarah Martin, Jeff Martin, Ramona Long, Paula Matter, Lee Lofland, Cynthia D'Alba, and my Sisters in Crime. I am grateful to you all.

Foxy Roxy

❧ 1 ❧

The only witness to the arson was a one-armed marble statue of a naked man with ivy growing where his fig leaf should have been.

Julius Hyde, the sixty-something heir to a massive Pittsburgh steel for-tune, had been pouring oysters down the throat of his twenty-year-old manicurist when his wife came home unexpectedly from an Arizona spa. Seeing her husband attend to his pubescent mistress while blowing cigar smoke all over the silk Scalamandré draperies pushed Mrs. Hyde to the brink of insanity. So said the newspapers.

But it was the sight of the couple's Great Dane, Samson, wantonly sprawled beneath the table so the manicurist could rub his belly with her bare toes that truly pushed Mrs. Hyde over the edge.

She set fire to the house using a Bic lighter and an airline bottle of cognac.

The house and contents were insured for eighty-five million dollars.

Weeks later, when the police and insurance company gave up their investigation and the Channel 4 helicopter quit hovering over the estate, the neighbors began to complain that the burned-out house was a safety hazard.

That's when the scavengers showed up.

On the evening of October 13, Roxy Abruzzo drove the Monster Truck between the stone gates of the Hyde estate, downshifting and roaring up the cobblestone driveway to the remains of the Norman-style mansion.

What had once looked like a grand French castle was now little more than a ruined hulk. Tattered streams of yellow caution tape left by the fire department fluttered from the shell like the forgotten decorations of a frat party busted by the cops. A blackened swag of wisteria hung from the portico's crumbled stone arch.

In a city full of grand houses built by millionaire industrialists, this one had been spectacular in its day. Now, it was sad to see it looking so forlorn.

"On the other hand," Roxy said aloud, "somebody ought to make a buck out of this."

Happily, she drove under the portico to the back of the house.

Beside the garage, sitting on the dented remains of an overturned washing machine, was her right-hand man, "Nooch" Santonucci. On his lap, he protectively clutched the Dunkin' Donuts box she'd given him that morning. The box was empty. He was licking the last memory of frosting from his thumb.

Nooch had weighed three hundred pounds back when he played defensive tackle in high school, and he'd gained another fifty since then— all muscle, no additional brain cells. Now he could bench-press a beer truck although he likely couldn't read the words painted on it—both qualities that made Nooch the ideal employee for Roxy. All by himself he could carry a marble mantelpiece out of an old house, but ten minutes later he'd forget where he'd put it.

Which was useful.

"Where you been?" he asked before she shut off the engine. "I been waiting an hour."

"Easy, big guy. I stopped to pick up some dinner."

Nooch sat up like a hungry bear catching wind of a picnic basket. "From the restaurant?"

Roxy waved a foil packet out the truck window. "Flynn put out rigs and pigs for the staff meal. He sent some just for you. Look, I even brought you a fork."

Truth be told, Roxy was so broke she had resorted to pilfering a hearty portion of rigatoni and sausage from the steam table where the kitchen staff at Rizza's ate before their evening shift. Flynn, the upscale restaurant's chef, had appeared out of nowhere and caught her slipping out the back door.

"Are you stealing food again?" he had demanded, grabbing the hood of her sweatshirt like he was pulling a troublesome puppy out of mischief. "Damn it, Roxy, you've been busting my balls since high school. What am I going to have to do? Beat your butt?"

"Kinky," she'd said, knowing leftovers would be going to the homeless shelter in a couple hours, anyway. "But I don't have that kind of time right now, sorry." She wriggled out of her top layer of sweatshirts and escaped.

Nooch noticed her wardrobe change. "Where's your shirt? Were you doing something with Flynn you shouldn't be?" His big ears turned pink at the possibilities. "I wish you two'd just get married," he said, "now that he's back in town."

"You gotta be kidding. Patrick Flynn is the last— Oh, the hell with it. Why am I arguing with you?"

"And you said you'd stop cussing," Nooch said. "So stop."

Beside her in the truck, Roxy's brindle pit bull, Rooney, perched on the passenger seat with his forepaws braced on the dashboard. Rendered blind in one eye long before Roxy rescued him from the pound, Rooney often missed easy targets. But he must have caught a note of Nooch's voice, because the dog suddenly gave a strangled howl before launching into hysterical barks. His slaver spattered the windshield.

Roxy grabbed his collar and hauled the dog off the dashboard. "Save your energy, fella. By now you know Nooch doesn't taste so good."

Rooney swung his big head around to lap her hand lovingly.

Giving Rooney a final pat, Roxy rolled up her window to about four inches and climbed out of the truck. She grabbed a pry bar from under the seat and slammed the door shut before the dog could scramble out. She put the takeout container on the hood of the truck.

"Can't I have it now?" Nooch asked, crestfallen.

"After," she said. "We've got work to do."

"It's all done! See?"

"You're not finished till I say you're finished."

"All right, all right." Nooch got to his feet. "Look," he said, continuing the conversation they'd broken off many hours ago. "I been thinking about what you said. About how I should get some character witnesses for my probation hearing."

"You can't ask your grandmothers. They don't count."

"I don't think either one'd have anything nice to say anyways. But Father Mike might."

Nooch didn't often get ideas all by himself. But she said, "Father Mike's not a good choice. He's not a priest anymore, for one thing." Roxy hated to dislodge Nooch's good opinion of his former boxing coach. "Besides, he's your cousin somehow, right? You need somebody who's not related to you. Also who isn't a felon, doesn't carry a gun, and doesn't work for my uncle Carmine."

Nooch frowned. "That's just about everybody I know."

"Present company excepted."

"Huh?" His favorite word.

"Never mind. We just have to expand your circle of friends."

He scrunched his meaty face in confusion. "How we gonna expand in a week?"

Getting Nooch off probation was one of Roxy's priorities at the moment. For ten years, since the day he'd beaten Eugene Poskovich to a bloody pulp, Nooch had stuck to the letter of the law—including no associating with known criminals, which was harder in their neighborhood than others. And Nooch had kept a steady job, because Roxy hired him to keep the big oaf out of trouble. She'd pretty much stayed out of trouble herself on his behalf, too. But life was complicated and temptations popped up every day. Getting Nooch off probation would make a hell of lot of things easier for both of them.

Roxy pointed the pry bar at his misshapen nose. "You been behaving yourself for ten years now, right?"

"I guess so." He must have thought of another small incident they'd managed to keep quiet, because he added, "Nobody really needs a spleen."

"Right. Well, what matters is you've done what the judge told you to do. So now you're due. Lemme take care of this hearing, okay?"

"But what about character witnesses?"

Sometimes there was no arguing with Nooch. He was an adult in most respects, except maybe his IQ, which was part of the reason the judge had ordered the long probation. But he could recite every word of the *Lord of the Rings* movies, so Roxy knew he was smart enough to get along in the world. He collected Spiderman comics the way other men kept porn, so he was harmless. No real threat to society. Though he could be relentlessly exasperating.

Roxy said, "I'll take care of the character witnesses."

Nooch's expression went from misery to relief in a heartbeat. "Thanks, Rox."

Roxy took a quick inventory of the day's haul. Lined up in front of the garage leaned a pewter chandelier and the two halves of a soapstone fireplace decorated with twin griffins. About a hundred spindles from the main staircase sat in tidy piles, tied with twine.

"See? I got it all done," Nooch said.

The trick to successfully scavenging architectural remnants was to let

Nooch do the heavy lifting while she stayed on the move. Roxy best spent her time poking into decrepit houses, befriending little old ladies and lonely old men. She had a list of demolition guys she called every week and a network of antique pickers who kept her in the loop. Over the years, she'd learned to drop her pride around know-it-all yuppies who wanted to get rid of the junk that cluttered up the homes they planned to renovate into *Architectural Digest* splendor. Acquiring the good stuff and selling it off before somebody with better judgment stepped in to screw up the deal—that was Roxy's gift. Lately, though, she'd been a little down on her luck.

"Ready to go now?" Nooch asked. "I'm hungry."

She'd been looking up at the ruined house speculatively. "Let's take one last look around."

"Why?"

"Why not? Tomorrow they're going to blow this place up. Let's see if somebody forgot anything."

"I hate it when you get this way."

"What way?"

"Sneaky."

"You want a paycheck this week or not?" Roxy could barely afford gasoline for the Monster Truck, let alone Nooch's pathetic take-home pay. They needed one more score. "C'mon."

Grumbling, he followed her around the house, past a parking area that was jammed with expensive cars.

Roxy took a look at the lineup. "What is this? The Mercedes dealership needs some extra storage?"

"Must be a convention," Nooch said, coming up with a line he'd heard before.

One car sported a vanity plate that read, BOOM. Probably the property of the demolition team, Roxy decided. And the demo business must be good if the owner could buy himself a new Mercedes.

She jogged up the back steps of the burned-out house. Nooch tagged along like an obedient dog. Inside the kitchen, they greeted a pair of surly dimwits who paused in their labor to remove a six-burner Aga stove. The Delaney brothers, who sometimes did a little dirty work for Roxy's uncle Carmine. If Roxy's moral compass occasionally pointed slightly in the wrong direction, these two had broken the needle. The aroma of marijuana clung to them in an almost visible smog.

The younger Delaney had his hair cut in a mullet and a herpes sore on his lip. He took one look at Roxy and joked, "Didn't I see you wrapped around a pole at the Pink Pony on Friday night?"

"Hey," Nooch said. "Don't talk like that."

"Yeah, very funny," Roxy added. "I should knock your teeth out, but you don't have any to spare."

"What's that supposed to mean?"

"Zip it, Jimmy." Vincent, the more sourpuss Delaney—and the one who didn't wear his glasses—must have decided Roxy was a security employee, because he pulled his salvage authorization paper from a hip pocket and handed it over to her.

She took a look—it never hurt to let people think she was someone to fear. The paper looked like the same one she had in her own pocket—signed by the honcho handling the disbursement of anything salvageable from the house. Handing it back, Roxy said, "What else have you lifted out of this place, Vincent? Besides what's on your list?"

"Nuthin', I swear."

Roxy cocked an eyebrow. "You sure? I've got a sick grandmother who says otherwise."

He understood the sick-grandmother code and dug a twenty out of his pocket. "That's all I got on me. We got some of the copper last week—a few downspouts, that's all. Somebody else got the rest of it, though. You know how sneaky the druggies can be."

The younger Delaney had chosen that moment to light up the remains of a smelly joint, but he dropped it and tried to snatch back the twenty. "Hey, that's Roxy Abruzzo, dude, not the city code guy. What the hell are you doing?"

With a smile for both of them, Roxy pocketed the bribe. "I won't tell a soul about the pipes. They're yours as far as I'm concerned."

"Bitch."

"You're a discerning judge of character, Jimmy. Look, if you two losers want to get out of here alive, you better hurry up with that stove. The demolition guys are supposed to blow this place up tomorrow. They're planting charges right now."

Jimmy responded to Roxy's show of concern for her fellow man with a one-fingered salute.

She laughed and left the Delaneys to their herbal refreshment. With their twenty bucks in her pocket for some gasoline and maybe a pitcher of beer later, she climbed over the rubble in the doorway and headed into the formal rooms of the ruined house.

In the foyer, the wooden floors were warped from a zillion gallons of water pumped in by the fire department. Likewise, the horsehair plaster had cracked and crashed down from the walls. Crunching it underfoot, Roxy led Nooch past the skeleton of the main staircase. Once the grand stairs had wound upward to the upper floors with a handsome chandelier lighting the woodwork, but now, evening sunlight slanted down from the open sky above. A blue jay swooped through the foyer.

Upstairs, they could hear voices calling back and forth—probably the demolition team figuring where to plant their charges. One of them revved up a power saw. Roxy decided to skip meeting them. Guys with dynamite always had a weird sense of humor.

The billiards room was a disaster site—nothing left except the cracked remains of the slate of the pool table.

The long dining room had two pairs of French doors at one end. Both hung off their hinges, not worth saving. The parquet floor was in bad shape—also from the fire hoses. Somebody had ripped out the coffered ceiling before Roxy had a chance to bid on the job, which was too bad. She'd been lucky to get the soapstone fireplace, though. Chances were she could sell it for a tidy sum to a developer building McMansions in the suburbs.

Nooch stopped in the doorway of the dining room and blinked up at the remaining plaster squares of the ceiling. Painted cherubs floated there, trailing garlands of flowers.

Nooch sighed. "It sure is pretty."

There was no sense agonizing over the painting—done by Joseph Laurencia at the turn of the century, if Roxy was any judge. Lots of these old mansions were decorated with fancy murals that would crumble when the house fell down, so she considered them a waste of paint.

She hefted her pry bar, itchy to find one last thing of value. "Very nice. But we can't scrape it off the ceiling, so I'm not going to lose any sleep over it. Let's have a look outside."

"Huh?"

"Just come on, will you?"

Roxy headed across the dining room floor, then pushed through the broken French doors to the terrace.

A broken patio table with a set of wrought-iron chairs stood on the flagstones. The scorched remains of the garden curved away from the house, and a line of tree skeletons framed the swimming pool. The water in the pool was green already, and some blackened leaves floated on the surface in a skim of greasy soot.

Pissing into the pool was Julius Hyde himself, the man of the ruined house. At Roxy's approach, the billionaire turned his head and grinned around the stub of a cigar.

She said, "You've still got a pretty good arc, Julius. Impressive for a man your age."

"Roxy Abruzzo. Still a wiseass." He took his time tucking himself back into his trousers. "Who are you trying to hoodwink today?"

"Not you, that's for sure."

"Don't lie to me, girl. I know a con artist when I see one." He zipped up. "Still shooting pool for lunch money? And reading all those library books?"

Roxy shrugged. "Now and then."

"I hope you return a few of them. The books, that is. I don't mind losing the lunch money. You played with admirable finesse. Either that or you cheated. And if I didn't notice at the time, you deserved your winnings."

Roxy had met Julius last spring when he wanted to modernize the old carriage house into a garage. The house had been beautiful back then. She'd taken a few pieces of the carriage house, and he'd offered her a drink on his patio while he wrote her a check. They'd shared a couple of laughs after that and played a few games in which Roxy showed no mercy. She cleaned his pool table and his wallet, but Roxy had liked the guy. Admired his tendency to make up rules as he went along. She appreciated that he didn't treat her like some kind of French housemaid when he'd made a pass at her. And he'd taken her rejection graciously.

Too bad his pool table had burned up. She could have won a few more extra bucks from him.

He said, "I see you're still babysitting that moron."

She should have hidden her tightened fists behind her back. "At least he knows when to keep his pants zipped."

Julius shrugged. "An underrated virtue."

Without his clothes, Julius Hyde might look like one of those half-animal men that played the flute at orgies—heavy in the thighs and hairy-chested. Even now, curly white hair bristled at the open collar of his crisp pink shirt. Roxy wondered if his legs were all woolly under his trousers—although she wasn't curious enough to find out. He wore his white hair long, combed back from his forehead and waved over his shirt collar. He looked like a rich man who enjoyed his pleasures.

"Damn shame, isn't it?" He cast a glance up at the burned remains of the house. "I'm sorry the old place ended up like this."

"The insurance company will make you feel better."

"My mother may feel better," he corrected. "Depending on what the insurance company decides. Funny, isn't it? A man like me still living in my mama's house?"

The question sounded like one of those rhetorical things men consider when they're feeling blue. But Roxy knew Julius had plenty of consolation prizes. He'd grown up in a filthy rich family, and when his father died he'd inherited enough dough to run a small country. When his old lady finally kicked, he'd inherit even more. He had dabbled in business, but gave it up to a younger brother when he'd lost interest in empire building and started making lousy friends and a few fierce enemies instead. He'd married a few times, but eventually stopped caring what anybody thought and did as he pleased. Roxy figured he was rich enough to get away with anything. His latest girlfriend made him a laughingstock in the city, but Julius hadn't cared.

Until now, maybe.

Julius took a slim silver flask from the pocket of his trousers and unscrewed the cap. He had a nostalgic look in his eye as he glanced around the grounds. "I grew up here, you know. Before they sent me off to school. There's a bomb shelter under that piece of lawn over there. A real bunker. I could have kept a girlfriend down there and nobody would have known. My wife Monica would never have fired up her curtains."

"That's creepy, Julius. Bad enough you have a girlfriend young enough to be your grandkid, but locking her in a bunker? Too freaky for me, and that's saying a lot."

He laughed shortly and removed his cigar to sip from the flask. "Do you have family, Roxy?"

"A daughter."

"Well, someday she might drive you to socially inappropriate behavior."

"It doesn't take my kid to do that."

Another laugh. "No regrets?"

"Not yet."

"Good for you." There was something else glimmering in his eyes, though. Sadness? Or maybe he's nipping at the flask for courage, Roxy thought. To her, Julius suddenly looked a little spooked.

"You feeling some regrets, Julius?"

"It's too late for that." He caught her looking curious and grinned. "What are you doing here, though, young lady? Picking at the bones like the rest of the vultures? Why aren't you out for dinner with a nice young man?"

"I'm still doing an honest day's work, that's why."

"Not so honest sometimes," he observed, then checked his watch as if he had an appointment. "I suppose that's why I like you. There's larceny in your soul. I'll leave you to your job. Time for me to toddle off."

With more sincerity than she usually felt, Roxy said, "Take care of yourself, Julius."

"That's what I do best." He straightened his shoulders, summoned his self-respect, and departed.

Roxy watched him swagger around the house, but shook herself of the notion that maybe she should go after him.

"He okay?" Nooch asked.

"He'll be fine. Amazing how a billion dollars can brighten your day. C'mon, let's take a look around. I need to pay my kid's school fees by next week or the nuns kick her out."

She led Nooch the opposite way—around the terrace and past a row of burned hydrangeas.

On a previous visit, Roxy had found a shopping cart and some ragged blankets in the remains of the pergola at the end of the pool—evidence that homeless people had moved in after the fire. But today the shopping cart was gone. Left behind was a black barrel full of ashes. The scavengers had probably burned the plastic coating off copper wire here. They'd left nothing of value.

Roxy pushed past the bushes.

A marble statue stood in the flower bed behind the pool, half hidden by the collapsed pergola. A naked man, maybe a gladiator, judging by his stance. Forgotten, he stared nobly into the distance, as if watching his troops march off to victory. A tangle of ivy swarmed up his muscular leg, evidence that he wasn't marching anywhere anytime soon.

"Whoa." Nooch stopped short behind her. "Who's the dude?"

"Some hero, I guess."

He must have been holding a sword or a javelin at one time, but now his whole right arm was gone. The back of his head and most of his helmet were missing, too, but that didn't matter much. Judging by the way he jutted his jaw and curled his lip, he had an ego bigger than his dick.

But Roxy could see he was special. A kind of energy coiled beneath the surface of his marble skin. He was very old, she guessed. And the owners of the house had forgotten about him. Otherwise, why was he still standing here? The night before demolition? A final ray of sunlight slipped through the tree branches overhead and danced along the curve of his magnificent shoulder.

With her pry bar, Roxy tore away some of the ivy.

"What are you doing?" Nooch asked. "You don't want that, do you?"

"I sure do."

"Why? It's broken. You always say condition, condition, condition."

"Not in this case."

She slipped the blade of the bar beneath the base of the statue. Crusty with decay, the pedestal flaked a few crumbs, and then a splinter of marble broke loose and skittered down into the weeds. The statue rocked gently above her.

Roxy steadied him with a hand on his knee. "Easy, big boy."

"Are we supposed to be here?" Nooch glanced over his shoulder in the direction Julius had gone. "Aren't we just supposed to take the stuff we already got?"

"How am I supposed to pay my kid's tuition bills if I don't show a little creativity? Besides, they're blowing up the house tomorrow, right? So whatever's left behind is going to get destroyed. It's free for the picking."

"What if Mr. Hyde comes back?"

"Just go get the handcart."

"But—"

"Go!"

With a sigh, Nooch lumbered off to do as he was told, and Roxy patted the statue's bare butt. "No worries, fella. I'm going to find you a nice new home."

❧ 2 ❧

Henry Paxton, attorney-at-law, newly divorced at thirty-five, lived quietly in the former chauffeur's apartment of Hilltop, the bucolic Pennsylvania estate thirty miles outside of Pittsburgh. The estate had been built by a Pittsburgh steel magnate who died richer than anyone except maybe John Rockefeller. Since then, subsequent Hydes had summered at Hilltop, raised horses, apples, and Charolais cattle in a gentlemanly way, leaving the dirtying of hands to their employees while they partook of the fruits of the estate. They had turned the land around Hilltop into a park the likes of which Capability Brown would have wept over.

For Henry, it was like living in a Merchant-Ivory movie. And while his former fraternity brothers were still sitting in sports bars watching arena football and scoring with pretty waitresses who needed orthodontia, he had found real luxury. And he loved it.

He stayed on the estate thanks to the largesse of his only client, Dorothy Richardson-Hyde, the ninety-two-year-old matriarch of the Hyde family. Conveniently for Henry, Dorothy spent most of her time in a coma in a nursing home, regaining consciousness only now and then to assure her family that the well-being of Hilltop should be entrusted to her law-yer, Henry Paxton, Esq., who didn't mind dirtying his hands.

The rest of the family resented the arrangement, though, and Henry frequently uncovered evidence of their Machiavellian plots to get him kicked off the premises.

But so far, he'd hung on.

On this Friday evening in October, he had dressed himself for a gala at the nearby country club. Many members brought along their daugh-ters for such evenings—young women who had long, suntanned legs and seemed to be studying art history at European graduate schools. None of the young ladies hung out in sports bars. They were all beautiful, and they were gracious—if a little unimaginative—when bestowing their sex-ual favors. But it was their parents whose faces lit up when Henry arrived in his evening clothes—a young, eligible, and presumably successful young man who would provide well-behaved grandchildren and vote Republican when the time was right. For the moment, Henry was very popular at the country club.

Upon returning home late that night, he stripped off his dinner jacket. As he unfastened the cuffs on his crisp shirt sleeves, he almost heard the voice of his ex-wife, Pamela.

"You look smooth, Henry."

He smiled at his reflection. Perhaps the compliment hadn't been given with sincerity at the time—Pamela had decided to leave him after a series of mistakes including a drunken kiss he'd shared with her best friend, Nikki Viets—but Henry appreciated the word. Smooth. If anything, he endeavored to be smooth in everything he did. Even the less than savory duties.

The phone rang, interrupting the admiration of his reflection.

By habit, he checked the caller ID.

Fair Weather Village. The nursing home where his benefactress currently resided.

Henry winced.

For years, he had braced himself for this phone call. Eventually, Dorothy was going to slip gently into that good night, and the estate would pass into the hands of her moneygrubbing heirs. When that happened, Henry would be tossed out of his happy home. Of course, even if other plans failed to project him into the financial stratosphere, his legal fee for the estate work was going to be enough to buy himself a beach condo in the Caribbean as well as a ski house in Vail—perhaps with one of the long-legged art history students in tow by then—but Henry would be sorry to leave Hilltop.

With regret, he thumbed Tiger Woods off the plasma TV, then sat down in an armchair and picked up the phone. He adjusted his voice to sound both somber and crisply efficient. "Henry Paxton."

"Paxton? You need to get your ass over here to Fair Weather."

He recognized the foghorn bellow of that awful woman in charge of Dorothy's care. One-handed, he opened a fresh can of cashews. "Sharlane? What's going on?"

"Mrs. Hyde's awake, that's what's goin' on. And she wants you here on the double."

"Is she all right?"

"Of course she's not all right! She's been in a coma!"

"Is she conscious?" Henry asked.

"How else would she be saying she wants to see you?"

Henry had noticed that Dorothy's coma seemed to come and go depending on what channel the television in her room was tuned to. In the back of his mind lurked the suspicion that Dorothy wasn't comatose at all, just biding her time while forming more Byzantine plans.

"Has she been listening to Fox News as I requested, Sharlane?"

A short silence, then an exasperated sigh. "I can stand only so much of that bullshit. And I didn't want her hearing any local news either, you know? First the fire at her house, and now her son. We heard about Mr. Julius just an hour ago. Did you?"

"Yes."

"Damn shame him dying before his mama."

"Yes, a tragedy."

Henry kept his voice pitched professionally. Even the sudden death of Julius Hyde should not rock the estate's attorney.

"I sure won't miss him sneaking around here," Sharlane said. "But there's no sense her learning about her son getting shot if she can't do nothing about it. So I changed over to SOAPnet."

"You probably did the right thing, Sharlane."

"Thank you." Then Sharlane's defensive shield snapped back into place. "You get yourself over here pronto, slick. You know how impatient she is."

Henry did indeed. He drove to the nursing home in record time and found Dorothy Hyde sitting up in the bed in her private room. Fresh flowers stood on a table, as Henry had ordered. Civilities must be observed. An antique rug lay on the linoleum floor beside the defibrillator. Keeping his client alive as well as happy was Henry's priority.

And tonight, he hoped the news of her son's demise would not necessitate the use of the defibrillator.

"I want champagne," she said as soon as she saw him in his evening clothes. "That silly nurse thinks it will interfere with my medications. Why does she imagine I'm asking for some, if not to interfere with all these damn medications?"

"Mrs. Hyde, it's a pleasure to see you looking so well."

The old woman's arthritis-deformed hand traveled instinctively to her hair, which was snow white and flowed around the shoulders of her embroidered nightgown. "You're a silver-tongued devil, Henry. All my granddaughters say so. You're not trying to marry any of them, are you?"

Of course Henry had thought of marrying into the Hyde family, but all of Dorothy's anorexic granddaughters were obsessed with shopping or obscure subjects that bored him silly. None of them could possibly be worth the thirty million that came along with her. No, Henry had better plans in mind.

He placed the day's *Wall Street Journal* on Dorothy Hyde's bedside table. Then he set his briefcase on the edge of her bed and popped the latches. "I didn't bring champagne. Considering the season, I thought you might prefer a nice Pinot Noir."

He drew the bottle from the case and showed her the label. His selection had come from her very own cellar, which Henry kept fully stocked and rotated to avoid any wine aging past its prime. It was one of many responsibilities he took very seriously.

Dorothy wore a set of gold-rimmed glasses on a chain around her neck, and she lifted the lenses to her eyes to read the label.

"Chilean! Have you been speculating on my behalf again, Henry?" She tapped the bottle with one long, gnarled finger. "This is the primary reason I keep you on retainer, you know. Your good taste in wine."

"Thank you, Mrs. Hyde. May I pour?"

She handed him a plastic cup from the bedside table and sat back against her pillows to watch as he managed the cork. "What have I missed?" she asked. "Everybody here is tippy-toeing around like somebody died. Are you going to break the bad news, or do I have to hire myself another attorney?"

"Can't we just be happy you're so alert?" Henry asked.

He found himself surprisingly pleased, in fact, to see Dorothy's pert face and button blue eyes glaring at him with such vitality. She had aristocratic features—a long nose and pointed chin carved out of alabaster skin—but the sharpness of her gaze was anything but refined. And several weeks of deep sleep seemed to have invigorated her.

"Who's gone?" she demanded. "One of my daughters? It's Patricia, isn't it? She drinks too much. I told her time and time again—"

"It's not Patricia."

"Who, then?"

Henry passed the wine into Dorothy's hand, careful to support it until he was sure her grip was strong enough to hold the cup. "I'm sorry to tell you, Mrs. Hyde, that Julius has passed away."

"Julius! Finally got himself shot by a jealous husband, did he?" Her voice remained gruff, but Dorothy suddenly appeared to need a sip of wine. She swallowed carefully, then rested her head against the pillow and looked at the ceiling. "He was a sweet boy, my Julius. In his middle years, I thought he might enjoy collecting something or running the family foundation. But, no."

Julius's only interest in the family foundation, Henry suspected, had been how quickly it might be dismantled upon his mother's death.

"And then he started marrying over and over. That was the beginning of the end for him. The start of his debaucheries. Who was the lucky wife when the music stopped? Who gets a whopping share of my assets?"

"Monica."

"Oh, yes. The philanthropy queen. She was trying to polish up his image, last I heard, by being charitable with my money." Dorothy sat straight again. "Has he been buried yet? There was no awful press, was there?"

Henry cleared his throat. "We'll have little control over that, I'm sorry to say. The circumstances—"

"Good heavens, he didn't really get himself shot, did he?"

"He did," Henry replied solemnly. "It happened earlier this evening. Just a few hours ago. Someone shot him, and he died instantly. He didn't suffer, Mrs. Hyde."

It took a moment for Dorothy to absorb that information. Then she pierced Henry with those rheumy but intelligent blue eyes. "Were his brothers both accounted for at the time?"

"I don't know if either of your younger sons were even in town tonight. They're often away on—well, business."

"My business," Dorothy said. "What about the police investigation?"

"It won't be pretty. Of late, there's been an unfortunate amount of media attention focused on Julius's personal life. But it will die down. It's football season, you know. The Steelers have a shot at the playoffs."

"Where did it happen?"

Gently, Henry said, "Julius was shot on the grounds of your Pittsburgh home. And there's more bad news where the house is concerned, I'm afraid. A few weeks ago, it was destroyed by fire."

"A fire!" Dorothy immediately forgot about her son's demise. Aghast, she cried, "You say it was destroyed?"

"Essentially, yes. Julius's attorneys have been handling the insurance issues and so forth. The property will probably be sold to one of the nearby universities for a campus expansion. I thought you'd find that a suitable use for the land, so I didn't object to the plan."

She waved off the subject with one hand. "The house was a hideous pile of bricks. It's the contents that matter! What about the paintings? They're gone? The Van Gogh? The Pollock?"

Henry concealed a smile, pleased to have anticipated Dorothy's certain interest in the most valuable works of art. "The Van Gogh was rescued with minimal damage and it can be restored. Monica had the presence of mind to carry it out of the fire herself. It's with a gentleman in New York right now. Monica directed the firefighters to rescue all the important pieces. The Pollock, I understand, was moved to Julius's home in Palm Beach last year. Monica's idea, too."

Dorothy snorted. "That Monica still fancies herself an expert in art, doesn't she? After a few years of working as some curator's secretary? Well, the Pollock doesn't belong in Florida, for God's sake. Any fool can see that."

Henry decided not to go into the details of Monica's current situation. Not yet. He said, "A few lesser paintings were saved, and some glass. Unfortunately, quite a few pieces of furniture were lost, along with rugs, a pair of Audubon prints, and a small watercolor of boats, artist unknown."

"The so-called artist was my father. It had sentimental value, nothing more. And the furniture was insured. I never cared much about furniture.

At least the Van Gogh and Pollock are safe." Dorothy shot another sharp glance up at Henry. "I never liked the Pollock much, but it was a good investment. On my death, it's supposed to go to the Metropolitan. It's my farewell gesture to the art world. You'll remember that, Henry?"

"Of course, Mrs. Hyde."

"I never liked the Metropolitan. Too political." She folded her slender hands on her lap, fingers touching—her usual gesture before getting down to business. "I suppose you'd better file an injunction or whatever you call it. Stop the distribution of Julius's will, please, Henry. I don't want anyone inside or outside the family poking their noses into that document until I have a grasp of the situation. Heaven only knows what nonsense Julius promised the various women in his life. His ego got the better of him in the last few years, didn't it?"

It was Henry's private opinion that Julius suffered from the Prince Charles syndrome—waiting for his mother to kick the bucket so he could live his life. Julius had lost sight of his priorities during the waiting game. But he said, "I'll take care of the injunction immediately."

"Good. And get me a copy of his will from his lawyers, will you?"

"That might be tricky."

"Tricky is what you're good at, Henry. Surely you play golf with the right person?"

"Well . . ."

"Excellent. Now, what about my Achilles?"

Henry hesitated. "Your . . . ?"

"My statue. We found it in Greece fifty—no, sixty years ago. My husband was an amateur archaeologist, you know. Well, he was drinking gin on the terrace of our Greek getaway place while locals dug us a new well in the backyard. And guess what the diggers uncovered?" She smiled at the memory. "We had quite a time getting it out of the country. I borrowed my cousin's yacht, but never mind that now. Where is it?"

"Your statue," Henry said.

"Yes, damn it, the marble sculpture of Achilles. It was in the garden.

None of my offspring would appreciate him, so I parked him out by the pool where they wouldn't take any notice. If I'd placed him on a plinth under some fancy lights, they'd have figured out he was priceless. So that's why he's been standing in the garden all these years—right under their silly noses."

"A statue by the pool," Henry said. "How clever of you, Mrs. Hyde."

"Except my granddaughter Arden, of course. She'd have figured it out. Which is why I began sending her all over the world when she was a girl. Got her a passport when she was twelve, and she never looked back. It was a good excuse to get her away from her mother, too, the pill popper." Dorothy skewered him with a look that had certainly caused many an investment adviser to squirm. "You're keeping tabs on all my valuables, aren't you, Henry?"

"I don't believe I've ever seen a statue noted on any of your lists, Mrs.—"

"For heaven's sake, do I need to tell you every damn detail?"

"No, but—"

"It's an antiquity, Henry! Probably worth fifty million dollars by now. That is, unless the Greeks start yammering about his return like he's one of the Elgin Marbles. He's my favorite piece in the whole collection. I want to know where he is."

"I'll look into it immediately."

"Good," said Dorothy. "Because I can find another lawyer, Henry. But there's only one Achilles."

"Yes, ma'am."

❈ 3 ❈

Arden Hyde took off her sunglasses to evaluate her appearance in a mirror in a women's bathroom at Frankfurt airport. Bloodshot eyes? Nothing new. Gorgeous black Italian sweater with Dior ruffled tank underneath? Appropriate for stylish transatlantic travel to a funeral. Complexion? She peered closer at her face and shuddered. Best not to over-analyze. But her family was going to take one look and think she was ready for the coffin, not her uncle Julius.

In preparation for reentry into family life, Arden scrounged in the bottom of her bag and came up with a handful of pills. Her fingers hovered over a slightly linty collection of pharmaceuticals. Maybe half a Xanax? An Ambien, too, of course. She could always pop something else in the air for added serenity, if needed. She gulped them dry, ignoring the American mother scrubbing her grubby child's hands in the adjacent sink and giving her a disapproving frown in the mirror.

Instead of acknowledging the disapproval—there would be plenty more of that soon enough—Arden dug into her bag and found her ticket. She congratulated herself for snaking the last first-class upgrade. Served Hadrian right for schmoozing in the lounge instead of dropping by the check-in desk for himself.

Her boss, art dealer Hadrian Sloan-Whitaker, made it his business to troll airport lounges for possible celebrity clients. But he was going to sulk in coach the whole way home on this trip.

Technically, though, Arden reminded herself, Hadrian hadn't been her boss since a rather hideous scene in Florence.

"We're supposed to sell art *to* museums," Hadrian had roared at her on the steps of an institution where a nearly done deal had gone woefully awry. "Not convince the bastards to sue us!"

"It was the right thing to do," Arden replied. At the time, she was under the influence of a Tylenol PM with a glass of white wine, so she kept her calm in the face of his rage. "The provenance makes it clear that our client's Nazi uncle stole that triptych out of a Latvian church."

"We don't *know* that!"

"Oh, Hadrian. We both read the research. Don't we have enough money without aiding and abetting war criminals?"

"Some of us," Hadrian said, swelling up like a toad, "don't live on trust funds, Miss Hyde. And we need to put food on the table. You're fired."

Hadrian's idea of putting food on the table meant fois gras at starred restaurants. So he wasn't exactly hurting, either.

In the airport bathroom, Arden's cell phone rang. She carried it out into the concourse because who really wants to listen to toilets flushing on the phone?

Arden checked the screen.

And, despite the fact that the Xanax hadn't kicked in yet, she took the call.

"Daddy?"

"Arden, I have bad news."

"I've seen CNN, Daddy. I heard about Uncle Julius." She'd watched a

25

whole report on a television in a convenient airport bar, and even now her throat closed with grief. She clutched the tiny phone with both hands. "Are you all right?"

"Of course I'm all right!"

Quentin Hyde's voice sounded blustery. Arden knew her father liked to think of himself as the family's commander in chief, a captain of industry who showed no weakness—a gruff, heartless businessman who slew the bulls and bears of Wall Street. Even the death of his elder brother would make no dent in his emotional armor.

"Are you on your way home?" he barked long-distance.

"I'm getting on the plane any minute."

"Good. I'll send the jet to meet you in New York. We need you here immediately."

"What's wrong?"

"It's important to show family solidarity in a crisis, that's all. I don't want anyone thinking Hyde Communications might be weakened by recent events."

"I'm sure the company will survive." Arden checked her watch and tried to calculate the minute she might feel emotionally capable of coping with her family.

If Quentin heard something negative in her tone, he pretended otherwise. "I want everyone in upper management to be on alert. Your presence is required."

"I'm not management, Daddy—upper or lower. I've never been employed by Hyde Communications, and I don't—"

"Can anyone hear you? Don't be talking company business within earshot of the press. Those media bastards will screw us to the wall if we leak the wrong message."

Most of her fellow passengers were making their way to the gate. Arden could see them gathering their comfort measures—cashmere pashminas, spritz bottles of moisturizer, little bags of cosmetics. She wanted to remind Daddy that she wasn't working for the company. Not now, not ever. But the Xanax was stealing blissfully into her brain.

"You're an important part of the team," Daddy was saying. "I need reliable help if we're going to weather this storm."

Hyde Communications didn't need any help in its inexorable march to world domination. Pretty soon her father would have control of cell phones, television, and Internet coverage in every country and most of outer space.

The only thing he couldn't dominate was his youngest daughter. One by one, her siblings had given in, taken his money, and done his bidding—even if it meant giving up their right to think their own thoughts. But Arden managed to resist. She had more esoteric interests than cell phone towers. There was art and history. Wonderful books to absorb and—

"It's time you left that dead-end job, Arden." He interrupted her thoughts. "The market for fine art has collapsed completely. I read about it in the *Journal*. You should reconsider joining Hyde Communications."

Feeling almost serene, Arden asked, "Are the funeral arrangements made?"

He took the bait. "There are legal issues we must iron out first. Right now, though, I'm too busy doing damage control where Monica is concerned."

"Monica?" Arden was surprised to hear the name of Uncle Julius's latest wife, who she thought was a pleasant woman with a passing good understanding of impressionist painters. "What's she done?"

"Well, she set fire to the family homestead," Quentin said quite unnecessarily. Who hadn't heard about the blaze started by the outraged wife of a billionaire? Even the European press printed photos. He continued, "But turns out Monica has been systematically raiding my mother's house for anything valuable. Silver, furniture, porcelain—everything. The woman's been acting like a drunken sailor on shore leave! All in the name of charity, for God's sake. She may have given away dozens of masterpieces!

I need your help getting back the most important items. Surely there are loopholes in these museum deals."

"What's Monica given away?"

"Who knows? Why Julius let her run rampant, I'll never understand. You can look around and see what's missing. It wouldn't surprise me to learn that woman was getting kickbacks. There had to be something fishy going on."

Arden noted that her father was focusing all his rage on Monica, when he was probably feeling angry with Julius instead. Redirecting emotions was nothing new in the Hyde family.

Arden said, "My flight arrives at noon. But don't send a plane, Daddy. I'll fly commercial."

"It's no trouble to—"

"No, really, I can manage for myself."

"All right," he said, sounding doubtful. "But get home soon. We need you here, Arden."

He terminated the call with that.

She shut off her cell phone and thought about how much nicer it would be to find a pleasant hotel and just hole up for a while. Maybe wander some galleries. Hike in the Black Forest to absorb the clear air. But she shouldered her bag and got into the line to board.

Although she hadn't really enjoyed the many pleasures of her family's fortune—no boats, no long visits to lavish vacation homes, no cosmetic surgery, no runway shows or lunches with movie stars—the one thing Arden might actually mind losing would be the Hyde family art collection. Or perhaps—if she were truthful with herself—the right to bask in the glow of the reflected good taste of her relatives. It was easier to enjoy the company of art than the people who'd collected it.

But it was very trying to spend more than an hour with her grandmother Dorothy, fondly known as Dodo. Too many questions, too many expectations. Uncle Julius's death was going to send everyone scrambling to restructure the family hierarchy, too.

The dread of seeing everyone again bubbled up in Arden's throat like bile.

She closed her eyes and tried to conjure up the soothing Van Gogh. And the Calder mobile that slowly spun in the sunlight cast from the skylights at the family's island getaway. Dodo's Rauschenberg hung in the corporate headquarters of Hyde Communications, where it was hardly appreciated by the employees, but served its purpose when competitors needed to be impressed. While they admired the painting, they often didn't notice they were being consumed by her father, absorbed into the massive corporation, stripped of their own identity, eaten alive.

So why had Julius died? Why hadn't Arden's father been the one murdered instead? Quentin was the ruthless corporate raider with enemies all over the globe. Julius had become little more than a harmless, aging playboy.

"Miss?"

Arden woke and handed over her ticket.

"Have a nice flight."

She shuffled onto the plane and found her seat. The man in the window seat looked pleased to see a well-dressed young woman stowing her Gucci carry-on next to his, but she ignored him as she settled in.

The flight attendant appeared with a tray of beverages. "Something to drink, miss?"

"Yes, a vodka rocks, please. Just a small one."

"Right away."

As the steward went away, Arden groped in her bag for that other half Xanax. She found a stray Ativan, too. A lucky, just-in-case find. By the time she had to face her family, she would be fully anesthetized.

❧ 4 ❧

It was late when Roxy helped Nooch stash the statue in a back corner of her warehouse—a damp and smelly area so skeezy where even the most determined snoopers were unlikely to explore. They threw a tarp over the statue, bound it loosely with twine, and walked away.

With a feeling she might score big with this find, Roxy happily filled various buckets of water for Rooney while Nooch scattered chewie bones and nuggets of kibble around the perimeter of the chain-link fence to keep the dog roaming throughout the night.

She was reaching to haul down the garage door when a small, dented pickup fishtailed into the yard and slid to a stop on the gravel in front of her. The driver's window was down, and the shriek of guitars burst into the night air. Some crazy Irish punk rock. Punching off the CD player, the driver leaned out the window.

"Flynn," she said when she recognized him. "Shouldn't you be washing dishes?"

"Shouldn't you be home in bed?"

"Sorry to spoil your fantasy." Roxy sauntered over to the pickup, but didn't lean down to get intimate.

The light from the dashboard illuminated the sharp cut of Patrick Flynn's cheekbone and the stubble on his jaw, but his eyes were in shadow, so she couldn't gauge his mood. He probably wanted to keep it that way.

The back of his truck was cluttered with a bunch of little cages full of straw that had a definite stink. Roxy took a step away from it. "What the hell are you doing? Hauling livestock?"

He grinned a little. "Free-range chickens."

"You're kidding, right? You're a farmer now?"

"I'm experimenting for the restaurant. Fresh ingredients, you know. Nothing but the best."

"I remember a time when you ate only hot dogs and onion rings. Now it's fancy food and guys saying, 'Yes, Chef' when you give orders?"

Instead of answering, he grabbed a rumpled sweatshirt from the passenger seat and threw it at her. It was the hoodie she'd wiggled out of earlier. "You dropped your glass slipper earlier, Cinderella. I'll trade it for my hockey helmet. Which I believe you stole last week."

She caught the sweatshirt with a grin and slipped it on. It was two-sweatshirt weather these days. In another month she'd add a flannel shirt to her layers. "You playing tonight? This late? Don't you have to get up early to milk cows or something?"

He shrugged, his gaze slipping down her body as he watched her dress. "Some of the guys rented the rink in Harmar. It's the only time available now that even five-year-olds have a hockey league."

Flynn used to have a cute dimpled face and curly dark hair, not to mention melting blue eyes that he'd used to full advantage back in high school. But after flunking out of community college for too much partying and doing two tours in Afghanistan, not to mention bumping around parts of the world where tourists didn't venture, he was no longer cute.

Now he radiated something lean and hard—something dangerous that made little girls nervous, but turned grown women's heads.

Not Roxy's, however. Not anymore. She said, "Don't you and your friends have anything better to do at this time of night? Like go home and sleep?"

"Life's too short. What about you? I thought you might be singing somewhere tonight."

Roxy shook her head. "Only occasional weekends."

In the last couple of years, she'd been asked to sing backup vocals for some local bands. Not a career or anything—more of a hobby, although she liked the extra bucks. She was surprised that Flynn knew about it. She hadn't told anybody. Not even Nooch.

He said, "Where's my helmet?"

She jerked her head. "Inside."

He stayed where he was, engine running, but with a ghost of a smile tugging at the edges of his mouth. "I'll wait. You might pick my pocket if I go in there."

Roxy went into the office and came back a minute later dangling a battered hockey helmet by its strap. She tossed it to him. "Sorry about the scratches."

He turned the helmet in his hand, examining the minor damage. "How does the other guy look?"

"Worse." Roxy grinned and slid her hands into the hip pockets of her jeans. "I wore it to figure out who was breaking into my office for petty cash. Good thing, too, because he took a swing at me."

"I presume he's in jail now?"

"Why would I call the police? He'd just come back. Which he won't now."

"You took a shot at him?"

"Unlike you," she said, "I don't keep guns around. No, I belted him with a two-by-four. Sent him home crying to his mommy. He was just a methhead kid. Easy to scare."

Flynn shook his head. "Eventually there's somebody in this world who is going to outfox you, Roxy."

Nooch appeared out of the darkness, along with Rooney. The dog jumped up and planted his forepaws on the door of Flynn's truck, looking for attention. Flynn reached out and roughed up the dog's big head.

Nooch said, "Hey, Flynn, thanks for dinner. You sure learned how to do some good cooking while you were away."

"Glad you liked it."

"Next time, how about some dessert?"

Flynn laughed. "Anything in particular?"

"I like marshmallows. Anything with marshmallows."

Wagging his head, Flynn shoved Rooney away and put the little pickup in gear. "I'll see what I can do."

He drove off, leaving Nooch with a smile on his face. The bumper sticker on the back of the pickup read, Marine Corps: When It Absolutely, Positively Must Be Destroyed Overnight.

Rain began to spatter on the gravel.

Roxy turned away and thought about hoisting the Monster Truck up onto the lift to work on the rattle in the driveshaft, but her cell phone rang. She grabbed it.

"Yeah?"

"Roxy?"

She recognized the voice of Trey Hyde, slippery youngest brother of Julius. Although it was a surprise to hear from yet another Hyde in the same night, she said, "Long time, no see, Trey. You gonna steal from me again?"

"I thought you made me a loan." Trey laughed musically. "For cab fare to get to the airport. Didn't I pay you back?"

"You will," she said. "One way or another."

"How about another?" he said just as playfully. "Can we get together? We could talk about economic Darwinism again. Or just—you know. Screw around. My place?"

Roxy knew all she needed to know about Darwin and the strong devouring the weak. Hang up on a jerk? Or let him satisfy the urge that had been building inside her all day?

She said, "I'll see you in half an hour."

When she clipped the phone shut, Nooch was chewing on an already ragged fingernail. "I know that look on your face," he said. "Are you going to do something that'll send you to confession?"

"I'll take you home first."

Suddenly it was raining like hell. Typical for October—balmy one minute, then blowing sleet the next. Tonight, the rain pounded down hard, washing grit from the streets. Roxy drove Nooch home with the wipers clacking on the truck's windshield.

Fifteen minutes after Trey's call, she arrived at a former riverside factory that had been converted into lofts for the city's young elite. Thomas Xavier Hyde—Trey to those who associated with him—kept one of the lofts for when he returned to Pittsburgh.

Trey spent most of his time in the Caribbean doing modern-day treasure hunting. With sonar, radar, and Inspector Gadget wizardry, his expedition team looked for sunken pirate ships and the Spanish gold they'd taken down with them in hurricanes. More accurately, Trey paid for the gadgets and stayed onshore with various American girls gone wild while others did the grunt work.

Whenever Trey did give up the fun and sun to come home, it was for the purpose of wheedling more money from his mother to pay for the next expedition. Hunting for another long-lost man-of-war seemed to need so much cash up front, Roxy often wondered why Trey didn't just take the dough from his family and forget about using the million-dollar vacuum cleaner to suck gold ingots and brass cannons from the ocean floor.

But everybody, she supposed, needed a hobby—especially the loser third son of a powerful family.

Roxy slipped past the doorman and rode the elevator to the fifth floor.

Shaking the rainwater from her hair, she walked down a long hallway to the last unit.

Trey must have been pacing inside the loft and checking the peephole, because the door suddenly opened and the Pirate of the Caribbean seized her arm to pull her inside. He snapped shut his cell phone and tried to kiss her.

Roxy fended him off with a stiff-armed block to the shoulder that sent him glancing off the doorjamb. "Down, boy. Save the mushy stuff."

"Sorry. I forgot." Grinning, he closed the door and dropped his cell phone on a pedestal by the door. "It's always your rules. Great sex and no declarations of undying love."

"Just the way you like it, too." She put out one hand, palm up. "Before we get to the main event, I want the hundred bucks you stole from me."

"There was less than twenty in the pocket of your jeans!"

She wiggled her fingertips. "You owe me for pain and suffering. I'll settle for an even C-note."

He dug out a gold money clip in the shape of a shark, peeled off a hundred-dollar bill, and slapped it into her hand. He added a few more bills with a flourish. "There. Forgive?"

"Sucking crap off the bottom of the ocean must be more profitable than it used to be." She gave back the tip and kept the hundred.

"It could always be better." Trey leaned back against the door to look at her. His face was pale and sweaty—excited. "You're looking good, Roxy."

She knew he went for classy, girly girls most of the time, so Roxy's combination of wild black hair, no makeup, and less fashion sense wasn't what drew him back to her. She looked great naked, that was the main thing. Sometimes she gunked her lashes with mascara and made her mouth juicier with plum-colored lipstick, but not tonight.

"You're going to make me feel even better, right?"

"I'll do my best."

Trey Hyde was several inches taller than his much older brother, and he'd have been a few degrees more attractive if he'd laid off the costumes.

People magazine had once photographed him in a skipper's cap and full yachting regalia—the photogenic front man for the treasure-hunting venture—and he'd taken to dressing that way all the time. Tonight he wore sand-blasted jeans, deck shoes, and a collarless blue sweater with a sailboat logo. All he needed was a white cap and a long cigarette holder to look like Thurston Howell III on his way to a desert island with Gilligan.

Roxy folded his money into her pocket and walked past Trey into the apartment. Polished concrete floors, no walls. The foyer was a cool, empty space except for a pedestal with a large openmouthed pottery jar—Aztec, to hear Trey tell it. One of his expeditions brought it up from the bottom of the Caribbean, he said, but it could have come from Pier 1.

The foyer expanded into a living-dining area furnished by a decorator who obviously thought a *Moby-Dick* theme would be dandy. A harpoon on one wall, a stainless-steel table with a sailing-ship model on top—sails tilted as if catching a stiff breeze. A shallow glass case filled with gold coins lay displayed on a side table. A diver's helmet had been converted into a lamp. The rest of the loft was dark except for the undulating underwater colors of a muted television. Gave Roxy the feeling she was inside a fish tank.

Through a doorway lay a king-sized bed, silver sheets pulled tight, gray pillows neatly stacked. Ready.

Trey hung back behind her, probably admiring her ass, but Roxy could almost feel the vibration of his nervous energy.

Across from the bed, a huge television hung on the wall, tuned to the eleven o'clock news with the sound turned off. Beside it, a window framed a spectacular view of the city—all sparkling lights and the shining blackness of the river with a glitter of rain glistening around it all. A tugboat was passing by the building, pushing three barges laden with coal upriver against the deluge.

Roxy turned back to Trey and unzipped her top sweatshirt and pulled it off. She noticed a new affectation flashing in his earlobe. "Nice earring, Captain Blood. But isn't it supposed to be a gold hoop?"

He fingered the diamond, smiling a little nervously now that they'd reached the bed. "Do you like it?"

She flicked his earring with her finger, ignoring his question. Which was what he wanted, really. The tougher she treated him, the shinier his face got. Make him wait, she thought. Make some conversation while his imagination stimulated the rest of him. She hooked one finger behind the snap of his jeans and unzipped him. "Did you come home to help your big brother dynamite what's left of the mansion tomorrow?"

"I guess you haven't heard."

"About?"

"My brother died tonight."

Roxy pulled away, foreplay forgotten. If he'd punched her in the gut, she wouldn't have been more shocked. "Died?"

Motionless, Trey said, "You look surprised."

"Of course I'm surprised. Jesus Christ." Blown away, more like it. And sick. Her last glance at Julius—walking away from his pool, looking forlorn—suddenly surged up in Roxy's mind.

And now he was dead?

Trey said, "I thought you might have known already. Considering you were at the house tonight."

The air in the loft was suddenly too cold for Roxy to breathe, but it snapped her back to reality. "How do you know that?"

"I was there, too."

"You—? What do you mean?" Roxy frowned. "What happened to Julius? Did he have a heart attack or something?"

"He was shot. Somebody shot him."

"Somebody who?"

One-handed, from underneath his sweater at the small of his back, Trey drew a handgun. A Colt 1911.

The hair on the back of Roxy's neck prickled as he dropped the weapon onto the bed. "Jesus, Trey. Did you kill him?"

"Did you?"

She held her ground as he stepped closer. Trey wasn't the kind of guy to be afraid of. Not usually. He was a little bent sexwise, but nothing Roxy couldn't handle. She held still while he pulled her second sweatshirt over her head and dropped it on the bed. Then he put his face against her bare shoulder, and a moment later his fingers were under her camisole, on her skin. He nuzzled her neck. But she could feel his hands shaking.

Then his act collapsed. He said, "Oh, my God, Roxy. Julius is dead. My own brother." He shuddered, and then he clutched her.

Roxy stiffened. It was easier dealing with the crazy Trey. Trey with a hard-on and too much coke in his bloodstream. Not blubbering Trey. "Hey, cool it."

In the biblical sense, men were pretty much the same. Except some liked it standing up or outdoors, on the bottom, or on top. Maybe mirrors. Sometimes batteries. It didn't matter. The only ones she said no to were the camera buffs. Even the men who despised women, they could be fun. The trick was figuring out how to provoke them all into doing what she liked, no strings, no personal shit.

Trey was crossing a line with the wimp routine.

She pushed him to sit on the bed. "Don't weird me out like this, Trey. Tell me what happened."

He sat, not bothering to wipe the tears from his face or to zip his pants. The blue light from the television played across his features. "Somebody shot him, I guess."

"Who? You? Did you pull the trigger?"

His breathing got rapid again, like he couldn't get enough air. "Not me. I don't know who."

"Tell me what happened. What did you do?"

"I've got a new deal cooking, and I pitched it to him. All I need's a little capital, but the rest of my trust doesn't kick in until I'm forty. So I asked

Julius to help me get the financing from Dodo. But he blew me off. Said I should run it past Quentin. Like Quentin's the boss now? So I walked away tonight, I swear. I was in my car when I heard shots. I ran back, and—look, he was already dead."

"Jesus."

"I didn't know what to do. I got the hell out of there. I knew how it was going to look."

It still looked that way to Roxy. Trey had a gun. And probably enough frustration with his brother to pull the trigger.

Roxy tried backtracking through her own timetable at the Hyde mansion. The habit of self-preservation. "When did you first get to the house?"

He frowned, struggling to focus. "I don't know exactly. By the time I got there, lots of people were already—I mean, there were some cars in the driveway and your truck out back, too. I didn't talk to anyone but Julius, though."

"But you argued with him. Did you threaten him? With the gun?"

"No, no, nothing like that." The denial came too fast, and he made an effort to look convincing. "We just yelled a little, and then I left, that's it."

Roxy figured he was lying. But she said, "You took off when you heard the shots?"

Trey avoided her gaze. "No, I went back. And there he was—sprawled out on the grass like he was making snow angels or something." Trey glanced up at her, perhaps trying to gauge if she was swallowing his story. "That's when I heard your truck leave."

Roxy knew she couldn't have heard the shots over the noise of the Monster Truck's engine.

Trey's composure loosened at the edges again. "Somebody else must have seen what happened and called 911, because in a couple of minutes I heard the police sirens coming. I didn't want them to see me—not with the gun." He dashed tears from his face. "So I got into my car and left."

"And then you called me. What for?"

39

"Well, you were there at the house. I thought you'd—I don't know. Help me." He unraveled completely and began to cry. "I—I got blood on my shirt when I touched him, Roxy. So I took it off. Changed into my sweater."

"Where is the shirt now?"

With a shaky thumb, he wiped snot from his upper lip. "I threw it out the car window on my way here."

Roxy squinted at Trey to figure out if he was lying or in shock. "You really didn't see who killed him?"

"I saw you, that's all."

"Who else saw me?"

"I don't know."

"The police?" Sharper.

"Really, I don't know. Can we talk later? I really need a fuck. It might clear my head. I—I'm scared, I guess. Should I take off my clothes? I'll do what you want, Roxy. Anything. Please. I don't want to think about it for a while."

The television screen changed, suddenly filling the room with the flashing lights of police cars. Light-headed, Roxy watched and saw the familiar hulk of the Hyde mansion. White noise hummed in her head as the news of Julius Hyde's death unspooled on the news. Trey sat forward and reached for her. When he slid his hand up under her camisole, the cops were roping off the crime scene. The camera zoomed in on the face of a bearded vagrant being dragged from the bushes.

Roxy had the psycho sensation of floating up on the ceiling at that moment, watching from a distance as Trey tried to coax her detached body into action. She thought of Julius sipping from his silver flask with the odd smile on his face flicking back and forth between bravado and fear. Had he guessed he might be dead within the hour?

Roxy pushed Trey's hands away, in no mood for sex now. He pulled his halfhearted erection out of his pants and tried to peel down her jeans. Then someone knocked on the door of the loft.

Trey jumped to his feet, his face ludicrous with surprise.

Roxy yanked down her camisole and reached for her sweatshirt. "Somebody joining us?"

Trey gulped. "No, Roxy."

In the hallway, somebody knocked again, harder this time.

Police, Roxy thought. Her head cleared fast. She pulled her sweatshirt over her head. Then she grabbed a handful of Trey's sweater and pulled him around to face her as he tried to get his penis put away. "Get a grip," she commanded.

"But—"

"Don't open the door yet. Just look. And ask."

Before she could stop him from picking up the gun, Trey snatched the weapon from the bed. With his pants still open, he went out into the foyer, where he crept to the door. He swiped one hand through his hair as he peeked through the peephole. The gun hung in his other hand, his finger on the goddamn trigger.

"Hey," he said, surprised. "It's Kaylee."

"Who the hell is—?"

At least Trey had the presence of mind to drop the gun into the open mouth of the Aztec pot before he opened the door.

Midknock, a young woman tottered into the foyer on a pair of high-heeled shoes tall enough to make her interfere with incoming airplanes. Her toes looked blue with cold. She was almost as tall as Roxy and skinny in a pair of stovepipe jeans. A pink sweater the color of bubblegum slid off one shoulder. Mascara smeared her face. A cloud of cigarette smoke engulfed her figure like exhaust from a tractor trailer.

"Trey!" She threw herself into his arms.

He barely dodged getting his ear burned on her cigarette, but he hugged her automatically. "Kaylee—"

She burst into sobs. "He's gone! Dead! What are we going to do? Everything's ruined!"

"It's okay." Trey patted her bare shoulder. "But we have to be smart now."

Tears poured out of her like water from a faucet. "Oh, God. I miss him already! What will I do?"

"Take it easy. Calm down."

"I had to get out of there. I ran away. I saw—I saw—"

"You did the right thing."

The girl had a baby-doll voice, ratched up high and strangled. "Oh my God, I'm so scared!"

"I know. Me, too."

"I ran away. I took a bus back to my place. I can't believe it! He's really—"

"It's okay, it's okay."

"No, it isn't!" She hit Trey on the chest with her fist. "How can you say that? Julie—my Julie!"

"Easy now." He tried to subdue her with a tighter hug.

But she fought him, punching harder, eyes squished shut. "No, no—it's awful! He's gone!"

Trey dodged blows. "Kaylee—"

She stopped fighting just as suddenly as she'd started. "Wait a minute. Who is she?"

She looked over Trey's shoulder at Roxy, and her tears dried up. But her one hand remained knotted in a fist. The other managed to hang on to her cigarette.

Roxy said, "Let me guess, Trey. This is your big brother's pop tart."

Roxy had read the newspaper and seen the pictures of Julius Hyde's manicurist girlfriend—the one he'd been wining and dining the night his wife came home early and discovered her marriage was kaput. Since then, the local media had had a field day with Kaylee—the barely adult sex kitten who'd slept with a man old enough to be her grandpa.

Gently, Trey disengaged himself from the hysterical girl. And he finally zipped up. "Roxy, this is Kaylee, my brother's—uh—friend."

"Fiancée," Kaylee corrected, frowning at Trey as he snapped his fly.

"Right. She's—Julius was very fond of her."

"He loved me." Kaylee took a puff of her cigarette and blew a stream of smoke out the side of her mouth while she did the math of Trey's zipper and Roxy's presence in the loft.

"You were there tonight?" Roxy asked. "At the house when Julius was killed?"

"I wasn't anywhere."

"You'll need a better story than that one, honey."

The girl suddenly lunged as if to claw Roxy's face with her pink talons. "You bitch! Who do you think you are?"

Trey managed to hold her back. "Kaylee, please. Roxy's a friend. She can help."

Roxy had a hard time imagining what a man like Julius Hyde might see in a teenybopper, let alone one with a hair trigger. "Now what, Trey?" she asked. "Is this temperamental cutie a part of your inheritance?"

Trey pinned the girl's arms to her side. "That's not the way it is. Kaylee's just a friend."

"Who are you, exactly?" Kaylee asked with a sneer. "Besides badly dressed? I think my brother wears those boots."

"Does he use them to kick your ass? Because—"

"Please." Trey raised his voice before a catfight broke out. "We're all upset. It's been a terrible night. Let's take a deep breath, shall we?"

"How can I calm down?" Kaylee broke into tears all over again and slumped against Trey. "My Julie is gone!"

Roxy saw the fat tears spurt down Kaylee's face again and figured they were fake. She was no theater critic, but the scene didn't exactly look like an authentic family drama.

Trey spun the girl gently around. "Kaylee, why don't you powder your nose?" He gave her a harder push in the direction of the bathroom.

"Before I do," Roxy muttered.

Kaylee threw an anatomically impossible suggestion over her shoulder, but she went into the bathroom. Her jeans rode low enough that the tattoo on her lower back was revealed—a tramp stamp with Chinese characters and an arrow pointing down the crack of her butt. Like an invitation.

When the door closed behind her, Trey turned back to Roxy. "Baby, listen."

"I don't think so." Roxy zipped up her sweatshirt tight around her neck.

"I don't know what she's doing here, but I'll get rid of her. Give me ten minutes. Please. I need you. What if the police come? What will I tell them?"

"Oh, so this is why you called me? Not for slap and tickle. You want my special insight into crime prevention."

"Hey, I only thought—"

"I know what you thought."

"What do I know about this kind of stuff? What should I do?"

"For one thing?" Roxy hooked her thumb at the jar containing the gun. "The cops will be here faster than you think, and the first thing they're going to find is your weapon. So get rid of it."

He blinked, surprised. "It's brand-new. My grandfather had a big collection at our summer house. He always said the Colt .45 models are the best investments. I want a collection of my own."

"I don't care if it's a priceless family heirloom, idiot. Lose it. Permanently. Don't hide it or sell it, either. Throw it in the river. Make sure it's gone for good."

"Will you take it for me?" Trey grabbed her by the arm. "Please, Roxy?"

Roxy recoiled. "No way!"

"Please. I'll do it wrong, I know I will. Take it." He let her go and reached into the pot to pull out the Colt. "Get it out of here before Kaylee sees it. Please, I'm already in a jam."

"And you're pulling me in."

"You're already in. You were there tonight. But I won't tell the police."

His tone wasn't quite right, and Roxy's temper rose. "What are you saying, asshole? You'll keep me out of this if I take the gun for you?"

"Hey, I'm not threatening. I just— Please. Here. I trust you."

Against her better judgment, Roxy took the gun from his hand and checked it. Unloaded, thank God. She glared at him. "You'll forget I was at the house?"

"Sure, anything."

"I'm going to regret this. But I'll get rid of your toy. If you double-cross me, though—"

"I won't, I swear."

She tucked the weapon in the back of her jeans and pulled down her sweatshirt to cover it. Better to have the gun than knowing Trey might be waving it around and blabbing. She gave him one last quelling glance and turned to go. "Have a good time with your little friend."

Kaylee gave a wail from the bathroom, causing Trey to turn.

While he was distracted, Roxy scooped his cell phone off the pedestal and slid it into her pocket, too. She went out and pulled the door closed behind her. Then she took the stairs and walked out of the building into the rain.

In her truck, as she drove across the Sixteenth Street Bridge, she rolled her window down. She pitched Trey's cell phone over the railing and into the river. No sense helping anyone pinpoint who the murder victim's screwy brother had called right after ditching his bloody clothes.

The gun, though, she kept.

❊ 5 ❊

On Saturday morning, Henry drove across the suburbs to Teed Off, a golf shop owned by a former stockbroker. The broker had already made his millions on a sweet retirement bonus and now spent his days telling other golfers what was wrong with their game. After picking up his golf clubs subsequent to their being regripped, Henry listened to a condescending lecture on his backswing. Fortunately, a more important customer soon entered the store, and the owner hurried off to bully that poor slob into buying the latest and greatest titanium driver.

Henry took a leisurely browse through the new selection of Calloway shoes before putting his clubs into his trunk and climbing back into his BMW.

His dad had been a cop, back in Buffalo. Sitting in his car with autumn sunshine warming him through the windshield, Henry thought again about how Dad might have started an investigation. He tried to summon up the voices of Dad and Uncle Rodney at the dinner table on Saturday nights, bitching about the job. But it was no use. The two brothers had inevitably squabbled about their gambling debts—they took turns owing big money to someone Henry knew only as "Sal"—while getting stupid on Miller Lite. Had they ever talked about procedure? Ways of tracking down information? If so, the memory had been washed away long ago.

Henry took out his cell phone and made a few calls. Then he stopped at a strip mall liquor store for a fifth of Glenlivet and dropped in on a friendly judge. The whiskey helped take care of Dorothy's injunction.

Finally driving into the city, he tracked down Monica Hyde by cell phone. She agreed to meet him at the museum, where she had been allotted a small office. In the years before she'd met Julius, she'd been a pretty little divorced church mouse transplanted from Texas and working in the museum. Some department or other required her to write catalog copy and entertain a lot of big donors at cocktail parties. She'd encountered Julius at a splashy museum function. The clever minx must have danced nude on a tabletop, because he dumped his previous wife and married Monica faster than most men get off a golf course in a thunderstorm. The museum graciously allowed her to keep the office—perhaps a reward for landing the biggest donor in the institution's history.

By the time Henry reached the museum, Monica wasn't in her office as she'd promised. On a hunch, Henry bought a ticket and followed a throng of parents and their yelping tots as far as the turn to the dinosaur exhibit. Henry proceeded a little farther down the cavernous corridor and found Monica standing in the hall of architecture at the back of a group of committee ladies who were discussing plans for decorating Christmas trees. The ladies all carefully ignored Monica and instead focused with intense concentration on their committee chairwoman.

Monica was looking fierce, but a little weepy around the edges.

Nips, tucks, Pilates, and an impressive force of will had kept Monica's true age at bay so far. She looked about forty, which meant she was at least fifty. Her absurdly conservative tweed suit was a uniform of political wives or women under suspicion of murder. She had a diamond pin lanced through one lapel, and a stately string of pearls tangled around her throat with the folds of a silk Hermès scarf—perhaps too much froufrou for a petite woman, but she was making an effort to carry off the look. On her forearm she steadied an ugly handbag no doubt worth thousands. Being from Texas, she likely carried a lady derringer in it.

Monica snuffled up her tears when she laid eyes on Henry.

She reached out, seized his arm, and pulled him around a pillar for some privacy. "Henry, I'm so glad to see you."

"I couldn't stay away." He cupped her elbows to convey steadfast support. "Monica, you shouldn't be here. Let me take you home where you won't be on display like this."

She trembled with suppressed emotion. "Things are so awful at the hotel where I've been staying. The press has staked out the place. They're always shoving microphones in my face. But it's even worse here. My so-called f-friends are acting as if I k-killed my husband with my b-bare hands."

She began to lose her considerable composure. Botox prevented her forehead from crumpling, but her eyes filled with woeful tears. A cooler head needed to prevail.

Henry tucked her hand into the crook of his elbow and drew Monica out of the hall of architecture and away from the eavesdropping commit-tee. He kept his voice low. "I'd have come to you last night, you know. You should have picked up the phone, Monica."

"The last thing I need right now is to be seen with another man, right?"

"I—"

She suddenly blushed. "Oh, Henry, I'm sorry. I didn't mean—I've never thought of you as—well, you're a friend. A family lawyer and a—my good friend."

"All of the above," he said stoutly. "I'd have a heart of stone if I stayed away. I'm sorry about Julius. You must be devastated."

"I am." She stopped in the middle of the doorway and made a good show of devastation—stiff and trembling. It was a display of emotion as unnatural to her social class as stripping off her clothes in the middle of a city intersection. She looked up at him tearily. "But I'm angry with Julius, too. That old fool got himself killed, and—and now I'm a pariah!"

"Well, you look wonderful. Have you lost weight since I saw you last?"

With a little sob, she bowed her head. "That's what catastrophe does to a woman like me. It's honed me down to bone and sinew."

Henry gave her his handkerchief.

He had bonded with Monica during several of the marathon weekends Dorothy insisted everyone in the family attend to hear speeches by financial planners. There were dry, tasteless meals, too, and long hours of sitting around listening to Julius—supposedly the male head of the family—wrangle with his mother about The Trust and The Will and The Shares. Then Quentin, the second son, would get in on the act about The Company. While the more vociferous family members argued, Henry managed to find a spot to sit in the background—on the same window seat with Monica, both of them sipping sherry and endeavoring to look interested in the proceedings, but actually stealing small smiles at each other as if sharing witty bon mots but being too wise to say them aloud.

It had been a strategic flirtation.

Today, despite the tears, Monica's mouth looked juicy—plumper, perhaps—maybe the result of some kind of injection that made Henry squeamish just to think about. But his mind wandered involuntarily to the possibility of sex with the newly minted widow fifteen or more years his senior.

While Monica dabbed her lashes, she surprised the hell out of him by looking up into his eyes and saying with a lot of southern honey, "Somehow I knew you'd be the one to come to my rescue. I need help so desperately."

Henry took her hand again. Time to get her away and explore the possibilities. He set off leading Monica to the privacy of her office.

He said, "I'm not a litigator, Monica. But I can help you find an expert team. You'll need someone who can protect you if you're questioned by the police."

"*If* I'm questioned by the police? They practically used rubber hoses last night! They think I killed Julius! They had to let me go while they check my alibi. Can you believe it? I need an alibi! But now I've got even bigger problems."

"Bigger problems than a murder charge?" Not to mention the whole issue of setting fire to her home with her husband inside.

"It's Samson."

Henry missed a step. "Who?"

"Julius's chauffeur thinks he can wrestle custody away from me. He called this morning. He says I'm an unfit mother!"

Henry's brain sputtered like a faulty lawn mower. "I—I didn't realize you had children, Monica."

"He's not a child, he's Samson! I raised him from a puppy, brought him home on a plane myself from a Great Dane breeder in Bavaria."

With another sob, Monica headed for the elevator. A gigantic vase of flowers sat in a niche, lighted from above and scattering pollen on the marble floor. Monica touched the call button. She said, "I know Julius was plotting to steal him away from me in our divorce settlement, but this is too much!"

"Divorce settlement?"

"Well, of course. Long before the fire, Julius and I were preparing to separate. Naturally, I've kept that a secret from everyone."

"A wise decision."

"But then I caught him with his little paramour, and I could hardly stay married another minute, could I?"

They stepped onto the elevator. Henry adjusted his tie as they wooshed upward. "I'm surprised you were leaving your husband, Monica. The golden goose, so to speak. But then, you're a woman of high principles."

She took the compliment like a largemouth bass grabbing bait. "I am.

Honestly, Henry, I understand a man's pursuit of youth, but couldn't she have a few IQ points more than a tortoise? It's very insulting."

Henry wondered if Monica had told the police about her coming divorce. If so, they might rightfully assume that Monica had knocked off her husband before the divorce was final—the better to inherit her prenup-decreed portion of his gargantuan share of the Hyde family fortune as a widow instead of an ex.

"Did the tortoise cause you to lose your self-control last night, too, Monica?"

She gave him a suddenly frosty glance. "Are you inquiring whether or not I killed my husband?"

"Forget I asked. It was rude of me."

Monica softened and took his arm to step off the elevator. Her composure under control again, she steered Henry past the executive offices and the desk of a wan young secretary who was dressed entirely in black, including her nail polish. Monica didn't acknowledge the girl—who might very well be holding down the same job Monica had before her advantageous marriage—and she pushed open the door to her own office and snapped on the desk lamp—Tiffany school, with dragonflies.

The office overlooked a courtyard with a fountain and sculptures. An expensive view, Henry decided, probably paid for by the Hyde donations. Furniture included a petite lady's writing desk with a modern chair behind it and a pair of leather armchairs for visitors in front. All of the furniture had probably come from a Hyde house. On the desk stood a promisingly sensuous piece of Venetian art glass, the color of arterial blood.

The surrounded walls were artfully papered with clippings of Monica making donations. The headlines trumpeted her philanthropic largesse— the activities that had bought her way into a level of society she would never have achieved otherwise. Her work had also kept Julius from being completely ostracized for his steadily declining social conduct.

Looking at the collage of her charitable work on her husband's behalf, Henry said, "You're a complex person, Monica."

She sent him a sidelong glance. "And you're a smoothie with the compliments, Henry. Most women must be putty in your hands. Once they sleep with you, they do your bidding. Am I right?"

He summoned an innocent expression. "Why do you ask?"

"Well, I—" She faltered. "I thought you were—never mind. For a moment I forgot my age."

"What does your age have to do with anything?"

She smiled tentatively. "You're a dear, Henry. Forgive me for thinking you might have motives unbecoming the gentleman you are. Once anyone joins forces with my mother-in-law, I immediately worry about his motives."

"Speaking of Mrs. Hyde, I was with her last evening."

Monica closed the door—perhaps more sharply than she intended. "Was she conscious? Or still napping?"

"Wide awake. And concerned."

Unwrapping the Hermès scarf from around her neck, Monica asked, "Did you break the news about Julius?"

"Yes." Henry sat in a leather armchair. He crossed one leg over the other and smoothed the crease in his trousers. "She was dismayed. But it was also the first time Dorothy heard about the fire, and frankly, she became very worried about her property—primarily the artwork."

"Well, at least she has her priorities straight."

Henry chose to ignore her tart tone. "Julius's death, of course, took her by surprise, but their relationship was difficult, as you know. Monica, forgive me for asking an indelicate question when Julius isn't even—well, help me put Dorothy's mind at ease concerning the art."

"Why should I care about her mind?"

"Let me put it a different way. It might be beneficial for some of us to know where her things are. For safekeeping. And for proper distribution . . . later." Letting Monica ponder her mother-in-law's demise, he went on smoothly, "In your predivorce due diligence, I presume you made an inventory of Julius's assets?"

"You can only chair so many ladies' luncheons, Henry, before you start thinking about detonating the centerpieces."

"So you made a complete list? Of the paintings? Antiques? Statuary and whatnot?"

She dropped the scarf into her handbag and perched on the edge of her desk. "What are you asking?"

"If you made a list of valuables, perhaps we could share information. Just you and me."

"Not Dodo?"

"It's not necessary for my client to know all the details."

Monica crossed her legs and made the mental leap to the time when Dorothy's estate would be divvied up. She seemed to grasp the benefits of cooperating.

Henry said, "I seek nothing more than a relatively accurate inventory of family assets, Monica. Whatever Julius gave you during your marriage, I'm sure you deserved."

She smoothed one hand down her kneecap. "His brothers might disagree."

"Good thing they're not here, then."

She considered a moment longer, then relented. "When we were first married, it was quite a shock to discover what a short financial leash Dodo kept everyone on. She still does. But then, I suppose you know all about that."

"I do write all the checks for Mrs. Hyde."

"Well, would it do any harm to add another zero now and then, Henry? If Dodo were a little more generous, everyone would stop having to be so devious."

"Julius was devious?"

"The whole family is!" Monica's voice rose petulantly. "With all that money sitting in stocks and shares? And everyone on allowances? They're always looking to finagle a little extra cash. I had to be very creative about our donations to the museum." She lowered her voice to a whisper. "And Julius was especially hungry for spending money. For his girlfriends, I suppose. And lavish meals with friends. Jaunts to Las Vegas on the jet. A trip to the Super Bowl with his buddies cost nearly forty grand! So, back in January, Julius consulted with some dealers."

Henry decided not to remark upon Monica's idea of restrained spending. "Art dealers?"

She nodded. "I caught him, of course. He had the discretion of a marching band. I thought maybe he was buying that adorable little beach shack in Costa Rica for me, so like an idiot I told him that if he wanted to sell off his mother's pictures while she was comatose, he ought to at least get top dollar."

"Did he?"

"I put him in touch with a lot of contacts. Why should he do business with the small-time dealers when there was big money to be made?"

The idea that Julius might have been selling off his mother's property had occurred to Henry, but here was Monica throwing prudence to the wind and saying he'd done just that. Henry said, "Now that the house and contents have burned up, we'll never know exactly what he sold, will we? Except by your list."

Monica recrossed her legs demurely. This time Henry couldn't stop himself from looking. She wore her tweed skirt with no stockings. Her legs were smooth—no blue veins, either. He began to think a fifteen-year difference in their ages meant very little these days.

Perhaps guessing the direction of his thoughts, Monica smiled at him. "Truth be told, I might have sold off some silverware myself, for pin money. Who needs four sets?"

He smiled, too. "Who, indeed? Did you mention your pin money to the fire insurance people?"

"Maybe I forgot. They were very rude to me, Henry."

No doubt they'd wanted to strangle her. She'd burned up millions they'd never see again, Henry knew, if the family decided to close ranks against her. Or the family could help Monica by somehow helping her duck responsibility for the blaze. Of course, insurance issues were going to drag on for years, no matter what. With luck, Henry would be long gone to his new life by the time the final checks were cut.

But killing her husband before he could divorce her? Smart move. Now she might gain a significantly larger share of the Hyde pie. Hundreds of millions larger.

"You were very wise to keep your own counsel, Monica." Now that they were cozy conspirators, he asked, "Did you send Julius to any dealer in particular? One of the New York auction houses, perhaps?"

Monica ticktocked her forefinger at him. "They're too fussy about the rules for Julius. Reporting to the IRS—that kind of thing. No, he went the other route—using people with few scruples about where their art comes from."

"Care to share any names?"

"What will you give me in return, Henry?"

Matching her light tone, he said, "Name your price."

The luscious tears suddenly returned to her eyes. "Help me get my dog back," Monica said in a broken whisper.

Henry took her hands and said he'd do anything in the world to help her. He could have kissed her, he supposed later, but that might have scotched the deal.

Monica rattled some keys on her BlackBerry, and they were soon bending their heads close together over a list of art dealers on the small screen.

Then a commotion erupted in the outer office. At the same moment, the door burst open and a large, red-faced man thrust himself into the room.

"Quentin!" Monica jumped away from Henry and managed to avoid looking guilty.

"Damn it, Monica, why can't you answer your cell phone once in a while?"

Her Texas vowels returned. "Reporters kept calling me, Quen. So I shut off the ringer. Would you rather I talk to them?"

"Of course not," Quentin snapped. "We had enough bad press after the fire. It drove the company stock price down to an all-time low." He gave a shudder at the catastrophic financial memory. "We don't need another downward spiral, especially now. Hello, Paxton. What the hell are you doing here?"

Quentin Hyde, Julius's younger brother, had inherited all of his mother's smarts, but none of her gentility. Which probably explained why he was the one who wrested Hyde Communications from the more ineffectual family member and rolled the company from a small venture in cable television into a conglomerate that fed television, Internet, and phone access into most North American households. Word was, he had his eye on Europe and Asia now.

Glaring at Henry as if challenging his right to be anywhere but his mother's bedside, Quentin said, "Is something wrong with Dodo?"

"Not a thing," Henry replied. "Except she's grief-stricken about your brother." A little hyperbole didn't hurt every now and then. Gravely, he added, "My condolences, Quentin."

"Right." Quentin couldn't hide a nervous twitch. "She's awake?"

"At the moment, yes. She'll be looking forward to seeing you, I'm sure."

Quentin winced at the news. He probably hated reporting to his mother, who tended to ask uncomfortable questions that probed more deeply than a proctologist. Gruffly, he said, "I'll be in touch with Dodo as soon as possible. But I'm sure you understand I'm very busy right now."

"Of course. I expect I'll be meeting with you in a few days."

"What for?"

"Julius and I were cotrustees of your mother's estate. Standard safeguarding practices. Mrs. Hyde will probably choose you to represent Julius's part from now on. You or," he said gently, "one of your siblings, I suppose. Whomever she selects, I look forward to working together."

The situation had clearly occurred to Quentin already, but his closed face indicated that he wasn't prepared to discuss control of his mother's vast estate just yet. Not until he'd figured out a plan to his own advantage.

Quentin turned to Monica. "You shouldn't be subjected to unwanted attention, Monica. I'll take you home."

"I don't have a home at the moment."

"Find another hotel, damn it." Quentin's temper erupted once more. "You shouldn't be out in public. What will people think? We can't have your face in the papers all over again." He glared at the collage of newspaper photographs on the wall, and his bulldog jaw tightened—perhaps at the thought of all that money draining away.

Monica said, "I could wear a veil, I suppose. It might look very Jackie Kennedy. Or maybe I should stay with you for a little while, Quen? That way, you could keep an eye on my activities."

"What activities?"

She waved a graceful hand at her publicized good deeds. "My museum work."

"That kind of work," Quentin said, turning purple, "is going to stop immediately. We can't have you—well, we'll discuss it when we're alone."

"So I'll be moving in with you?" The honey thick.

"No, no!" Flustered, Quentin said, "With my wife in Mexico, I can hardly have my brother's widow staying in the same house."

"She won't be coming home for the funeral?"

Unless Quentin's wife spontaneously enjoyed a miracle cure for her various prescription drug addictions, Henry knew there was no chance she'd be home before hell froze over.

Henry watched and wondered. There was some kind of dynamic going on between the big ox and Monica. Quentin was the opposite of his brother Julius—not a womanizer or a lavish spender, or even a man who enjoyed many pleasures, so it was hardly a flirtation. Businesslike—that was Quentin. Devoid of subtle people skills. Probably lousy at intimacy. No wonder his wife turned to pills.

But Monica was looking like a startled doe—ready to dash into the forest if Quentin flashed his big antlers at her.

What was going on? Quentin ought to be furious with her. She'd lit a match to a considerable part of his inheritance. But there was something else in the air.

Abruptly, Henry found himself wondering if Quentin was capable of murdering his own brother.

Monica's deerlike body language hinted she was thinking precisely the same thing. And yet her eyes sparkled with interest. Confound it, was she actually attracted to Quentin?

To ease tensions, Henry said, "Monica, why don't you move into Hilltop? While Mrs. Hyde stays at the nursing home, you'd have all the privacy you could ever want. The staff is engaged part-time at the moment, but it only takes a phone call to gear up for you. I could drive you there myself, if you like."

Quentin's glare was suspicious as he tried to decide if Henry might be outmaneuvering him or whether having Monica out of the public eye was preferable.

Monica said, "Oh, Henry, you're so sweet."

"Nonsense." He patted her hand. "Mrs. Hyde will want you to be comfortable."

Quentin's complexion turned an even more dangerous shade.

Monica gently bit her lower lip, then said, "But the police told me not to leave town."

"I'm sure they meant you aren't supposed to abscond to South America. I can make a phone call on your behalf. Let them know how to reach you."

"It's not a bad idea," Quentin said at last, apparently concluding it would be best if Monica were to disappear from the public eye. He checked his watch. "I'd take you myself, but I'm meeting my daughter Arden."

"Arden's come home?" Henry couldn't stop himself from asking the question, and immediately regretted his slip.

Quentin zeroed in on Henry. "Yes, she's back from Italy or Budapest or wherever the hell she's been wasting her time."

"It will be good to have Arden around," Monica said. "She'll be a comfort to her grandmother."

Obviously, the last thing on Quentin's mind was his mother's comfort. He whipped out his cell phone. "Let me make sure her flight's on time. Maybe I can rearrange my schedule and take you to Hilltop."

While Quentin made a call, Henry got back to business. With Monica's BlackBerry in hand, he ran his finger down the long line of local and distant dealers who might have done business with Julius Hyde before his demise. He paused when he came upon a female name.

Leaning toward Monica, he asked softly, "Who's this?"

Monica's reading glasses had the Chanel interlocking Cs on the frames. She peered at the list in Henry's hand. "Oh, that's some woman Julius hired to haul a few things away last spring when we renovated a garage. It was just junk."

"Her listing says 'architectural salvage.' What does that mean, exactly?" Henry's radar had begun to hum.

"I don't remember. Maybe she was the one Julius played pool with. Quite the tomboy." Monica took off her glasses and looked into his eyes. "But listen, Henry, Julius was being positively nefarious once he decided he needed more income. He picked the least scrupulous associates. If you're serious about tracking down things Julius might have sold, you should look for someone who's one step from being a thief."

Good advice. But first he'd see Monica safely ensconced at Hilltop, just a stone's throw from his own apartment.

❧ 6 ❧

Arden Hyde took a US Airways flight to Pittsburgh, where the terminal was as empty as a bowling alley. She stopped in a bathroom to wash her face and check her bag. The Ambien and Xanax had worn off, leaving her feeling low. She contemplated her choices for revival. Half a caffeine pill? Just the thing.

She caught a taxi and sat in the back feeling her energy coming back. Great! The weather was fantastic! Autumn in Pennsylvania—what could be nicer? It made her think of a line from Proust, but she couldn't quite summon it up. And the view coming out of the tunnel and bursting across the bridge into Pittsburgh—breathtaking!

Arden heard herself chattering at the driver and realized maybe she needed to come down a notch, so she swallowed half an Ativan and sat back, confident she had sufficiently medicated herself to avoid too much reality but maintain the appearance of sentience. She'd put off her father's offer to pick her up at the airport, and he'd suggested they meet at the

Hyde house. The cab arrived at the burned-out mansion in the late afternoon. Her first glimpse of the old house was quite a shock. All that remained was an ugly hulk. Manderley after Mrs. Danvers.

In the driveway, Arden found her way blocked by police tape and a gum-chewing security guard. And Quentin Hyde.

Daddy climbed out of his long black Mercedes, holding his cell phone to his ear. He was shouting at someone about a merger. The other half of the Ativan called to Arden from her bag.

The security guard asked Arden to respect the crime-scene tape, so she stopped at the edge of the driveway, put on her sunglasses, and waited for Daddy to finish his shouting. The security guard left her alone and watched the passing traffic, sharpening his attention when a car slowed down so the passengers could gawk. She was back in Pittsburgh, all right, where even security guards took their work seriously.

As he bellowed into the phone, her father looked like he was holding off a heart attack by force of will. Since she'd last been home, he'd grown a little beard—carefully trimmed to give him the firm jawline that had long ago been lost to too many steak dinners at Morton's. He wore a too-tight camel-colored sport coat over a black sweater, and dark trousers that had been chosen, Arden was sure, to look slimming. His efforts were rather endearing.

Whoever was on the other end of his phone call was getting royally reamed, though.

Arden tuned him out. With her hands shoved into her pockets, she turned and stood looking at the remains of the once magnificent house. What she saw made her incredibly sad. She had no cherished childhood memories of the mansion—years of boarding school prevented that—but the idea that so many things of value had been destroyed gave her a surge of sorrow. And nausea.

Or maybe it was that last vodka on the airplane.

Quentin pocketed his phone. "Idiots."

"Hello, Daddy."

"You should go to law school," he said without greeting. "I need to get the new headquarters built. You could run the project while I focus on the merger."

The career path he outlined might have sounded wonderful fifteen minutes ago, before the Ativan. Now it was too dreary to think about. She kissed him on the cheek anyway and patted his chest with more fondness than she expected to feel. "It's nice to see you, Daddy."

He grabbed her shoulders—half hug, half something more demanding. "Why won't you work for Hyde Communications?"

She looked up into his fierce face and couldn't help smiling. "Because I'm no good at business."

"Nonsense. You're young! What, twenty-two? Twenty-three?"

"I'll be twenty-five in the spring."

"Plenty of time to finish your education. You have more intelligence than all your brothers put together."

"I have no ambition."

"You would, once you got your teeth into things. It's glorious, Arden. It's truly glorious."

She loved seeing the fire in his blue eyes. She couldn't bring herself to say how little she thought of cold-blooded business. Not when her passion lay in the power of the arts. "Slaying all those corporate dragons? Daddy, I'd be a total failure."

He let her go, perhaps seeing her distaste for commerce. "I won't give up, you know."

"That's rather nice to hear," she replied.

He fondled her hair. "Why are you so skinny? Don't you eat anything?"

"I want to fit in my clothes. You like?"

He seemed baffled by her wardrobe, which maybe looked a little worse for the plane ride. "Sure."

She sighed. "Tell me what's going on with the police. Have they decided how poor Uncle Julius died?"

"There was nothing poor about him." Quentin's face flushed all over again. "He was murdered. Shot and killed by a coward." He glared at the blackened house as if his keen vision might spot an important clue that the police had missed. "They tell me it was some homeless fellow who did it, but they don't say it with much conviction. The pathetic bastard doesn't look as if he could organize his own breakfast, let alone a killing. It's damn frustrating not to have answers."

Arden found herself saying, "What must he have thought when it happened? Was Uncle Julius frightened? I hate to think he was frightened, Daddy."

Quentin gritted his teeth. Maybe to hold back grief. "He wasn't."

"No?"

But her father didn't argue his opinion. Funny how he could flatly deny a fact if he didn't like hearing it. Perhaps that was the quality that had made him most successful in life.

Briskly, he changed the subject. "I want to know what things are missing from the house. The insurance bastards don't want to pay for anything because that damn Monica set fire to everything. Maybe we'll have to prove she was temporarily insane, but we'll plan a strategy for that soon enough. I want to know if anything was removed from the house before the fire. A list is our first step. There used to be a weird painting in the upstairs hall. Remember? All squares and squiggles. Ugly as sin. Surely it was valuable. But I noticed it disappeared last May."

"I think it was a Braque print, that's all, Daddy. A tourist thing. Monica probably gave it away when she redecorated the bedrooms. It was hardly worth getting upset about."

"She had no right to give anything away! The house and contents belong to Dodo. But Monica's been throwing family assets at any museum that will shovel it up. All to curry favor with people Julius alienated when he had his midlife crisis. What a waste."

"Maybe some things are better off where they are now."

"What do you mean?"

"Important art belongs in a museum where it's safe and everyone can be uplifted by it."

"Are you crazy? She had no right! And worse yet, I saw her with that sneaky lawyer of your grandmother's."

"Henry?" His name startled Arden more than the involuntary way it popped out of her mouth.

"That snake, Paxton," Quentin confirmed. "He's been up to something, too, since the fire. Julius mentioned they were at odds over Dodo's trust, but I never got the full story. We'll have to sort it out. But first we should know exactly what was lost in the fire. You can help with that?"

The thought of seeing Henry Paxton again gave Arden a pang. He was an unfortunate chapter perhaps best forgotten. How had they left things? If she could think straight, she might remember. "I could try," she said faintly.

"Good. I have some paperwork in my office. Some lists and notes. It's all Greek to me. You can take a look."

"Can it wait?" Arden felt herself crumbling inside. "I—I can't think, Daddy, while I'm looking like this."

"Like what?"

"This." She pulled at her hair, tugged at her clothing. "I'm a mess. I need to drop in at the salon and see if I can't get a haircut, maybe a facial."

"You look fine."

"I need to relax, too. I've got jet lag or something." Now that she'd made the decision to cut and run, she said with more conviction, "Really, I'll be much more useful if I could just have a couple of hours to pull myself together."

Quentin looked impatient for an instant, but he mustered some kindness. Maybe they disagreed about a lot of things, but he'd always had a soft spot for Arden. "All right, I'll drop you wherever you want to go." He took her elbow rather gently. "Come on. Get into the car."

Arden did as she was told, and after he'd closed the car door and was walking around to the driver's side, she put her palms together and gripped her shaking hands between her knees. Trying to distract herself from all the crap that was suddenly raining down around her, she sat looking at the grounds of the house. What had been lost in the fire?

One thing she'd spotted already, of course. In the little glen near the swimming pool, the sculpture of Achilles should have been keeping watch. But he was gone.

When Quentin climbed into the car, she nearly asked him. Had someone moved Achilles after the fire? Or had Monica made off with him before all that? Had she sold him? Or given him to a museum?

Instead, she said, "Is Mummy coming home? For the funeral?"

"No. She needs to work on her treatment."

"Of course."

Drug addiction, Arden knew, was hard work. At least, that's the way it was with her mother. Which was why Arden kept good track of her own medications. She didn't plan on ending up like Mummy, living all the time in a spa with a locked gate and a lot of awful people.

Quentin started the car. "Where to, honey?"

Arden gave him the address of the salon in Oakland where she knew people. If her father talked about anything on the drive, she could muster only humming noises of agreement. The hum seemed very loud in her head. But ten minutes later, she gratefully walked through the door of the nearly deserted salon. A college student was getting a noisy blowout at one station. Another student sat waiting, leafing through a limp magazine as tufts of hair blew along the floor. Things hadn't changed much.

Jody was doing her own nails at the counter. She looked up, unsurprised to see Arden after a year. "Hey."

"Hi." Arden put her slouchy bag on the counter and leaned on it. "Busy?"

Jody blew on the wet nails of her left hand. "Need something?"

"You still in business?"

Jody twisted her lips. "I wouldn't be sitting here if I wasn't. What do you want?"

Arden paid with traveler's checks and took her first bump in the salon lavatory. Just a little. Oh, it had been too, too long. The drug felt like stardust in her system. She tucked the rest of the cocaine in her bag— enough to survive a week with her family.

❧ 7 ❧

On Sunday people in Pittsburgh went to church and then watched football. No murder case could supplant the city's obsession with the Steelers, not even a billionaire who got himself shot. Roxy watched the game with some musician friends at a bar. They drank beer, ate hot wings, and held a sloppy rehearsal afterward.

Early on Monday morning, she walked a couple of blocks over to the Rite Aid store for a package of Lorna Doone cookies and a pocketful of Slim Jims. Then she stopped at the corner coffee shop.

Unfortunately, the coffee shop had changed hands again, and this time it was two nice Russian ladies running the place, and they didn't sell coffee. Or speak English. After some chattering and a lot of hand gestures, they made her a cup of tea, though, and Roxy bought a newspaper, too. She walked back to her house reading the headlines about Julius Hyde.

His photo made him look noble. Quotes from his friends made him sound like a saint. Well, that's the way things worked in his tax bracket.

The paper made his pyromaniac wife out to be Lady Macbeth and Annie Oakley rolled into one.

Roxy's current neighborhood was a section of the city called the Mexican War Streets for reasons she still hadn't figured out. The narrow two-story houses—jammed together with no space between for lawns or even clotheslines—were in various states of repair, ranging from a palatial renovation recently completed by a couple of gay lawyers, to a crack house on the corner. A few months back, Roxy had purchased three dilapidated houses with the idea of flipping them. But she'd run out of money. So she had moved into one place herself and put a couple of tenants in the others to prevent less law-abiding neighbors from dealing drugs in them.

On one side of her house lived Dolores, who made her living by prostitution and needed a place to hide from her bullying shithead of a boyfriend. Roxy rented the house on the other side to Adasha Washington, an ER doc who worked at the nearby hospital.

Roxy finished her breakfast, put on her sneakers, and ran once around the park. She found Adasha stretching her hamstrings on a park bench. Adasha was still wearing her hospital ID on a lanyard around her neck over a scrub shirt and a pair of shorts that showed off legs that had surely caused attention deficits in her anatomy class.

"How was the night shift?"

Adasha stood up and tried to mash her hair into a ponytail. "Two gunshot wounds, a baby delivery because the father fainted in the parking lot, and assorted cases of viral infections, common colds, sprains, and a broken leg sustained by a robbery suspect whom the police officers refused to unchain even while we set the leg. Oh, and an infestation of lice that would make an ant farm look deserted."

"Delightful. You ready to burn off some of that resentment?"

"Let's go."

They took off jogging at an easy pace, but as soon as they were warmed up Adasha quickly accelerated. She'd been a track star back in high school, a state champion distance runner, and Roxy only hoped she could keep up for the first couple of miles. After that, there was no use trying.

When they reached the river, running smoothly in the same rhythm, and started on the path upstream toward the old Heinz food plant, Adasha said, "I had a patient last night who could use your special brand of TLC."

"Oh, yeah?"

"A girl whose live-in boyfriend beats her up. She needs a fresh start. A place to live for a while, maybe some help getting a new job."

"Why didn't you call Social Services? Sounds like a case right up their alley."

"Her boyfriend's another doc. He could snoop the records and find out her whereabouts. I think he's liable to go after her again. The present situation is toxic, and normal channels just don't cut it. So I thought maybe you could find her an apartment—a place she could hide until she gets her shit together."

"How much time do I have?"

"Five days is my best guess. Plenty of time, right? She'll be in ICU for two, on a step-down floor for three or four days after that. Maybe longer if we find previous injuries that require care."

"Jesus. What did he beat her with?"

"A crockpot to the head, then a meat tenderizer to the bones of her face."

Roxy quelled the emotion that roiled inside her. It was the kind of story she should be used to by now. "He in jail?"

"Hell, no, he's some kind of hero in orthopedics. Rescues professional athletes from career-ending injuries. We wouldn't want a Superman like that to spoil his reputation, now would we? His girlfriend, on the other hand, is expendable as far as the bosses can see."

"I think I know a place she could crash for a while. And one of the neighbors is a nurse. Meanwhile, somebody needs to end his career."

"I'm working on it," Adasha said, and she sprinted ahead to a foot-bridge on the path.

Roxy sucked in some air and chased after her friend.

When they reached the opposite end of the bridge, Adasha settled into a slightly faster pace than before. Her breathing seemed no different when she asked, "How was your night, sister friend? Anything you want to tell me about?"

"Nope."

Adasha laughed. "Who was the guy? Anybody interesting?"

"Nobody you know."

"C'mon, honey, you gotta give me some vicarious sex. Was he hot? Good in bed? Don't hold out on me. I haven't had a man in over a year. My best lover requires double-A batteries."

"The guy was no good at all last night, as a matter of fact."

Adasha shot her an amused look, still running easily. "A game player? Wounded cowboy and strong Indian maiden? I know you hate that stuff."

Roxy didn't answer. She pretended she had to catch her breath instead. She wasn't sure what she'd been looking for when she paid the visit to Trey Hyde last night.

After another couple hundred yards in which Roxy decided what to say, Adasha spoke again. "I know you, Rox. When you don't talk, you're off the bead. Things getting weird again? No longer going to bed with guys just for the fun of it?"

"I'm great. Everything's great."

"Shut up," Adasha said without malice. "What's wrong? Flashbacks?"

"Nothing I can't handle."

Adasha snorted. "You think you can handle anything. But I know better. I was there, remember? When your family imploded? So don't play the tough lady with me. I don't need my stethoscope to hear there's something wrong inside your heart."

"I'm okay, Dasha."

"Sage?"

The mention of her daughter's name made Roxy grin. "She's great."

"How's your business?"

"A little slow."

"You broke?"

"You bet."

"I could lend you a few bucks."

"You've got the scariest student loans I ever heard of," Roxy managed to say. "So forget it. Jobs come in cycles. I'll come up with something soon."

"Oh, boy. Something like doing another little favor for your uncle Carmine?"

Carmine Abruzzo was the guy you called when you needed an arsonist to torch your failing but well-insured used-car dealership. But sometimes he needed jobs done that were a little less felonious—like asking for repayment of debt or settling disputes among other employees. Those things Carmine didn't like taking care of personally.

"I'm not that desperate," Roxy said. Not yet, anyway.

"Okay," Adasha said. "But let's get together soon, all right? You need somebody to talk to besides Nooch. You keep him around because he doesn't ask any questions. Just lets you alone. Not me. I'm going to push your buttons till you give it up, girlfriend. I have a couple of days off next week. Let's do some shopping. Surely you need a new pair of jeans, right? Or maybe it's time to buy yourself some girl shoes? Heels for once?"

"I need heels like a fish needs a bicycle."

Adasha laughed, sounding relaxed at last. "C'mon, Rox. Let's get some real exercise, what do you say? Ready to start running?"

Roxy begged off and let Adasha go ahead, probably headed for a ten-mile run that would allow her to sleep through the day until her next shift. Roxy turned around and jogged back to her neighborhood.

As Roxy stepped through her front door, her cell phone rang. She grabbed it off the newel of the staircase and opened it.

Her daughter's voice was loud and clear. "Mom, hey, can you come over here today?"

"Why aren't you at school?"

"I'm home sick."

"Senioritis?"

Sage said, "I don't need the third degree. I just need you to sign a permission slip."

"In high school, you still need my permission?"

"Can you come or not?" She sounded testy. The constant mood of the teenager.

Roxy said, "Sure. I have to stop by the yard first. I'll bring lunch."

Sage disconnected without saying good-bye, which meant Roxy was in the doghouse again. What her latest parental infraction was, she couldn't guess. She closed the phone.

Parenthood had come to Roxy early. She'd been seventeen, pregnant, and the size of a cow at her own high school graduation. When Sage was born, they were both lucky to have Roxy's aunt to live with. Even now, Sage lived at Aunt Loretta's place, and Roxy moved in and out, depending on the houses she renovated. Maybe the three of them together were a family therapist's dream team, but the arrangement worked most of the time. Adasha came around now and then to spread some calm if things got tumultuous.

Roxy ran up the stairs. Her current house was a construction site. Her furniture consisted of a bed and a tattered Salvation Army armchair, plus a couple of Tupperware storage containers for her clothes. As usual, a heap of library books was piled on the floor around the bed, their late fees growing daily.

She showered, threw on her jeans, a camisole, a T-shirt, and a couple layers of sweatshirts, then drove across the river. Chewing on a Slim Jim she sang along with Gracie Slick on WDVE. Nobody could rock and roll like Gracie Slick. Except maybe Aretha, but that was another stratosphere. At the first commercial, she flipped from classic rock—the traditional music of everyone in the construction business—to an all-news station. The headlines hadn't changed. Julius Hyde, philanthropist, shot and killed.

Some pathetic homeless guy was the suspected shooter. The police had found a gun in his nest behind the Hyde garage.

Roxy turned a corner and saw Nooch waiting nervously at the gate of the salvage yard.

Behind him, a rattletrap squad car sat in the middle of the yard, the idling engine sending up a noxious cloud of blue smoke.

Nooch hustled over to the truck before Roxy shut off the engine. His eyes were round with anxiety. Through the window, he said, "It's the cops. They want to talk to you. What did you do?"

Roxy killed the engine and climbed out of the truck. "Walk down the street and buy us some bagels. Some of those pecan-flavored ones. Take your time."

She handed over twenty bucks. Nooch grabbed it and obeyed, glad to get away before any trouble started. He glanced over his shoulder as he went.

Roxy slammed the door of her truck and crossed the gravel, still humming the old Jefferson Airplane.

Bug Duffy got out of the passenger side of the cruiser, balancing himself on two crutches. In high school, Bug had once punched Roxy, but he had since matured, gone to college, worked as a substitute teacher in the city schools for a while, then joined the Pittsburgh police force and worked his way up to detective. He didn't seem to regret punching her, though.

"You deserved worse than a fat lip," Bug said after they'd shaken hands. "You called my mother names."

"You were picking on Nooch, remember? You almost knocked out my front teeth. One's still crooked, see?" She showed him the damage.

Bug gave her teeth a closer look, grinning. "You took care of Nooch, even back then. What's he doing for you now?"

"Heavy lifting."

"What did he lift out of the Hyde mansion a couple of nights ago?"

Roxy eyed Bug sideways. "Nothing I didn't tell him to. What? You missing something? Or do you think Nooch killed Julius?"

"You know about the murder?"

"Hell, Bug, it's all over the news."

"I just wondered if maybe you have some information we hadn't heard yet."

Although his tone was still jaunty, Roxy gave Bug a once-over. He'd gotten his name in elementary school when he showed off for classmates by eating insects on the playground. Now he had a wife and a couple of redheaded little boys, Roxy knew, and a reputation for being a good cop. He was stubborn and thorough—exactly the kind of detective she didn't want hanging around her place of business.

She pointed at his crutches. "What did you do to yourself? Get wounded in the line of duty?"

His leg was encased in a blue strapped-up thing. "I tore up my knee playing touch football a couple of weeks ago. Nothing permanent. But the Hyde case brought everybody back on duty—even the ones in worse shape than me. You have time to talk a little, Roxy? Your name is on the list of contractors who were hauling junk out of the mansion. I drew the short straw, so I'm here to interview you."

Best to make like she was happy to see him. Roxy hooked her thumb at the garage. "Sure. I've got the Hyde job paperwork in my office. Want to take a load off while you read it?"

"That'd be great."

Bug's partner got out of the driver's side of the cruiser. She was a middle-aged woman with a ponytail that seemed to yank her face so tight she looked like a hawk. With obvious distaste, she glanced around the yard.

The place was littered with the usual stuff Roxy collected—piles of building materials, a few Victorian toilets, and some broken garden accessories, all sitting in mud. A lion's head fountain, propped against the fence, was going to bring in a couple of hundred bucks as soon as the right customer drove by. Some general refuse was lying around, too. Roxy hadn't had time to make a trip to the dump lately.

The centerpiece of the yard, however, was the old hydraulic Al-jon car crusher, a piece of heavy equipment once used to smash automobiles down to stackable size. The rusting hulk hadn't been used in over ten years—back when some of her uncles had run a junkyard on the same property. The whole setup was a city block in length, surrounded by a chain-link fence topped by razor wire to keep out the druggies and the homeless looking for a place to camp.

Roxy acknowledged that maybe the yard didn't look very tidy.

The neighborhood was what some people were calling "postindustrial." The streets were laced with bone-jarring potholes. A couple centuries of soot coated the cobblestone streets with a greasy black layer of crud. Surrounding blocks featured no-name warehouses, a restaurant supply house, and some "collision repair" shops that probably included at least one dealing in stolen car parts. Half of the other buildings sat empty while their owners hoped a developer might come along and convert them into trendy condos. But the ballet theater's rehearsal space and a flower wholesaler—signs of hope for the gentry—lay several blocks eastward. The smell of the nearby Allegheny River hung around most days. But the city had installed fancy new streetlights—high-tech and green—with hopes that good things might follow.

Bug said, "Roxy, this is Crystal Gaines. She's stuck driving me around today. Crys, this is Roxy Abruzzo."

The lady cop didn't acknowledge Roxy except to say, "What are you? Some kind of junk dealer?"

"Read the sign." Roxy pointed at the board that swung over the open door of the garage: Bada Bling Architectural Salvage.

"Looks like junk to me," the woman muttered.

"Crystal," Bug said, "why don't you wait with the car? I'll talk to Roxy alone."

"You better stay in the car," Roxy said. "My dog doesn't like girls."

Crystal opened her mouth, but Bug shot her a look and she shut up.

"This way," Roxy said, leading him toward the garage.

Her office had once been a barbershop that opened onto the side street, but she'd blocked off that door with some sheet metal, then busted through the wall to the garage to connect the two. Which made for an almost civilized space for her desk, dusty computer, and files. The office was warmed by a temperamental electric space heater. The floor was pock-marked linoleum. The barbershop mirrors had been broken long ago, but the counter remained and now functioned as a place to heap the mail. She kept a broken hockey stick on the counter in case trouble walked through her door.

Inside, Bug said, "Don't hold anything against Crystal, Roxy. She just got her promotion, but she's stuck playing chauffeur to me until the Hyde case cools down. She thinks of it as *Driving Miss Daisy* in reverse, so she's feeling pissy."

Roxy closed the door. "Does she suspect Nooch, too?"

"Aw, c'mon, we're just asking around for information, that's all."

Roxy grabbed a couple of Red Bulls out of the case on the floor. This time of year, the office was usually cold enough that she didn't need a refrigerator. She handed a can to Bug. "Sorry. Best I can do. A methhead stole my coffeepot. Sit down while I find the paperwork."

Bug leaned his crutches against her desk and eased himself down onto the sprung leather sofa that had been part of the original barbershop. It hadn't gotten any more comfortable, but Bug didn't seem to mind. He stretched his bad leg out in front of him. "I hear Nooch's probation hearing is next week. He ready for that?"

"Sure, why not? He's behaved himself for ten years."

"Except for that thing last Christmas. He helped his cousin steal an old lady's Toyota?"

"That was a mix-up. Nooch thought they were helping Mrs. Sedlak find her car in the Macy's parking lot."

"But the cousin drove it off and sold it two days later."

"Hey, a judge decided Nooch was innocent in that situation. Even Mrs. Sedlak said so. He carried her shopping bags, for crying out loud. He stays out of trouble."

Bug cocked an eye at her. "That first conviction of his? Nooch beat up

Poskovich real bad, Roxy. Brain damage and everything. Okay, Poskovich was a lowlife, but still. Everybody figures the only thing keeping Nooch from doing something like that again is you."

"He won't go nuts again."

"Unless he thinks he needs to protect you. He's as bad as that dog of yours—loyal and vicious. Not a great combination."

"Don't worry about either one of them." She shuffled some papers, counting to ten. Then, "You still married to Marie?"

"Yeah, eight years."

"She okay? I heard . . ."

"She's doing all right. Lots of tests."

"What do they think it is?"

"Maybe just exhaustion. Or that, whaddayacallit, Epstein-Barr." He ran his thumb around the top of his pop can. "Or MS."

"You tell her I said hi, okay?"

"She may not want to hear I've seen you." Bug grinned a little. "She's still mad about her brother Darrell."

"I didn't do anything to Darrell."

"Took his girlfriend. Hid her for a month."

"He was beating her up, Bug, and you know it."

"She could have gone to a shelter."

"Where her kids would get onto some CYS list? Once that starts, she'd be living in constant fear they'd be taken away from her. Which would have made Darrell perfectly happy, by the way. It was only a matter of time before he started beating on them, too."

"Darrell went to jail."

"For a grand total of five weeks."

"And somebody put an open can of anchovies under the seat of his car. Only he didn't find the can for weeks. He had to get rid of that car. It stunk permanently."

Roxy grinned. "No kidding?"

"Marie's whole family blames you for everything."

"I can take it. His girlfriend couldn't."

Bug shrugged. "The system would work, if you'd let it."

Roxy knew better.

Bug said, "You're looking good, though, Rox. I hear you're singing, too. For a couple of bands on the South Side, right? You're just as hot as you were in high school. I had a crush on you back then. But who didn't?"

"Believe me, I'm feeling my age at the moment." Roxy popped open her Coke and slurped off the foam. "How old are your kids?"

"Justin's seven. Trevor's five."

"Wait till they're teenagers, then we'll talk."

Bug popped open his Red Bull, too, and held it away so the foam dripped on the floor. "What's wrong? Your daughter giving you trouble? How old is she?"

"Seventeen, going on thirty."

"Wow. Has it been that long? You have any more kids?"

"Hell, no."

"Married?"

"Nope."

"Seeing anybody? I heard Flynn's back in town. He's got a job working as a chef, right?"

"What are you, some kind of dating service?"

There had been no flirtation in his tone, and Roxy found herself glad that Bug was one guy she hadn't seduced in high school. For her, the teenage years had been a struggle figuring out how to make the world spin in a way that gave an iota of power to a girl who didn't have any to begin with. Plus the sex had been fun.

She shook off the memories and said, "Can you tell me about the Hyde murder? I heard the rainstorm messed up your crime scene."

"A little."

Roxy hoped the rain had obliterated all footprints and—more important to her—the wheel tracks of the handcart. She said, "I saw a homeless guy on the TV. He's really the shooter?"

Bug rolled his eyes. "That's the prevailing theory. Seems he lived be-hind a garage off and on for months. Had a few run-ins with Hyde and the chauffeur. That'll all be in the newspaper tomorrow. For the last year or so, various people from the house called us to sweep him out. So there was a history of antagonism. We're spending a lot of man-hours on him but you know as well as I do it's a long shot. It keeps the media off our backs, though."

"The news said something about you guys not finding any shell casings at the scene."

"Whoever killed Hyde either used a revolver or had the presence of mind to pick up the shell casings after shooting him."

"Professional hit?"

Bug laughed. "You a conspiracy theorist? Some international cartel decided to visit Pittsburgh to terminate Julius Hyde? We doubt it. Maybe the homeless guy ate his shell casings. Me and sixteen other cops are try-ing to dig up somebody else who had a reason to kill Hyde."

"Good luck."

Bug took a slug from his can. "I'm supposed to run down all the guys who were stripping stuff out of the house that day. When I saw your name on the list, I figured I'd come here first." He smiled. "I mean, you've always had a temper, Roxy."

"I hope you shared that opinion with everybody at the station house, too."

"Nah, I want all the credit for arresting you."

"Maybe somebody will give you a parade. Here's the list of stuff I took from the Hyde house."

She had ruffled through the mess on her desk. She found the paper-work for the Hyde job under the hammer she used to weigh down the stuff that hadn't made it into the file cabinet yet.

Bug set his Red Bull on the floor and accepted the papers. He glanced down the list of items she'd been authorized to take from the burned-out mansion. "You still have everything here?"

"Yep. I sold some of the staircase spindles to an antiques dealer, but he won't show up until tomorrow. You want his address? Phone number?" She reached for her Rolodex.

Bug asked, "When did you pick up the stuff?"

"Friday night. I was there until about six."

"I heard that. Who else did you see?"

Roxy noticed he had waited for her to volunteer her whereabouts. "A couple of other contractors. And Julius, of course."

Bug couldn't hide his surprise. "You saw Hyde? Talked to him?"

Roxy propped her feet on the desk and linked her hands behind her head, making herself the picture of relaxed calm. "Yeah, I did some business with him before, so we were old buddies."

Bug sat back on the sofa. "Hell, Roxy, maybe you know more than I thought. What was going on up there?"

"Last I saw him, Julius was peeing in the pool. Otherwise, nothing much."

"Did you see our homeless guy?"

She shook her head. "Sorry."

"Anybody else?"

"Couple of morons moving a stove."

Bug nodded. "The Delaney brothers. Not exactly upstanding citizens."

"I know them a little. Maybe one of them shot Julius?"

"Not likely. Jimmy was the one who called 911 when they heard shots."

"They see anybody else?"

"You and Nooch." Bug went back to studying the paper. "Except Vincent thought you were some kind of city inspector." He glanced up. "You didn't disabuse him of that idea, did you?"

Roxy smiled, remembering the twenty bucks she'd scored. "Nope. You gonna bust me for taking a bribe?"

"Split it with me?"

"Sure." Smiling.

Bug said, "They also saw some other people. Hyde's youngest brother, for one. Thomas the third."

She nodded. "He goes by Trey. I didn't see him there."

"You know him? Wow, Rox, you get around better than ever, don't you?"

She shrugged. "Julius paid me to dispose of some stuff when he tore down part of the old carriage house last February. Two gargoyles. I sold 'em to a company in New York—and I made some real money on them. Just in time to pay Sage's spring tuition, thank heaven. Trey was in town at the time and thought his big brother should have gotten a piece of the profit, though, and the three of us had an argument. Eventually, they saw it my way. Nothing unusual in my business."

"Which business is that, exactly?" Bug asked in a different tone.

"Salvage," Roxy said evenly. "I buy and sell stuff from old buildings."

Bug let a pause fill the space between them before he said, "And what about your family business? The Abruzzos have had their fingers in a lot of pies over the years. Heck, Carmine was making book back when we were in school."

"He probably still does," Roxy said.

Most everybody in the old neighborhood knew a little about Roxy's uncle Carmine and his crime organization—or they pretended they knew all about it—and certainly all of the cops in the city kept pictures of Carmine and his crew handy.

Roxy said calmly, "I don't know what Carmine's doing these days, except getting old."

"I hear he's sick."

"News to me."

"Okay," Bug said. "What about you? With Nooch as your knee breaker, you got anything else going on?"

Roxy had grown up fielding questions about her family. Carmine's operations were loosely connected to the larger, more complex Abruzzo family activities in New Jersey and New York. Locally, Uncle Carmine was smart enough to stay out of jail, but his various employees had done time for loan-sharking, illegal gambling, fencing stolen goods, and other, even less savory offenses.

Most of the time, Roxy had kept her distance from the Abruzzo family businesses. With Sage to protect and Nooch to keep out of trouble, she'd found her own path, which didn't stray into Carmine's territory unless she could keep her involvement completely quiet. The cops came nosing around with questions now and then, though.

Roxy looked him dead in the eye. "You're fishing, Bug. If you had something on either one of us, you'd have come here with more backup than your lady driver."

Bug said, "With Carmine sick, everybody's wondering what happens to his empire."

"Empire? You mean some old video poker machines and a restaurant that serves lousy spaghetti? C'mon, Bug, I'd make a better living if I sold burgers out of a drive-up window."

He smiled again and shrugged. "I figured I have nothing to lose by asking. As far as I know, no Abruzzo ever killed anybody in this city."

"As far as you know?"

Easily, Bug switched topics. "So you know Trey Hyde, too?"

"I know him a little. He isn't part of the family company—Hyde Communications, or whatever it's called. You talk about organized crime, that cable TV business is a license to print money. But Trey pays for those deep-sea exploration things—ships that go looking for old treasure."

"I heard about that. He get along with his family?"

Roxy pulled a face. "Does anybody get along with their family?"

"Sorry. I forgot about your folks. You ever hear Trey and his brother argue? Anything to make you think Trey held anything against Julius?"

"We didn't get into that kind of conversation." Truth be told, her conversations with Trey were mostly about where to put which body part and how fast. But telling Bug might make him blush.

Bug said, "In your acquaintance with Julius, did you ever get a hint that anyone thought ill of him? Might want him dead?"

Truthfully, Roxy said, "He was a pretty easygoing guy, as far as I could see. Paid on time. Enjoyed a dirty joke. Didn't blow a gasket if Rooney peed on his lawn. I don't know why anybody would want to kill him."

"Yeah, that's what we hear from everybody. So far." Bug put the papers on his knee. "Okay, here's the deal. I'm going to report back what you had to say, and somebody else will probably come calling. The two guys running this case are under a lot of pressure to wrap things up fast. Could be you might remember something they think is important. Between now and then, if you think of anything, here's my card. Call me. I mean it, Roxy. If you've got some real information, everybody including you is going to be much happier if you call us, not the other way around."

He flipped his card onto her desk.

She didn't reach for it. "Is that a generic threat you use with everybody, Bug?"

"It's a friendly suggestion, that's all. I mean, we could put you in one room and Nooch in another and see if the two of you remember the same stuff."

"You aren't going to do that."

"I probably wouldn't, no, but I can't speak for the whole department. Nooch is a scary-looking guy, and he hasn't been an angel all his life. They're looking at everyone for this murder, Rox. If anything comes to your mind, give me a call. You might spare Nooch an interrogation."

"Thanks for the preferential treatment." Roxy used her toe to kick Bug's crutches toward him.

"You're welcome."

After Bug left, Roxy turned up the space heater. She sat in the barbershop and thought about things. The Hydes, damn them. She should have known better than to get mixed up with that family in the first place. It didn't pay to stray too far out of her own neighborhood.

She unlocked her desk drawer and took a peek inside. Trey's gun lay there, just where she'd left it. Maybe she should have given it to Bug. On the other hand, the gun might be valuable later. And it would only cause more questions and maybe lead to the statue. She closed the drawer and locked it again.

Her safest bet was to unload the statue fast, before the cops really started nosing around. She reached for her Rolodex and flipped through it, hoping a name might jump out at her.

The desk phone rang. Roxy considered letting it go to voice mail, but what the heck—it might be necessary to eat this week.

"Roxy?" a voice shouted when she'd identified herself. "You there?"

If she were paid a nickel every time she was asked if she was in the office, she'd never have to work. "I'm here, Freddie. What's up?"

Freddie Manfredo, a guy who demolished buildings for the city, bellowed as if he were standing on the moon. "I'm here at a teardown in East Liberty. We got some kind of pictures in white plaster."

Roxy rubbed her forehead to stave off a headache. She liked Freddie, and he often called when he found stuff he didn't understand. She was usually glad to hear from him. Unlike most demo guys, he didn't destroy everything in his path. "A bas-relief."

"You're the best, kid." The noise of a bulldozer roared over the phone line.

"Thanks. Good condition?"

"Coupla cracks, nothing major. It's a jazz band or something."

The neighborhood of East Liberty had been a thriving kind of second "main street" for the city until the Johnson administration edict came down to create cheap housing for the poor. Half the beautiful art deco buildings had been razed to build sterile high-rise apartment complexes that quickly became nests of family dysfunction and crime. Fifty years later, the city was trying to undo the mess by tearing down more buildings to make way for big-box stores and peripheral office space for the nearby hospitals. The theory was that all the indigenous people would move to pretty houses in the suburbs, but it didn't work that way. Roxy's observation was that more poor families were getting broken up just like back when LBJ gave the orders.

But there was a good chance the bas-relief Freddie found was a left-over from one of the old East Liberty theaters. With luck, she might be able to sell it to the fancy new August Wilson cultural center downtown.

"Save it for me, Freddie?"

"I'll be here till noon tomorrow," he yelled, and hung up.

Roxy wrote Freddie's name on a Post-it and stuck it to the side of her computer screen. Maybe the bas-relief was one of the kind made during FDR's time, when real artists were paid to create public art. In which case it might be worth a pretty penny. If not—well, it would probably be worth the gasoline to drive up to East Liberty.

Outside, Rooney threw himself against the office door to pop it open. The door burst inward and banged against the wall. The dog trotted into the office, panting hard and tracking mud on the linoleum. He skidded to a stop, made eye contact, and gave a woof. Then whirled around and dashed outside again.

Roxy sat looking after him. "What's the matter, Lassie? Timmy fell down the well again?"

She could hear him barking outside. Thinking he'd maybe cornered a couple of skateboarding kids on her property again, Roxy followed.

But Rooney stood in the shadow of the car crusher, his head cocked at an angle, listening. Roxy shoved her hands into her pockets and listened, too.

Which is when she heard two gunshots. Then two more.

Followed by the distant squeal of tires.

A silver Monte Carlo—vintage with fancy hubcaps and a tattered lan-dau roof—roared laboriously up the street, took the corner with another scream of rubber, and disappeared around the block.

"What the hell—?"

Rooney followed Roxy to the gate, and they stood together looking in the direction the car had gone.

A minute later, a red Mustang came lurching up the street, too. The driver was swerving like a drunk on his way home from a bachelor party.

Surprising the hell out of Roxy, the Mustang turned into the salvage yard and slid to a stop in the loose gravel. Screwed to the front bumper of the car was a pink vanity plate that read SEXY BABY.

But it was Nooch who popped the passenger door and heaved himself out of the car. "Rox, you won't believe what just happened!"

By that time, Roxy had already noticed the bullet holes in the driver's-side door. She squinted to see who was behind the wheel and wasn't happy to recognize the face.

Nooch handed over a bag of bagels. "They were all out of the Parmesan cheese kind," he reported. "That's what you wanted, right? I asked them if they were going to make another batch, but they said if I couldn't get there before nine, I should—"

"Nooch," Roxy said. "What happened? And what are you bringing her around here for?"

"This is my cousin Kaylee. Kaylee Falcone. Well, she's kind of a second cousin, really."

Kaylee climbed out of the car, all long legs on another pair of expensive-looking high-heeled sandals. Today she wore a wraparound dress with matching leggings, no coat. The wind had kicked up, and she hugged herself against the cold, trying to hide her nipples. She'd been crying again, and she didn't look as if she'd gotten much sleep. Her smeary mascara gave her the look of a high-fashion raccoon.

She looked at Roxy and hiccupped. "Somebody just took a shot at me!"

"Kaylee," Nooch said formally, "this is Roxy. Roxy, this is—"

Roxy pushed the bag of bagels into Nooch's chest. "I know who she is. What the hell is she doing here?"

Kaylee leaned on the hood of the car and gave a gasping sob. "I don't know what's going on. Last week my life was just perfect and now—now everything's gone crazy. I saw Nooch down at the bagel shop and we were just talking and I said I'd give him a ride, but then—then a car zoomed past and—and—y'know, this city isn't safe anymore. And holy shit, I think I'm gonna faint."

Roxy grabbed her just as Kaylee's knees gave out. The girl sagged against her, all skin and bones and goose bumps.

"Help me get her inside," Roxy said to Nooch.

He picked up Kaylee and carted her clumsily across the yard to the office. Rooney ran around them in circles, panting with excitement. Roxy pushed open the door and stood back. When Nooch dumped Kaylee on the couch, Rooney jumped up and licked her face.

"Oh, gross!" Kaylee sat up, woozy, but mad. "That dog is totally dirty!"

"Her boyfriend got killed," Nooch said to Roxy. "And now somebody's shooting at her, too."

"Get this dog out of my face!"

Roxy snapped her fingers, and Rooney flopped onto the floor at her feet. She handed Bug's Red Bull to Kaylee.

"I told her you'd help," Nooch said.

"What am I supposed to do?"

Kaylee wiped the dog slobber from her face with the back of one hand, further smearing her makeup. She took a sip of Red Bull and grimaced. "Believe me, you're not my first choice, either."

Nooch said, "The police arrested her."

"They didn't arrest me! The cops came to my apartment to talk. They think I killed Julius."

"Did you?"

"Hey," Nooch protested. "Kaylee's a nice girl. She's got a temper sometimes, but she's nice."

"The police don't think so," Kaylee said, looking tired.

Roxy folded her arms across her chest. "You don't need me, honey. You need a lawyer."

"I've *got* a lawyer. I called him when the cops questioned me. But I can't pay him, because Julius didn't give me my allowance yet this month. Look, I don't like you any more than you like me, but Noochie said—"

"Hold it. Rewind." Roxy put up her hand to stop the flood of idiocy. "The cops really think you killed him?"

"They asked a bunch of questions."

"When?"

"All day yesterday! And again this morning! It's a wonder I got any sleep at all. They kept pushing and pushing until I finally gave those guys a piece of my mind."

Nooch said, "Kaylee knows how to do that. She was in this fight once in a drugstore—"

"A salon," Kaylee corrected. "If you're talking about that time I shoved a lady into a display of hair products. She was the one mouthing off, but they made me pay for the damages!"

"No, the drugstore. When you hit a guy with magazines or something."

"Oh, that! It was the post office." Kaylee seemed pleased to recall the story. "I threw my grandmother's mail at a cop behind me in line. I was picking up her mail because she was in the nursing home, you know? And he gave me a hard time about my skirt being short or—I forget exactly. So I let him have it. How was I supposed to know he was a cop?"

"Okay, okay." Roxy steered them both back to the crisis of the moment. "What about the night before last at Trey's apartment?"

"What about it?"

"Did the police come visit you then?"

"Not while I was there. Trey threw me out, the bastard. I was upset, but he made me go home! There's something wrong with him. Then Sunday the cops came to my house and talked for, like, hours."

"But they let you go? Didn't charge you?"

"The *lawyer* charged me."

"I mean—never mind."

Nooch flopped onto the sofa and opened the bagel bag. "Roxy can help. There's all kinds of people she helps."

"I don't think so." Kaylee stood up unsteadily. "This was a bad idea. I'm going back to my apartment."

"Sure, go ahead," Roxy said. "Those guys in the Monte Carlo are probably waiting for you there."

Nooch pulled out a bagel and frowned at it. "Was I supposed to get Parmesan? Or pecan? I forget."

"What do you mean?" Kaylee asked Roxy.

Roxy stood looking down at the bedraggled girl and almost felt sorry for her. It must be hard going through life with shit for brains. "You think it was random that a couple of guys shot at your car? After your boyfriend is murdered?"

"Who said anything about shooting at me? Those guys probably robbed a store or—or—" Kaylee began to doubt her own theory and frowned. "Why would anybody shoot at me?"

"Face it, Kaylee. Somebody doesn't like you."

"Who?"

"Besides me?" Roxy shrugged. "I don't know. One of Julius's friends? Or his family? His wife? Somebody who's pissed about all the stuff he gave you?"

Kaylee's face scrunched into a surly pout. "There was lots of stuff. Not just jewelry. Big stuff."

"Such as?"

"A building, for one thing. A warehouse or something down on the river. He took me to see it once. He said I could sell it, if I wanted to, as soon as I got the title. Why a building needs a title, I don't know. He wanted the best for me. Said I deserved a break in life. He actually said that."

"You're still a kid if you believe the pillow talk." Roxy didn't feel like explaining how come a rich man's family might be unhappy that their heir apparent had been generous with his tattooed ho. Chances were, they wanted to repossess her car and everything else he'd given her. And what easier way than scaring her first?

Or maybe there was more to the story.

Kaylee suddenly looked forlorn. "I shouldn't have quit my job at the salon. Good jobs like that are hard to find."

"Look, Kaylee, you don't have to take my advice, but unless you want your pretty red car to be further air-conditioned, I think it might be a good idea for you to disappear for a while."

"Disappear?"

"Don't go home. Do I have to spell it out? Find someplace else to stay for a few days, until the police figure out who killed Julius."

"Where am I supposed to stay?"

"With friends?" When Kaylee looked blank, Roxy said, "What about your family?"

The girl's expression loosened. "Except for Nooch, they'd sell me out for the price of a pizza."

"So stay at Nooch's place."

Nooch chose that moment to let out a bodily noise. He looked sheepish, and Kaylee rolled her eyes.

"I see your point," Roxy said, then began hating herself for being such a soft touch. "Oh, hell, I'm going to regret this. There's a house I've been renovating across the river. Nothing fancy, but at least you won't get shot at over there. How are you with a paintbrush?"

Kaylee blinked. "Paintbrush?"

"I don't suppose you know how to fix a leaky toilet? I haven't gotten around to that yet, either."

"What kind of house is this?"

"A nice house. Or it will be eventually." It was a waste of breath explaining the lack of furniture. Or the missing floor in the kitchen, either. Kaylee would find out all the shortcomings for herself. "If you want to crash there for a little while, it's fine by me. But I'm not your babysitter, understand? If you need anyone to bring you bonbons and fashion magazines, Nooch can do it."

Kaylee mulled over Roxy's offer, the steam practically shooting out of her ears while her brain processed the situation. Finally, she must have decided she didn't have any other choices. "Okay. Maybe just for a night or two."

"I wasn't asking you to be my permanent roommate."

Kaylee stuck out her tongue, then asked, "What about my car? Everybody knows my car. Should I ditch it?"

In a city as small as Pittsburgh, a dingbat blonde in a red Mustang with a SEXY BABY plate was pretty obvious, Roxy had to admit. "You can leave it here. Nooch can take you over to the house in my truck."

Nooch looked astonished, as if she'd suggested he should run for president. "You're gonna let me drive the truck?"

"I don't have time to play taxi service." Roxy turned to Kaylee. "If you want to make yourself useful, take Nooch to the mall first. Find him something to wear for his probation hearing on Friday."

"Something to wear? Like a suit?"

"Make him look like normal."

Together, they looked at Nooch.

Kaylee said, "He's never going to look like anything but an ape."

Roxy almost socked her. "Just get him some nice pants and a decent shirt. A belt, maybe."

"Shoes?" Kaylee glanced at Nooch's gigantic boots.

"Sure, whatever."

"What am I supposed to use for money?"

Roxy searched her pockets and peeled off Trey's C-note. "See how far this goes." She handed the bill to Nooch.

"Okay." Kaylee wrestled with her thoughts for a moment and finally said, "Thanks, I guess."

"Don't thank me yet," Roxy replied.

Because if Bug Duffy came around looking for ways to connect Roxy with any part of Julius's death, she knew what diversion she could toss in his path. Add a bad temper and some expensive gifts from the dead man, and the cops would have lots of reasons to put Kaylee into the center of their investigation. Maybe they'd spend less time wondering what Roxy and Nooch had been doing at the Hyde house.

When the truck rumbled out of the yard, Roxy went into the garage and walked deeper into the vast building past her inventory—a couple of stair-cases, a slew of doors, a bunch of garden urns, and a lot of stuff she should have unloaded by now. She unlocked a door, passed through a tunnel and another door before she entered the old fur storage. In the back of a vault where water dripped down the wall, the statue stood under his splotched canvas tarp.

Roxy tugged the tarp down and took another look at him. His face looked empty, just the way she liked her men. But, God, he was beautiful. Probably worth a fortune.

"Are you going to be a lot of trouble?" she asked. "Because I prefer to get rid of trouble fast."

8

On the phone from her bed in the nursing home, Dorothy Hyde said, "Can we pin it on Monica?"

Henry nearly choked on his morning coffee. "I beg your pardon?"

"Don't get the vapors," Dorothy snapped. "Pretend it's my dementia talking. If Monica killed my son, a lot of problems would be solved. The insurance company would have to pay us the settlement on the house, and the share of Julius's estate that would have gone to his wife could stay in the family."

"Have you suggested this scenario to anyone else, Mrs. Hyde?"

"Of course not. I'm old, but I'm not crazy. What do you think? Can we come up with some evidence?"

"I'm not entirely comfortable with—"

"Comfortable! I'm the one they tie to the bed at night! Don't talk to me about comfort. I'm getting irritated with your lack of enthusiasm, Henry. I don't suppose you've found my Achilles yet either, have you?"

"I have some promising leads."

"Leads! What are you—Philip Marlowe? Leads are not good enough. Call me when you've got something worthwhile to say for yourself."

She banged down the telephone and left Henry's ear ringing.

He turned off his phone and threw it onto the sofa with more force than he intended. The old bat was a menace to his mental health. A few calming breaths, and then he could think clearly again.

It occurred to him for the first time that perhaps he had miscalculated.

But with Monica settled into a suite of rooms at Hilltop and her wishes attended to by the hastily reassembled staff of the estate, Henry decided he could leave her for a day. In fact, it might be smart to let the widow contemplate her options for a while. She seemed entirely unaware that the family was putting up with her only as long as it took them and the insurance company to decide her role in the settlement of the house fire.

Not to mention Dorothy's brainstorm.

When Henry told Monica he needed to make a trip into the city, she got teary-eyed all over again. "Oh, Henry, you're going to find Samson for me, aren't you?"

He assured her Samson was his highest priority, and Monica nearly kissed him good-bye. He'd seen the impulse glowing in her eyes. Perhaps a little Texas two-step was in his future.

Armed with a list of people Julius Hyde might have contacted to sell off his art—a list Monica had been happy to collaborate on as long as Samson was still in the picture—Henry made only a few phone calls from the car before he realized he was going about his investigation far too straightforwardly. It would be much smarter, he decided, to ambush people.

Which is how he found himself pushing through the plate-glass door of a pizza parlor at lunchtime. A plate-glass door, in fact, that had obviously been kicked in by burglars and was now held together with duct tape.

The heavy smell of garlic hung in the humid air of the shop. A heart-stopping menu was posted on the wall above the antique cash register. The printed prices of various cholesterol-heavy items had been crossed out with a marker and replaced with new numbers.

The patrons of Bruno's Pizza and Subs—most of them hunched over sandwiches at small, wobbly tables and watching *Judge Judy* on a small television behind the counter—turned to look at Henry when he entered. He made a mental note to leave his Burberry raincoat behind next time if he had any hope of blending into the neighborhood. Everyone including the proprietor—who had just skimmed a hot pizza onto the counter with a big wooden paddle—seemed to favor multiple layers of the hooded sweat-shirt as their sartorial statement.

One guy with his mouth full of calzone and a severe case of plumber's butt gave a particularly loud snort at Henry before turning back to his lunch.

At the counter making conversation with the swarthy proprietor stood a leggy brunette in jeans and boots and a shapeless sweatshirt that somehow managed to convey a spectacular shape beneath its folds. Her derriere was a thing of beauty. A crucifix dangled on a thin chain around her neck, and she leaned one elbow on the counter with the confident air of a woman who knew every male eye in the establishment had lin-gered on her for a moment's fantasy.

Henry took a second to formulate on an appropriately working-class pickup line and headed across the pizza shop toward her. But in a heart-beat, the scene of blue-collar lunchtime tranquillity turned to chaos.

A man sitting at one of the small tables struck a flame on his plastic cigarette lighter and stuck it under the brunette's beautiful bottom.

And with the speed of a striking rattlesnake, she scooped one hand under the pizza and flipped the whole pan—hot cheese and all—straight into the side of her attacker's head. He howled, dropped the lighter, and used both hands to claw the steaming cheese out of his fa-cial hair. His dining companion—snickering one instant, then leaping to escape a similar fate—was no match for the brunette. She clocked him with her fist. He grabbed his nose and fell straight back into his chair, which somersaulted over backward. Two soft drink cups flew into the air, and the customers at nearby tables jumped up to avoid getting splashed.

Everybody in the shop was suddenly cussing like truckers.

Henry stepped over the man who'd been punched—he was writhing in pain as he clutched his nose—and he took the elbow of the furious brunette.

Henry said, "May I escort you outside?"

She socked him in the gut, and Henry doubled over. When he could breathe again, he realized she had charged outside. He staggered after her, and arrived on the sidewalk in time for her to spin around with one fist cocked.

He grabbed his stomach and braced for another blow. "Miss Abruzzo?"

She withheld the punch and stared at him. "Who the hell are you? Prince Fucking Charming?"

"My name is Henry Paxton," he replied, his voice strained. "And if I'm not mistaken, you are Roxy Abruzzo."

Her dark eyes narrowed to slits. "Do I know you?"

"Not yet." He straightened cautiously. "But we have a mutual acquaintance. Julius Hyde."

"Had." She took a step backward and lowered her fist. "I get it. You're another cop? Boy, Bug does fast work."

"I'm not a cop. But I'd like to talk to you about Julius."

"If you're not a cop, you can take a hike." She turned on her heel.

Unaccustomed to being summarily dismissed by women, Henry experienced a dumbfounded moment before following her down the sidewalk. One hand still protectively clutched his stomach, so he made a conscious effort to stop the milquetoast business. "Miss Abruzzo, I think you and I have a similar stake in Julius's death."

Over her shoulder, she snapped, "I doubt it."

"We're both interested in his property," Henry said. "And we'd both like to turn a buck, so to speak."

She spun around at that, and he realized she was potentially beautiful. Her eyes were a fathomless black and disconcertingly direct. She had good bones and an athletic carriage. Not to mention a show-stopping body and those dark, velvet-lashed eyes that were probably best appreciated in intimate circumstances. But her hair looked as if it had been plugged into a light socket. And her clothes needed to be burned.

She jammed her forefinger into his chest, however, with all the charm of a longshoreman. "Listen up, chum. I've heard enough about Julius Hyde's death to last the rest of my life. So you can pussyfoot around somebody else for information, got it?"

He grabbed her hand hard and didn't let go. Two could play the tough game. "Let's talk, Miss Abruzzo. You and me. About the things you got out of his house before he died."

It wasn't the manhandling that got through to her. Because he felt her tensile strength and knew she could knock him down like a fly. But she stared directly into his face—her own going poker blank as she took stock of the situation.

Rather than confirm or deny, she said, "Not here. I don't need the whole damn neighborhood knowing my business."

"Excellent." Henry regained his good cheer. "Where should we go?"

Roxy Abruzzo glanced down his body, perhaps taking in the Burberry or his neatly pressed shirt, his newly dry-cleaned trousers, his pair of Gucci loafers. Or maybe she took an entirely different measure of his manhood.

She disengaged her hand from his. "You live around here?"

Did her question suggest a different kind of meeting than the discussion Henry had proposed? "Unfortunately, no."

She shrugged. "Okay, then, come with me."

Henry had already identified her vehicle. He'd staked out her place of business a little before noon and followed her when she left the property.

The little red Mustang had been easy to tail, and he'd watched her stroll into the pizza shop ten minutes ago. Sexy baby, indeed.

She'd left the car parked next to a fire hydrant.

He opened the passenger door and froze at the sight of an ugly speckled dog growling murderously on the front seat.

"Don't mind Rooney," she said. "He's just a pup."

The animal had a basso profundo growl and a thick, quivering strand of drool that hung from his lower lip. Spikes studded the heavy collar around his thick neck.

Roxy climbed into the driver's seat and with a smack on the dog's haunches sent him into the backseat. "Get in," she said to Henry. "He'll definitely shed on you, but he probably won't bite."

Henry eased onto the passenger seat. "Is this a dog or a rhinoceros?"

"Don't worry. You won't be getting to know him well." She started the car and pulled away from the hydrant with neck-snapping acceleration. She turned down an alley and left the busy commercial street behind. The dog, meanwhile, panted at the back of Henry's neck. The radio blasted an old rock song, and she sang a couple of bars—her voice low and full and sexy with vibrato.

She cut the radio and said, "What's your name again?"

"Henry Paxton." He handed over one of his ivory vellum business cards. "Attorney-at-law."

She tossed the card onto the Mustang's console without glancing at it. "And what do you want with me?"

"Straight to the point. I like that in a woman. I found your name on the list of contractors who helped dismantle the Hyde mansion. You deal in architectural salvage."

"Where'd you get the list? You work for the city?"

"Monica Hyde was helpful."

She glanced across at him. "You working for her?"

"Why so worried about who I work for?"

"What do you think I am, an idiot? A lawyer doesn't come looking for me to hand over a lottery check."

Despite her rough talk, she had a Cleopatra profile—a prominent nose counterpointed by a femininely sharp chin and a full mouth. He guessed her age to be early thirties, but it was hard to be sure. On the steering wheel, her hands were strong—short nails not exactly clean. She wasn't skinny, but lean like one of those Olympic volleyball players who stripped down to a bikini to crush the competition.

She said, "I'm a 36C, if that's what you're wondering."

"Good to know if I need to buy you lingerie."

"You buy your wife a lot of lingerie?"

"No wife. Not at the moment, anyway."

She took a corner very fast and beat another car into the line of traffic, then touched the brake and glanced at him. "You almost look like a nice guy from the suburbs, Paxton—big house, two kids and a dog. But something's not quite right."

"You don't like my tie?"

"That's not it. You doing Monica?"

He replied, composed, "Monica is considerably older than I am."

"And she was Julius Hyde's wife. Well, you look smart enough not to shit where you eat. So tell me what you're after, Counselor. You want I should go looking for some oak flooring for your snazzy office? Or maybe a nice stained-glass window for a Hyde mausoleum?"

Henry decided he should be careful not to show too many of his cards to this one, or she'd clean him out. "I'm trying to track down valuable items that disappeared from the Hyde house. Some of the family members have sentimental attachments, and now that Julius is dead, they'd like—well, mementos, you could say. I'm willing to pay for their return."

"Things that disappeared? You mean stolen."

"Things that have gone missing."

"You calling me a crook?"

"No, no. I'm willing to buy back items that the family let go."

"Like what?"

"The Hydes are known for their collection of art. Porcelain. Fine glass. Objets d'art."

"Objets what?" she mocked. "That's not what I deal in, Paxton. I buy and sell the heavy stuff—things that need to be hauled in a truck, not packed in tissue paper. You need an antique picker, not me. Those guys are the ones with dirty hands."

"We're afraid some of the larger objects in the collection may have gone missing, too."

"Gone missing, huh? Nice euphemism." She wagged her head. "I see this kind of thing in families all the time. The older generation decides to pay for their prescriptions by selling the farm when the rest of the family isn't looking. Or they send their junk to the Salvation Army at tax time for a big tax deduction? They think they're doing the world a big favor by dumping their broken lamps on the loading dock of some charity."

Amused, Henry said, "You Pittsburghers are all alike."

"What's that supposed to mean?"

"You all have the same chip on your shoulder. The attitude that the whole world's against you."

"Fuck you. Want to know what usually happens? They take the tax deduction, then call the insurance company and say Grandma's silver teapot got stolen. They get an insurance payoff, and the police come around my neighborhood looking for somebody who stole an ugly teapot, which is now taking up shelf space at the Goodwill store. You think I'm wrong?"

"I think you're a reverse bigot, as a matter of fact."

She made a crude suggestion, then drove through a yellow light, hung a right, and a moment later crossed traffic and pulled through a set of imposing wrought-iron gates. A cemetery. Elegant headstones appeared on either side of the car. Some of them decorated with flags, some with plastic flowers. One grave site sported a black and yellow bow with trailing ribbons.

She pulled over, braked, and threw the transmission into park.

Henry cleared his throat. "Sorry. I think we're getting off on the wrong foot here, Miss Abruzzo."

"Damn straight we did."

"You have no earthly reason to trust me."

Roxy Abruzzo turned in her seat and said, "You mean, why should I trust a guy who dresses like an FBI agent? And talks like he just fell off the HMS *Pinafore*?"

"A Gilbert and Sullivan aficionado. Now that's a surprise."

"Save the patronizing routine, will you, Paxton? I'm a busy woman." Her dog emphasized her point by sticking his head between the seats, shoving his wet muzzle into Henry's arm, and growling ominously.

Thinking the dog might snap his arm like a matchstick, Henry hastened to the gist of the matter. "I'd like to buy any pieces Julius Hyde or someone else might have given or sold to you. Price is no hindrance."

"No hindrance?" She laughed. "You must think I have something really valuable."

"Do you?"

"I have some spindles from the stairs and a big fireplace with griffins. Is that what you want? The fireplace?"

"No."

"Then what?"

Her eyes flickered with intelligence. Had he made an error in judgment? Was asking to buy the sculpture of Achilles a tactical blunder? He wondered if she might already be two steps ahead of him.

He tried another tack. "Perhaps you know some of the other dealers Julius might have spoken with. Is there someone else I should approach?"

"Dealers?" She grinned coldly. "Or do you mean fences?"

"Are you always this defensive?"

"When somebody insults me, yes. Next thing that's going to happen is you saying maybe I killed Julius while I was hanging around his house."

"Did you?"

"See what I mean?" She had a harsh laugh.

"Miss Abruzzo—"

Her phone rang, interrupting Henry. She arched her lovely hips off the seat to wrestle the cell phone out of her jeans. She flipped it open. "Yeah?"

A voice squawked on the other end of the line.

"I'm coming. I got sidetracked."

The other voice again.

"I ordered a pizza, but something happened." She glanced at Henry. "No, nothing like that. Give me ten minutes."

Her caller hung up.

Henry said, "Problem?"

"You ask a lot of questions and don't give many answers." She slid her phone back into her jeans. "I've got places to be, Paxton."

"So do I. But maybe we can come to a mutually beneficial arrangement."

"You're looking for stolen goods," she said. "I've got a fireplace to unload, but that's it. If you want anything else, I suggest you keep going down that list of yours. Unless you've got something different in mind?"

Her direct gaze challenged Henry, and this time he felt sure she was measuring him.

He'd never met a woman with her particular brand of sex appeal— blunt, yes. Putting the possibility right out in the open. But simultaneously daring him to make the first move and warning what short work she could make of him. The SEXY BABY plate on the front of the car was half true. She was plenty sexy, but there was nothing babyish in her manner. No childishness in her frank gaze. No nonsense in her tone. As if communicating that sex with her would be an entirely different experience from anything else he'd ever known.

He found himself saying, "It's a shame we didn't meet under difference circumstances, Miss Abruzzo."

"Circumstances," she said, "can be changed."

What happened next didn't make sense.

Four big thuds hit the car, and then they heard four short cracks of noise from somewhere among the cemetery monuments.

Roxy ducked, cursing. Then, "Get down!"

"What's—?"

She grabbed the back of his head and jammed his face into the solid muscle of her thigh. "Damn," she said. One-handed, she put the car in gear and peeled out so fast the dog tumbled onto his back.

When she put both her hands on the steering wheel, Henry was freed enough to struggle upright. "What was that?" He grabbed the door handle as the car whipped around a curve and Roxy accelerated toward the gate.

"Somebody just took a shot at us!"

"A shot?"

"Four bullets, didn't you hear them?"

By that time, Roxy was driving like a NASCAR champion. "Whoever it was can't shoot for shit," she was saying in a voice laced with adrenaline. "This car is going to need some serious body work. I didn't see anybody. Did you? Serves me right, too. Losing my concentration."

"You get shot at frequently?"

"Who says I was the target?" She braked for a light, but checked the rearview mirror. A spot of high color showed on her cheekbone. "Maybe you're the one with the bull's-eye on his back. You work for the Hydes, right?"

"I sincerely doubt anybody's trying to—"

"What, you're too classy? Okay, smart guy, tell me why somebody would kill a nice fellow like Julius Hyde."

"Class has nothing to— Look, I've too been busy taking care of family matters in the wake of his death to concern myself with—"

"Maybe you ought to start concerning yourself, Counselor. I get the feeling whoever offed Julius has some loose ends to take care of."

"Should we call the police?"

"Should we?" She laughed shortly, taunting him. "You're an officer of the court, right? Somebody just shot up the car we were sitting in."

"Right. We should call 911."

"So why haven't you done it yet?"

The light changed, and she drove forward.

Henry was still working on an answer when she pulled up in front of the pizza shop where he'd found her in the first place. She threw the car in neutral and turned sideways in the seat to look at him. "Nice meeting you, Counselor. But this is the end of the road for you and me."

"That's it? We're done?"

"Well done," she said. "Cooked before we even got started. Which is a shame. You're kinda cute."

"Look," he began.

She put up one hand as if stopping traffic. "I don't think so, Henry. You've got something going on that I want absolutely nothing to do with. Understand?"

"But—"

"Don't make me kick your ass," she said. "Sayonara."

Henry had no doubt she could give his ass a good kicking. He got out of the car.

She leaned across the seat to look at him. "I don't know what you're up to, Counselor, but here's a piece of advice. You come to this neighborhood? Bring your A-game."

He stood on the corner while she drove away. When she disappeared into traffic, he got into his own car and checked his reflection in the mirror. He was disconcerted to discover his face looking pale.

His phone rang, and Henry checked the screen. The number was Monica's. Probably asking if he'd found her damned dog yet. He decided not to answer.

Putting his phone away, he discovered his wallet was missing. And rain started to spatter his windshield.

❊ 9 ❊

Nooch phoned to tell Roxy the shopping trip hadn't happened. Kaylee had refused to set foot inside the Mr. Husky store.

Roxy cut across his explanation and told him she needed a pizza, fast. Ten minutes later, she drove into the salvage yard, where he was standing beside the truck in a gray drizzle. Driving the nimble little Mustang seemed like a good idea for the moment, despite the bullet holes, so Roxy leaned over and opened the passenger door. He barely squeezed into the front seat beside her.

"Where's Kaylee?"

"At your house. She needed a nap before she could face taking me to the mall." Nooch rubbed the rain from his hair. "I think she could use one. She's scary when she's mad, but I like it even less when girls cry."

"She'll get over it. If she's lucky, another old rich dude will start looking for her kind of manicures. She tell you anything interesting?"

"Huh?"

"About that building she mentioned?"

"What building?"

"The one Julius gave her."

"Why'd he give her a building?"

No sense beating his brain. Nooch had a hard time remembering what he ate for breakfast.

"How mad does Kaylee get?" she asked instead. "Sounds like she's been arrested a couple of times for losing her temper."

"She can get pretty ticked off. At the last family reunion, she threw potato salad at Uncle Stosh. I thought he was gonna shove her head in the kiddie pool and hold her down till she drownded, but she got away. She keeps going to anger-management classes, but it never seems to take."

Uncle Stosh had a legendary temper, too. "Think she could get mad enough to shoot her boyfriend?"

The idea scandalized Nooch. "Kaylee? She's just a girl! She couldn't hurt nobody!"

Roxy wanted to say that girls hurt people all the time, but Nooch had already staked out his position on the subject.

"Did you call for the pizza?"

"I forgot."

Roxy tossed him her cell phone, and he dialed.

Under a steadily lowering October sky, Roxy headed uphill through the Lawrenceville neighborhood, a mix of empty nests, college students looking for cheap rents, some budding artists, and a few junkies—young and old. While she drove, she thought about being somebody's target practice. Had the shooter been aiming for her? Or Kaylee's car? Or the Hyde family lawyer? The chances of it being a random shooting, she decided, were nil.

She drove farther up the hill into Bloomfield, the city's version of Little Italy, pulled next to the curb near Bruno's, and parked. She gave Nooch all the cash left in her pockets, and he clambered out and headed into the pizza shop in the rain, leaving Roxy alone to further wonder about Henry Paxton.

Had he guessed she had the statue? His fishing trip seemed to say so. Had she successfully diverted him? She figured the answer was no. She listened to the clack of windshield wipers and idly rubbed Rooney's head, thinking about her next move.

Her cell phone rang, and she picked up.

"Roxy? Charlie McManus. You want to take a look at a duplex I just bought in Morningside? We're cutting it into apartments and there's some windows and shutters and shit we're tearing out."

Charlie McManus, absentee slumlord extraordinaire. He tended to buy lousy houses and make them lousier rentals, meanwhile living in a fancy suburb. Chances were good the windows were broken and he simply wanted somebody to haul his junk to the dump.

"How long are you there today?" Roxy asked.

"For another two more hours, that's it. Take it or leave it."

Definitely he wanted a run made to the dump. Roxy wasn't that desperate this week. She said, "I'm tied up today, Charlie. Call me next time."

"You got it," he said, no hard feelings, and they hung up.

The passenger door popped open, and Roxy yelped.

"Jeez," Nooch said, apparently forgetting he'd been shot at once already today. "Why so jumpy?"

He climbed into the car balancing a wet pizza box in one hand. He pulled a smaller package out from under his sweatshirt. He handed it over, fighting off Rooney's interest in the pizza.

Roxy hefted the package. "What the hell is this?"

"Your uncle Carmine gave it to me. For you."

The hair on the back of Roxy's neck prickled.

She glanced into the rearview mirror, which had an excellent view of the sidewalk in front of Annamaria's Italian Specialty Market, home of the best hot Italian sausage in the city. The market was also a hangout for a handful of old men from the neighborhood.

At tables set up under the market's awning out of the rain, a bunch of old guys sat huddled in layers of coats and sweaters, sipping espresso, same as every day, except Sunday, no matter what the weather. They came to get away from their wives for a couple hours, to buy lottery tickets and gossip in Italian. Roxy didn't have to get out of the car to know the codgers were reminiscing about the days when they ran the neighborhood.

The old mobsters liked to think they were still in the game.

Like most of the small neighborhoods in Pittsburgh, Bloomfield started when immigrants were attracted by good jobs in the steel mills. The men walked down the hills to work in the mills while their families built up the various ethnic neighborhoods on the hillsides above the smokestacks. The Polish immigrants located on one hillside, the Slovaks on another, and Bloomfield grew into a Little Italy. Each had its own markets, restaurants, and version of the Catholic Church. And petty crime. When the steel industry left for the Far East, the families who could manage it left the crime for a better life elsewhere—the suburbs or other cities with jobs, like Charlotte or Houston. Those who stayed were too poor or too old or too stubborn to get out. But now, students from the universities were edging in, making the crazy quilt of neighborhoods even crazier.

And her uncle Carmine Abruzzo kept watch over it all.

In the car's mirror, Roxy could see him watching her. The shriveled old man looked a lot like a lemur—hunched over, big eyes staring.

Before she ripped open the edge of the package—a thin plastic grocery bag wrapped around a hunk of something approximately the size of two pounds of Land O Lakes butter—she knew what was inside. Cash. Plenty of it.

"How much?" Nooch asked, elbowing Rooney's big tongue away from the pizza box.

Roxy ran her thumb down the side of the twenty-dollar bills. They had been neatly bundled, probably counted. At least twelve thousand dollars, she decided. "Enough to fly you and me to Vegas, if we need to make a quick getaway."

Enough for Sage's school fees, too. With some left over to live on.

Sounding wistful, he asked, "Is Celine Dion still in Vegas?"

Roxy ignored the question and contemplated her situation. "Unless Carmine is giving me an early birthday gift, this must mean the old coot still makes a living with the video poker machines. Why'd he give it to me?"

"Phil went to jail last month."

Phil Tolucca had passed himself off as a mob lawyer for as long as anyone could remember, but mostly he took care of moving Carmine's cash around and fixing whatever trouble popped up. Everybody knew Phil—grandmothers, and little kids who begged him for the penny candy he kept in his pockets. He wore silk suits and imported ties. For years, he had been the smiling face behind Carmine's operation. The money launderer. The bag man. The guy who took care of problems, too. Sometimes with rough stuff. Roxy remembered him as the "uncle" who bought her a gold wristwatch for her high school graduation and told her which shops she shouldn't use when it came time to hock it.

Nooch said, "Maybe he'll meet your dad in jail."

"Shut up," Roxy said automatically. "What did Phil go in for? Jaywalking on his way to the bank?"

"I forget. No wait, I think they got him on indecent exposure."

"Get out!"

Nooch shrugged. "That's what I heard at the gas station."

Chances were good Nooch heard the story wrong or some asshole was pulling his chain for the fun of it, but Roxy made a mental note to ask around.

She rewrapped the package again and plunked it on the dashboard, not pleased with the new situation that seemed to be coagulating around her.

Nooch said, "Maybe Carmine heard how good you are at helping out friends."

Salvage being mostly a cash business, Roxy often found herself turning cash into gift cards and phone minutes to help friends conceal income from the IRS. Or she accepted cash and wrote checks out of her account to help people who worked at jobs that didn't look good on a tax return.

No big deal.

There were other favors, too. Sometimes she helped straighten out misunderstandings or ran errands others were afraid to run.

Then, of course, there was the whole business of finding apartments for a few women who needed to start their lives over.

To Nooch, Roxy said, "I don't want to be Uncle Carmine's new gofer either."

Nooch nodded. "Doing favors for Carmine is dangerous. You say that a lot."

Being a girl in the Abruzzo family used to mean learning to cook large quantities of food and getting knocked around on a Saturday night when the man of the house had a few drinks. But the feminist movement had finally come to the family. Her cousin Connie ran a sports betting operation in Jersey, and there was an aunt who collected on loans for another cousin. Neither one of them had any kids, though.

Seeing her half brother Mick after he'd come home from jail—a tough guy all spooked and half dead inside from his stint—Roxy had decided to stay out of the family trade. It had taken Mick nearly ten years to recover. But now, with all her male cousins either in jail or swearing off the organization, here was Carmine offering Roxy a piece of the action.

Roxy said, "I gotta find a steady income to pay for Sage's college."

"Oh, man." Nooch stared at her. "You're gonna take Carmine's money?"

"Shut up."

"Maybe I should just deliver it back to him." Nooch reached for the package.

"He'd be insulted," Roxy predicted. "Maybe shoot you for dissing him."

Nooch snatched his hand back. "Forget it, then."

This was a development Roxy hadn't seen coming. Carmine was asking her for something. He was just paying her before he told her exactly what.

Roxy started the Mustang's engine. "Why does everything happen at the same time?"

"What everything?"

"Never mind. Hide this package under the seat until I decide what to do. Meanwhile, let's take some lunch to Sage."

Nooch brightened. "Great! Maybe she's baking cookies."

Roxy drove around the block and past Annamaria's, but Carmine was gone already. Sneaky SOB. She took the side streets, weaving her way through Bloomfield before hanging a left at a defunct car dealership.

Over the car dealer's empty lot hung a giant billboard advertising a law firm that specialized in elder law. Three lawyers were pictured on the ad, including one woman with huge breasts barely contained by a business suit. To offset the *Playboy* aspect of the picture, she wore eyeglasses. Her two partners—dead ringers for Hugh Hefner—appeared to be admiring her cleavage, but the printed message said, "Seniors! Protect your assets!"

Roxy turned right onto the side street where her aunt Loretta's home stood.

Like all the other houses on the narrow street, Loretta's brick Foursquare had a wide front porch with an aluminum awning. Autumn leaves from a lone maple tree had already been raked out of the front yard—hardly bigger than a parking space—and the walk was swept. The windows gleamed. The grass had been mowed one last time before winter.

Loretta owned the house next to her late husband's parents, Mr. and Mrs. Radziewicz, who lived next door even after their son passed away. For reasons beyond Roxy's understanding, Loretta kept the house and even took occasional meals to her ungrateful in-laws. The in-laws reciprocated by spying on Loretta and criticizing everything she did. They couldn't forgive her for using her husband's life insurance to pay for law school. Apparently, they expected her to set up a shrine in her front yard instead.

Nooch wrestled his way out of the car and moved the broken kitchen chair Loretta kept on the street to save the parking space in front of her house. Roxy slid the Mustang into the space. Rooney jumped into the front seat and landed on the pizza box.

Loretta came out of the house, but stood on the front porch to keep her hair out of the drizzle. Like many Pittsburgh women, Loretta wore her blouses cut low and her hair big. The bigger the hair, the closer to God. At all times, her gold crucifix lay nestled between her voluptuous breasts. She had been saving for breast reduction surgery for twenty years, but other expenses always seemed to pop up to delay her doctor appointments.

Father Pete over at St. Dominic's once speculated that maybe some men in the parish had sabotaged Loretta's roof back when it looked as if she had finally saved up enough for the surgery. Seeing as how Father Pete might have gathered insider information in the confessional, the rumor hung around long after Loretta paid for new shingles.

Meanwhile, Loretta's cup size was going to waste, because she was a pious widow who attended mass every morning at St. Dom's before she went to work.

Roxy had run away from home after her mother died and arrived on Loretta's doorstep as a teenager. Newly widowed and childless, Loretta welcomed Roxy into her house. Since then, they'd forged a sort of family of their own—made stronger when Sage came along. Between the two of them, they managed to attend all of Sage's parent-teacher conferences and sat in the stands at all of her basketball games. Loretta had been thrown out of the gym once for telling a ref where to stick his whistle.

Today, Loretta was dressed in a gray pin-striped suit with a tight, short skirt that showed her spectacular legs. She carried a fancy briefcase, fancy purse. Her shoes were probably some fancy brand, too, but Roxy couldn't keep all the designers straight. Her mascara had been laid on thick, and her makeup was flawless.

Rooney dashed up the sidewalk, barking with joy. Next door, a curtain twitched, and the pinched face of Mrs. Radziewicz appeared in the window long enough to register disapproval. Nooch waited at the curb.

Loretta did a dance to keep her shoes away from the dog's dirty paws, but she patted Rooney on the top of his huge head, crooning to him. He crooned back.

Roxy said, "Damn, Loretta, I just saw the billboard on the corner. You look like a porn star."

"I thought the eyeglasses might help, but, no." Loretta looked up at Roxy. "Where's your truck? Did you trade it for that cute car? It's adorable."

"The car's borrowed."

"You should consider making it permanent. Red is the color that most catches a man's eye, did you know that?"

The other thing she claimed would attract a suitable husband for Roxy was the ability to make pasta. Despite her law degree, Loretta still had the mentality of a Bloomfield housewife, circa 1953. But Roxy would rather stick a fork in her eye than learn to roll her own ravioli.

"Who's car is it?" Loretta asked.

"One of Nooch's cousins'."

"It's got holes in it."

"I got stuck behind a truck in traffic. It kicked up a bunch of gravel."

Loretta looked unconvinced.

Roxy went on the offensive. "I just heard about Phil Tolucca."

Loretta's whole face turned a rosy pink. "I don't want to talk about it."

"How come you didn't mention it before?"

"I don't want to discuss that man or anything else associated with him." Loretta's blush spread southward down her neck and into the foothills of her cleavage. "We were barely acquainted. We simply nodded in church a few times, that's all. Nothing more."

"Right. Sure." Roxy decided not to mention the dinner dates at a neighborhood restaurant known for its private alcoves and gossipy waiters. "But, wow, embarrassing, huh? Was he really exposing himself?"

"Certainly not to me," Loretta said. "I'm putting that whole sordid chapter out of my life."

"I don't blame you." Dying to learn more, Roxy figured now wasn't the time—particularly within earshot of Loretta's in-laws. So she said, "Why aren't you at work?"

"I had the mother of all hot flashes in the office this morning. Soaked clear through my blue blouse."

"Wow."

"All the men in the firm avoid me now, for fear I'll start gushing sweat. Or they're afraid I'm going to snap their heads off and prop their dead bodies in a room with the air-conditioning turned so low they'd never decompose. Anyway, I was on my way home to change my clothes when I got an emergency phone call from Abby Ricci. Can you deliver a covered dish for me to St. Dom's? It's Abby's night to supply the soup kitchen, but she's having a gallbladder attack."

All of Loretta's neighborhood friends were twenty years older than she was and had lives that revolved around St. Dom's, the Catholic church behind the hardware store. These days, they were coaching Loretta through The Change. Thanks to her friends, Loretta now carried little Ziploc bags of edamame in her purse the way other women carried Tic Tacs.

Roxy said, "Abby still uses that government cheese in her lasagna?"

Loretta shuddered. "Yes. Nobody will miss that at the soup kitchen. My rigatoni's thawing on the counter. You could take it to the church, or you could drop it at Abby's house. Her nephew Richie is in town, back from Miami. The handsome one."

"The handsome gay nephew?"

Loretta's mouth popped open. "He's gay?"

"He dropped out of seminary and started calling himself Richie Ricci. Of course he's gay."

"I'm stunned. Abby has no idea. She thought you'd hit if off." Loretta looked shaken at the thought of an Italian gay man. "Well, I'd take the rigatoni over myself, but believe it or not there's a cancellation at Valentino's. I can have a nail appointment if I go over there right now."

The only event that took precedence over everything except mass and

gallbladder attacks was an appointment at Bloomfield's premier salon.
Roxy said, "I'll deliver. Can it wait an hour?"

"The rigatoni can, but my appointment can't."

"Memorize the gossip for me, will you?"

Loretta narrowed her eyes. "Anything in particular?"

For a moment, Roxy considered how much of a pain in her ass Loretta
could be if she thought Roxy was bending the law. But she decided to risk
it. "Ask around about the Hyde family. I seem to remember Valentino's
grandmother took in laundry for rich people. And isn't one of her sons a
chauffeur now?"

"Sewing. Not laundry. She still alters fancy dresses for brides and
debutantes. In her younger days, she spent quite a bit of time upstairs in
those houses. Rumor has it, her youngest son wasn't her husband's child.
Yes, I think Valentino's uncle is a chauffeur or mechanic or something.
He learned auto mechanics in reform school. Whatever happened to reform schools? Boys used to learn useful skills in places like that. What do
you want to know?"

"Maybe one of the family has some good gossip about the Hyde
murder."

Loretta continued to look suspicious. "That's all?"

"I knew Julius a little bit," Roxy admitted. "I liked him. I'd like to hear
who killed him."

Already in a rush to get her nails done, Loretta said, "All right, I'll see
what I can find out." She leaned close, smelling of White Rain, and gave
Roxy a kiss on the cheek. "I told your uncle Carmine that you'd take him
to his bowling league tonight, too. Buy him a hamburger on the way. He's
not eating enough these days."

Aha. Loretta was playing go-between. But Roxy needed to think
through what she wanted to tell Carmine when he offered her a job in his
organization.

"I can't. Appointment with Nooch's probation officer." Carmine's "bowling league" didn't involve rolling anything down an alley, unless it was the

bruised body of somebody who owed him money. Roxy frequently used nonexistent probation appointments. It was an excuse nobody doubted, not even Loretta, who usually had good instincts for lies.

Loretta shook her head. "Nooch is seriously cramping your social life. It's time he went back to his own people."

"He's harmless."

"As long as he's your constant companion, you'll never date anybody nice. Who would want to share you with a caveman?"

"After the hearing, things will change. His uncle Stosh thinks he can get Nooch into the union."

"The steamfitters? Well, that's something. I just wish there weren't so many steps to get him out of your life."

"It's his life, too."

Loretta gave up trying to influence her. She reached out and tousled Roxy's hair. "We miss you. Come back and stay here for a while. You need to be with your daughter."

Roxy shrugged. "She's better off under your watchful eye."

"Yes, but only you can help with her calculus homework. That boyfriend of hers just got here, so go inside and make sure they're not up to something." Loretta went down the steps, putting up a bright umbrella and shouldering her briefcase and purse. "Nooch, keep your feet off my coffee table."

"Boyfriend?" Roxy said. "What boyfriend?"

Next door, two faces appeared at the window to watch Loretta leave the house in her short skirt and low-cut jacket. Chances were good she'd cause a fender bender or two on her way to the salon.

With Loretta safely gone, Nooch came up the short sidewalk to the porch. He had the squashed pizza box in his hands. "The two of you are just the same. Never anything nice to say. Why does she think I'd put my feet on her old coffee table?"

"Just remember, or she'll tear your head off when she gets back."

"Don't I know it," Nooch muttered. "Look, the dog got into the pizza. He ate half of it, and the rest of it probably's got his drool all over it."

Lunch hardly looked appetizing anymore. "Leave it in the car. Loretta's got rigatoni thawing on the counter."

The soup kitchen always had too much food anyway.

❧ 10 ❧

Arden ended up at her father's house—a drafty, rambling place in a woodsy suburb. Mummy had never quite finished decorating, so the house had a flaky ambience. Fragile French furniture in the living room. Horsey prints in the study. Chinese wallpaper here. A refectory table there, purchased after seeing a movie with Diane Keaton. But Arden's bedroom was still girly with a canopy bed and dotted Swiss curtains.

She rolled up the shades around noon and peered outside.

Beyond the trees, the neighborhood was full of executives and doctors. Their tiny wives drove the winding roads in gigantic SUVs. In the autumn, they hauled home cornstalks, bales of straw, and pumpkins and built displays beside their front doors. Someone down the road had a scarecrow lounging against her mailbox like a drunken Dean Martin.

Arden intended to do a little jogging along the nearby walking trails. It would be good to get in shape again—strengthen her core, build her endurance. But she flinched back from the window, remembering how the trails attracted whole herds of deer and some aggressive kind of wild turkey. Plus inquisitive white-haired ladies with Labrador retrievers that tended to shove their noses in a girl's crotch—the dogs, not the ladies.

So Arden went back to bed.

Ambien at night for the jet lag. Some diet tabs to wake up in the morning. A little Xanax to ease the heart palpitations. Coke in the afternoon for a zing. Under control, though. Totally under control.

One morning, Daddy knocked on her door with a partial inventory and a long lecture about preserving family assets. When he left, Arden dropped the papers on the bedroom floor and tried to think about Dorothy Hyde's art collection.

The sculpture in the garden, for one thing. It niggled in the back of her mind.

"What became of it?" she said aloud. Only her Malibu Barbie doll— still dressed in her original bikini—stood at the top of a bookshelf and listened with sloe-eyed attention.

So far, Arden hadn't seen the sculpture listed on any family paperwork.

"Did Monica sell it?"

Or was it floating around one of the many Hyde family homes, Barbie seemed to suggest. If so, which one?

So far, Arden hadn't mentioned the statue to anyone else. For one very big reason.

If she could find it without alerting everyone in the family, she intended to give the statue back. Somebody needed to make a statement in the art world—set a precedent for other collectors to give their antiquities back to the country of origin.

"That's what I'm going to do," she said to Barbie.

If she could just concentrate, Barbie almost said.

"Shut up," Arden replied.

She fell asleep again, and when she woke in the afternoon, Barbie was still looking at her. So she dragged herself downstairs and found the house bustling with people she didn't know. She poured herself a glass of wine and sneaked into the study. Snuggled down in a club chair, she telephoned Hadrian Sloan-Whitaker at his gallery in New York. He was surprisingly frosty on the phone.

"I'll mail a check for the balance of your salary," he said. "I don't want any trouble. Where shall I send it?"

"Just hang on to it, Hadrian. I'll stop by next time I'm in New York."

He didn't seem to hear. "I put up with you long enough, Arden. Nobody could fault me for how patient I've been. The erratic behavior. The opinions that come out of nowhere. I can't risk my reputation on you anymore."

Apparently, he took the whole firing thing seriously. Arden popped a Xanax and said, "I understand."

She could picture Hadrian standing in his shop, surrounded by a collection of heavy-framed pictures hanging on the ecru walls and a few gewgaws sitting under lights waiting for the last of the hedge fund wives to come looking for ways to decorate their Hamptons homes. They wanted to do business with an Art Dealer, not just a decorator. He would be standing at his desk, perfect posture, of course. Wearing one of his Hong Kong suits. Pastel tie, matching pocket square. Shiny shoes with a subtle amount of heel. But those awful British teeth. He was just old enough to not care about his teeth. You'd think a finicky guy like Hadrian would get himself some decent veneers, but no.

Before he could berate her again, Arden said, "Listen, Hadrian, my grandmother's art collection seems to be in play right now. Some of the pieces were in my uncle's keeping, but there was a fire, you know, so we're—well, sorting out what to do about everything."

He must have smelled a lucrative role for himself, because suddenly he wasn't quite so rude. "Does the family envision a way my firm could be useful?"

His firm included Hadrian himself, now that Arden had been cut loose, plus a grad student from the Art Institute who answered the phone while the boss traveled. Otherwise, his "firm," as he put it, was a fax machine and the smelly Persian cat that slept in the window. But Arden decided she could be magnanimous.

She said, "We're wondering if a few things might have gotten away from us."

Hadrian didn't respond, but Arden could almost hear the gears whirring in his mind. Although euphemisms abounded in his network of contacts, Arden knew he dealt in more stolen art than he cared to admit.

Hadrian said, "Should I put my ear to the ground for anything in particular?"

"Have you heard anything about Greek or Roman antiquities?"

An intake of breath indicated how much the goods might be worth. "There was a sale at Sotheby's two months ago. Some helmets, I believe. And a very fine Hellenic sculpture purchased by a Japanese corporation for the CEO's office."

"Anything more recent than that?"

"Nothing that I've heard about. Oh, except a chariot they say was dug up last summer. I think the Greeks are taking the archaeologist to court, though, so it won't be on the market." Coolly, he added, "Quite your thing, I suppose."

"No, this would be something that's been out of sight for a while."

"Sounds clandestine." He paused. "I can ask around. Discreetly, of course."

"Thank you."

"It could be the Russians, you know. They're always the first to spark a trend these days. The first to spend big money. And unlike almost everyone else who collects, they hate advertising their latest acquisitions. I'll see what I can learn."

Arden sighed. If there was any villainy going on in the art world, rumor had it that unnamed Russians were always behind it. They supplied a convenient smoke screen for dealers who wanted to keep things on the downlow.

Arden felt her enthusiasm slipping. The Xanax and wine mixture had kicked in, too hard. Time for another bump, maybe. Preparing to hang up, she said, "Thank you, Hadrian. I knew you were the one to ask. And we'll keep it between the two of us for now, all right?"

"Of course," he said. "Arden?"

"Yes?"

"I may have been hasty in Florence."

Arden thought longingly of a nap. "Don't think twice, Hadrian."

"No, seriously," he began.

He talked. He made a pitch. A very flattering one.

Then he said, "If you think your grandmother is interested, I have access to some terra-cotta figures from China. Nothing I can talk about on the phone, of course. But very valuable. I could cut you in as a partner on this, Arden, if your grandmother wants to add to her collection."

Arden's attention drifted. She sipped her wine and stopped listening to Hadrian and his Chinese warriors.

Then a door banged somewhere in the house and woke her. She realized she hadn't hung up the phone. Thank heaven Hadrian had stopped talking about terra-cotta.

A giant spotted dog suddenly barged into the study. Her first hallucination. A black and white beast with a head the size of a mailbox. Arden screamed.

Then Uncle Trey burst into the room, not a hallucination at all. He looked surprised to see her.

"Arden! Did we wake you up?"

Arden realized she had somehow climbed up onto the top of the wing chair. Balancing there, she pointed a shaky finger at the dog. "Is that—? Is it vicious?"

"Hell, no, it's Monica's dog, Samson. He's harmless, see?" Uncle Trey wrestled the Great Dane down onto the carpet. The dog chewed on Trey's arm. His tail, as big as a buggy whip, wagged happily. His huge blotches of black and white made him look like the Hound of the Baskervilles crossed with a Holstein cow.

From the floor, Trey said, "Julius's chauffeur wanted rid of him. Apparently, he's not entirely housebroken. But we're supposed to keep him out of Monica's clutches. Boy, those two must have had a hell of a feud."

Arden cautiously climbed down from her perch on the chair. "Uncle Trey, you scared the daylights out of me. My heart's beating like crazy." She clutched her chest and sank onto the seat cushion again.

"Sorry, Ardy. I thought I could put the dog in here during our dinner. I didn't know you were snoozing."

"I'm jet-lagged, that's all."

From beneath the gigantic dog, Uncle Trey smiled up at her. "You look a little jagged, all right, Ardy. You spilled your drink."

"Did I?"

"Carpet's all wet." Trey climbed out from under the dog and picked up her wineglass. He set it on the table by the phone, but remained crouched beside her.

In his younger days, Trey had a feckless streak—perhaps the curse of being the baby of the family. He used to instigate games with his nieces and nephews, like how to taste the difference between scotch and bourbon. How to make a peanut butter and banana sandwich. Water balloons, though, were his specialty. Now, however, he looked too old for water balloons. Too old for his youthful clothes. Too old for his salon haircut. He was turning into Julius—a dissipated playboy.

"You okay, Ardy?"

"Yes. No thanks to you."

He smiled. "Where's your dad? He's here, right? Or did the big man go to the office? Quenty calls a family powwow, and then he leaves?"

"He'll be back." The Great Dane came over and sniffed Arden's shirt. With ineffectual hands, she tried to push the dog away, but he snuffled her with a wet nose and gave her arm a tentative lick.

123

Trey patted Samson. "Is your dad going to make us an offer for our shares? So he can run the company free and clear? Do you think that's what we're here for? I could go for that. Little extra cash in my pocket. We're not really here to talk about a funeral for Julius, are we?"

"I don't know." Arden watched the dog make a loop around the room, sniffing everything. Her heart was beating very fast, making her head light.

"Is Quentin going to try selling the property down on the river?" Uncle Trey asked. "That was Julius's but maybe its in play? We'd get a nice chunk of change for that now. What'd he tell you, Ardy?"

"Nothing at all." She took a deep breath to steady her heart. "I saw you on the Discovery Channel."

He perked up and smiled. "You did?"

"Something about a ship that sank during a hurricane. With gold coins and slaves."

He grunted, losing the smile. "That one, we never found. At least that's what the guys on the boats told me. Which happens a lot. Sometimes I think they put out marker buoys and plan to go back when my money runs out."

"Why don't you go on the boats with them?"

He made a face. "I get seasick. Besides, they like my money better than they like me."

Arden couldn't stop herself from putting her hand out and patting his face. "Poor Uncle Trey."

He patted her back, then said kindly, "Ardy, you're blitzed. You gotta give up that stuff before you turn into your mother."

"What stuff?"

"You know what I mean." He got to his feet and went over to the desk. "I saw the caterer in the kitchen. Looks like a great dinner—if you're look-ing to boost your cholesetrol. Anybody else arrive yet?"

Arden frowned, trying to remember what Daddy had said about din-ner. The whole family, she recalled, was getting together. Everybody under one roof. To talk about the funeral, Daddy had said, but they'd probably discuss company business, too. That's why everyone would show up, of course. It all sounded insensitive, actually.

Everybody would be looking at her, Arden thought. Wanting to know things. Like how much they could sell paintings for.

She said, "Does Samson need to go for a walk?"

Uncle Trey was busy snooping on the desk and probably didn't absorb the question, but he said, "Sure, maybe."

"Did you bring his leash?"

☙ 11 ❧

Roxy sent Rooney into Loretta's fenced backyard, where he could bark his head off at the Radziewiczes' Chihuahua. Then she let herself into the house. Right behind her, Nooch sniffed the air for cookies.

"Go watch some TV," Roxy said. "I have to talk to Sage."

Nooch slouched onto the flowered sofa in the flowered living room and turned on the television. The television was probably the only thing in the room that didn't have flowers on it. Even the rug swirled dizzyingly with roses. Nooch looked like a brontosaurus that had wandered into that Sissinghurst garden in England.

"Don't yell at Sage," he said.

"Why would I yell at her?"

"Just don't."

With the remote, he clicked around until he found cartoons. Then he put his boots on the coffee table and settled back to watch.

"I wasn't going to," Roxy said.

On Loretta's dining room table sat an open shipping box with a Gucci handbag inside. With the onset of menopause, Loretta wasn't sleeping well at night and tended to do a lot of shopping on QVC. Looked like she was revving up her credit card again. The breast reduction must be on hold.

Roxy tripped over a pair of enormous sneakers at the bottom of the stairs, dropped the car keys on the newel, and called upstairs to her daughter. "Sage? Sage, you here?"

Instead of Sage, a rangy boy appeared at the top of the stairs, hitching his loose jeans and pasting some charm onto his face. "Hey, Mrs.—Miss A. You're looking really hot today."

The kid thumped down the stairs in his sock feet. He had a buzz cut that made his head look pasty white. His T-shirt said Rookie in big black letters.

Roxy squinted. "I know you."

"Yeah, I'm Zack. Zack Cleary. I started hanging with Sage last spring when the girls won the basketball championship." He plunked himself on the bottom step and reached for his sneakers. "Sage is upstairs, ralphing in the bathroom. She must have had some bad cafeteria food last week."

Roxy kicked the sneakers out of his range. "What are you doing here, Zack Cleary? I thought you were going to college somewhere."

"Sage didn't tell you?"

Sage hadn't bothered to mention she had a boyfriend at all, let alone this one. "No, she didn't. What did you do? Join the army?"

When the kid had first appeared, he'd looked like a character in a vampire movie—all skinny good looks and long hair. He still had the good looks, Roxy noted, but with muscles now and no hair.

He rubbed his hand on top of his bristly head and grinned. "Does it make me look tough? Because I started at the police academy a couple of months ago. We're on break for a week before we start training at the gun range."

"Is that shirt some kind of official uniform?"

"Hell—heck no. It was my dad's. I stole it out of his closet. I'm not a real rookie until I get hired on the force."

Zack, Roxy remembered suddenly, was the idiot son of the city's new chief of police.

Roxy thought about what it meant that her daughter was dating the one kid with the most direct line of communication to the police department. She steadied herself on the newel. The chief of police's kid coming around on the exact week Carmine asked her to join his crew—that's all she needed. "You think you can be a cop, huh? I guess there's hope for the criminal element after all."

He laughed and reached for his shoes again. "Yeah, I'm heading into the family business. It was either police work or Laundromats. Hey, was that you last week at that club near Station Square? With the band? Singing?"

"That was past your bedtime."

Zack grinned. "I didn't know you could belt it out like that. Plus you looked—you know—sexy up there."

"Sweating, mostly."

"Sexy, though. Hey, I'm starving to death. I don't suppose you'd make me a sandwich, y'know, for the road?"

Roxy controlled the urge to snatch off one of his gigantic sneakers and beat him over the head with it. The last thing she wanted was Sage's friends recognizing her at club gigs. "There's half a Bruno's pizza on the front seat of the red car out front. It's a little squished, but help yourself."

"No kidding? Thanks." Zack finished with his shoes and lounged to his feet. "I'm outta here. Behave yourself, okay?"

Roxy debated kicking him through the front door. But the thought of Zack chowing down on the pizza Rooney had slobbered over was good enough.

When he was gone, she took the steps upward, two at a time.

Her daughter's bedroom was frighteningly tidy. Unlike every other teenager on the planet, Sage kept her clothes and many books in perfect order. Even the poster of Colin Firth in a velvet suit was attached to the wall in a frame, not with masking tape. Such tidiness wasn't something Sage learned from her mother.

While her girlfriends loved boy bands and gift cards to Ambercrombie & Fitch, Sage read the *Onion* every day and watched Jon Stewart. Roxy was increasingly at a loss about her increasingly adult daughter. It was only calculus that Sage couldn't conquer alone.

"Sage? Where are you?"

A voice croaked from the bathroom. Roxy went down the narrow hall and pushed open the door at the end. Sage lay on her back on the poufy pink bathtub rug, staring at the ceiling with a blank face. Her long legs—when had they gotten so long?—were draped over the edge of the bathtub.

"Hey." Roxy rested her shoulder against the doorjamb. "What was Zack Cleary doing here?"

"He just left."

"I know that. He said you ate some bad cafeteria food or something?"

Sage groaned. She still liked wearing her dark curly hair in pigtails that stuck out on the sides of her head, but today they didn't look so perky. Her lanky body was encased in a Steelers football jersey, with a pair of nylon basketball shorts on her legs and tall athletic socks on her feet. Her fair skin looked as white as marble.

Sage turned her face away. "Leave me alone."

"You want some ginger ale?"

"Mom." Sage sounded as exhausted as if she'd just staggered out of the Amazon jungle.

"Okay, I just—it was a surprise to find the Cleary kid hanging around."

Sage flung one arm across her face. "He dropped off some stuff, that's all."

"What stuff?"

"A basketball. I left it at the court over the weekend."

"You saw him over the weekend? I thought you were working on a biology project with Kiryn."

"I see him around. He's not a total jerk, Mom."

Could have fooled me. Roxy almost said it aloud.

Without moving her arm, Sage grumbled, "You're so judgmental."

"I didn't say a word."

"I know what you're thinking. Zack was just being nice."

"Okay, okay." Roxy knew better than to argue any longer. So she said, "Actually, I was hoping you could find a book for me. About ancient Rome. Or Greece. I forget which. With pictures. You were reading it last spring for a report. You know the one I mean?"

Sage opened her eyes and looked up, suspicious. "I wrote a paper about Sparta. But there must be, like, a thousand books available about ancient Greece. Have you gone to a library?"

"I've been banned until I pay my late fees. I figured I'd just ask you instead." Roxy stepped over Sage's prone body, put down the toilet seat, and sat on it. "I thought you'd like to give your mom a little help."

Sage closed her eyes again wearily. "Do I look like I feel like helping?"

"C'mon, it'll take your mind off your stomach." Roxy put her hand down and felt Sage's forehead for fever. "What do you know about old statues?"

Sage pushed Roxy's hand away, but said, "What do you mean by old? Like, old-old?"

"Really old. Naked guys throwing spears—that kind of thing."

"Are you referring to some kind of antiquity? Like the sculptures celebrating the athletes at Olympia? In ancient times, the winners were immortalized by carvings that lined the walkways of the original Olympic village."

"Yeah, okay, are there any in museums and stuff?"

"Of course there are. And more are being discovered every day, so it's still an emerging field of scholarship. Why are you asking?" Sage propped herself up on one elbow. "What's going on, Mom?"

"Nothing."

"Bullshit."

"Watch your mouth or Loretta will wash it out with soap. I wonder how much one of those Olympic statues might be worth now."

"A lot." Sage lay back down, her intellectual curiosity waning.

"What about the book?"

"I'll check the library. Maybe I can find a general history for you."

"Great. Thanks. Want me to make you some toast?"

Sage blew a long-suffering sigh. "God, no."

It hadn't been too many years ago that Roxy had spent hours on the bathroom floor, too, just moaning about being a misunderstood teenager. She'd spent even more hours raising hell, but Sage didn't find hell-raising all that therapeutic. Sometimes Roxy wondered how she could have produced a kid so different from herself.

So Roxy thought for a minute before guessing what had Sage moping.

Roxy said, "Did you get rejected by Yale?"

"No, I won't hear from admissions for weeks."

"Is that idiot chemistry teacher proving his manhood by giving pop quizzes again?"

"No."

"Then what? Some dickhead hassling you?"

Sage covered her face with both hands. "Sometimes you totally gross me out, Mom."

Deciding to take a general stab at the situation, Roxy said, "Hey, nothing's worse than high school, kiddo. I know that. But you're almost finished. Pretty soon you'll go off to college, and everything will be great. I know we've been worried about the tuition, but maybe I've got that figured out. You've just gotta make it through the stupid stuff of senior year, that's all. Keep studying and—"

"Stop," Sage said through her hands. "Just—stop with the cheesy pep talk, Mom."

"I'm serious! You've got everything going for you. Look out world, here comes Sage. The greatest kid to ever graduate from this—"

"Mom." Sage raised her voice. "I'm not graduating."

"What?"

"I can't graduate."

"Why the hell not?"

"I think I'm pregnant."

Roxy sat very still. "You're . . . ?"

"Yes," Sage said. "It was a stupid mistake, a onetime thing, and I was completely dumb about it. Now I've missed my period."

The whole bathroom spun, and no words made any sense. Roxy grabbed the toilet seat with both hands to keep from falling off. "What?"

Sage sat up unsteadily. "I missed my period, and I've been throwing up for days. I'm pretty sure I'm pregnant. I mean, I did everything wrong. And now I can't graduate in May because—because I'm going to have a b-b-baby."

Roxy tried to focus on Sage's words, but the colors in the bathroom all whirled together in a sickening jumble. "How can you be pregnant? Do you even know about sex?"

Sage's face contorted with tears. "You're kidding, right?"

"What's that supposed to mean?"

"For crying out loud, I'm not blind! And I'm not stupid. You're like a walking sex bomb. Maybe Loretta doesn't see it, but God, Mom, I— Look, I just thought I could try it, too, you know?"

"No," Roxy said. "You're too young."

"I'm the same age as you when you got pregnant."

"That was different. You're different! You've got a real future ahead of you, Sage."

Sage burst into sobs. "Now I don't have any future! Everything's ruined. Yale, basketball—everything."

"Have you taken a test?"

"How can I walk into a store and buy a p-pregnancy test? Everybody knows me!"

"Who's the father?"

"Zack, of course."

"Zack?" Roxy almost shouted. "Of course?"

"Well, it's not like I'm dating anybody."

"Except him!"

"We're not dating." Sage used the word as if it were something disgusting. "We just— We're friends, that's all. I didn't want to go to college a virgin, for crying out loud. So we were fooling around. It was nothing serious."

"It's plenty serious now. Haven't you heard of birth control?"

"Of course I have! I just never thought I'd need it."

Another motherly shortcoming to add to her list. Roxy bit back a few more choice words on the subject of sexually transmitted horrors and nearly choked herself with the effort. Better to save that lecture for when the hysterics had passed. Then she thought of Zack's smug grin. "Does your boyfriend know?"

"He's not my—no! I can't tell him." Sage groaned again. "Not yet, anyway. Eventually I'll have to. It's not like I'll be able to hide this for long." She hiccupped. "I'll be f-f-fat by Christmas. Huge at Easter."

Roxy felt her anger crumble. "Easy, now."

"It's so awful!"

"It's not awful until it's official. What you need is a test."

"I can't just walk into a store and buy something like that!"

"I'll get you one. There's no sense panicking until you know for sure."

"I'm sure." Sage gave a miserable sniffle. "You're going to be a grandmother!"

The word felt like a shard of hot glass stabbing Roxy through the heart.

"And me," Sage said, starting to weep again. "I'll have a kid to take care of. Oh, how could I be so dumb?" Sage buried her face in her arm and wailed.

Roxy should have patted her shoulder. Done the consoling mother thing. But all she could think of was how she could possibly murder Zack Cleary and get away with it.

The next thing she knew, Sage was lunging for the toilet and up-chucking. Roxy held her hair and listened to the echo of her daughter's first throes of pregnancy. It took her back. Not in a good way.

Her cell phone rang.

Sage waved her away, then went back to clutching the toilet.

Roxy grabbed her phone and went out into the hall, hoping against hope she could hear some good news for once.

Bug Duffy's voice said, "Roxy? I need to talk to Nooch."

"On the phone?"

"No," Bug said. "The detectives want to see him. We have a few questions. Can you bring him down here?"

Oh, hell, Roxy thought. Why couldn't disasters happen one at a time?

☙ 12 ❧

Henry walked into Fair Weather Village carrying a small potted calla lily and trying not to inhale the smell of old people getting older. A herd of codgers in wheelchairs clustered by the closed door of the dining room watched him pass by. Henry checked his watch. It was ten thirty, and they appeared to have nothing better to do than listen to Muzak and breathe the unappetizing scent of boiled sauerkraut.

As he hurried past the observant group, somebody muttered, "Nice flowers. Too cheap to get the big pot, huh?"

Henry hastened his step. Outside Dorothy Hyde's room, Sharlane, the formidable nurse, sat at a desk, glowering like a gnome guarding a bridge.

"You can't go in just now, slick." Sharlane focused on her paperwork. "She's on the phone with one of her daughters."

"Which one?"

Without lifting her pen, Sharlane said, "The one who asks for money all the time."

That could be any of Dorothy's offspring, but Henry decided not to continue the subject. He lingered at the desk, though, and summoned some cheer for Sharlane. "How are we feeling today, Miss Oaks?"

Sharlane finally glanced up. "We're just peachy. She's constipated, and I've got cramps. Want more details?"

"Uh, no, thank you."

She leaned her elbow on the desk and put her substantial chin in her hand. "How's the funeral coming along? You gonna get Julius buried this week?"

"I don't know about that," Henry admitted. "We're waiting to hear from the police."

Sharlane picked up her ballpoint pen again and used it to scratch an itch under her earlobe. "The police aren't known for hurrying up, are they? At least, not around here."

"I beg your pardon?"

She shrugged and went back to making tiny ink marks on her paperwork. "I got nuthin' to say."

Henry put the lily on Sharlane's desk. "I get the impression you have an opinion you'd like to share."

She shook her head.

"You have a problem, Sharlane? Something I can take care of? Something that concerns Mrs. Hyde?"

Sharlane held back for a full thirty seconds, clearly bursting to talk, but unwilling to admit anything of value to Henry. But finally, she said, "I called the police the last time Mr. Julius came to see her." She nodded toward Dorothy's closed door.

"Why?"

"I may not be the sharpest knife in the drawer, but I know when a man's got ugly intentions."

"Sharlane, you're going to have to be more direct with me. What are you talking about?"

"I'm talking about the time I told Mr. Julius that his mama was wandering at night. When she's not in her coma, she sometimes gets out of bed and walks around in the dark, sometimes goes out on that balcony. In the pitch dark, she could fall right off, down onto the patio below. You know what I'm saying? It's dangerous for a lady like her to be walking around by herself, especially when that balcony needs to be fixed."

"What do you mean, it needs to be fixed?"

"I told him he needed to get a contractor out here. This whole wing, you know, belongs to the Hyde family. It's not really part of Fair Weather Village. So he's responsible for fixing stuff when it's broke. Like the door to the balcony. And the balcony railing. But Mr. Julius says to me it's too expensive to fix. Tells me she'll be okay."

"So you called the police?"

"I did. Of course, around here, you mention the Hydes, and the police get all twitchy. They don't want any trouble, you know?"

"Why didn't you call me?"

"Mr. Julius said not to bother you." Sharlane brought her gaze up to meet his. "And anyway, I'm not too sure whose side you're on."

"I'm on the side of keeping my client safe," Henry said.

"Well, I didn't know who to trust. So I got my brother DeWayne to come fix the door and the balcony. Do I want Mrs. Hyde falling down in the middle of the night? Breaking her head? No way. I paid DeWayne myself for the materials, and he donated his time."

"That was very generous of you, Sharlane. But I will reimburse both of you."

Sulky again, she said, "I only want the best for my patient."

Half to himself, Henry said, "Doesn't sound as if Julius wanted the best for his mother, does it?"

Sharlane shook her head. "It most certainly does not. I can't say as I'm sorry he's gone."

Henry considered Julius's behavior. It was obvious that he'd wanted his inheritance sooner rather than later, but Henry hadn't expected Julius to take action. Certainly not such clumsy action.

Henry nudged the flowerpot across Sharlane's desk. "I can't stay any longer, Sharlane. Will you give my regrets to Mrs. Hyde? And tell her I'll telephone later? And perhaps you'd accept these flowers as a thank-you for telling me what happened."

Sharlane poked her ballpoint into the lily's soil. "Looks dry. Needs some water."

"I trust you'll take care of it. Meanwhile, if anyone else endangers Mrs. Hyde, I want you to call me immediately. Understand?"

Sharlane didn't answer, but watched Henry depart.

He skipped out on his client, glad to avoid another lecture about finding her damn statue or losing his job. Yet somehow, hearing about Julius Hyde's attempt to hasten his mother's demise motivated Henry to return to his investigation. He visited a few more contacts on Monica's list: An annoying guy with curry on his breath who bought and sold silver. A nervous pair of women who dressed like Gypsies and purchased a collection of bird prints from Monica to sell on eBay. Plus a loudmouth who sold huge slabs of stone, marble, and slate while screaming at his wife on his cell phone.

It was the loudmouth who gave Henry one tidbit of useful information.

"If you're asking about artsy stuff from big houses, you need to see Roxy Abruzzo. She's the damn expert in all that shit. Now, get outta here!"

So it was time to make another run at Roxy Abruzzo.

The next day, Henry waited across the street from her salvage yard all morning. The red Mustang sat parked on the gravel, looking abandoned. Henry went to a coffee shop for some revitalizing caffeine and returned in time to watch the arrival of a large black pickup truck. It had wheels that looked as if they'd been inflated by a giant, and an engine that sounded like a jetliner. The ugly guard dog ran out of the garage and barked a happy greeting. Roxy herself got out of the truck and proceeded to unload something wide, flat, and very heavy, wrapped in a tarpaulin. She used a winch on the back of the truck, and then rolled her treasure into the garage with a two-wheeled cart.

Her dog trotted circles around her, wagging his tail, and then they both disappeared into the garage.

Eventually, Roxy came out of the garage and rejiggered the winch on the truck. Then she stood back and took off her gloves. She slapped them against her shapely thigh.

Henry took a deep breath, stepped out of his car, and walked across the street. He handed her a cup of Starbucks cocoa.

"I figured you for plenty of whipped cream," he said.

"If it isn't my favorite flunky." Roxy accepted the cup and sniffed it suspiciously. "You still doing legwork for the Hydes, Paxton?"

Today she looked coltish in snug jeans, a black turtleneck sweater, and a fitted leather jacket that had seen better days. She tucked her work gloves into her hip pocket. She'd pulled her wild hair back in a plastic clip, but dark curls escaped around her face and tumbled down her creamy white neck. Botticelli with overtones of Harley-Davidson.

Her evil rhinoceros dog flashed out of the garage and lunged at Henry as if to take a chunk out of him. It took all of Henry's self-control not to jump up onto the nearest fire hydrant.

"Can you call off Cujo?"

"Down, Rooney," she said and the dog backed away. She took a tentative sip from the cup, looking at Henry with those dark, knowing eyes.

Henry cleared his throat. "I'm not always on the Hyde payroll. I do freelance flunky work from time to time."

"I'll remember that next time I need to flunk something."

"Have you taken any more bullets since I saw you last?"

"Nope. But I found something of yours."

"Oh?"

She walked around the truck, opened the door, and leaned into the cab, showing Henry a breathtaking view of her denim-clad bottom. He admired it while she rummaged in the glove compartment. When she stood back and slammed the door closed, she tossed something compact at him.

"I found your wallet in the car last night."

He caught it one-handed. "What a relief. Now I won't have to cancel my credit cards."

"I should have taken your American Express out for exercise, but I've been busy. You must have dropped it in the car yesterday. Go ahead and count the money. It's all there." She smiled. "I wouldn't want you to think I'm some kind of criminal."

Henry noted the arch in her brow, the twitch on one side of her delicious mouth. "Where would I get such an idea?"

"I could have returned it sooner, I guess. But I had a hunch you might turn up again."

Henry figured she'd gone carefully through every detail of his wallet.

Roxy smiled, denying nothing, and leaned against the truck. If Ford Motors had used her in an ad campaign, they'd have put the other car companies out of business years ago.

She took a sip from her cup. "Thanks for the hot chocolate. You trying to make up for something?"

The dog made another circle of him, hackles bristling, but Henry managed to say calmly, "I can do better than chocolate. How about a late lunch? Early dinner?"

She sipped more coffee, eyeing Henry speculatively. "I have a better plan."

"I'm listening."

"Do you know Kaylee Falcone? The manicurist?"

"Julius Hyde's girlfriend?"

"That's the one. This is her car." Roxy nodded at the red Mustang. "Somebody took a shot at her while she was in it. And an hour later, you and me nearly got ourselves killed, too."

"Do the police know about either incident?" Henry asked.

"Did you call them, Counselor?"

"I hate to distract them while they're so busy. Investigating Julius Hyde's murder must be grueling work."

Her smile developed an even more cynical twist. "Then, for whatever reason, we're on the same page."

"For whatever reason," he agreed.

They smiled at each other, making a pact, of sorts.

Henry said, "Were you thinking of taking some kind of immediate action, Miss Abruzzo?"

"Yes, as a matter of fact. The police are interested in somebody I care about."

"Anybody I know?"

"The big guy who works for me. His name is Nooch. Despite a complete lack of evidence, the police took him in for questioning yesterday. They haven't released him yet. They're asking him about the Hyde murder."

She kicked at a loose rock in the gravel, and it skittered a few dozen yards. Henry thought maybe she was more agitated than she let on.

"Does your friend know anything about the murder?"

"Nope. But that won't stop the cops from putting the pressure on. I'd like to give them something else to think about. I know a couple guys. Guys hired to scare people every now and then. I'd like to ask them what they know."

"They scare people? Or do they shoot people?"

"Both."

"You mean . . . hit men?"

She grinned. "More like intimidation. They haven't actually killed anyone yet."

"It's only a matter of time?"

"My money's on one of them killing the other, probably by accident, probably when they're drunk as skunks." She pulled the Mustang's keys from her pocket and dangled them in the air. "Until then, they're free agents. I thought I'd go see them and ask a few questions. You game?"

141

"Depends. What are the chances these gentlemen are drunk as skunks today?"

"Pretty good, as a matter of fact."

A moment later they were climbing into the Mustang. The dog sat down on the gravel, looking unhappy to be left behind. Henry enjoyed a moment of relief before he took the precaution of fastening his seat belt.

She drove fast, humming along with the radio. Within minutes, Henry's faulty internal compass was thoroughly confused. He had no clue what part of the city they were in. But the farther she drove, the more dilapidated houses flashed by his window.

To make conversation, he said, "Did you take care of that problem you had yesterday?"

She stopped humming, which had been almost an unconscious accompaniment to the blaring radio. She turned down the volume. "Which one? Right now, I have a shitload."

"The pizza delivery."

"Oh, that." She slipped through a red light to make a right turn, but a mail truck blew through the intersection, blasting his horn at her. Unruffled by the near-death collision, she put her foot down hard on the accelerator. She said, "Actually, that problem turned out to be a big one. One that could last a long time."

"Anything requiring legal advice?"

"As long as it's free. Can I kill the kid who got my daughter pregnant?"

Henry couldn't hold his surprise. "You have a daughter?"

"Yep, seventeen years old. Yesterday she announced she thinks she's going to make me a grandma."

"Wow." Henry tried to calculate Roxy's age. "That news must have been a shock."

"Yeah, a humdinger. I was having sex when I was fourteen, but the fact that she even talks to boys at her age makes me crazy. So, can I kill him? Maybe slow dismemberment? Starting with his dick?"

"You might get off if you draw a grandmother for a judge."

"Those odds aren't good." She cracked her window and let the cool air rush into the car. "Of course, I was a pregnant teenager, too, but I figured her for smarter than me."

"There's nothing like hormones to lower SAT scores."

"Exactly. But it's not like the sex is even good at that age."

"Sex is good at any age."

She shook her head and laughed. "Then you haven't learned enough, Paxton. Not nearly enough."

The traffic thinned out, and she whipped down a street pocked with potholes the size of craters. She slowed down and began peering through the windshield at the house numbers.

"In general," Henry said, "I think women who talk about sex are trying to decide if I'm worth going to bed with. They're flirting, but they're also making up their mind. Picturing the outcome. Will I pull on my pants and leave or want to spend the night? Make stupid small talk afterward or turn on the game? Fall madly in love and become an annoying stalker? Or leave them with nothing but good memories? But with you, I get the feeling that you've already decided what we're going to do."

A bigger laugh this time, very throaty. "Which way do you think I've decided to go?"

He was saved from answering when Roxy made a life-endangering right turn in front of some oncoming traffic. She seemed unfazed by the horns blown by other drivers and continued to concentrate on reading house numbers.

Henry said, "What about the big guy the police are interested in? What did you call him? Nooch?"

"What about him?"

"You seem to care what happens to him. What's the relationship?"

"Relationship?" She seemed amused by the word. "A while back, he got into some trouble on my behalf, and I'd like to be sure he's okay. He works for me. I keep him employed and out of trouble."

"How long has this been going on?"

"Ten years."

"That must have been some trouble he got into."

"Bad enough," she acknowledged. "I was with a man, and it got out of hand. Nooch came to my rescue, I guess you could say. And he got into a lot of trouble for it. So I owe him."

"And you want to keep him away from the police?"

"Far away," she said.

Expertly, she squeezed the little Mustang into a tiny parking spot between a rusted car on cinder blocks and a van that looked as if it had been entered in a demolition derby and lost. Across the street sat a late-model Monte Carlo with a shredded roof.

Roxy cut the engine.

"Now what?" Henry asked.

She popped her door open. "Follow my lead."

Henry climbed out of the car. "You have a plan?"

"It's a little hazy at this point. How are you at improvising?"

"I've learned a few tricks over the years."

"Then let's see what you've got, champ."

She led the way to the front door of a two-story frame house that should have been condemned long ago. The paint had blistered off. The roof was missing shingles. The concrete steps looked as if they'd been broken by a madman with a sledgehammer.

The yard was a mound of weeds. Henry looked closer and thought he recognized marijuana plants among the desiccated stalks.

A skinny cat bolted off the porch, leaving behind a lot of junk. An over-turned plastic garbage can, a broken chair, and a baseball bat.

Roxy picked up the bat. She didn't bother knocking. She reached through a broken pane on the front door and released the lock, then barged into the house, shouting, "Hey, Delaneys! Anybody awake in here?"

Two thugs were sprawled side by side on a lumpy sofa in the living room, watching ESPN on a brand-new television with the WalMart stickers still pasted on the side. It was balanced on top of another, ancient television, presumably broken. In a large, filthy aquarium next to the TV coiled a gigantic sleeping snake.

The door crashing back on its hinges made both men jump.

One thug had been eating SpaghettiOs from the can. He was a skinny, weasel-eyed man with a pulsating sore on his upper lip.

He dropped his spoon and reached under the sofa cushions.

Roxy pointed the tip of her baseball bat at his nose. "Don't do it, Jimmy."

Jimmy swallowed his mouthful of SpaghettiOs and eased his hand out from inside the cushion.

His brother—swinelike down to the stubble on his double chin—sat still on the sofa. He had a guttural whine. "Did you have to bust down my door?"

"It was already busted, Vincent." She jerked her head at Henry. "This is a guy from the DA's office, Henry Whatsit. He wants to know about the bribe you paid me."

Henry endeavored to look official and tried to remember if state statutes included a mandatory sentence for such an offense.

Vincent sat up straight, and the bulge of his hairy belly popped out from under the bottom of his sweatshirt. "That wasn't no bribe," he said to Henry. "She tricked me. She pretended she worked for the city, that's all."

Roxy said, "And you're in the habit of bribing city officials?"

"In the habit—? Hey, no, man, that's not what I meant. She's doing it again, see?"

"Take it easy," Henry said. "Nobody's accusing anybody."

"The hell I'm not," Roxy said. "I want him arrested."

"For what?" Vincent demanded.

"Influence peddling," Roxy shot back. "It's a felony, right? And you're already on probation, Vincent. This could land you in jail."

"What the hell are you talking about?" Jimmy asked.

"I'd like a little clarification myself," Henry said.

"Here's the deal." Roxy bulldozed them all. "You tell us what the story is with Kaylee Falcone, and we let the whole matter slide."

"Who?"

"The chick," Jimmy clarified. "Hyde's girlfriend."

"You took some shots at her yesterday," Roxy said. "Remember? Down in the Strip. Only you missed. Or did you just plan on scaring her?"

"We don't know nothing about that," Jimmy said, trying to bluff.

"And afterward, you tried to shoot me and Henry here. We were in the car in the cemetery."

"We didn't!"

"Where'd the new TV come from? You win the lottery? No, somebody paid you to shoot at Kaylee Falcone."

"It wasn't me," Vincent insisted. "I had nothing to do with it. All I did was drive the car."

"Jesus," Jimmy said. "Do you have to be such a moron?"

He hurled his can of SpaghettiOs at his brother's head. The glancing blow prompted Vincent to throw a punch, connecting with Jimmy's upper lip, splitting open the sore. In an instant, the two were pounding each other. Vincent wrestled Jimmy off the sofa onto the floor in a splatter of tomato sauce.

Grunting and punching, they rolled clear of the sofa, whereupon Roxy stepped over the two brothers and dug under the cushions until she came up with a handgun. She picked it up by the barrel and smoothly handed it off to Henry.

Before he knew what was happening, he was standing there holding a gun on the two brothers.

Roxy started kicking them and yelling. "Cut it out, you idiots! Stop it! I'm gonna bash both your heads in!"

Eventually, Vincent sat up, dazed and rubbing his ribs where Roxy's boots had done some damage. Jimmy clutched his bleeding lip and cursed. His eyes streamed tears of pain. Then they both noticed that Henry had a gun on them, and they fell silent.

"That's better," Roxy said. "Now come clean, the two of you. I know you do work for hire. You've been auditioning for Carmine for years. It was the two of you who tried to cap Duke Slansky two years ago. Everybody knows that."

Vinnie stared at the muzzle of the gun. "It wasn't—"

"Shut up. Everybody but the cops knows you did it, so don't bother lying. Who else is stupid enough to use Duke's credit card at a gas station with security cameras—except you, Jimmy? You were just lucky everybody in your family covered for you when the TV stations ran the tape. Tell us who hired you to shoot Kaylee Falcone."

Jimmy was mesmerized by the gun, too. "I didn't—"

Roxy kicked him again, then put both hands on the grip of the baseball bat and prepared to hit a line drive.

"We weren't supposed to shoot her," Vincent quickly confessed. "Just scare her."

"Who bought your new TV?"

Vincent shook his head stubbornly and didn't answer.

Lightly, Roxy tapped Jimmy upside his head. "How about it, Jimbo? You want to know what it feels like to have your brains all over the floor?"

Henry raised the muzzle of the gun a little higher. "Tell the lady a good story, okay?"

Sullen, Jimmy said, "It was Hyde himself."

"What?" Roxy said, "You mean Trey?"

"No." Jimmy cut his eyes at Henry. "The old man."

"Are you lying? Because I'll bash—"

"I'm not lying, bitch. It was the dead guy."

"Why would he want to intimidate his own girlfriend?"

Jimmy was pouting. "How should we know?"

"And if he hired you, why did you wait until he was dead to follow through?"

"He paid us a grand to shoot at her, that's all. We took the money, so we figured we better do the job."

Roxy laughed. "A grand? That's it? What are you, discount hit men?"

"Roxy," Henry said. Taunting seemed pointless at the moment, and he could see her getting out of control. The circumstances had pumped her up. Even her voice was different—harsher, louder. Any minute she was going to splatter somebody's brains all over the room.

"Yeah, okay." She held the bat loosely at her side. "When were you hired? The night Julius Hyde was killed?"

"We had nothing to do with that," Jimmy said quickly. "He hired us before. I dunno—a couple of weeks ago, maybe We met him down on the river, and he said—"

"Along the river?" Roxy asked. "Where?"

"An old steel mill." Jimmy looked at his fingers to see how badly he was bleeding. "Down off Butler Street. He said he owned the place. My uncle worked there twenty years."

Vincent said, "Who's the blabbermouth now?"

"Shut up," Jimmy said. "You got us into this in the first place."

"Did not."

"Did, too."

"Moron!"

"Asshole!"

Suddenly they were beating up each other again. Rolling on the floor, kicking and throwing punches, gouging at each other's eyes.

"Oh, hell," Roxy said.

She swung the baseball bat and hit the aquarium. Glass smashed, and then the huge snake began to uncoil into the room.

She dropped the bat and walked out of the house. Henry bolted after her, hearing the screams of the Delaney brothers as they scrambled to escape their pet.

In the car, Roxy was breathing hard, as if trying to get her temper under control. "Jesus, I hate snakes. But you did good work in there, Paxton. I'm impressed."

"Thanks. You're no slouch, either. Setting the snake loose was a nice touch. They'll be busy for a while." As his heartbeat returned to normal,

Henry fastened his seat belt. "But are you sure it was wise to take their gun?"

"I figure removing guns from the possession of idiots is a public service." She started the car. "It should happen more often. Got a handkerchief? Use it to wipe off your fingerprints. Mine, too. Then put it under the seat for now."

"A wise precaution." Henry did a thorough job of erasing his participation and stowed the gun as she requested. "What was that business about the steel mill?"

She frowned as she pulled out into the street. "I dunno. Something rang a bell. Kaylee mentioned a building. She said Julius gave her one."

Caught off guard, Henry said, "He did? Officially? With a deed and everything?"

"I don't know the details. But she claims he showed her a building and said he was giving it to her. I assume she means the old steel mill the Hydes used to operate. You know anything about that, being the family retainer?"

"The family did own a steel mill down on the Allegheny. It went out of business years ago."

"Believe me, I know that part. A lot of people in my neighborhood were put out of work back then. You want to see mass exodus? A spike in domestic violence? Drinking? Drugs? Fire everybody at the same time." She darted between a school bus and a slow-moving Buick, driving the car like a jet fighter.

Henry said, "If his will names his girlfriend, I can think of a few family members who'd have a motive to kill Julius. They wouldn't want such valuable property to leave the family."

"Why would he pay the Delaneys to shoot *at* her? Not just shoot her dead?"

"Maybe he regretted giving love tokens to her. Wanted to convince her to give back his gifts?"

"And he decided to bully her to get them back? That doesn't make sense."

"No, it doesn't."

"I mean, it's totally nuts. They're lying. I'd go back now to find out, except the snake is probably still loose Hyde's wife's still in the picture, right?"

"Unless she goes to jail for torching the house."

Roxy gave a wry laugh. "Anybody who can afford the right lawyer can stay out of jail these days."

"Miss Abruzzo, your prejudices are showing again."

She stopped for a traffic light and grabbed a pack of gum from her jeans. She thumbed out a stick and offered it to Henry. "You don't know anything about me."

He accepted the gum. She peeled a stick for herself and folded it into her mouth. He could see her thinking. He realized his own prejudices were showing, too. He hadn't expected her to be smart. And despite her rough edges, he was starting to like her.

She said, "Tell me about the Hyde family politics."

"Have you heard of attorney-client privilege?"

She ignored that. "Julius Hyde wasn't a bad dude. He liked his pleasures, that's all, and he could afford them. Why would somebody want to bump him off? He never really harmed anybody."

"Depends on what you call harm. I just learned he tried to stage his own mother's accidental death."

"Oh, yeah? That's not nice."

"No, it isn't. And in addition to physical harm, say, done with a baseball bat, there's financial harm."

"Financial harm. Twenty years ago, there would have been a list of guys who'd want to kill the man who closed the steel mill. Not now."

"But Julius never ran any of the Hyde businesses. His father was the steel magnate. His brother runs Hyde Communications."

"What are you saying? Wait—when Julius died, what happens? Do his kids get his money right away? Do not pass go, collect your two hundred dollars?"

"It's his share of his mother's estate that's got the most value. And his share doesn't necessarily go to his children. Julius has two brothers, plus two sisters. Don't forget about them." Henry couldn't afford to forget about the dragon sisters. They demanded their fair share. "And nobody gets money immediately. All the lawyers will start revising the estate plan."

"Aren't you the lawyer?"

"In a family like this, everybody has his own lawyer. Plus shared lawyers. And lawyers to watch the other lawyers."

"What about more girlfriends? He thought he could get away with anything, right?" Roxy asked. "A guy like Julius only needs a checkbook and a Viagra prescription to keep a lot of women happy."

"As far as I know, he had the manicurist, that's it. But of course, I can't be sure."

"What does his wife say? If anyone knows the truth about that, it's probably the wife."

"I think Monica chose to turn a blind eye."

"Until she found out about Kaylee, and then she lit a match." Roxy slid the car through a stop sign and drove into a park. "Maybe she's the one who paid the Delaneys to take potshots at Kaylee. They're got to be lying. She has the most to gain from Julius's death, right? The wife gets half of everything and the kids fight over the rest?"

"That's usually how it goes, but not in this tax bracket. Monica won't go hungry, though, that's for sure."

"Except she torched the house. That has to jeopardize her piece of the family pie, surely."

"Depends. Quentin is focused on the price of Hyde Communications stock, which is affected by bad publicity. As long as Monica is kept under wraps, the stock price is good. But once his brother is buried and a decent interval is past, Quentin will go back to gobbling up any small communications company he can get his hands on. For which he will need capital. And he'll want Monica's share of Julius's inheritance. That's my guess, anyway. He's sticking close to her now and making a show of caring about her, but she's going to be a grease spot on his driveway before it's all over."

"So Quentin's a viable suspect, too. He wanted Julius's share of the estate."

"And he has the right personality."

"He could pull a trigger?"

"Yes," Henry said. "I think he could. For all his Wall Street talk, he's basically a bastard who'll do anything to build his empire."

"Another CEO with a heart of gold." In a murmur, Roxy added, "His brother Trey always needs money, too."

"But does Trey have the stomach for killing?"

"For him," Roxy said, "it would have been panic, more likely. He's emotional, impulsive. The kind of guy who wouldn't plan a murder. But only an idiot would try to pull off an execution will all those people around. Maybe it wasn't planned at all. Maybe it was a crime of passion."

"Monica's impulsive. As setting fire to the house shows."

Roxy turned to him. "Could she have killed her husband?"

"If angry enough, maybe."

"Kaylee could have been angry enough," Roxy said.

"Oh?"

"She's a hot-tempered chick." Then Roxy shook her head. "But I don't see her having the stones to shoot her boyfriend. I see a lot of women who get in over their head with men. Hardly any of them can pull the trigger. Maybe she had some kind of conspiracy going with Trey, though. Jeez, they all have motives. It makes me dizzy."

Henry sighed. "Everybody wants Dorothy's money. And she's not even dead yet. Funny, because she's the one who'd be easiest to kill. A pillow over her face, and *poof!* You'd have your inheritance."

Roxy glanced at him measuringly.

Henry caught himself, chagrined to find he'd mused so much aloud.

Roxy gave him a cold smile. "Interesting how the other half lives."

"Don't pretend the people in your world don't squabble about money."

"Sure, we fight about money. And for us, it's just as important, maybe more. But our everyday concerns are more about the work we do, the people we know, the family we protect. Not about which brother or sister we can screw over to get what we want. Even those lying scumbags, the Delaneys. See them? Together through thick and thin. Not like the Hyde brothers."

Roxy braked the car and pulled over onto a grassy area. In the distance, the buildings of the downtown rose between a gap in the trees, looking like a storybook city. None of the grit showed from this distance. Around the car, rolling hillsides converged on the curving asphalt road. Closer, the ivory towers of a couple of universities glowed. It was a bucolic spot in the middle of the city.

"Where are we?" he asked.

Roxy shut off the engine and unfastened her seat belt. She said. "A park. I come here to let off steam."

Henry turned to face her. "What kind of steam?"

She grinned. "I'm not exactly America's Sweetheart. I like sex. That doesn't surprise you." She rolled down her window and spat out her gum. Rolling it back up, she said, "Sometimes I take guys to my house. Sometimes, I go to theirs. But some afternoons, I've been known to come here."

He felt himself respond at once. She must have guessed, because she smiled. "I could take care of business in the car, Henry, but that would be all about you. It's too cramped for me to get what I want. I need more space."

"You have this kind of rendezvous well choreographed. Is the gum part of your routine?"

She unzipped her leather jacket and let it fall open. "I don't like bad breath."

Henry could imagine what her mouth would taste like right now. How her strong body might feel against his. He could see her contemplating the same about him. In a few seconds, he wasn't going to be able to conceal his willingness to try.

With a smile, he said, "If you're trying to turn me on, you win."

She reached over and unfastened the top button on his shirt, allowing her fingertips to linger at his throat. "Here's what I'm saying, Henry. If you come around again, we could make each other feel good and have some laughs. But I don't fall in love or let any man use me—for sexual gratification or whatever you're trying to learn about the murder. If that's cool for you, okay. If not, this is good-bye."

The fact that she kept her emotions out of the way was enough incentive for Henry to spit the gum out of his mouth. He stuck it on the gear shift and reached for her. "I could be cool with that."

She met him halfway. She had a lush mouth and a sure tongue. Her curves felt softer than he expected, and a ripple of warmth seemed to pass through her body as he touched her. Hot-blooded, that was Roxy Abruzzo. Even better, a laugh bubbled in her throat. And he liked thinking maybe she could lose her cool head just a little with him.

"What the hell," she said. "C'mon, Henry."

She had a condom, and she made a show of putting it in her mouth. She held it poised for a heartbeat between her teeth, her eyes alight. He hardly felt it slip on, so swiftly did it happen, with the mane of her hair in his lap and the suction of her mouth exquisitely strong. Everything happened very fast after that. Instinct told him to hold her head to guide her, but there was no need. He was out of his league. Instead he held on to the car for dear life while she performed an intensely powerful act. In the middle of it, Henry heard a whimper and realized it was his.

No stardust and angels singing celestial praise. Just mind-bending, top quality sexual performance.

When he was on the brink of nuclear detonation, she sat up and crawled over the gear shift, telling him what she intended to do next in a husky voice and laughing at his expression. Probably one of near delirium. While he braced himself, Roxy slid one long leg out of her jeans and neatly straddled him. Henry groaned as she sank down on him, hot and sweet. She was a female force against his belly, her thighs gripping his, her breasts firm against his chest. Supple and powerful, she was an animal. He was her prey.

He forgot to be a partner, forgot about what she might prefer, and let it happen. His hands on her tight ass, that was all, he gasped for breath and hoped he'd survive.

He came too fast, of course, before she'd found a rhythm that pleased her, and when he remembered himself, Henry felt the heat leave his penis and flush his face instead.

She didn't seem to mind. She hadn't broken a sweat, but she smiled against his mouth anyway.

"Interesting." She rocked back on him, keeping him snug inside with admirable muscle control. But Henry felt trapped, actually. And both of her hands were linked around his neck as if she considered whether or not she should snap a few vertebrae as long as she was in the neighborhood.

He tried to sound collected. "Interesting?"

"Yeah."

She released him slowly, perhaps to prove she was still in control. And when she was behind the steering wheel again, he was left to the embarrassing business of putting himself back together. All while trying to catch his breath.

She said, "I learned something about you, Henry."

Part of him felt as if he'd been tricked. Like his brain had been sucked dry, not the rest of him. Nervously, he wondered what exactly she'd figured out.

Another part of him just wanted to roll over and go to sleep.

❈ 13 ❈

Arden's phone rang several times during the day, but she couldn't manage to wake herself up in time to answer it. Finally, though, her bladder insisted she get out of bed, and when she dragged herself out of the bathroom, the phone was ringing again, so she picked up.

"Arden?" The silky voice of Hadrian Sloan-Whitaker purred in her ear. "I have some news for you."

"News?" Arden collapsed on the bed again and racked her fuzzy brain to find some context. A sliver of sunshine glowed at the bottom of her window shades, but she had no clue what time it might be.

"Yes, I put my ear to the ground as you suggested, and there's definitely a seismic shift going on."

"An earthquake?"

"Nothing that significant yet. But a buzz."

What the hell was he talking about?

He said, "Someone contacted me through my Facebook account. Someone asking about antiquities."

"You have a Facebook account?"

"Leave no stone unturned," Hadrian said. "I embrace all technologies that put me in touch with people. We texted for a while and I then realized I may have been inadvertently communicating with the party you wanted to reach. She's asking all the right questions."

Arden groped a random capsule from her nightstand and swallowed it dry.

Hadrian continued. "She wants to know about Greek statuary, perhaps second century BC. She's very cagey, but I put two and two together. I wonder if she is someone with knowledge about your grandmother's collection. It might be best if you were in touch with this prospect yourself." After a pause, Hadrian sounded pained. "I sense she thinks I might be a sexual predator of some unpleasant kind."

The information finally began to penetrate her fog. Arden dragged herself to a sitting position. "What did she say about the statue?"

"Nothing specific, but she's definitely fishing. I suspect she's in possession of something very valuable. Either that, or she's looking to acquire. Either way, it's good. For us."

Since when were they an "us"? Arden remembered her own plan and didn't recall Hadrian being a part of it. "What did you tell her?"

"I gave some basic historical information, but it was clear she already knew a thing or two. She mentioned Pittsburgh, and that's when the penny dropped. Arden, if I put you in touch with this person, you'll remember me when the time comes, won't you?"

"When what time—? Oh, of course, Hadrian." Suddenly she liked the note of fawning in his voice.

"I'd like a shot at placing your item."

Arden said coolly, "With a museum?"

Hadrian barely held back a here-we-go-again sigh. "If an institution of 'origin is in a position to pay the going rate, of course we should consider its offers. But we'd certainly do better by—"

"You know how I feel about private collectors, Hadrian. If an important piece falls into the hands of dilettantes who simply warehouse history, the whole world suffers."

"I know, I know," he soothed. "Arguing is moot if there's nothing in our hands yet, don't you agree?"

"Ye-es," Arden said slowly.

"So talk to my contact. See what you can learn."

"All right. Give me the phone number."

"Promise you'll report back to me?"

"I promise."

Arden copied down the phone number Hadrian dictated, then sat staring at it long after she terminated the call. Who was this contact? A collector? A scholar at the local museum, perhaps? Or someone more sinister? Sage Abruzzo. Arden didn't recognize the name.

She would need to have all her wits when she made the phone call.

Arden began sorting through her pill bottles. If she was going to pull this off, she needed to mix the right combo to sharpen her mind.

✳ 14 ✳

After dropping off Henry Paxton at his car, Roxy discovered he had stolen the crucifix from around her neck.

Somehow during their interlude in the park, he'd managed to distract her and snitch it. And the whole time she'd mistaken him for a weakling.

"You naughty boy," she said aloud, one hand on her throat. "This could mean war."

Or something much more delicious.

Stealing her necklace showed he had more juice than she'd first thought. She liked the guy. Didn't trust him—especially now that he'd paid her back for lifting his wallet—but she liked him. He had a good laugh and a nice body—two qualities Roxy especially appreciated in a man. Too bad he had a brain, but that was a fault she could overlook. The sex had been barely acceptable for her, but after all, she had ambushed him. Given different circumstances, he'd be better. Stealing her crucifix showed that, surely. A weekend in a hotel with him to find out sounded pretty damn good. Maybe after Nooch's hearing.

Her phone beeped—a text message from Adasha Washington.

Free for dinner? Adasha asked.

With a pang of guilt, Roxy decided not to respond.

She closed her phone hastily. She didn't want to tell her friend about car sex with Henry. She wasn't sure why.

Shoving that uncomfortable thought down into her subconscious where it belonged, Roxy went back to the yard and switched Kaylee's red convertible for her truck. She remembered to take Carmine's money out of the car and stow it under the seat of her own vehicle. The Delaney gun she locked carefully in her desk drawer. Safer there. While in the drawer, she found some cash. It was only a few bills left over from lunch a few days back, but it would come in handy.

Then she checked her cell phone and found a voice message from Nooch. He'd called to say he'd been released by the police.

Roxy drove over the river to pick him up.

With the windows rolled down, she sang along with Annie Lennox. Nothing like Annie to lift a girl's spirits.

She found Nooch in a North Side diner, a cop hangout. The place was packed with officers in uniform as well as in plain clothes. At the counter, Nooch was finishing off a double order of eggs, bacon, and pancakes with a piece of banana cream pie waiting. He spotted Roxy coming and started to wolf down the pie.

His lawyer sat on the stool beside him, awestruck by the amount of food Nooch could consume. Roxy took the stool beside Marvin Weiss.

"Marvin," Roxy said, "is your mom still buying your clothes?"

The young lawyer glanced down at his suit—a size too big and with pants that hung down over his Florsheims. The outfit made him look like a kid who'd graduated from high school at twelve, Princeton at fifteen, and law school at seventeen. Which he had. Then, too young and socially inept to be successful in a big firm, he'd come home and hung his shingle adjacent to his parents' dry cleaning shop.

He said, "What's wrong with my clothes? That getting paid by my clients once in a while can't fix?"

"Carmine doesn't pay you?"

"I don't work for Carmine Abruzzo," he said quickly. "Never have, never will."

"Half your client load comes from his recommendation."

"I am not a mob lawyer."

Marvin had been sitting in his little office doing a slow business in real estate transactions for people in his synagogue when Uncle Carmine called him out of the blue. Carmine liked to pretend he plucked his employees from thin air, but there were actually a lot of backroom shenanigans that went on during the process of finding minions with just the right personality type. For his first gambit, Carmine asked Marvin to help out a cousin who needed a lawyer to attend his tax audit. When the tax audit turned out well, Marvin was soon getting calls from lots of Carmine's "cousins." Roxy thought it was cute that he continued to deny helping anyone connected with Carmine.

"Whatever you say," Roxy replied. "Where's your bill?"

Marvin scrawled some numbers on a napkin and handed it over. "And you can pay for your goon's food right now, too. I know you have some cash at the moment. In fact, Carmine's a little concerned that he hasn't heard from you."

"I've been busy."

"Right. PTA meetings and bake sales, I'm sure. You'll be in touch with Carmine? Soon?"

"What does he want?"

"A little help, that's all. Now that Phil's out of the picture, there are some errands. He thought you might be interested. You should call him."

"When I get a chance," Roxy said, with enough edge to remind Marvin that Carmine wasn't the only one with the last name of Abruzzo. "And not a minute sooner."

Marvin put up both hands. "Okay, okay."

She pulled some bills from her pocket to pay for Nooch's dinner. "What did Nooch have to say to the cops?"

"Nothing at all." Marvin stood up and rocked back on his heels, smug. "That's what you pay me for."

"He didn't give any information?"

"He looked at some photographs and picked out the Delaney brothers, that's it. Otherwise, you can rest easy."

"Hey," Roxy said. "I have nothing to hide."

Marvin smirked. "Sure."

"While you were in the station, did you hear anything about the Hyde murder?"

"Why do you care?"

"If the cops are interested in Nooch, I want to know what's going on."

Marvin grabbed a toothpick and began to use it like a pneumatic drill around his molars. "I got a gander at the homeless guy they think pulled the trigger."

"And?"

Marvin shrugged. "They're not so sure about him anymore. Attention is turning to the wife—Monica. But I heard your name mentioned."

"As a suspect?"

With another smirk, Marvin said, "As someone to call for a good time."

Roxy patted her butt. "You couldn't handle this much fun, Marvie."

Nooch looked up from the last crumbs of his pie. "Be nice, Marvin."

The kid lawyer flushed at being reprimanded by a guy who had never been within a hundred miles of Princeton. He grabbed his rumpled raincoat. "In case you end up in jail, pay my bill immediately, will you? Not in cash. I don't want any trouble with the IRS. Meanwhile, make sure Nooch stays available. The police are going to want to see him again. I'm guessing soon."

He walked away, and Roxy spun on her stool to look at Nooch. "What did you tell Marvin?"

Nooch pushed away his empty pie plate and burped. "Why? Was I supposed to tell him something?"

"What did you tell him about the thing we did at the Hyde mansion?"

Nooch rubbed his face. "Man, I'm sleepy. What thing?"

"At the Hyde mansion. The house that was burned up."

The carbohydrate content of Nooch's meal began to hit him like a sedative. "Can I just go home to bed? Please, Rox?"

She settled his bill and took him outside, aware than half the cops in the diner watched them leave. They climbed into the truck, and Roxy pulled out onto the dark street. "Did the cops bring Kaylee back to talk, too?"

"I didn't see her. Not since yesterday."

"Did you tell them about her?"

Nooch frowned. "I don't think anybody asked about her."

"Because we didn't see her at the mansion."

"But she was there," Nooch said sleepily.

Roxy stood on the brake. "What?"

Sometimes Nooch plucked random memories out of the otherwise pondlike stagnation of his brain.

Nooch caught his balance on the dashboard. "She was at the burned house. The night her boyfriend got shot."

"Jesus, she said that? Why the hell didn't you mention this before? Never mind. What did she see? Anything important?"

"I don't know. You know, cussing just lowers people's opinion of your intelligence."

"I don't care about anybody's opinion. Did Kaylee see her boyfriend get killed or not?"

Nooch surprised the hell out of Roxy by saying, "Yeah, she did."

She pulled over and parked before turning to her passenger. She tried to stay calm. "She said that? She told you she saw Julius die? Did you say so to the police?"

"I don't know," Nooch whined. The barrage of questions stymied him. "Marvin kept interrupting me. They didn't ask about Kaylee. They asked me about you."

"What did you tell them?"

"Nothing. Marvin kept interrupting me."

Roxy shoved her hair away from her face and ended up holding the sides of her head. The news shook her up. It meant Kaylee had seen a lot more than she'd originally said. Maybe that explained why Kaylee had been so bitchy to her. She'd seen Roxy talking to Julius before his death.

And Trey had lied outright about his final moments with Julius, too, Roxy realized.

She pulled back into traffic again and drove the truck across the bridge, thinking it was a good thing Nooch hadn't spilled these particular beans to the cops. She decided she needed to give Marvin an early Hanukkah present.

But Kaylee, she thought. Had the girl really witnessed the murder?

If so, had she watched Roxy and Nooch steal the statue? And had she blabbed to the police about it?

Roxy clamped her hands hard on the steering wheel. There was no use asking Nooch for more details. He had put his meaty face in one hand and gone to sleep in the passenger seat.

Roxy drove Nooch home, pushed him out of the truck, and watched him stumble through the front door. She bit her lip. If the police discovered he'd helped steal the statue out of the Hydes' yard, his probation hearing was screwed.

Half an hour later, Roxy parked the truck by a fire hydrant in an alley in the Strip District and cut the headlights.

In darkness, she slipped out of the cab and locked the truck. A couple of upscale restaurants backed onto the alley along with a nightclub that appealed to rowdy college students. It was an appealing neighborhood for enterprising car thieves. Pricey cars belonging to the restaurant patrons who were too cheap to pay for valet parking were left in open lots that drunken students trolled hourly.

Pocketing her keys, she hustled down a cobblestone alley behind the restaurant, nimbly dodging a swampy pothole. Out front, the restaurant was very tony, but in the back, homeless guys were Dumpster diving for their evening meal. Near them, a young drunk had wandered away from the nightclub and was taking a furtive leak in a shadowed doorway.

A bright light knifed from the back door of Rizza's, illuminating the haphazard crush of motorcycles parked in the alley by the restaurant staff. As she walked closer, luscious late-night scents from the kitchen mingled with the less appealing stench of trash.

Dougie Calderelli came out the door lugging two bags of garbage in his good hand. He grunted a greeting.

"Hey, Dougie."

Roxy caught the screen door from him and slipped past Dougie into the kitchen, where the rest of the guys were cleaning up for the night. Already, the stainless-steel counters gleamed. The floor smelled of disinfectant. At the dishwasher, Ray rinsed a mountain of pots with his hose. He wiped sweat from his brow with his tattooed forearm, nodded at Roxy, and went back to the job.

Someone had nailed to the wall a Support the Troops ribbon. And draped an old athletic supporter from the nail. Above it hung a framed photo of the guys when they'd served in Afghanistan together. They were all smiles then, holding their weapons lightly in the harsh sun, leaning against a battered Humvee. Dougie's baby face bore a broad smile, but back then he'd had two good hands.

As if there weren't enough testosterone in the air already, they were blasting rock and roll from the speaker by the walk-in cooler—harsh shouting over a screaming guitar. The Clash, *Combat Rock*.

Roxy let the screen door bang shut behind her.

The noise caused Carl, Rizza's longtime sous-chef, to glance up from packing his knife kit. He was short and stocky, and his black T-shirt—the standard uniform with the restaurant's logo printed on the chest—was still soaked with sweat. He wore lime green Crocs beneath his black jeans— one concession to a job spent on his feet. "I didn't hear the Monster Truck pull up," Carl said. "What'd you do, Roxy Road? Trade it in, finally?"

"Never."

"Good. We like a little warning before you show up."

"How was hockey the other night?"

"I didn't play. We have a baby now."

"I heard. Congratulations. A baby tends to change a lot of things."

"I hear you. Am I ever gonna get a decent night's sleep again? Or a little nooky with the wife?" Over his shoulder, he called, "Flynn! Look what the cat dragged in."

From his executive chef's office, Patrick Flynn scooted on his swivel chair and glanced around the doorway. He had a phone pinned to his shoulder—probably ordering truffles from France or maybe exotic fruit from the planet Jupiter. He held up one finger to Roxy, asking her to give him a minute's patience. He'd already peeled off his bandanna, and his shaven head gleamed under the fluorescent lights.

Roxy leaned one hip against the stainless counter. To Carl, she said, "Busy night?"

Carl shrugged. "Not bad. We did two hundred plates. Only one idiot sent his tuna back for being undercooked."

"Did you deep-fry it for him?"

Carl grinned. "You bet. And added some cocktail sauce to make him happy." Carl shouldered his knife kit, then used a key on his ring to un-lock a drawer and pull out a handgun. Casual as could be, he checked his Sig's magazine and the chamber before tucking it into his belt at the small of his back. "Keep your powder dry, Rox."

She shook her head. It creeped her out that all Flynn's guys carried weapons. "Don't shoot off a testicle, Carl. You may want more babies."

Roxy hadn't figured out the whole ex-military attitude about guns yet, but she had a gut feeling it wasn't much different from the mind-set of guys they'd grown up with who went into breaking and entering with the occasional convenience-store mayhem on the side. Except the Marines thought they were entitled.

Carl laughed, saluted his boss, and disappeared into the night. A moment later, she heard his motorcycle engine bark to life.

The rock and roll cut out abruptly. Then Flynn strolled from his office, rolling his neck as if to work out some hard-earned kinks. Tonight the black T-shirt clung to his shoulders like red on a Roma tomato, and his jeans rode low on his hips. His shaven head already showed a stubble of black hair, which would grow in curly if he'd let it. He'd been a good-looking hellraiser back in high school, but time in the mountains around Kohat and a couple more years of bumping around the world learning to cook had changed that.

He said, "Where's Nooch?"

"I dropped him off to referee his grandmothers."

With a grin, Flynn said, "I remember those grandmothers. One of them has a pretty good arm when it comes to throwing a frying pan."

The memory popped up in Roxy's mind. A Halloween night of soaping windows at Nooch's house to irritate the grandmothers grew into smuggling pints of Wild Turkey into school dances and stealing cars in the neighborhood—only to joyride and park them in front of the wrong houses for the fun of watching irate people hunt up their vehicles in the morning.

She couldn't help smiling. "Good thing you're a fast runner."

"You, too," Flynn said. "And it's a good thing you showed up tonight. You saved me a trip."

He pulled open an under-the-counter fridge and put his hand on a takeout container. He skidded the food across the stainless counter to her.

"You made me dinner?"

"Nope. Call it an *amuse-bouche* for your uncle Carmine. I hear he's not very hungry these days. Maybe this will tempt his appetite."

"Where'd you hear that? Somebody paint a billboard?"

He grinned again, this time with sincerity, and the killer dimple popped briefly in his cheek. "I heard from Gino Peppo, buying mahimahi down at the market. Gino plays pinochle with Carmine every Tuesday. Says Carmine started chemo last week."

Seemed everyone in town knew Abruzzo family business except Roxy. Suddenly Carmine's job offer took on a different meaning. But with Flynn watching, she said, "Apparently you haven't heard that I have no known association with Carmine."

"I figured since he was sick, you might have eased up on that policy. He may be a crook, but he's family."

"He's probably using the sick thing as a smoke screen. You'll have to make your own delivery."

"Okay. Hungry?"

She shrugged, not quite sure why she'd turned up here, but knowing it wasn't for the food. Dougie called good night from the doorway, and Ray went out behind him, leaving Roxy alone with Flynn.

"What brings you here?" He had been watching her. "Looking for more leftovers?"

She summoned up some self-control. "No, I need information. I thought maybe you might have heard some good stuff from your fancy customers."

Flynn looked surprised. "Wow. You're asking for help. From me?"

"Just information."

"That's all?" Flynn asked, barely holding back a smile.

"Do you have time to talk, or not? Or is there somebody waiting at home in your bed tonight?"

"I have time," he said without really answering the second question. "What do you want to know?"

Roxy took a deep breath. "Your dad still owns some riverfront property down on the Allegheny?"

He leaned against the counter and nodded. "Good thing, too. The newspapers say the city's going to develop that stretch like they did down on the Mon River."

Usually, Roxy kept up with local news, but the paper rarely seemed to have actual information anymore, so she didn't bother to read it regularly. And reading the online version was a scattershot thing for her, too. But with Flynn's family connection, she figured he'd have the scoop.

She was too tired to think up a way to finesse the information out of him, so she asked flat out, "What kind of development?"

"Condos and shopping, that kind of thing. Not industry. Some developers brought the mayor in here a couple of nights ago to talk about it. My old man thinks he's going to hit the Powerball. He still owns the dock and the river salvage company property."

To Roxy, any development along the stretch of river currently occupied by crumbling steel mills, dilapidated warehouses, and slum housing sounded like a gold mine. For somebody.

"Do you know anybody else who owns riverfront properties?"

"I grew up down there on the river," Flynn reminded her. "Still keep a boat myself. I know a lot of those guys. You want a list?"

"Sure."

Flynn reeled off a few names. Roxy knew some of them. "What about the Hyde family?"

"They owned the steel mill when it was in business. I suppose they still do. You could check the tax records to be sure. That's public information. Why?"

"You know anything else you can tell me?"

By way of an answer, Flynn made a fist and planted it warmly on her breastbone, then pushed Roxy onto a stool. She sat.

From the little fridge he conjured another package. With a practiced flip, he unwrapped the white paper from a glistening hunk of fish. Stretching as easily as a cat, he pulled a clean sauté pan down from the overhead rack and cast it onto the stove. As flame licked up to heat it, he swiped a knife from its sheath and a handful of something wispy and green from a nearby pot. With easy speed, he chopped the herbs, cracked some pepper, and set about seasoning the fish.

If he was tired after a long night of feeding the city's most discriminating palates, Flynn didn't show it. As his body moved in the steady rhythm of a man who knew how to do something very well indeed, Roxy decided he had the look of a warlock casting a spell over the sauté pan.

She sat back and watched, letting exhaustion take hold of her mind at last. It had been a long couple of days, full of anxiety, hard work, and a few shocks she wished she could forget. But here was Flynn, cooking for her. For a moment, Roxy's troubles receded as the heat of the kitchen warmed her bones.

Flynn flipped the fish in the pan, then slid the whole thing under the broiler. Next, he snapped the tips off some very thin green beans and dropped them into another pan with a knob of butter, salt, and pepper. His strong hands bore a dozen tiny scars—broiler burns. He set down his knife.

And said, "You thinking of buying some riverfront real estate?"

"Next time I win a bet, why not?" Roxy touched the handle of his knife, thinking. "Who else profits from development of all that property along the river besides owners?"

"Construction companies. Suppliers. Concrete and asphalt guys. Middlemen."

"Right. You have a lot of middlemen in and out of this restaurant."

"That's us. Chefs to the lesser stars." Flynn removed the knife from her hand and used a clean towel to wipe the blade. "Why do you mention the Hydes? Your buddy Julius is dead."

"I talked to somebody he might have given the steel mill to. A girlfriend of his."

Flynn slipped his knife back into its sheath. "Whatever happened to flowers and Whitman samplers?"

If Julius had given Kaylee cheap gifts, Roxy wouldn't be wondering what the girl's connection to his murder was.

Flynn walked away from the food for a moment and returned with a bottle in one hand and two long-stemmed glasses suspended from the fingers of the other. He set the glasses down in front of Roxy and splashed two inches of white wine into each.

Flynn picked up one of the glasses and broke across her thoughts by saying, "So, forget about real estate for a minute. What's the real problem?"

"I don't have problems."

He sipped the wine and eyed her as he held it on his tongue a moment. Then he swallowed and said, "You've got that funny wrinkle in your forehead. And you don't ask for help from anyone unless something big's going on. Now you're here with me, of all people."

Roxy rubbed the knot between her eyebrows. "It's nothing."

"We've known each other too long to start lying now."

For a second, Roxy wondered exactly how long she'd known Flynn. Raising hell on Halloween seemed a long time ago. But time didn't matter anymore. It felt as if they'd been some kind of unit forever. More than friends. Less than lovers.

She took a slug of the wine. It was crisp—a word he'd taught her. And perfumey. She actually preferred Uncle Carmine's sweet homemade red wine, but she drank Flynn's choice so as not to insult his taste.

She said, "Aren't you related to the Clearys?"

If the change of subject surprised him, he didn't show it. "Which Clearys? The cops or the ones who own all the Laundromats?"

"The cops. Specifically, do you know Zack Cleary?"

Flynn tilted his head and squinted into the middle distance. "Tall kid? Basketball player? Cocky little bastard?"

"That's the one."

"Yeah, he's some kind of distant cousin. Or an in-law, I guess, if you want to be accurate. Why?"

Roxy clenched her teeth, unable to say the words.

"What?" Flynn paused in the act of taking another sip of wine. "Wait, he's not hanging around Sage, is he?"

"It's worse than that."

He laughed. "Dating her?"

Suddenly Roxy's throat felt tight, and her eyes were stinging.

All trace of amusement left Flynn's face. He put down his glass, hooked another stool close, and sat on it, bumping Roxy's knees with his. He reached for both her hands and held them hard. "What's wrong? Is Sage okay?"

"No," Roxy managed to say. "Yes. I mean—she—thinks she might be pregnant."

"Jesus. How did—? Shit. With Zack Cleary?"

Roxy could only nod. She'd managed to hold it together this long, but now—with Sage miles away and Flynn's sympathetic face in front of her—the whole puzzle of Julius Hyde's death faded from her mind and she was suddenly a bowl of mush. His hands were hard to the touch, yet gentle.

"She's just a kid!" Flynn said.

"Sage turns seventeen in April. He's a little older. Twenty or twenty-one, probably." Roxy eased her hand free of Flynn's. "She's—I can't believe I'm saying this—she's the same age I was when I had her."

"Jesus. It happened fast, huh? Her growing up."

Roxy glanced up into his face. Sage had his deep-set Irish blue eyes and his dimple, too. And the same quickness of expression—the ability to show a lot of emotion, then shut down fast to prevent revealing more than he wanted. Tonight the force of his understanding felt like the heat of an oven.

She looked away from his probing gaze. "I feel like—I don't know—like I blew it. I thought Sage was going to have it all, you know? Great education, great life."

"Don't write her off yet."

"I'm not. But it's . . . hard. Believe me, I know what it could be like for her, and I—I guess I should have done something sooner. Talked to her more, I guess. Been a better mom. I left the hard stuff to Loretta."

"You're a great mom. Loretta's been good, too, but not like you. Look at her! Nobody's happier than Sage. And smart? She's goddamn brilliant. Kids don't come more well-adjusted than she is."

"She's a little adult," Roxy agreed, sneaking a glance at Flynn. "I'm the kid in the family."

Flynn said nothing, but he held her gaze, and an odd moment ticked by.

Roxy felt her cheeks get hot. "I thought Sage could make it out of her teenage years without messing up the way I did."

"The way both of us did."

She let out a short laugh. "Yeah, both of us."

He hesitated. "I haven't tried, Rox. To be a part of her life, I mean. I thought you wanted it that way."

"I did," she said firmly.

If he noticed her use of the past tense, he chose not to remark on it. Abruptly, Flynn touched her shoulder and got up to check the fish. Using a towel to protect his hand, he pulled the pan from the broiler and slid the food onto a clean white plate from the stack. It was perfectly cooked, as if he had a timer in his head. A wrist flip sent the green beans from the second pan cuddling against the fish. He used a squirt bottle to paint a wave of bright pink sauce.

While his back was turned, Roxy used her sleeve to wipe her nose.

At last he was satisfied, and he set the plate in front of her. It was a pretty presentation of color, balance, and heady steam. He grabbed two forks from their bin and handed one over to her.

"C'mon," he said. "Since when do you turn down a free meal?"

"I'm not in the mood."

"You know how long it takes to get a reservation in this joint? Even if you come in the back door, the food's going to be fucking brilliant. So eat."

Obediently, Roxy took a bite of fish. It was good. Maybe even delicious. She forked another piece. "Tasty. What is it?"

"Ahi with a mango foam. And some technique I picked up in Singapore." Flynn tasted the fish, too, nodding once with approval. Then he put his fork down. "There's just one thing I've got to know."

"What's that?"

"Have you killed Zack yet? Or just hit him with a tire iron a few times?"

Roxy smiled grimly. "I'm weighing my options."

"I'll be your alibi," he offered. "It's the least I can do."

"Thanks. I don't know why I came here, really. Maybe because I knew you'd help me bury the body."

Flynn watched her eat a few more bites of fish and try the beans. Seriously, he said, "Roxy, don't beat yourself up about this. You've done your best with Sage, and until now that was pretty damn good."

Roxy toyed with her fork. "I haven't been, you know, an exemplary role model."

He gave a half shrug. "Maybe not. Who are you dating now?"

"Dating? I've never 'dated' in my life."

"Okay, who are you sleeping with?" he asked bluntly. "More important, are you sleeping with anybody Sage knows?"

"No," Roxy said, just as harshly. Then, "I figured if I didn't stick to any one specific guy, it would be better for her. I guess I hoped she'd never catch on."

"Unless she's slower than I think she is, she's known about your sex life for years. And she still loves you, no matter where you unzip your jeans. Or," he added, "where you make your money."

Roxy glanced up and met his steady gaze.

"Hey, don't worry," he said. "I'm not calling the cops. But I heard you're maybe going to work for Carmine."

Neighborhood gossip moved fast. "Since when do you get an opinion about my life?"

"Since never, and you know it. Consider this a friendly suggestion. You need to be careful. I heard Carmine wants to cut you in. But Sage is going to need you now more than ever. If you go to jail for whatever, what happens to her?"

"I'm not going to jail. Not unless you and your battalion of misfits start blabbing all over the neighborhood—"

"Shut up," he said.

"Just because I come to you once doesn't make you her father, you know. So don't butt into my life."

He didn't argue.

Roxy dropped her fork, suddenly not hungry, but annoyed for reasons that were just beyond her grasp. "I gotta get going."

"I thought you wanted information."

"I got enough. I'm going home." She headed out. She should have delivered the pregnancy test to Sage long ago anyway.

"Hey," he said when she reached the door. "Don't go off and do something stupid because you're upset about Sage. Or mad at me."

"What the hell do you think I'm going to do?"

"We both know each other's weaknesses," Flynn said.

"I take care of myself." She pushed out through the door and didn't look back.

She stormed down the alley away from the restaurant. She was mad, yeah. And feeling unsatisfied after her encounter with Paxton. Probably too distracted to make any kind of smart decision. And letting down her guard with Flynn had been a mistake. It never paid to get emotional.

She should have gone home right then. Or gone to find Adasha to talk it through. But sometimes girls just wanna have fun.

The college kid who had been taking a leak in the alley earlier was hanging around her truck when she got there. He had his hands cupped around his face and he peered in the window, looking to see if she'd left the keys in the ignition.

"Oh, hey," the kid said, leaping away from the window. "This your truck?"

He had the name of his college printed on his shirt in big letters, and

his haircut—blond tufts carefully combed back from a widow's peak—
had cost his mommy a pretty penny. He was still drunk, but just a little.
She guessed he was twentyish. Old enough.

"Yeah, baby, it's my truck." Roxy pulled the keys from her pocket and
looked him up and down. Nice body? Check. Brainless, too? Very likely.
The perfect man. For tonight, anyway.

"Must get lousy gas mileage." He smiled.

Roxy smiled, too. "You need a ride somewhere?"

With a blink, the kid said, "Sure."

Inside the truck with the kid, Roxy dug a condom out of the glove
compartment. She tossed it into his lap. "Put this on, baby. Let's see what
kind of mileage you get."

She began to peel off a few layers of clothes, ready to rock and roll.

The kid laughed nervously, but he had his shirt off a minute later, and
they wrestled a little. The truck's windows began to steam up, and the
kid proved he was very teachable. Nothing like a little love with the perfect stranger to take a girl's mind off her troubles.

❋ 15 ❋

At the crack of dawn, Henry took another browbeating phone call from Dorothy Hyde. A call that reminded him how much he preferred his client comatose.

"Call me when you find my Achilles," she said after a tirade about his lack of progress. "Or you can polish up your résumé, Henry. I haven't got long to live, and I want that statue."

So he swallowed a Rolaids tablet with some coffee, showered, and dressed while watching a little *SportsCenter* and thinking up a new plan. Trouble was, he kept thinking about Roxy Abruzzo instead. And how he'd somehow lost a round with her. It made him feel uneasy. The sex was great. The afterglow, unsettling.

Revived by the caffeine, he went outside into the sunshine. He'd left his BMW parked outdoors in the brick courtyard between the great house and the stables instead of parking it inside the carriage house with the other vehicles that belonged to the estate.

Outside in the cool October air, Monica Hyde galloped up on a black horse the size of a rogue elephant. She wore jeans, boots, and a red fleece jacket, and she looked like a girl. Her blond hair danced in the breeze, and Henry wondered if maybe she had intentionally worn it loose, just for him. The horse's hooves clattered on the bricks, and the noise echoed against the tall walls of the nearby house, very *Masterpiece Theater*. The scene needed only Helen Mirren to be perfect.

Henry might have tossed Monica a gallant compliment, but the damn horse was snorting and stamping, and he looked capable of biting Henry's arm off.

"Good morning, Henry!" Monica sat happily on the enormous animal and seemed unconcerned by the beast's antics. "You're up early!"

"Good God, Monica, be careful up there!"

Monica laughed. "Isn't he amazing? I'd completely forgotten Dorothy still kept the horses here."

"Just two. I pay their feed bills. They eat like—well, horses. The vet and the farrier cost a fortune, too."

"Worth every penny," Monica declared. "Do we still have a membership in the hunt club? I'd love to ride this Saturday, if they're going out."

"They have archaic rules, but I'm sure they'd bend a few for you." He kept his distance from the horse. "Unless you think it might be inappropriate, Monica. How are the arrangements coming along for Julius?"

"Quentin's working on the funeral. Several business leaders have expressed interest in attending. And the Dow inquired about paying respects, too. It's quite a fraternity. I had no idea. But there's some awful business about releasing the body, you know."

"I see."

The television news was still full of Julius's death, the investigation into his murder, and the plight of the poor homeless chap who was still the prime suspect. But there was plenty of media speculation about the family, too. Lots of recycled photos of Monica in handcuffs, Quentin's

CEO portrait, and Trey looking silly in a scuba suit. Someone had found a picture of Julius's children all gathered around a polo pony.

Thankfully, Quentin had managed to control the family, it seemed. Not one of them made any statements or teary appearances on camera. Quentin's daily press releases were predictable and succinct: The family appreciated the public outpouring of condolences and had nothing further to say.

Most everyone else on the local television stations burbled briefly about Julius's good works before plunging into tawdry talk about his private life. Some intrepid reporter found Kaylee Falcone's high school photograph, mortarboard and all. Henry expected the fraternity of CEOs all wanted to know the circumstances of Julius's death before hopping on their jets and putting themselves in front of any cameras on his behalf.

Monica seemed unconcerned. She patted her horse's neck. "Have you had any luck finding Samson?"

Damn. Henry had wanted to avoid the subject of Monica's dog. He'd found his attention thoroughly distracted by Roxy Abruzzo.

Before Monica noticed his involuntary flush, however, they were interrupted by the arrival of a large black Mercedes that barreled through the gates of the Hilltop estate and came roaring down the tree-lined alley that led straight to the garages. Fallen leaves blew attractively behind the car, and the sunlight glinted off the immaculately waxed vehicle.

It would have made an ideal automotive commercial except for the scowling man who sat behind the wheel.

"Quentin," Henry said. "What's he doing here?"

Monica put her gloved hand to her forehead to shade her eyes from the morning sun. "Oh, dear, he's early."

"Early for what?"

"We've scheduled a meeting with Dodo this morning."

"You're seeing Dorothy?" Henry knew he was sounding like a fool, but the news that Monica and her brother-in-law intended to visit Henry's client suddenly made him wish he'd put a few extra Rolaids in his pocket. "What for?"

The Mercedes rocked to a stop nearby, sending the black horse into another frenzy of snorts and bucking.

Quentin got out of the car and slammed the door. "Monica, have you forgotten? Or do you intend to ride Kensington over to Fair Weather Village?"

"You're early, Quen."

Irritated, Quentin checked his watch. "Now we're going to be late. You know how Mother feels about punctuality. Good morning, Paxton."

"Hello, Quentin. I didn't realize you were seeing Mrs. Hyde today. I'll get my briefcase and join you."

"There's no need for that." Quentin spoke gruffly. "My mother is perfectly capable of talking to me without counsel."

"It's no trouble. I'm happy to tag along."

"This is purely a family visit."

Henry ground his teeth. There was no telling what Quentin had up his sleeve. Or what Dorothy might be plotting. Which one had called the meeting? he wondered. And how did Monica fit into their plans? He tried again, saying, "Well, I can certainly drive separately, if you'd rather have time alone with Monica. I can be there in case Mrs. Hyde wants something done, you see. I'm always happy to help her in any way."

"We'll be having a private discussion, Paxton. Can I say it any plainer? You won't be needed."

From astride her horse, Monica said sweetly, "It's not that we don't appreciate your services, Henry. Of course we do. But we need to talk about Julius, you see, and what's to be done."

"Well, if I can provide any—"

"We'll muddle through without you this morning," Monica said. "But thank you, Henry."

The rear door of the Mercedes opened, and a person who had been invisible in the backseat climbed out of the car.

"Arden!" Monica cried. "How nice to see you!"

Henry's insides contracted with a force he hadn't experienced since a bout of dysentery in Portugal.

Arden Hyde wore large black sunglasses. She was skinnier and paler than he remembered, and her hair looked both fashionable and dreadful. She yawned. "Hi, Monica. Hello, Henry. How's life treating you?"

"Hello, Arden. Very well, thank you."

Henry endeavored to keep his voice neutral, but he must have failed. Quentin came alive like a dog on point, and Monica sat up straight and glanced from Arden to Henry and back again.

Henry said, "How was Jerusalem?"

"Florence," Arden replied. "I was fired. For encouraging the Italian government to return artwork to its rightful owner."

"How interesting," Monica cried, not noticing Quentin's wince. "I can't wait to hear about that!"

Arden said, "How's your rash, Henry?"

"All gone," he replied. Quentin's head looked as if it might explode all over the courtyard. "Nothing serious. Just an allergic reaction."

"Too bad," Arden said. "It was kinda cute."

Quentin took charge of the moment. "Monica, we're wasting time here. Get down from that animal, and we'll leave immediately."

"I have to put Kensington back in the stable."

"Let Paxton take care of him."

"Me?"

"Hurry up, Monica."

Monica slid down from the saddle and tossed her horse's reins in Henry's direction. Was her manner slightly cooler than it had been before Arden's arrival? She said, "I don't know why you're in such a hurry, Quen. It's not as if Dodo's going anywhere."

"I don't like to keep her waiting. Besides, I have other appointments later."

Monica remained cheerful. "I'm very curious to find out what you have planned. Are you staging a family coup? A corporate takeover?"

"I'm taking care of the day-to-day matters, as always. Dodo likes to be kept informed. Let's go, shall we?" He took her elbow and pulled.

"I should change my clothes—"

"Never mind about that. Paxton, you understand."

"Of course." You greedy bastard.

Henry wanted to warn Monica. He wanted to pull her aside and tell her to be careful or Quentin would hang her out to dry. She was just one small obstacle in his plan to get as much of the Hyde fortune as he could for himself and Hyde Communications.

Monica threw a smile over her shoulder at Henry. "Take Kensington down to the stable for me, will you, Henry? You're such a dear. Jerry's there. He can take care of Kensington properly."

Arden gave him a flat expression. Then she got back into the Mercedes and slammed the door, the memory of a single unfortunate indiscretion obviously clear in her mind.

Henry got a tentative grip on the extreme ends of the reins and tried to keep a safe distance between himself and any part of the horse that might kick or bite. Meanwhile, Quentin hustled Monica into the Mercedes, and a moment later they were roaring up the driveway and headed for the nursing home.

To himself, Henry muttered, "I wish there was a way to prove Quentin killed his brother."

Kensington gave a declamatory snort and tossed his head.

Henry said, "And he's setting her up for a murder charge."

And what the hell was Arden doing back in town? What role did she play in Quentin's plan?

The horse must have decided to throw in with Quentin, too, because he suddenly yanked the reins out of Henry's hand, spun around on his haunches, and took off running across the lawn. Before he disappeared from sight, the horse kicked his heels in Henry's direction—as if he were making a final editorial comment on the situation.

Henry watched the animal gallop away—probably a quarter million dollars on the hoof. At least he was headed for the stable. Didn't all horses have some kind of homing instinct?

Henry stood for a moment, weighing his options.

That damn statue. If he could lay his hands on it, a lot of things would fall into place. Long enough, perhaps, for him to help Monica inherit Julius's share of his mother's fortune. And maybe need a younger man for a husband.

His best lead was still Roxy Abruzzo. He reached into his trouser pocket and pulled out her necklace. Smiling, he watched her crucifix glint in the sunshine. Perhaps she had bested him once. But Henry had a flare for comebacks.

❀ 16 ❀

After her refreshing recreational hour with the college kid, Roxy had driven to Loretta's place. She'd let herself into the silent house with her key and taken a shower before crashing on the sofa for a few hours. When she woke—way too early—she smelled coffee and something delicious.

She followed the murmur of voices and pushed through the kitchen door to find Sage at the kitchen table, talking with none other than Patrick Flynn. Sage was looking teary-eyed, but she was smiling.

But her smile faded when Roxy appeared wearing the rumpled clothes she'd slept in. Sage blew an exasperated sigh. "Mom, couldn't you at least comb your hair? We've got company."

Flynn eased back in his chair. He looked freshly showered and annoyingly relaxed in a black fleece pullover and jeans. "You look more rested than you did when I saw you last. What happened?"

"None of your business," Roxy said. "I hope you're here to make breakfast."

He tipped his head to indicate the cast-iron skillet on the stove. "Frittata. We saved you the crispy edges."

Roxy peeked into the skillet and used her fingers to pluck out a shard of cheese. Half the frittata remained in the pan, brimming with veggies and fluffy eggs. The cheese melted on her tongue, and Roxy closed her eyes to savor the taste. It sure beat Pop-Tarts for breakfast. "You can stay."

"I brought fresh coffee, too. But Sage tells me Loretta only uses instant."

Sage said, "I think she says that so I won't want to try it. She says coffee will stunt my growth."

Roxy tugged the quilted cover off one of the many small kitchen appliances on the counter—all items Loretta had purchased on QVC. The existence of an expensive chrome version with an espresso feature indicated that Loretta—like all women of their ethnic background—knew exactly how to brew an excellent cup of coffee.

"I see the light," Flynn said, and he got up to make a pot with the bag of freshly ground beans he'd brought. He said, "Pretend you don't see what I'm doing, Sage. You're not supposed to be drinking caffeine now anyway, right? Just in case? I mean, it's bad for the baby, isn't it?"

Stopped in the act of cutting herself a large wedge of the frittata, Roxy turned on her daughter. "You told him?"

"Why not?" Sage bristled. "Aunt Loretta's been crying in her bedroom since I told her last night. And you weren't exactly supportive when I broke the news."

Since Flynn's return to town, Sage had steadily been getting used to the idea of having a father. They all were. But Sage had a continuous pink blush whenever Flynn came around, which Roxy found both kinda cute and extremely annoying.

Sage also exhibited signs that she thought her mother was an idiot not to marry Flynn immediately and make them one big happy family.

Sage said, "Did you buy me a home test, by the way?"

"I did, but Nooch sat on it," Roxy snapped. "I'll pick up another one."

"Thanks heaps." Sage matched her tone.

Flynn said, "Take it easy, the both of you. Either way, it's good news, right? Babies are good news."

Sage looked unconvinced, and Roxy knew her own face wasn't exactly reflecting joy.

"Okay, so it might be happening a little earlier than you'd like." Flynn poured water into the coffeemaker. "But, c'mon, it could be fun."

"Fun?" Roxy couldn't stop herself and turned on him. "Exactly how many times did you host the birthday party at Chuck E. Cheese? Wash the sheets in the middle of the night during the stomach flu from hell? Dodging bullets in Afghanistan is a hell of a lot easier than—"

"Mom," Sage warned.

Flynn didn't need anyone coming to his defense. "You were the one who wanted to prove you could handle everything on your own. You threw me out of your life, remember? So eat your breakfast," he said to Roxy. "It'll improve your mood."

Roxy grabbed a fork from the drawer, plunked her plate on the table, and straddled a chair. She cursed herself for going to see him last night. Stupid move. And now here was Sage with stars in her eyes.

Stabbing her food, she said, "So I guess all the important decisions have been made?"

"What decisions?" Flynn asked.

"Like whether or not she's really going through with this. If she's really . . ."

"Pregnant," Sage said. "You can say the word."

"If you are," Roxy said, "there are other options."

"Dear God." Flynn sat down at the table and stared. "Are you kidding?"

"There's adoption." Roxy ignored Flynn.

"Okay."

"Or you could go for a clean slate, Sage. Forget this ever happened. I'll help you and stand by you, if that's what you want."

Flynn was flabbergasted. "Are you saying what I think you're saying?"

"Shut up. It's easy for you to judge, Mr. I'm Gonna Join the Marines and See the World. She's the one who'll have a person depending on her for the rest of her life. She could have an abortion."

Sage said, "If I'm having a baby, I'm not getting rid of it."

"You sure?"

"No adoption, no abortion. No way." Sage lifted her chin.

Roxy remembered how it felt to finally have something of her own after both her parents essentially disappeared from her life. She had something that gave her purpose against the world. It hadn't been just the lessons taught at St. Dominic's that gave her the conviction to hang on to her baby.

"Okay, okay. I get it. I did the same thing, in case you didn't notice."

"I noticed," Sage replied, with a little less heat. "Look, I know this isn't going to be easy. But I can handle it."

Flynn took a deep breath to calm down. "You're going to need help. That means your mom and Loretta."

Sage shot him an unsure look. "I have to ask their permission to go through with this?"

"No, that's your decision. But if you want them to pitch in once in a while—well, it's only polite to ask."

Roxy was starting to get really annoyed by Flynn's presence. If not for the fragrance of life-giving coffee brewing on the countertop, she'd kick him out the door. "We don't need you to play referee."

"Maybe we do," Sage snapped. "It's kind of a novelty to have a voice of reason around."

Roxy forked another large chunk of frittata and ate it. "What about

Zack?" she asked around her mouthful. "What's his opinion on all this? Or are you keeping it a secret until you know for sure?"

Again, Sage sent a glance at Flynn—an appeal for help.

He said, "We were just talking about the best way to break it to him."

Sage reached for the glass of milk in front of her. "I think he should know. It's not fair keeping it a secret. He should have a say. But it's tricky right now."

"What's so tricky about it?"

"Zack," Flynn said carefully, "may not be the monogamous type."

Roxy dropped her fork. "He's screwing other girls? Oh, that's great, Sage. You get pregnant by a jagoff who—"

"Let's try to keep this discussion productive," Flynn said. "Name-calling isn't helpful."

Roxy slammed the table. "I'm sick of this! Since when did you get to be the boss all of a sudden?"

"Mom—"

"How come you're here, anyway? Did Sage call you?"

Flynn remained unruffled. "I dropped by after going to the market this morning. She was pouring herself a bowl of cold cereal when I came to the back door. And she was crying. So I came in and made breakfast."

"I had to tell him why I was crying," Sage said, fighting down another blush. "About the baby. He said congratulations right off, by the way, which is a hell of a lot nicer than the reaction you gave me."

"I just don't see why we need him butting into our—"

"I could use a male perspective! Flynn thinks I should tell Zack now. Right away. Not months from now when I'm all—you know, puffy. Maybe I should invite him over for dinner."

"Alone," Flynn clarified. "Without having your mother or Loretta around."

Roxy rolled her eyes. "What are you going to do, Sage? Sedate him with pizza before you break the news? You think giving him dinner will make him suddenly want to marry you? Haven't you learned anything by living in this neighborhood?"

"It could happen!"

"Sage, it should be obvious to you that a onetime donation of sperm doesn't magically turn a guy into a devoted father."

Sage was suddenly fighting tears. "Do you have to be so negative?"

"I'm being realistic! In my experience, a young guy is not going to jump for joy when he hears he's going to be a baby daddy before he can legally buy himself a beer."

"Well, your experience is extensive," Sage shot back. "So I guess you're the expert."

Flynn reached out with one hand and pinned Roxy to her chair before she could jump up and explode. He said, "Okay, so I was a jerk. Let's not assume everybody is. Maybe Zack is more mature than you think. He wants to be a cop, for one thing. Surely that means he's got a sense of responsibility."

"Or he's a cowboy who wants to carry a gun."

"Roxy—"

"All right! But if you plan to ask him about child support, Sage, don't get your hopes up."

"I'm not asking him for any kind of support! I'll get a job."

"An after-school job?" Roxy couldn't believe her ears. "No way! This is your senior year. You've got to focus on your grades and those college applications. You're not going to spend your life making more babies and taking welfare to raise them—not while I'm still kicking."

"How am I going to pay for everything?" Sage cried. "Doctors cost money—even at the clinic!"

"I've got it covered," Roxy said. "Don't worry about money right now."

Both Sage and Flynn looked at her with surprise.

Roxy couldn't keep the defensive note out of her voice. "I've got options. So don't worry about paying for things." She sent a glare at Flynn.

But Sage said, "Thank you. So can I invite Zack over for dinner?"

"You'd better ask Loretta. It's her house."

Sage picked at the tablecloth with her fingernail.

"Okay, okay," Roxy said, getting the message. "I'll talk to her for you. I know she can get emotional sometimes."

Flynn got up to pour coffee, but he wisely kept his mouth shut.

Roxy punched his arm. "Cut her some of that frittata. And pour plenty of coffee. I'll take some upstairs to Loretta."

Sage got up from the table and gave Roxy a noisy smooch on the cheek. "Thanks, Mom."

Gee, it was almost a cozy family moment. Then Sage shouldered her book bag and said, "I got some info about statues, by the way."

Roxy forgot about being mad. "Like what?"

"I'll tell you later. Tonight, maybe, after I learn more. I'm meeting someone today."

"What someone? I thought you were just going to the library."

"I did some Internet research instead and talked to some people on the phone. I'm meeting an art dealer lady at a coffee shop."

"What did you tell her?"

"I was completely circumspect," Sage said. "I can keep my mouth shut."

Aware of Flynn watching from over the rim of a coffee cup, Roxy attempted to control the rising concern in her voice. "When are you meeting?"

"This afternoon, after school. Don't worry. I'm not going to get roofied and kidnapped, all right? Jeez."

"You're not meeting this person alone."

"I'll take Kiryn along."

"No, I mean I'm going, too."

"Mom, sometimes you act like I'm still twelve!"

"This is business, and I need to be there. When's your appointment?"

"I don't know yet. I'm supposed to call today to set up a time."

"Give me the number." Roxy put her palm out. "I'll talk to this person myself. What's her name?"

Handling a knife and plate, Flynn said, "If this meeting is so scary, how come Sage is involved at all?"

"She's not involved. She was just looking up stuff for me." Roxy sent a hard look at her daughter. "At least that's all it was supposed to be."

"Arden something," Sage said at last. "She is a very nice person. She's classy. Friendly. You'll say something wrong, I just know it."

"You think I can't handle friendly?"

Flynn laughed. If Roxy had been closer, she'd have kicked him.

"You'll scare her off," Sage said. "Besides, I'm already involved, so let me keep going."

"No," Roxy said flatly. "Call me when you know what time you're meeting. We can do it together. I'm serious about this, Sage. I have to be there. Got it?"

Sage poured herself a glass of orange juice and drank it down in four long swallows. She put the glass in the dishwasher, letting the suspense build. Finally, she turned to face Roxy. "Okay, okay. Anything you say. Go talk to Loretta, will you? I'm going to be late for school."

Flynn said, "I'll take you."

Roxy said, "You're really getting into this dad thing, aren't you?"

"Mom—"

"Something wrong with that?"

"There is if you screw up."

Sage said, "He's not going to screw up."

Roxy and Flynn shared another long stare. He'd screwed up before. He didn't deny it. Nor, Roxy noted, did he make any promises that he wouldn't again.

Roxy went upstairs, leaving Sage alone with the man who had provided some DNA, but nothing else in seventeen years except a decent breakfast.

Another fancy business suit lay ready on Loretta's bed. But instead of getting ready for work, Loretta was stretched out on the pillows wearing nothing but a slip that clung to her many curves. She fanned herself with a copy of *TV Guide*. She had the TV remote in her other hand, and she was watching Matt Lauer interview some starlet.

When Roxy edged the bedroom door open, Loretta put Matt Lauer on mute and dropped the clicker on the bed. "What are you doing here?"

"I came last night. Slept on your couch. You okay?"

Loretta fanned herself harder. "I hate menopause. Am I all red?"

"Purple. Here, I brought you some breakfast."

Loretta forgot about sweating and sat up. "Smells wonderful! Is Patrick Flynn here? This looks like something he'd make. And I'm so sick of soybeans I could cry."

"Flynn's downstairs, talking to Sage." Roxy handed her the plate and pulled a fork from the hip pocket of her jeans.

Loretta accepted the fork. "Is that wise?"

Roxy kept the coffee for herself and sat down on the bed. She swung her sock feet up onto the quilt. "He says you need to stop buying instant coffee."

"I hide the good stuff in the back of the freezer alongside my Dove bar stash." Loretta cut a delicate bite with the fork and nibbled it, eyeing Roxy. "Patrick didn't sleep on the couch with you last night, did he?"

"No, he didn't."

"Thank heaven for small blessings." Loretta began to eat with enthusiasm. "He's got more baggage than most men in this neighborhood. Does Sage know his whole story?"

"I haven't told her anything."

"Good call. Let him do it when the time is right. You've got enough problems without him. Especially now."

"So, Sage told you the big news."

"I started worrying days ago. I hoped I might be wrong."

"How'd you guess?"

"I heard her vomiting. She sounded exactly like you did. With a little squeak at the end of your retch."

"Thanks. It's good to know that I have a memorable gag."

Roxy sipped coffee. She'd spent a lot of time in this room. Her relationship with Loretta hadn't been quite the average foster parent and rebellious teenager dynamic. It wasn't sisterly, either, but somewhere in between. Around her, Loretta's bedroom was crammed with clothes. On rolling rods, hanging on padded hangers, organized by color—all probably according to some diabolically anal Martha Stewart plan. She had business suits lined up along one wall—each one specially tailored to fit her extravagant figure. Church clothes along another wall—Easter colors, lots of lace. Their labels meant nothing to Roxy, but she saw brands that were not available at JC Penney or Target.

On the dresser, Loretta had arranged a photo tribute to her dead husband. Pictures of Lou looking a lot like Archie Bunker. One large picture of Sage sat in the middle, though. A ninth-grade school photo with Sage still in braces.

Loretta set down her fork, also perhaps thinking of Sage at that moment. "Roxy, where did we go wrong?"

Roxy eased back against the extra pillow and stared up at the cracks in the ceiling. The ceiling was easier to look at than the walls, which featured Jesus on the cross—three different versions, including a modern Jesus who looked like Keanu Reeves.

"It's my fault," Roxy said. "I didn't think she was paying attention to boys yet. I thought she was playing basketball and studying."

"She was studying! But boys had her on their radar. You didn't notice at the basketball games? It was only a matter of time before one of them worked up the courage to seduce her. A bad boy, of course. All of us are drawn to bad boys."

"Was Uncle Lou a bad boy?"

Loretta's husband, Lou, had died just two years into their marriage. He'd had a heart attack in a strip club at a bachelor party, but his buddies

had dragged him across the street to a Burger King, where he'd died waiting for an ambulance. To this day, his parents thought their darling son
went to meet the angels after choking on a French fry. They blamed his
wife for not cooking him decent meals at home.

"Lou was wonderful." Loretta got misty-eyed. "At first, I thought the
only reason he married me was to get into the mob. He was a nice Polish
boy who wanted to be Don Corleone. I thought he'd settle down eventually.
I'm just sorry we never had children," Loretta said for the ten thousandth
time. "You and Sage—you became my children. And look what happened.
Just goes to show, a family needs a man around, doesn't it? To balance the
yin and the yang."

"I've got too many men around," Roxy said. "Some are more helpful
than others with my yin yang."

Loretta radiated disapproval of Roxy's sex life. She knew few details
and clearly wanted to keep it that way. "Don't let Sage hear you talk like
that."

"Maybe I should have. If she treated sex like I do, she wouldn't be in
this predicament."

"I remember you had a few romantic dreams when you were her age."

"Are you kidding?" Roxy snorted. "Watching the way my dad treated
my mother? He broke her nose three times before she died."

Loretta fell silent, her fork toying with the last bites of her breakfast.

"Okay," Roxy said. "I had a weird childhood."

"It would be hard to be well-adjusted, considering."

"I survived. Not everybody did."

As always when things got uncomfortable, Loretta changed the subject. "It's going to be expensive, you know, if Sage is really expecting.
Prenatal care. The hospital. And then the baby."

"I know, I know."

"Will you let me help?"

Roxy shook her head. "We've had this discussion a hundred times, Lo.
Okay, maybe I'm a rotten mother, but at least I pay for everything. I can't

let you start chipping in—not if you're going to buy into the partnership at the law firm. And I can do it. I've got possibilities."

Cautiously, Loretta said, "Are you considering working full-time for Carmine?"

"You know about that?"

"He's ill, Roxy."

"You sure he's not faking?"

"Don't be a smart-ass."

Although a lawyer and technically an officer of the court, Loretta tended to ignore the "crime" part of "organized crime" and looked upon Carmine's activities as simply a family business—one with a few more twists and turns than other businesses, perhaps, but a respectable source of income.

"I can't get mixed up with Carmine. Not until Nooch gets off probation. He could go to jail if he associates with known criminals, and—"

"Nooch, Nooch, Nooch." Loretta set her empty plate sharply on the nightstand.

"It's about Sage, too. If I start working for Carmine, what will she think?"

For all of Sage's life, Loretta and Roxy had worked hard to keep Carmine's business a secret from Sage. So far, it had worked.

Roxy said, "Besides, I like my own job. Sage wants to invite Zack over for dinner, by the way. To break the news to him gently."

Loretta perked up at the mention of food. "I'll fix some veal. A nice scallopine."

"No offense, but she wants to do the cooking herself." Roxy gave Loretta a kiss good-bye and rolled off the bed. "I gotta go. I'll tell Sage it's okay with you for her to have her rendezvous with Zack."

"Let's you and me have a nice dinner together. You can wear something other than your jeans for once. Rizza's? If Flynn can work magic like this with eggs, think what he could do with a nice lamb chop."

"Sure, whatever."

"Run along. I need another shower. I'm going to be late for work."

"Hang on a minute. Did you hear anything at Valentino's salon?"

Loretta flashed her fingernails—coral pink. "New color. You like it?"

"Sure, but I meant about Julius Hyde. You know—from Valentino's grandmother."

"Oh, yes. It's Valentino's uncle who worked for the Hydes. He married and divorced one of the Calderelli sisters—the family that owned the penny candy store, remember them? Anyway, he's called a chauffeur, but he's really a mechanic who does a little driving for the family. Mostly when Mr. Hyde had too much to drink. His name is Valdeccio—Valentino's real name."

"Did he know anything about the murder?"

"I don't know. Valentino didn't mention anything. You know he's always touchy about gossip that's too close to home. That family has a lot of dirty laundry."

"Don't we all. Okay, thanks." Roxy lingered at the door. "One more thing."

Loretta was climbing off the bed. "What?"

"Nooch's hearing is on Friday."

"What does that have to do with me?"

"How about representing him?"

Loretta began shaking her head before Roxy stopped talking. "I practice elder law. When Nooch is ready for a nursing home, he should call me."

"What about being a character witness?"

"In your best interests, I should keep my opinions of Nooch to myself."

"You'd be a big help, Lo."

"You don't want to hear what I think about your sidekick. Tonto he ain't."

"It's not what you'd say that's important. Just show up. You'll make a good impression on the judge. As long as you're not hot flashy. C'mon. Wear your red suit. The one with the slit in the back of the skirt."

Loretta went into the bathroom. Through the door she said, "Don't you have work to do? Surely there's some other weak-minded soul who needs your help today."

Disappointed, Roxy grabbed the doorknob to leave. But she stopped. Loretta's choice of words triggered an idea.

Suddenly she remembered a weak-minded soul who might buy the statue.

Loretta stuck her head out of the bathroom, a mascara wand in her hand. "You okay?"

"Terrific," Roxy said. "Gotta run."

❦ 17 ❦

With Malibu Barbie watching, Arden made an overseas call to an old boyfriend.

"Arden!" Tiki Papadakis cried warmly. "How often I think of your funny narrow bed at Brown! Do you still make that little snore in your nose when you sleep, I wonder?"

"Hello, Tiki." Although the memory of his golden shoulders was still quite powerful in her mind, she attempted to divert him back to civilities. "Is the weather warm in Athens?"

"Glorious. When can you come? My family's house on Mykonos is available this weekend. Bring sunscreen. You haven't been topless since senior year, have you, my blushing little American?"

"That's a sweet invitation, but I'm sorry, I can't get away right now. I'm swamped with— Well, listen, do you remember me telling you about my grandmother's garden?"

"With the sculpture, early classical period, perhaps a Hercules or a gem from Olympia. It had a pleasing angle of the hips and shoulders—quite unusual. Yes, of course I remember."

Arden avoided looking at Barbie, who was no doubt staring at Arden with deep disappointment for forgetting how perfect Tiki's memory could be, particularly where art was concerned. His mind was the proverbial steel trap for details—dates, artists, materials, everything. He'd grown up in a family of museum folk and studied anatomy and painting at Brown—emphasis more on American female anatomy, of course. Arden had a vague memory of sketching Dodo's statue for him once, with the Rhode Island moonlight streaming in her window.

"Uh, yes, Tiki, as a matter of fact, it's that statue I'm calling about. You see—"

He crowed with pleasure. "I'm delighted, Arden! Your family is ready to give it back!"

"Actually, I'm just hoping to learn a little more about—"

He wasn't listening. "I can be on the next plane. I work with my uncle Christos now at the Ministry of Antiquities. Oh, he'll be overjoyed! It will be a coup for us to recover such a masterpiece!"

"It's not exactly in my possession at the moment—"

"No? Well, we'll get it for you. We have the power to seize Greek property now, did you know? Well, at least we can kick up a fuss, draw attention. International scrutiny, you see. It's as simple as alerting Interpol, and they take care of all the legalities. Even the inevitable squabble with the State Department. I can get Interpol on the other line right away."

Arden's heart had begun to pump hard enough to send a rocket into orbit. Already, things had gotten out of control.

"We can be there in a trice," Tiki said. "Maybe the FBI will join us. Wouldn't that make all the newspapers? A grand photo op! It will be an international triumph!"

Or an international scandal, Arden thought with dread.

❋ 18 ❋

Roxy picked up Nooch on the sidewalk outside his house, glad she didn't have to ring the doorbell. His grandmothers were legendary for hating each other. They conked each other with frying pans and broomsticks, inflicting damage that frequently ended in ambulances. Repeated citations for domestic disputes finally required a clear division of labor in the household. One night Nooch's nonna cooked spaghetti and meatballs. The next night, his bubbe made pierogies. The grandmothers still squabbled all day long in their respective languages, but the police weren't needed as often.

Except for Nooch and his uncle Stosh, all his male relatives were in jail. Neighbors claimed they committed their crimes to get away from the grandmothers.

"Feeling better?" Roxy asked when Nooch climbed into her truck.

"I'm okay." He yawned like a lion who'd just awakened from a three-day snooze.

"Have you heard from Kaylee lately?"

He frowned, flummoxed by the simple question. "Huh?"

"I'll take that for a no. I have to go see her."

"She sleeps late. And she hates to be waked up."

With no desire to cope with Kaylee's temper so early in the day, Roxy said, "Okay, after lunch we'll go see her."

Glad Nooch didn't bug her with a bunch of questions, Roxy drove down to the yard, and Rooney greeted her with delight. Roxy herded Nooch into the warehouse, where he wrestled the griffin fireplace from the Hyde mansion onto the handcart. Together, they loaded it onto the back of the truck just as sunshine broke through the clouds. Roxy lashed it down with bungee cords, and they got back into the cab of the truck. Rooney jumped in, too.

"Where we going?" Nooch asked, sitting as close to the window as possible to stay away from the dog.

Roxy said, "I'm not telling, because I don't want you getting hysterical again."

"When did I get hysterical?"

"Never mind."

"Oh, wow! Are we gonna see Lapraxo again? Oh, wow! Oh, *wow!*"

"We are not seeing Lapraxo! Probably, that is. So calm down."

But Nooch was bouncing in his seat at the thought of meeting his hero, professional football player Lapraxo DuPree. Rooney began to bark as Nooch crowed, "I want his autograph! I wanna shake his hand! I wanna see his Super Bowl ring!"

"Get a grip, will you? First we have to find his house. Damn, I hate the suburbs."

Roxy found her way out of the city and into a far-flung burb where every house was built to impress the hell out of the Joneses. While Nooch chattered on about his favorite Steeler, she got lost twice and was cursing up a storm as she roared through the labyrinthine streets.

"All these McMansions look the same to me," she snapped. "All the same, ugly sprawl. I feel like that kid who went up to Alaska and just kept walking until he found a school bus and died of starvation."

Nooch halted his gush of praise for Lapraxo long enough to look puzzled. "Why didn't he drive the school bus to get something to eat?"

"It wasn't that kind of bus. And where do they get these stupid names? Buckingham Way? Northumberland Lane? Some developer must be hoping for a knighthood from the queen."

"I think it's real pretty. A guy like Lapraxo shouldn't have to live in the city anymore."

"What are you all of a sudden? A social worker?"

"I'm just sayin', a guy has enough money, he ought to have some trees and playgrounds without needles on the ground."

Finally, Roxy found the right cul-de-sac perched on the rolling curves of a golf course. Houses under construction lined the circle. Rooney clambered into Nooch's lap to stick his head out the window. With his tongue hanging out, the dog slurped up the suburban smells, maybe looking for a sexy poodle.

One house looked like a Moorish palace that was being constructed by the same people who built McDonald's restaurants. Twin minarets on either side of the front door were clad in vinyl. The shutters bore the initials DuP.

Standing impatiently on the mud-packed driveway, an ex-fashion model in a fur coat tapped the toe of her pointy shoe and glared at her watch. "Where have you been?"

Roxy slid out of the truck, wondering only for a second what might happen if she kicked mud up on a fur coat purchased by a Heisman Trophy winner who'd once been arrested for beating up his mother.

She slammed the door before Rooney could jump out and pasted on a friendly smile. It took a monumental effort, especially after Nooch scrambled out of the truck and began scoping out the site, hoping for a glimpse of Lapraxo. But Roxy doubted the famous running back would be caught dead spreading Weed 'N' Feed on his own lawn.

Roxy approached her client. "I stopped to pick up something for you, Shanna. I think you're going to love it."

Shanna DuPree narrowed her eyes with suspicion. "What is it?"

"The fireplace of your dreams. Take a look."

The trophy wife of Lapraxo DuPree had been serving as her own building contractor for at least a year. Which only meant the job was taking twice as long as it should. All the tradesmen on the project were delighted Shanna kept changing her mind, because they charged her over and over again for essentially the same work. Also, most of them hung around hoping to meet Lapraxo. Today a panel truck marked with the logo of a plaster company sat parked near the house.

Roxy led Shanna around to the back of her truck and unfastened the tarp protecting the soapstone fireplace they'd pulled out of the Hyde mansion. With some luck, Roxy might sell the statue to Shanna and be done with it. Maybe not for what it was worth, but enough. But first, she had to finesse her customer a little.

Shanna leaned over the tailgate from a distance that assured she wouldn't get her coat dirty. She eyed the fireplace. "Not bad."

"Not bad? It's stone from France! Hand carved, too."

Shanna rubbed her forehead as if the strain of thinking was too much. "Are those supposed to be lions?"

"They're griffins. Mythical beasts. Half lion, half dragon or something. See the claws? And it's beautiful workmanship. Just the thing to give your family room some pizzazz."

Shanna shook her blond hair extensions very firmly. "It's not a family room. It's a great room. And I don't want pizzazz. I want elegance."

"How much more elegant can you get than French carving?"

"Oh, my God!" Shanna suddenly took a step back from the truck. "I know that fireplace. It came out of Julius Hyde's house, didn't it?"

"How did you—?" Roxy decided to fall back on her professional policy of keeping her mouth shut whenever possible, and she swallowed her involuntary question. "Yeah, it came from the Hyde mansion. Which only means it's top quality. Look, Shanna, you need a little vision. It needs some polish, that's all. I know just the guy who can buff it up."

"I don't care how much buffing you can get, I'm not buying a fireplace from a dead guy—certainly not Julius! My husband would kill me."

Roxy couldn't help herself. "You knew Julius?"

Shanna gathered the folds of her fur coat closer. "Of course we knew him. He came to a charity fund-raiser at the Hilton one night. My husband does them all the time, and Julius was—he was rude as hell. Grabbed my boob in an elevator."

"Are you sure?"

"Of course I'm sure! The man was a pig. If Lapraxo had known that night, he'd have flattened Julius's face."

"Julius must have charmed you back to his house, though, if you recognize this fireplace."

Shanna managed to convey anger without the use of her Botoxed muscles. "If you say that to anyone, I'll sue."

"Take it easy," Roxy said. One look at Shanna's suppressed panic said there was more to the story. "I didn't know Julius was like that."

"Give the man a martini and he tried to pork every woman in sight. He was one of those guys who think inheriting a few million dollars gives them the right to do anything they please. Add alcohol, and he was disgusting. I'm glad he's dead. At least my husband will finally stop talking about beating him up."

Nooch said, "Is Lapraxo around?"

An expert at ignoring big men with dumb questions, Shanna said, "Everybody thinks Julius Hyde was some kind of philanthropic prince, but that was all his wife's work. I liked Monica. She was always nice, and she looked good. But Julius deserved that lowlife slut he was shacked up with."

Kaylee was no prize, but Roxy suddenly wanted to bop Shanna on her surgically perfect nose for taking the side of a woman whose big claim to fame was giving away her husband's dough and keeping her hair combed.

Roxy managed to say, "Why don't you take another look at the fireplace?"

Shanna snicked her tongue. "I don't like it. I want something really classy, not a bunch of animals, okay? It's not a children's room, it's a *great* room. That means everything needs to be *great*. You have to keep looking."

Roxy had already made three trips to show architectural materials to this gum-cracking trophy wife of a jealous millionaire Neanderthal. Nothing was going to please her.

But Roxy fought down her exasperation. "Okay, sure. That's what you pay me to do, right?"

"I don't know," Shanna said. "So far, you haven't demonstrated an understanding of my taste."

Of course Roxy understood Shanna's taste. She wanted gigantic and obnoxious. If Roxy could find a giant Mickey Mouse straight from fucking Disney World—that's what Shanna would grab in a heartbeat.

Roxy tried another strategy. "Well, if you've got somebody else in mind—someone who works cheaper—I understand completely."

"I'm not looking for cheaper," Shanna said quickly. "I just want to see some results."

"Quality takes time." Roxy pulled the tarp back down over the fireplace. "But I have a couple more ideas up my sleeve. I just don't want you to be shocked at the price tags."

"You can't shock me."

Shanna used that as her parting shot before she headed back to her Hummer, mincing across the mud in her silly shoes.

Grinding her teeth, Roxy climbed back into the Monster Truck and started the engine. Rooney licked her face for consolation.

Nooch got into the truck, glum with disappointment. "She's never going to buy anything."

"Yes, she will. She just needs the right kind of nudge. And then I hope she wanders out on an ice floe, and gets mistaken for a baby seal and beaten to death."

"Did you tell her about that naked statue?"

Surprised that Nooch remembered it, she said, "No. She doesn't deserve it. Besides, now I'm thinking we shouldn't sell it locally, you know? Obviously, Julius had a lot of people in his house. Eventually, somebody will recognize the statue and start asking the wrong questions. I need a new plan."

Nooch sighed. "I was hoping to see Lapraxo."

"We'll try again."

He perked up. "Yeah? Soon?"

"Soon," Roxy promised.

"Is it lunchtime yet?"

Roxy made a detour into a suburban fast-food drive-through—it was much cleaner than the one in the city—and bought Nooch a couple of sandwiches with a supersized order of French fries. For Rooney, she bought a hamburger, no condiments. Pickles did bad things to Rooney's digestion.

Driving while they ate, Roxy said, "I've been thinking about your hearing."

"Mmph?"

"We definitely need a couple more character witnesses. People who like you. Upstanding citizens. Got any ideas?"

Around a mouthful of fries, Nooch said, "What about Flynn? He's upstanding."

"No, he isn't. He's got a record. It's old, but it's still on the books."

"What books?"

"Never mind. Not Flynn. Who else do we know?"

Nooch scrunched his face in concentration and finally said, "I know the lady at the bank where I cash my checks."

"You go to the same bank teller every week?"

"Yeah, she shows me where to write my name."

"No, we need somebody who knows you more intimately. Somebody who likes you. A friend." She added, "A friend who hasn't been arrested for anything."

Nooch said, "I don't have any friends like that. Except Sage."

"Sage isn't old enough." Reminded, Roxy checked her watch. Too early to call Sage yet. She'd still be in school.

The little alarm bell beeped on the truck's dashboard. The gas gauge blinked—almost empty. Fortunately, Roxy thought of a stop she could make that might result in some much-needed gas money.

She pulled into the rutted parking lot of an old church scheduled to be demolished to make room for a highway. There, Roxy left Rooney in the truck and took Nooch for a stroll past the trucks of a bunch of other scavengers who'd also come to check out the church. Roxy gave the building a once-over. The Gothic arched windows might be worth saving if Nooch could wrestle them out of their mooring without breaking anything . . . including his neck.

"You want the pews?" asked the sad-faced volunteer standing inside with a clipboard. He might have been part of the small but stubborn Croatian community that had kept the old church going for generations.

Pews were a dime a dozen. "No, thanks. What moron smashed the front door?" Roxy nodded at the splintered remains of a handsome mahogany doorway—another Gothic arch decorated with the lives of saints, but now sporting the kind of damage inflicted only by heavy machinery.

The volunteer winced at the damage. "Some kids hot-wired a backhoe in the parking lot and rammed it around for an hour before the cops showed up. Maybe you could fix it?"

"For what? Firewood?"

He sighed. "I'll take your bid for the big windows. A couple other people want them, too. But there's a small stained-glass panel in the lavatory behind the nave. Did you see it? It's too small to interest anybody else. It's got a shepherdess with a flock of lambs."

"I'll take a look." Finally, Roxy let herself feel sorry for the volunteer. "Thanks."

The window was pretty. Easy to remove, too. The volunteer gave her permission, and she wrote him a check. A check that was going to bounce if he beat her to the bank. But the window was an item Roxy knew she could flip fast. In half an hour, Nooch was carrying the little window out to the truck. Roxy went looking for some bubble wrap under the driver's seat.

What she found was the package of money from Carmine.

"Shit," she said to herself. She couldn't keep driving around with all that cash in the truck. She needed to hurry up and decide what to do with it. On the other hand, she could really use the dough. She peeled off a hundred.

She pushed the rest of the money back under the seat and took the bubble wrap to Nooch. Together, they made a neat business of protecting the window.

Back in the truck, she tried calling Sage. No luck. Roxy checked her watch. School should be over by now. But Sage wasn't answering. Had she decided to skip her meeting?

The truck's engine was sucking on fumes by the time she pulled into a gas station near the Thirty-first Street Bridge. Nooch climbed out of the truck to pump the gas, so Roxy strolled into the convenience store inside the garage. She checked out the aisles and found a home pregnancy test. She read the expiration date and was glad to see the test hadn't lost its potency five years ago. She took it to the cash register.

Pepper Patrone was counting cash on the cracked glass counter, but stopped at the sight of the box.

"Whoa. What's that about, girlfriend?"

"It's not for me, Pepper." Roxy plunked Carmine's C-note down on the counter. "So don't start any nasty rumors."

Pepper laughed wheezily. She sold cigarettes by the carton, but her best customer was herself. She had one cigarette slowly burning on the window-sill and another on her lip.

Pepper had grown up in the neighborhood and—a pretty and petite little fireball with a cute butt and a red ponytail—was voted Most Likely to Marry Before Graduation. But she defied all predictions and ran off to join the army instead. When she returned, her hair buzzed in a crew cut, Pepper announced she was a lesbian and moved in with a beautiful young woman just out of college who taught kindergarten somewhere on the South Side. Pepper took over her dad's garage and did a good business in gas, tires, oil changes, and cigarettes.

Pepper rested a muscular forearm on the counter. Various tattoos showed—including one on her neck that read Doreen and featured a lip-smack. She said, "You going to tell me who's pregnant?"

"Nope."

"It's not you?"

"No way."

"Is it Loretta?"

"Not unless pregnancy can be caused by hot flashes."

"Is it anybody I know?"

"Pepper, I need a tank of gas."

Pepper transacted the business with a speedy slip of the cash and a bang on the cash register.

Watching most of her money disappear, Roxy said, "You know anything about Valdeccio, a guy married to one of the Calderelli sisters for a while?"

"Valdeccio? Yeah, sure, he's in here all the time." Pepper handed back a couple of small bills. "He takes care of all the cars owned by that dead gazillionaire Julius Hyde, you know. Drives him around a little. Drove him, I guess you could say."

"Have you seen Valdeccio since Julius died?"

"As a matter of fact, he was in here yesterday, filling up gas tanks. He charges all the gas for his own car and half the neighborhood, and he uses the Hyde credit card." Seeing Roxy's expression, Pepper said, "What do I care if he ripped off his employer? He's not the only one. I guess he was worried the card would get canceled."

"Nice guy. Did he say anything about the night Julius died? Was he around? Did he see anything?"

Pepper took the cigarette from her lip with her left hand. "Yeah, he did. He was pretty upset, in fact. Going to lose his job, which had a lot of perks besides credit cards."

"But did he see Julius get whacked?"

Pepper shook her head. "No, he left, he said, before the old guy got shot."

"I suppose he told that to the police."

With a grin, Pepper said, "I doubt it. He's a slippery dude."

Roxy supposed anyone who used his employer's credit card to buy gasoline for his entire family wasn't on the up-and-up.

Pepper put her elbow back on the counter. "I heard a couple of guys talking about you lately."

"Who?"

"I thought you didn't want me spreading rumors?"

"Pepper—"

"Okay, okay, a couple of guys who work in the kitchen at that fancy restaurant, Rizza's—they came in to get a price on new tires for their motorcycles. I hate that. They know exactly how much tires cost here, so why are they running around doing comparison shopping when they can see I'm busy? I had a minivan up on the lift and—"

"Pepper?"

"They were talking about Patrick Flynn. About how he's settling in real well at the restaurant."

"Am I supposed to care about Flynn and his job?"

"I guess not. But the guys told me that Flynn said you look just as good now as you did back before he joined the Marine Corps." Pepper scratched at one of her tattoos—an eagle with an olive branch in its beak. "They went to hear you sing at a club a couple of weeks back. Said you were dynamite. When are you gonna get me some tickets to hear you sing?"

"I'm only backup."

"Still, it's kinda cool." While Roxy put her change away, Pepper said,

"You know, as men go, Flynn's not bad. He's got a real nice butt, know what I'm saying?"

"If you decide to cross the railroad tracks, Pepper, don't leave Doreen for Flynn. He's not as upstanding as he looks."

Pepper cocked her thumb and forefinger into a gun. "Gotcha. He's seeing somebody else, anyway. They're living together."

"What? Who?" The information caught Roxy up short. She had guessed Flynn might be doing the dirty dance with someone, but this news took her by surprise. It wasn't like Flynn to commit to sharing a tube of toothpaste. "Who's he with?"

"Marla Krantz."

"Marla—? You're kidding me!" Roxy's chest locked up tight. "Is she still doing smack?"

Pepper nodded. "But you didn't hear it from me."

Roxy grabbed the pregnancy test, slammed out of the garage, and climbed into the truck. She loosened Nooch's teeth when she banged her door shut.

"What's the matter?" he asked.

"Why are men so predictable?"

"Huh?"

"Marla Krantz!"

"Oh," Nooch said. "The pretty one. What about her?"

"Shut up!"

Marla Krantz, well-known junkie, was now Flynn's live-in girlfriend. Great. Exactly the kind of people Roxy wanted around her daughter.

She dialed Sage's number again. This time, she left a blistering message.

"Call me back right away, you little sneak. Or you're so grounded, your kid will be in kindergarten by the time you get out. You hear me, Sage? Call your mother."

Back at the yard, just to make her life even more complicated, Roxy found that Bug Duffy had left a note jammed in the office door.

"Call me," it said. And provided two phone numbers.

Roxy let Nooch put the stained-glass window in the garage, and she went into the office to call Bug. Fortunately, he didn't take her calls. One went to his voice mail immediately, and the other was picked up by a secretary at the police station.

"They're in the squad meeting," the secretary said on the phone. She had a thick Pittsburgh accent. "I'll tell him yunz called. What's your cell number?"

Roxy gave it and hung up, glad to have avoided talking with the police. She called Sage again. No answer.

At least now Roxy could be reasonably sure Sage wasn't with Flynn. Because he was probably at home banging his drug addict girlfriend.

To Sage's voice mail, she said, "You'd better have a good reason for not calling me."

Tapping her fingers on the desk, she found herself thinking about men in general. Flynn, of course. And premature Henry Paxton. And finally Trey Hyde.

Trey. Okay, he was fun in bed. But Roxy didn't want to think about exactly why she let guys like Trey take her clothes off. She'd probably done it the first time just to get the upper hand with him. Ordering around a man from Trey's background, making him do her bidding—it gave her a kick, she had to admit. Plus he had a lot of stamina and some creative ideas.

The top drawer of Roxy's desk called to her, and she slid it open. She played her fingers lightly over the collection of items crowded there. A pocketknife she'd taken from a guy she'd had her way with in the men's room of a nightclub. A rabbit's foot that belonged to the artist who sloshed paint on canvases he bolted to the walls of a warehouse. The earring she'd nipped from the earlobe of the college kid in her truck last night. A key, a wristwatch, a class ring, a shirt button torn off in a moment of steamy excitement.

Her trophies? Were these trinkets reminders of her conquests— gathered the way a serial killer took mementos from victims? No, not quite. But they were a kind of list, she thought, a list of men she'd overcome, taken for a ride. Enjoyed and discarded before that elusive something changed and made life less about good times and got unpleasantly complicated.

Not even Adasha knew how many men there had been.

Uneasily, Roxy thought about her mother and the way she had groveled for Pop's attention. Being sexy for him. Coaxing him to be nice. Before he beat her face to pulp.

Roxy shut her eyes to make the mental image go away.

She fingered the earring and thought. In her truck, the college kid had done everything she'd told him to do. She'd had some laughs and a hell of a big climax. He'd done it happily and maybe learned a thing or two. And when she dropped him off at his apartment afterward, she'd felt satisfied. Which was good, especially after her spat with Flynn at the restaurant.

But it was weird, and she knew it.

Adasha guessed, too.

"Understand why you're doing it," Dasha had once urged.

But Roxy resisted.

Better sex than drugs, though. Of all the people from the neighborhood who had chosen drugs as their form of recreation, none of them had handled their addiction well. Some were dead, and others like goddamn Marla Krantz were making a mess of more than their own lives.

Then there were girls like Kaylee who used their God-given talents to hook up with sugar daddies. That hadn't turned out well, either.

Kaylee, Roxy thought. Time to pay her a visit.

❧ 19 ❧

Arden arrived at the coffee shop with time enough to walk Samson around the leafy residential block before her scheduled meeting. The Great Dane moseyed on his leash and snuffled all the bushes before leaving discreet messages for other dogs while Arden tried to organize a plan that would make the Greek government happy. Except no ideas sprang to mind.

During the bedside meeting at Fair Weather Village, Daddy had expounded about "company assets" until Dodo conked out. At first Arden was horrified, thinking Daddy had put her into another coma. But a nurse came in and pinched Dodo, which woke her up in a temper. Monica diplomatically suggested they leave Dodo so she could take a nap. Arden hadn't been able to get her grandmother alone to talk.

On the drive back, Arden wished she could have had a coma of her own. Daddy talked and talked and made Monica cry. Then he dropped her off at Hilltop—no Henry in sight—and drove back to the city, sulking while Arden tried to stave off panic about Interpol and the FBI.

Later, to Samson, Arden said, "I just hope we don't start a war with Greece."

Samson snuffled his way back to the Mercedes SUV Arden had borrowed from Daddy's garage. Two very tall girls with backpacks waited by the parking meter. They wore identical plaid skirts with white blouses.

The girl with an angelic face, curly black hair, and crazy kneesocks said, "Cool dog. What's his name?"

"Samson. Are you Sage?"

"Yeah, that's me." She took off her John Lennon sunglasses and stuck out her hand. Her nails were painted purple, and the same color rimmed her dark eyes. Her white skin made the contrast more dramatic. She had gorgeous cheekbones. Her sidekick had pink tips on the corona of her hair.

Sage said, "When you said to look for a big black and white dog, you weren't kidding. He's huge. You're Arden? This is my friend Kiryn."

Standing between the two rangy girls and the large dog, Arden suddenly felt like a hobbit. She wondered if all important art deals started out so unpromisingly.

Kiryn shook her hand limply. "Hi."

Sage tipped her head in the direction of the coffee shop's front door. "You want me to order something? We could sit outside. That way, you don't have to put Samson in the car."

Three outdoor tables stood on the sidewalk. One was occupied by a pair of young mothers with baby carriages, another by three elderly men in tracksuits arguing over a crossword puzzle. The third table sat empty. Sage didn't wait for an answer before tossing her backpack down onto one of the empty chairs.

"Sure. Good idea."

Kiryn said, "I'll order for everyone. What do you want?"

Sage said, "My treat. I'll have a chai with honey and soy milk."

Sage pulled a Hello Kitty wallet from her backpack. Judging by the various buttons clipped there—CoExist and Give Peas a Chance—Arden guessed the Hello Kitty was intended to be ironic. She realized she was already intimidated by this self-assured young lady.

Arden said, "I'll have the same."

Kiryn accepted some cash from Sage and disappeared into the coffee shop.

Sage flung herself onto the chair and proceeded to rough up Samson's face. The dog waggled his tail and tried to climb into Sage's lap. She laughed and hugged him impetuously. "What a nice boy you are! I love dogs. Don't you? They're unconditional."

Arden said, "I guess so."

"A dog is good training. You know, for bigger responsibilities." Sage looked up at her with a direct gaze. "I guess you're more into the arts. Committed to the cause, right?"

Had Arden said something like that to Sage on the phone? She didn't remember all the details of their earlier conversation.

Sage looked more carefully at her. "You okay?"

Arden realized she had zoned out for a moment. She sat down at the table. "Yes, fine. You talked to Hadrian, right?"

"Yeah, Mr. Sloan-Whitaker. He was really generous to spend so much time with me. And for putting me in touch with you. This is great. I hope you don't mind helping me with my project."

"Project?"

Sage pulled a notebook from her backpack. She had made a collage of magazine photos on the cover—pictures of rock singers Arden didn't recognize and an actor who played in the Bridget Jones movie. Sage's pen had floating confetti inside, like a snow globe.

Sage looked squarely at Arden. "This is for a school project."

Arden had missed more than a few important details. "Are you an art major?"

Sage laughed. "Hey, no, I'm just in high school. It's for Sister Mary Matthew's history class. We're studying antiquities and their cultural significance to the past and the future, and of course she's all interested in Vatican stuff, but that's why I thought I'd go Greek, you know? Shake her up a little."

"I must have misunderstood," Arden said. "I thought . . ."

Sage waited. Her blue eyes seemed to absorb a lot, and Arden remembered she was supposed to be clever enough to draw out information. But she felt inept, sitting there with this high school girl with a confetti pen.

Arden made an effort to be normal. "When we talked on the phone, I wasn't completely awake, I guess. I'm happy to help. What do you need to know?"

Inside Sage's backpack, an electronic device began to play Darth Vader's theme from *Star Wars*. The music made Sage roll her eyes.

Arden said, "Phone call?"

"My mother, that's all. She's been calling me for an hour." Sage checked the screen on her phone. "Yep. She thinks I still need a babysitter. Jeez."

"If you need to take her call . . ."

"No, no. She's just overprotective. Can we talk about statuary now?"

"Sure, of course."

From the jumble in her backpack, Sage pulled out a battered laptop. The case was plastered with more faded stickers—Think Green! And Free Tibet. Opening the computer, Sage quickly tapped on the keys. Her long fingers were decorated with an assortment of rings—one featuring a skull and another one a curlicue of silver. The third looked like something from a box of Cracker Jacks. While she typed, she said, "This coffee shop has wireless Internet, so I can show you stuff. I did some research on Greek statues—you know, the kind in museums. And I ran across this one in particular, see? Some fishermen pulled him up from the bottom of the Adriatic. They sold it to a museum for a bunch of money—"

Arden looked at the computer screen and recognized the photo. "Over three million dollars, if I recall."

Sage sat up straighter. "You know it?"

"Yes, of course. The question is, where was the piece discovered? If it was in international waters, the concern about its country of origin is fuzzy enough, perhaps, to justify the museum's acquiring it. But the Italian government is calling for its return."

"Why? It's a Greek statue, right?"

"Yes, but presumably some Romans were in possession of it when their boat capsized, so—"

"But why aren't the Greeks asking for the statue back?"

"Well . . ." Arden lost the thread of her own argument, so she started all over again. "Lately, there's been a flood of artifacts on the market from Iran and Iraq. It's because they've been stolen and smuggled out of their homelands during this time of political instability. Is it fair that those countries will lose their heritage?"

"I don't know. If their stuff stays in their country, isn't it in danger of getting blown up?"

"Should that be our concern?"

"Hell, yes," Sage replied. "If it's gone, nobody gets it."

In time to save Arden from flubbing another attempt at explaining, Kiryn returned with one cup of chai, which she set in front of her friend. She said, "The others will be ready in a minute."

Arden tried to form a reasonable argument. "The question of whether or not antiquities might be destroyed isn't really the point. It's the provenance that matters."

"You're saying a country has the right to preserve its heritage. But what about those horses in Venice? The ones that have been on top of the cathedral of San Marco since, like, the year 1200? Back then, they were stolen from Constantinople. Should they go back to where they came from originally? Or stay where they've been for almost a thousand years? Which country can claim them as part of its heritage? Both, right?"

"Well, that's—"

Kiryn caught the thread of their discussion easily and said, "I'm half

Colombian. Why should Colombian artifacts stay in Colombia when half the Colombians like me have moved elsewhere?"

"Yeah," Sage agreed. "The world is more global now, you know?"

Arden said, "Colombia is such an interesting country! And beautiful artifacts."

"Yeah, but the real growth industry is actually kidnapping. So maybe it's not the best place for artifacts right now."

Arden said, "You could see it that way, I suppose. Ancient civilizations belong to all of humanity—the whole world. At least, that's the argument of some of the big international museums."

"It's like musical chairs," Sage said. "Everything moves around. Maybe somebody needs to pick a time when the music stops and that's when everything stays where it ended up."

Kiryn whistled a few bars of "Pop Goes the Weasel."

Arden said, "Wasn't there a specific sculpture you were interested in learning about?"

"Oh, right."

Kiryn went back into the coffee shop, and once again Sage typed on her keyboard, then turned the computer so Arden could see the picture on the screen. "Yeah, maybe something like this."

Arden felt a thrill of recognition. Sage's statue wasn't the one from Dodo's garden, but it had surely been done by the same artist. Only a careful inspection by an expert like Tiki would confirm that, however. "It looks familiar. What do you know about it?"

"Some archaeologist dug it up on a Greek island a couple of years ago. At least, that's what it says here."

"Had it originated on that island? Or had it been made elsewhere and stolen? Moved to that location?"

Sage shrugged. "I don't know. I thought you'd know that kind of stuff. How much do you think it's worth?"

"It's priceless. That's why it belongs to its homeland."

"But if it wasn't going back to its homeland," Sage insisted. "How much?"

"Depends on the provenance," Arden said. "If you can prove its origin—"

"Here we go again," Sage said with a grin.

Arden's face got warm. "What I'm saying is, if it was legally removed from a licensed dig, it's more likely to find a legitimate home for a lot of money. But if it was looted—dug up and stolen, then smuggled somewhere, London or New York, say—you'd be dealing in the black market, where the prices vary."

Sage looked interested. "There's a black market?"

"Of course. Collectors who don't care about how they acquire their pieces drive a thriving black market now. Their money is incentive for looters to keep digging and stealing important antiquities. It's very cutthroat. People have died."

"Died? Really?"

"We're talking huge sums of money." Arden thought fleetingly of her uncle Julius. Maybe he died because of his foolishness with women, but he could just have easily been killed for art.

"Wow," Sage said, frowning.

"The commercial market for ancient objects should be curtailed. At least, that's my view."

Sage reached for the cup in front of her. "Cool."

Arden's buzz was definitely wearing down now. She wondered if the coffee shop had a bathroom she could slip into for a quick bump. Just a little one. She felt outgunned by Sage, who was only a kid, really. But a kid who was very observant.

Kiryn returned with two more cups and a sugar cube, which she fed to the dog. Arden accepted one cup and sipped the hot liquid. It was very soothing, she decided. But she didn't need soothing right now. She needed zing.

Sage's phone began to play the Darth Vader music again.

Kiryn giggled. "Your mom's relentless."

Sage laughed ruefully. "What did I do to deserve this?"

Arden watched the two teenagers. What had happened to all the smart girls in her classes at school? Had they outsmarted her then, too? Only she hadn't realized it? Arden wondered if maybe she'd been one of those people who peaked in high school. Or in a dorm room at Brown. And now a lot of other forces seemed poised to overwhelm her.

Sage said, "You okay, Arden?"

Arden snapped back to the present. "Sure, why?"

"You looked kinda—I don't know."

Arden pretended to check her watch. "Wow. Look at the time. Is there anything else you needed to know? Because I should get going."

Sage and Kiryn exchanged a glance, and Arden worried. She'd missed a point somewhere. Her meds were fading. She needed something to help her think straight.

"Sure, we don't want to keep you," Sage said. "But can I call you again sometime? If, you know, I need more information?"

"Okay." Arden tried to wrangle Samson. The dog had wrapped his leash around Sage's chair. "If I'm still in town. I just—I need to get away right now. I mean, I need to get home. To feed the dog."

"Need any help? With Samson, I mean?"

Arden let Sage coax Samson into the backseat of the SUV. Then she helped Arden into the driver's seat, too.

The two tall girls stood on the sidewalk and waved good-bye.

Arden drove away. She wasn't sure where. Next time she talked to Sage, she'd write a script for herself ahead of time. To ask the right questions. Right now, all she knew was that she'd failed to learn anything useful to deflect Tiki and the Ministry of Antiquities.

❧ 20 ❧

On her way to face Kaylee about witnessing more than just the murder of her boyfriend, Roxy tried phoning Henry Paxton. He didn't answer his cell phone, so she left a voice mail.

"I think you have something of mine, Paxton. My necklace? Did you take it to prove something, you slippery son of a bitch?"

Nooch waited until she hung up before saying, "You're cussing again."

"I'll go to confession."

Roxy parked the truck in an open space just a few doors down from her current crash pad. Evening light had just started to slant over the roofs of the tightly packed houses, which meant it would be dark in a few minutes.

"Stay here," she said to Nooch. She didn't want him to hear the talk she intended to have with Kaylee. "I'll be back soon."

She got out onto the sidewalk. A second later, somebody opened the driver's door of the parked car in front of her. Since she'd been approached by would-be muggers a couple of times, Roxy reached into the open door of her truck and put her hand on her pry bar. Then Zack Cleary got out of the car.

Roxy considered using the pry bar on her daughter's boyfriend, then decided against it. Nooch would disapprove. She tossed it back into the truck. "What are you doing here?"

Rooney jumped out and ran over to Zack, barking like he wanted a hunk of fresh meat, pronto.

Zack had good instincts. He jumped up onto the trunk of his car. "Hey, call off your dog!"

Roxy kind of liked seeing Zack on the run. Served him right, the little horndog. "He's just being friendly. Aren't you in the wrong neighborhood?"

Zack had automatically covered his family jewels and now sheepishly moved his hands away. "I wanted to talk to you."

"What about?"

"Don't you have a leash for that animal?"

Roxy whistled, and Rooney reluctantly sat at Roxy's feet, panting.

Zack carefully climbed down to the sidewalk. There, he managed to regain his cocky cool. "You're looking good, Mrs. A. As always."

"I hereby give you permission to stop calling me Mrs. A. I'm not married."

"I know, but—"

"Call me Roxy."

"Okay. Roxy." He bobbed his head nervously. "Thanks."

"How did you know where to find me?"

"Oh, Sage showed me once. We were driving around, you know, and she showed me the house you're fixing up. I thought I'd try to catch you here."

Although the afternoon light had faded, Roxy finally noticed that Zack's face was swollen. The beginnings of a black eye showed purple along his cheekbone.

Roxy stepped closer to take a look. "What happened to you?"

Zack reached to touch the bruise gingerly. "This? Another guy in my class and I had a disagreement. Nothing important."

"Does he look worse than you?"

Zack allowed a grin. "The sergeant broke us up before any real damage was done."

"The police academy allows fistfights?"

"It was no big deal. We just got a little hot. We'll get a lecture tomorrow. They discourage losing your temper at the police academy. No swearing, either."

"That's a fucking tough gig," Roxy said.

Zack laughed. "Yeah, it is."

"Don't disappoint your daddy."

His face sobered up. "No, I won't."

"What do you want with me?"

Zack glanced up the street, as if gathering his courage. "I guess I need your help. Is there someplace—? Could we go inside? There's something wrong with Sage all of a sudden. She's—I don't know. Weird."

"And you think I have some insight?"

He started to look genuinely unhappy. "I don't know. I thought I'd ask. You know. For advice."

It was Roxy's turn to laugh, but she kept it short. "Sure, tiger. Let's go inside. I'll give you a beer. Are you old enough for a beer?"

"Why not?"

Rooney took off and dashed up the sidewalk toward the house. Zack fell into step with Roxy, matching her long strides. He said, "This is a kind of scary neighborhood. You okay with that?"

"Sage won't be living here, if that's what you're asking."

"No, I wasn't asking."

"Isn't she a little young for you?"

The question startled him. "Sage? Hey, no, we're not really, you know, together. Like a couple or anything. But if we were, she's—well, she seems older than she is. Older than high school, I mean. She's smart."

"Maybe too smart for you?"

"I'm no dummy," he shot back.

"So what are you saying? You don't want to be with my daughter?"

"Sure, I do! I mean, you know, as friends."

Roxy stopped and faced him. "Friends with benefits?"

"What? No, I— Look, I like Sage. But she's mad at me or something. I was hoping you could tell me how to make her happy."

"Happy?" Roxy repeated. "Happy?"

"Yeah, you know. Like, do I buy her some jewelry, maybe?"

"That hasn't been my experience, tiger."

"Well, what has?"

Rooney barked and dug at the front door.

"Cut that out," Roxy commanded from the sidewalk. Then she planted a finger on Zack's chest. "Listen, kid, you don't want to know what would make me happy right now. But Sage? She's going places. And if she doesn't get anchored down by some jagoff who only thinks with what he keeps in his pants, she's going farther in this world than either one of us. Know what I'm saying?"

"Huh?"

"I'm saying what would make me happy is you keeping your distance from my daughter."

"But—"

Somehow, Rooney managed to push the front door open with his nose, and he disappeared into the house.

The open door surprised her. Roxy went up the stoop in one leap, forgetting about securing Sage's future away from Zack. "That silly chick left the door unlocked?"

"What chick?" Zack asked.

They could hear the dog barking inside. Roxy pushed the door the rest of the way open and went into the house. Zack hesitated behind her.

"Kaylee!" Roxy shouted.

The pitch of Rooney's barking suddenly changed. Roxy heard it and felt all her nerves contract. She went into the hallway of the empty house. A breeze hit her in the face, coming from the kitchen. Someone had left the back door wide open.

A lamp lay on the living room floor, casting a glare at a crazy angle.

"Oh, shit." Zack sounded like a little boy.

Roxy headed for the stairs, and when she turned the corner she could see Kaylee's shoe on the landing. Above it, Kaylee's bare foot.

Rooney whined. When Roxy arrived on the landing, she found him sniffing Kaylee's hair.

The dog had tracked her blood on the staircase. The girl lay sprawled on her back, her legs awkward, one arm bent beneath her.

"Oh, shit," Zack said again. He had followed Roxy up the stairs, but he suddenly turned and stumbled back downward. When he arrived in the living room, he kept going out the front door. Roxy could hear him gagging on the stoop.

Someone had chased Kaylee, she could see. She had run up the stairs to escape, but her attacker had grabbed her dress and dragged her down. She'd hit her head on the staircase—the blood was everywhere. She had probably fought with whoever it was. It looked as if one of her front teeth was missing in her half-open mouth. Roxy guessed by the crooked angle of her arm that it was broken.

And she'd been shot. The bullet had torn into her throat and exploded out the back of her head. The new plaster above her was splattered with something gruesome. The pillow from the bed lay on the upper stairs, the case shredded as if the shooter had wrapped the pillow around his gun to muffle the noise.

Roxy called Rooney to her, and the dog obeyed. Together, they sat down on the lower portion of the staircase. Roxy hugged Rooney, and he snuggled close. Roxy couldn't quite catch her breath.

When Zack staggered back inside, wide-eyed and catching his balance on the newel, Roxy pulled out her cell phone and called 911.

❄ 21 ❄

Bug Duffy wasn't the first cop to arrive, but when he did show up, he told Nooch to stay in the truck and invited Roxy to sit in the front seat of his squad car for a while. While he talked to his buddies, Roxy watched the Channel 2 people set up their remote. The on-camera girl wore a fluffy coat and a ludicrous amount of makeup. She joked around with her cameraman, then sobered up when the big lights came on, and she did her report in front of the police grimly going about their business.

Roxy thought about getting out of the car to throw up on the reporter's shoes, but she talked herself out of it.

After half an hour, Bug returned to the car. He'd given up his crutches in favor of a cane. He got in behind the wheel even though he hadn't been the one who drove.

"What a mess," he said to Roxy.

"In so many ways."

The sun had disappeared and a soft rain began to fall, speckling the windshield with tiny droplets that caught the streetlight. More fickle autumn weather. The Channel 2 girl opened a striped golf umbrella and lit a cigarette, clearly intending to spend some time hunkered down at the crime scene.

Bug's car was cold, and Roxy had to concentrate to quell her shivering.

"You okay?" Bug asked.

"I'm better off than Kaylee."

Bug nodded and pulled a notebook from his pocket. He seemed glad not to have to cope with an emotional female, so Roxy marshaled her feelings.

Playing the unflappable cop, he said, "You want to tell me what she was doing at your place?"

"I already explained to the officers who got here first. And to the Homicide cop."

"Well, tell me, too, and then we'll all know."

It was routine, she knew, so she didn't make a fuss although the exasperation of it was pressing behind her eyes. Roxy told him most of the truth—including what she knew about Kaylee being shot at the day before.

"You think it was the Delaney brothers who did that?" Bug asked, making it obvious that he'd already gotten the gist of things from his colleagues.

"I don't trust a lot of what the Delaneys have to say, but yeah, I think they were paid to intimidate Kaylee."

"Paid by a dead man?"

"That part I will quibble with."

"So they lied to you?"

"What a surprise, huh?" It was hard to say, but Roxy blurted it out. "Look, Bug, you should know I took a gun away from the Delaneys."

Bug didn't seem surprised. "Where is it?"

"Back at my yard. In my desk drawer."

"We're going to need that, like, an hour ago."

Roxy handed him two keys off her ring—one for the office door, the other for the drawer.

He took them. "We sent a car around to pick up the Delaneys," he said. "Those two shouldn't be on the street to begin with. But they're not anywhere we can find them right now. Know where they might hang out?"

"They're not my best friends."

"We'll keep looking. Shouldn't be hard to find a pair of idiots like those two." Bug craned around in the seat to look out the back window. "Where's Nooch?"

Although he'd seen where Nooch was, Roxy said unnecessarily, "Waiting in my truck. He's got an armed guard."

"Where's he been all day?"

"With you guys and Marvin. I picked him up just an hour ago."

"What about the Cleary kid?"

"He has nothing to do with any of this. He was here to see me. He's dating my daughter."

"Well, thank God for small favors. I don't have to tell the chief his kid is in trouble." Then Bug grinned fleetingly. "Abruzzos and Clearys. There's a match made in heaven."

From outside the car, a man approached Bug's window and knocked with one knuckle. Bug put the window down, revealing a uniformed cop who said, "Marx says to remind you they have to cut Hyde loose in four hours."

Bug, the back of his head to Roxy, made a cutting motion across his throat with his thumb, but said, "Hey, thanks. Is there any coffee?"

The uniform missed the point and leaned down to see who was in the passenger seat. He had no expression as he studied Roxy. "No, not any we've found yet."

Roxy waved at the cop using her fingertips.

Bug rolled up the window. "Sorry about that."

"You're just sorry you got caught. Which Hyde do you have in custody?"

"No custody. We're interviewing Trey."

Roxy's experience was that the cops could "interview" someone for twenty-four hours, after which time the person needed to be charged with a crime or turned loose. The fact that Trey was coming up on his twenty-four-hour deadline was a matter of urgency to the investigators, she could see.

Bug said, "I can't talk about Trey with you."

"You think he did it? Killed his brother?"

"You think he didn't?"

"He didn't kill Kaylee," Roxy pointed out. "If he's been with you for a whole day, he couldn't have chased her around my house and shot her on my heart-of-pine stairs. If you think Kaylee was killed to cover up Julius's murder."

Bug sighed, unhappy. "Yeah, Trey being with us today put a wet blanket on one theory."

"Trey was your new best suspect? What happened to the homeless guy?"

"We've been corroborating everybody's stories."

"Save that crap for the media. While you guys focused on the wrong guy, the real killer kept going."

The thought had clearly occurred to Bug a long time ago, but he said, "Maybe Kaylee was killed by somebody other than the guy who whacked Julius."

"Even I know there are too many connections for that theory to work. Unless you think it's a coincidence that a burglar broke into my house and Kaylee stopped him from stealing my underwear."

"Ballistics will tell."

"Not unless you have all the guns you need."

"What does that mean?"

"I have Trey's gun, too."

"Jesus Christ, Roxy. What are you doing?"

"I took it from him the night Julius was killed. Trey was acting all crazy, so I took it. It's in the same drawer with the Delaney piece. We can go get both guns now, if you want."

"Roxy—"

She said, "Look, it was stupid, but I'm coming clean now. Let's get going. I'd like to get home to Sage, if you don't mind. She's going to see this on the news. I don't want her to get upset about a shooting at her mother's house."

Bug shook his head. "Sorry. I've got to take you to Major Crimes. Some other guys want to talk to you. And they told me that before you said you have a gun collection."

Roxy wasn't surprised. But she said, "I'm not a part of this thing, Bug."

"No?" Suddenly he turned on her, and he was pissed. "You just happened to be at the scene of Julius Hyde's murder, and now his girlfriend is killed in your house? And you took firearms, then kept them a secret from me?"

"It looks sketchy, I know."

"Sketchy? You're up to your eyeballs in shit, in case you haven't noticed. The guy in charge of this investigation wants you to spend the night in an interview room! Me, I just want to punch your lights out."

"So I'll confess to something I didn't do?"

Bug pulled himself together. "Roxy, I'll be straight with you, since we went to school together. You need a lawyer. And not a mob lawyer, one of your uncle Carmine's friends. Not somebody you've slept with, either."

"Screw you."

"Nobody's going to take you seriously if you're banging your lawyer."

"If a man sleeps around, he's a hero. But a woman is automatically a stupid whore. I've heard that all my life."

Bug looked away. "I'm trying to be your friend for as long as I can. Get on the phone and hire yourself a good lawyer."

"Will Loretta do?"

"She's better than nothing."

Roxy made a call, and when Bug pulled out, she rolled down the cruiser's window to speak to Zack Cleary.

"Look after my dog," she said as the car went past him.

The kid's eyes bulged at the thought of taking care of Rooney.

"And you'd earn a few points with Sage if you call and tell her everything's okay."

Half an hour later, Roxy walked into the building on the North Side that headquartered Major Crimes. Within twenty feet of the front door, she spotted two cops she'd had sex with. One of them was Marty O'Brien, though, who'd been so drunk at the time he didn't remember her. The other guy had later admitted he was married, so Roxy had punched him in the gut and told him she'd better not see him ever again. She'd erased his name from her memory. He obviously remembered her, however, because he ducked his head and looked busy as she went past his desk.

Bug escorted her as far as an interview room, which had a linoleum floor, a mirrored wall, and furniture that looked as if it had been bought secondhand from a community college.

He left her alone in the interview room, and a few minutes later a couple of Homicide cops came in, offered her a can of pop, and tried to be her pals. Roxy declined, saying she'd wait for her lawyer. Disappointed, the cops went away.

In a while, her lawyer showed up.

The middle-aged cop who unlocked the door and let Loretta inside looked at her like she was a delicious slice of pie. He said, "A few years ago, we used to see you around here a lot, Loretta. Was it something we said?"

"I gave up being a court-appointed."

"Old people slipping and falling is more lucrative, right?"

She gave him her most twinkly smile. "Give us a few minutes, okay? And turn off the camera, will you, Dave?"

"Sure." Dave closed the door, maybe to go in search of a fork.

Loretta's twinkly look vanished. By the time she set down her leather briefcase on the table and folded her raincoat beside it, she had a warrior's glitter in her eye. But her hair was fluffy, her nails perfect. Her suit had gold braid, and her high-heeled shoes made her ankles look delicate despite the size of the rest of her.

She cocked one fist on her hip. "It's a good thing I already had my temper tantrum today, or you'd be dead meat."

"I'm innocent."

"If you were guilty, I'd hang you myself."

"What was your earlier temper tantrum?"

"Somebody tried to steal my briefcase on the bus. I knocked him down the stairs to the curb. That's one purse snatcher who will think twice before he tries to steal something from a menopausal woman. What does he think? After fifty we turn invisible? That it's okay to bully us? Take our things? Pretend we don't exist? I may be middle-aged, but I can still—"

"I'm not the enemy, you know."

Loretta sat down and picked up the can of pop. She pressed the cold aluminum to her neck to cool off. "At least you didn't fall for the full-bladder trick. That's got to be the easiest way to get people to spill the truth."

"When I'm ready to drink something, it won't be pop. Did you tell Sage I'm okay?"

"Yes. She'd already talked with her boyfriend. Was he with you? Maybe he's a nice boy after all."

Loretta put the can on the table and gave Roxy a steely, parental glare. "Bug Duffy says they sent officers to your place to pick up some guns."

"Yes."

"Roxy, what are you doing with weapons? First of all, you hate guns. Second, you'll jeopardize Nooch's probation hearing. Not that I care about that."

Roxy had been sitting there wondering if a good cry might help her feel better about everything. Seeing Kaylee dead, primarily. But Loretta's brisk manner helped her choke back the urge. "I was at the Hyde house a few minutes before Julius was killed—saw him, talked to him. And I met up with his little brother Trey later the same night."

Loretta didn't miss a beat. "For what reason?"

"He had an itch he wanted me to scratch."

"And did you?"

"Not that night, no. But a few months back, yes."

Loretta's mouth tightened. "A few months back, you were seeing the John Donne professor."

"Him, too."

"Roxana Marie, this self-destructive behavior of yours has got to stop. Your friend Adasha called me."

"What? When?"

Loretta reached into her briefcase for a notebook and a fancy ball-point. "She's concerned. She says you need to get over what happened with your parents. You can pretend it's done and doesn't mean anything, but here you are almost thirty-five years old and still acting like . . ."

"Like what?"

Loretta stiffened her spine. "Like sleeping with a lot of men is going to solve your problems."

"I don't have any problems."

Loretta clicked her pen. "Well, Pittsburgh's finest seem to think you do, so tell me everything before they start their interview."

Roxy knew how hard it had been for Loretta to express her concerns, so she gave her the lowdown without further resistance. About Trey and the Delaneys and the guns. Loretta took notes in an illegible scrawl and asked a few pointed questions. Then she repeated the facts back to Roxy and asked for corrections.

Roxy did not tell her about the statue or where she'd moved it. The only reason she'd told Bug where to find the guns was that she'd spent part of her day hiding a naked man where few people would notice him.

Finally, Loretta tapped her pen on the notebook. "How much of this are we going to tell the nice police officers?"

Roxy leaned forward on her elbows and managed to keep her voice level. "Let's get one thing straight. I want to help catch whoever did these two murders, Loretta."

"You need to protect yourself, too."

"That's what you're here for."

"Normally, I get three hundred dollars an hour, you know." Loretta reached around to rap her knuckle on the mirror behind her.

Two detectives came in and treated Loretta as if she were the Queen of England.

With Roxy, they weren't so polite.

Three hours later, Loretta walked Roxy out of the building.

"You did good," Loretta said. "I'll drive you home."

"I need to pick up my truck."

Loretta narrowed her eyes. "Whatever you have in mind for tonight, young lady, you can forget it. You need to see your daughter. You need to assure Sage you won't get arrested for anything."

"I'll go see Sage," Roxy insisted. "But I need to pick up my truck first."

"I'll take you to your truck. And then I'll follow you home."

Roxy stopped on the sidewalk. "I've got to do something else before I go home."

"Roxy—"

"Trey didn't kill Julius."

Loretta looked relieved that she wasn't going to go looking for a man to blow off some frustration with. "You know that?"

"He was with the cops today, so he didn't kill Kaylee."

Roxy hadn't liked the teeth pulling, but she'd answered all the questions posed by the police. The whole time, she'd been thinking about Kaylee—a girl who'd lived her short life using the assets God gave her to get out of the neighborhood.

"She was under my protection," Roxy said.

Loretta melted. She must have recognized the emotion that bubbled just beneath Roxy's exhausted control. She put her arm around Roxy's shoulders.

Roxy said, "Kaylee was my responsibility, Lo. I should have checked on her. I should have made sure the house was a safe place for her to stay. It's my fault she's dead."

Loretta hugged her. "Oh, honey. Let's get your truck and go home. I have a gallon of ice cream I've been saving for the right time. This is it—the perfect night to get drunk on butterfat. You can squeeze your daughter tight. Think about the joys of being a grandmother. Get some distance from all this. You'll feel better in the morning."

They climbed into Loretta's car, and ten minutes later, they pulled up to the intersection near Roxy's truck. The police still had the block roped off. Even the television trucks had been pushed back. The whole scene suddenly gave Roxy a headache. Her stomach felt like a sour, very empty pit, and ice cream wasn't going to fix that.

She had her hand on the door handle when Loretta reached across and grabbed her arm. "Roxy, don't go all vigilante about this Falcone girl, okay? Promise you won't do anything stupid?"

"I promise."

Loretta gave a bitter bark of a laugh and released Roxy's arm. "I can always tell when you're lying. Okay, come home when you can, will you? Let us know you're alive."

"Tell Sage everything will be okay."

"Sure."

Roxy bailed out of the car. She ducked under the police tape and headed for her truck, pulling her keys from her pocket. A few crime-scene techs were milling around her front door, all of them muttering into their cell phones. For them, it was business as usual. But all Roxy could think of was Kaylee's lifeless body.

Out of the tech group popped Zack Cleary. He spotted Roxy and made a beeline for her in long, loping strides.

"Hey," he said, subdued.

Roxy mustered some bravado. "You look healthier than the last time I saw you."

He blushed. "Yeah, sorry I lost my lunch earlier."

"Tomorrow you can get a hose and wash off my stoop."

"Okay, sure."

"Where's Nooch? Do you know?"

"I took him home. I hope that's okay."

"Did he fart in your car?"

"Huh?"

"Never mind." Surprised that he'd taken the initiative to look after Nooch, Roxy lingered. She wasn't ready to climb into her truck yet. She jutted her chin at the crime scene. "How's it going here? They find anything useful? Footprints in the dust? Fingerprints on the door handles? Any of that Sherlock Holmes stuff?"

Zack put his hands in his pockets and hunched his shoulders as he looked back at the techs. "Some of that, yeah. Looks like the dead girl let the guy into the house, though. No sign of forced entry."

"Kaylee. That was her name."

"Right. Sorry." Zack looked at her more closely. "You okay?"

"What else do they think? What kind of gun was used?"

"I don't know, but they think the guy wrapped a pillow around the gun when he shot her. Kaylee."

"I figured that out. What about shell casings?"

"What about them?"

"Were there any?"

Zack shook his head.

Same as Julius, Roxy thought. Either the killer picked up the ejected shells or used a revolver. "Are the cops asking all the neighbors what they saw?"

"Yeah, they canvassed the whole street. Not many people around here during the day, so nobody saw anything except a bunch of kids walking around like they wanted to break into a house, maybe."

"That's typical on this block. The cops will waste their time chasing down those kids. Did they talk to Dolores?"

"Who?"

Roxy pointed. "The lady who lives in this house."

"She hasn't been home."

"How about on the other side? The doctor, Adasha Washington. She was probably sleeping during the day. Her shift started at seven, I think. Maybe she heard something before she went to work."

"I don't know. Look, I have something to show you."

Roxy waited, jiggling her keys. Tomorrow she'd come back and ask a few questions by herself, without the cops watching. For now, she just wanted to get away, do some thinking. Find a few people and ask questions. The Hyde chauffeur, for one. He might know somewhere for her to start.

From underneath his jacket, Zak brought out a package. Wrapped in a plastic grocery bag.

Roxy almost stopped breathing. "Where the hell did you get that?"

Zack's face was smooth of any expression. He lowered his voice. "From under the seat of your truck. I searched the vehicle. Before the crime-scene cops looked. It's cash."

"I know it's cash." Carmine's chunk of bills looked the same as when she'd moved it from Kaylee's car to her own truck. "And you took it. What do you think? That I'm going to let you keep it?"

Zack was shaking his head. "It's not like that. I took it out of the truck because I figured you didn't want the cops to find it."

Once again, he surprised her. And Roxy didn't like that the kid was capable of keeping her off balance. "You're the cops, in case you haven't noticed. At least you're damn close. What the hell are you thinking, kid?"

Although her voice sharpened, Zack stood his ground. "I'm thinking maybe you should keep it a secret. You know, for a while."

"And you want some of it? For removing incriminating evidence? For saving me from an arrest, is that it? It didn't take you long to find a way to earn your protection money. Congrats, tiger. You're a dirty cop before you're even officially sworn in."

Zack opened his mouth to protest.

But her cell phone rang. When Roxy opened it, Flynn said in her ear, "Are you under arrest?"

"Nope."

"Then you'd better come over here."

She could hear the kitchen noise behind him. "Now?"

"Hurry up," Flynn said before disconnecting. "I'm feeding some Hydes."

Roxy closed the phone, opened the door to her truck, and climbed behind the steering wheel. Then she caught sight of Zack standing on the sidewalk.

"I'm not a dirty cop," he said, "I'm not. I just wanted to help you."

She knew she'd regret it, but she heard herself say, "Get in the truck."

❧ 22 ❧

To take the bull by the horns, Henry decided to telephone Arden Hyde. And a couple of hours later, they walked into Rizza's together for a late supper. The pretheater crowd was long gone, and even the second seating seemed to be thinning out. They were shown to a table near the fireplace in a high-ceilinged dining room with tall windows and pillars made of tree trunks. Using the Hyde name always got good service, but Henry backed it up. The hostess winked at him as she pocketed the fifty he slipped her.

At the table, Henry said, "It's good to see you again, Arden. Shall we order a bottle of wine?"

"Okay."

"Do you have a preference?"

"No."

She scanned the menu for a long time, nibbling the nails of her left hand.

Henry put down his menu. Arden looked sleekly blond tonight, with her hair pulled back in a ponytail and some kind of exotic textile thrown around her shoulders, hippie style. She was definitely more presentable than she had been earlier. But her foot jiggled incessantly, and he noticed all her cuticles were red. The front of her hair was cut in long bangs, which she tended to use as a screen.

He decided he'd chosen the right person to question concerning Quentin's plan for Monica and the situation with Julius's will. Henry planned to pop Arden like a cork.

After a few minutes of watching her obsess about the menu, Henry said, "I recommend the chef's choice. It's always an interesting culinary experience here."

"Okay. I like adventures."

She flattened her menu on the table and looked straight at him, a sign she had gathered her courage. "So what's this all about, Henry?"

His only mistake might have been the choice of restaurant. In Rizza's, there was always a waiter swooping in to refill glasses or a busboy slipping dishes away. The tables were tightly packed, too, with snippets of conversation flying around like mosquitoes. The tempo of the place was busy, but maybe that would work in his favor, Henry thought. If the atmosphere were too intimate, Arden would be even more nervous.

He leaned across the table. "I was delighted to see you this morning. You looked all grown up."

She linked her hands in her lap. "I am."

"So maybe we should get better acquainted."

With a brave tilt of one eyebrow, she said, "Now that I'm legal, you mean?"

He smiled genuinely. "You're beautiful, Arden. And polished now."

"You liked me pretty well when I was a kid."

"You were tantalizing."

"So you're a gentleman these days? That's the way you want to play it?"

"How would you like me to play it?"

The wine steward leaned over their table then, asking about drinks, so Henry ordered a bottle without any fanfare. The exchange gave Arden a chance to think things over.

When the steward went away, she said, "I always liked you, Henry. And I was flattered that you picked me to—well. But all my aunts and cousins said you were looking for a way to marry into the family, and after we—after that time we were together, I worried that I'd made a big mistake. So I went away. You're hard to resist, you know."

"It's a relief to hear your side of things. After you left town so suddenly, I feared my lovemaking wasn't up to snuff."

Her color changed. "How would I know? I'd never—well, I was ashamed of myself for getting seduced in a closet, so I ran away."

"It was more of a dressing room wasn't it? I remember a lot of hanging ball gowns and a very comfortable sofa. I'd had a little too much champagne at your uncle Julius's wedding to Monica."

"And then you had that allergic reaction to the champagne." She smiled shyly, but then Arden's face clouded, perhaps recalling the less appealing details of their tryst.

Gallantly, Henry said, "I remember how lovely you were. And deceptively mature. After I realized you were underage, though, I knew I'd made a grave mistake."

He also remembered a very messy interlude—not at all his usual conquest. It had been a low point for Henry—a clumsy attempt to seduce the least objectionable of the Hyde women, but a lapse in judgment nevertheless. With careful strategy, he might make amends tonight, though.

A waiter brought crusty bread and a dish of olive tapenade, and then came the water glasses. While the quiet flurry of service continued, Henry tried to keep the conversation rolling.

He said, "Julius seemed very happy at that wedding. He and Monica both."

"I can't believe he's dead." Arden fiddled with her silverware. "I keep thinking he'll walk into a room and say something funny. I really miss him."

"He loved you very much, I'm sure."

"Who didn't he love? He had a lot of joie de vivre. Okay, except maybe Dodo."

"Despite all evidence to the contrary, I think those two were actually very fond of each other. You shouldn't take their arguments to heart."

She glanced up to gauge his sincerity. "Uncle Julius never had anything nice to say about her."

"That was a game between them."

"Do you think so?"

"I know so."

Arden did the peekaboo with her bangs again. "That's actually very nice to hear."

The wine came, and they ordered food. Henry asked her about Florence and she babbled awhile. Gradually, she relaxed and became animated. From years of strategic dating, Henry had come to recognize that the best companions were women who knew how to get a man to open up about himself. But Arden talked and talked.

She talked so much that eventually he realized why. Between courses, she excused herself, and when she returned to the table, she was so radiant that the man at the next table got up to help her with her chair.

Arden leaned into the candlelight, refreshed by whatever she'd snorted in the bathroom. She was smiling at last. "I'm having a good time. I didn't expect that."

"Why did you come out with me if you didn't think you'd have a good time?"

"I don't know. It was like a dare, I guess. But I think I like you, Henry."

"You don't have to sound so surprised."

She laughed. "Monica likes you, too. But my dad? Not so much."

Henry split the remains of the bottle into their wineglasses, glad that she had brought the conversation around to where he wanted it. He signaled for a second bottle. "Why is that?"

Smothering a giggle behind the long fingers of one hand, she said,

"Maybe Daddy doesn't like another rooster in the henhouse. I saw the way Monica looked at you. So did Daddy."

"She's in a very emotional place right now. She can't be held accountable for her actions. Besides," he added with sideways smile, "she's too old for me. Surely Quentin sees that."

"I think he sees a rich widow and an opportunistic younger man making goo-goo eyes at her."

"I do nothing of the sort!"

"You do it with subtlety, of course. Just like you're flirting with me tonight."

"I'd have to be dead not to flirt with you, Arden. You've grown up so nicely. But really, we're just friends, aren't we?"

"Oh, yes," she said quickly. "Just friends."

Henry figured the time was right to lean across the table. "I'm actually glad to see your father so protective of Monica. Especially accompanying her to see Dorothy. That must have been brutal."

• "Yes, brutal," Arden echoed.

"It doesn't take a genius to see the whole family is distraught about Julius. But—true to form—they're trying not to show it, right? Everyone uses their own special coping mechanisms."

"Yes." Arden picked up her fork uncertainly. Her buzz was fading, so he guessed it had been cocaine in the bathroom.

"It's hard work sometimes," he said. "Playing referee in a complex family. That's your role, isn't it?"

"Yes," she said, although it was clear the idea had never entered her head until now. "Daddy's especially putting a lot of pressure on me."

Henry contrived to appear concerned. "Oh?"

"Trying to make me take a job with Hyde Communications. Maybe that would be easier."

"Easier than what?"

If he wasn't mistaken, she looked frightened. But the second bottle arrived, and it took a few moments for the cork and tasting ritual. By the time it was over, Arden looked more strained and anxious.

Henry filled her glass nearly to the rim. "What are you working on at the moment?"

Arden's head must have been fuzzy indeed. "I'm creating a master list—an inventory of Dodo's art collection for Daddy to present to the insurance company. At least, I'm trying to. Monica gave things willy-nilly to museums. And God only knows what Uncle Julius did. Daddy asked me to try piecing together a list—a complete inventory. I'm the only one who can do it. Tomorrow I have to go back through Monica's tax returns to find out what she claimed as charitable deductions, and who knows what's been stored away."

"There must be hundreds of items."

Another waiter appeared with a water pitcher. But he bobbled it, and water went splashing across the tablecloth. "Oh, wow. Sorry, dude." He had two small folders pinned in the pit of his arm, and he pulled them out. "Dessert, anyone?"

Henry used his own napkin to mop up the worst of the water spill. "I've never known a woman who didn't want to end a meal with a taste of chocolate. Or what about the baklava? I understand it's excellent here."

Arden shuddered. "Oh Lord, not baklava! Nothing Greek!"

"The apple tart instead?"

"Okay." She handed the menu back to the waiter. "One apple tart, two spoons, please."

"Coffee?"

"Espresso."

"Espresso?" the waiter said. He was a callow kid with a black eye.

"Yes, two espressos," Henry said firmly, annoyed and ready to be rid of the intrusion. "And the apple tart. That's all."

"Yeah, sure. Okay."

When the blasted waiter departed, Henry counted to ten and then gently prodded Arden back on course. "Did you mention your inventory to Dorothy today? I imagine she's the real expert on the family collection."

"I didn't have a chance. Daddy had business to discuss with her."

"What sort of business? Julius's will, I suppose?"

"Oh, yes, his will and Dodo's will and I forget who else's will. You know all about that stuff, I guess?"

"It's my job. Did Quentin discuss changes in Dorothy's estate planning? Now that Julius is gone?"

"He wanted to talk to Dodo about the amendments to her will."

Henry felt his stomach go cold. "He knew? About amendments?"

"I guess so. Daddy wanted to know what the changes were. Whether the steel mill was in play, because the city will pay millions for it now."

"Did Dorothy tell him?"

"She didn't know about any changes. She said if Uncle Julius had been scheming, it must have backfired. Daddy wondered if maybe you were in cahoots with Julius." Arden rested her elbow on the table to steady her grasp on her wineglass. "That's what he said. In cahoots."

"Did he?" Henry said.

"Something wrong?"

"Not a thing." Henry managed to smile. "You mentioned the art collection."

"Oh, yes. I'm doing the inventory. But I can't find the most wonderful piece of all. My grandmother's Achilles."

"Her—?"

Arden slurped more wine. "A marble sculpture of the Greek warrior. He's magnificent. He was standing in the garden before I went to Florence. But now he's missing."

"I don't remember any Greek warrior."

"No? Out by the pool. He had one raised arm." She lifted her own hand as if to hold a spear.

Henry forced himself to sound calmly intrigued. "Did anyone else notice he's missing?"

"I think he might have been sold or given away or maybe stolen." Arden lowered her voice confidentially. "But I talked to someone who may know where he went. She came out of the blue, asking me about Greek antiquities. In Pittsburgh, of all places! How strange is that? At the exact time we're missing a rare statue, what are the chances? It can't be a coincidence."

"Who was this person?"

"A kid, really. A girl. Smart, but just a kid."

"Name?"

"Sage. Isn't that a pretty name? Sage Abruzzo."

Henry felt another frisson of electricity, followed by a long moment in which all his brain synapses seemed to fire in perfect sequence.

With perfect calm, he touched her hand conspiratorially. "Arden, darling, I wonder if we couldn't help each other."

She smiled uncertainly. "To do what?"

"To find this statue you're talking about. We might make a good team, you and I." He rubbed the back of her hand with his thumb, drawing gentle, hypnotic circles on her skin. "And I could help you with your father."

Her smile loosened at the edges. "With my father? I don't need help with my father."

"That's the cocaine talking, sweetheart. You need more help than you know. Let's be honest. You'd like to go on keeping your cocaine use a secret from Quentin, wouldn't you?"

Her hand had stiffened beneath his.

Henry murmured, "And I'd like to find that statue. For Dorothy, of course. It's rightfully hers. And I think you're just the person to help me locate it."

Very pale, Arden said, "I don't understand."

"Yes you do." He turned her hand over and stroked her palm. "I'll help you keep the coke a secret from your dad. And you'll help me find the statue."

Like a snared rabbit, she tried to pull away, but he tightened his hold.

"Do we need to go into the particulars of your drug problem?" he asked. "I don't think so. The bottom line is that you'd like to keep it to yourself, right?" With the noise and activity of the restaurant busy around them, Henry said, "We should make a pact, the two of us. You help me, Arden. I'll help you."

❧ 23 ❧

In the restaurant kitchen, Roxy grabbed Zack as he came back from the dining room, clumsily carrying a tray and nearly tripping over the trailing ties of his hastily acquired waiter's apron. He dropped two menus on the kitchen floor and automatically bent to retrieve them.

Roxy yanked him up by his collar. Over the noise of the kitchen, she snapped, "Forget those! What are they talking about in there?"

"Art." Zack tugged at the bow tie they'd hastily fastened around the collar of his borrowed white shirt. "They're talking about paintings or something, I don't know. And they want a damn apple tart, too."

"What are they saying about the art?"

"About how priceless it is and— How should I know? A statue that belongs to somebody—"

"A statue?"

"Where's the espresso in this place?"

Flynn appeared with a butane torch in one hand. He said, "Carl will get the espresso. Here's the tart. I just need to put a crust on it."

Zack's eyes went wide as Flynn fired up the torch.

Roxy seized the kid by the front of his shirt to keep him upright while Flynn brandished the blue flame. "Don't screw this up, kid. I need you to remember every detail of what they're saying in there."

"It's hard! I have to hold the tray, take their order—I can't keep everything straight."

"I thought you wanted to be a cop! Think of this as your first undercover job!"

"Here." Carl hustled over with two espresso cups. An instant later, Flynn finished torching the dessert and skimmed it onto the tray, too.

Roxy spun Zack around by one shoulder and shoved him back into the dining room. "Stay around the table as long as you can," Roxy hissed after him. "Memorize their conversation."

The kitchen was controlled chaos. Jammed with many moving bodies, it felt much smaller to Roxy than before. Around her, waiters called orders, ran the computer, and moved fast to get back to the dining room. Runners carried hot food out of the kitchen to the tables. Busboys lugged tubs of filthy dishes back in. The cooks—all dressed like ninjas—wielded knives, flipped flaming pans and slapped steaming food onto hot plates, squirted sauces and wiped drips. If the dining room felt like an oasis for sophisticated palates, the kitchen was more like a downtown intersection at rush hour.

Roxy sidestepped the pastry chef and turned to Flynn. "Thanks for calling me."

"No problem." Flynn peeled the skullcap off his head. In his black T-shirt and black jeans, with a stiff set to his jaw, he suddenly looked less like the kitchen master and more like a marine dropped behind enemy lines. "We need to talk. My office."

He led her past the stove, where giant pots of soup and polenta steamed down to their last dregs of the night. One of the kitchen boys was scrubbing the burned remains of veal shank and ribeye off the grill with a wire brush. Wordless, he stood aside to let them pass.

Flynn's office was barely big enough for the two of them. His desk had enough space for a laptop and an empty coffee cup, nothing more. A couple of clipboards hung from hooks, very tidy. He kicked the swivel chair under the desk. With the windows and glass door, there wasn't much privacy, but he closed the door anyway. "I heard what happened to the Falcone girl. You okay?"

"Just peachy."

He turned his unamused gaze on her. "The police know who killed her?"

"Not yet."

"Same guy who killed Hyde?"

"The cops would be idiots to think otherwise." Roxy took a deep breath, surprised to feel shaky inside. "She shouldn't be dead. Not on my watch."

His stormy expression softened. "Don't talk like that."

Emotion welled up in Roxy's throat. "I was supposed to be protecting her."

"You gave her a place to stay, that's all."

Roxy shook her head, unable to say more. She felt guilty. And pissed.

Flynn squeezed her neck and released. "I know how you feel about this. But don't get all crazy, okay?"

"Yeah, well, you called me."

"I did." He folded his arms over his chest. "At the staff meeting before service, the hostess always tells us if we have any big names in the reservation book—anybody who needs special treatment. When she said we had a Hyde booked—I don't know, my radar kicked in. Do you know the guy?"

"Yeah. But he's not really a Hyde. He's Henry Paxton. Interesting that he used the name to get a good table, though."

"Happens all the time. Who is he?"

"He's old Mrs. Hyde's lawyer. I met him a couple of days ago."

"You sleep with him?"

Roxy didn't answer.

"Forget I asked." Flynn leaned against his desk, the picture of cold control. "Okay, who's the girl with him?"

"No clue who she is."

"Zack said they're talking about art. What's this about a statue?"

"Statue?"

Flynn laughed shortly. "Cut the crap, Roxy. I heard you talking with Sage about a statue, and now this. You're a good liar most of the time, but you were always the first to lose your shirt in strip poker. What have you got going on?"

Roxy hesitated. Flynn's tone meant business, and she could see the pilot light of his temper flickering.

She said, "The night Julius got killed, I picked up a bunch of stuff at the Hyde house. There might have been a statue in the load."

"What kind of statue?"

"Big. Made of marble. You know, like a lot of the stuff I get."

He cocked an eyebrow at her. "Something tells me this statue isn't exactly your usual haul. And Sage was talking about something really valuable."

Roxy tried to push past him to get out of the office. "You don't need to know."

"No, hold it." Quick as lightning, he grasped her upper arm and spun her around to face him. "What do the police say about it?"

"The police?"

"You told the police about the statue, didn't you?"

"The statue has nothing to do with Kaylee or Julius dying."

"Are you sure?"

No. Roxy almost said it out loud. No, she wasn't sure anymore. Slowly, she said, "I took the statue because it was going to get destroyed when they blew up the house. They were demolishing everything, so I took it."

"And then?"

"They didn't blow up the house. Nobody mentioned the statue until now."

Flynn locked his gaze with hers. "You need to tell the cops."

"I can't. I wasn't the only one who hauled the statue away from the Hyde house."

Flynn released her and groaned. "You're protecting Nooch, aren't you?"

"His probation hearing is Friday. It's been ten years since his last arrest, and he's been clean. He deserves to get off. But this—this would be a felony, the real deal."

"Roxy—"

"I can't admit anything. Not yet."

"You're keeping your mouth shut so Nooch stays out of jail."

"Yes."

"And if you're lucky," Flynn said, "you'll get away with stealing an expensive statue."

"Put it any way you like." She noted his expression and snapped, "I've got bills to pay. Look, there was a day when you weren't lily white. You joined the service because your other choice was jail. That's why you and all your pals here went to Afghanistan in the first place. The guns and the action—it's legal over there. Well, things are a little hot for me at the moment, but not—it's not too bad."

"Yet."

"Shut up. The only reason I'm telling you is . . ."

When she didn't say more, he prodded, "Is why?"

"Because you get it. About Nooch. About me. You won't go blabbing to the cops. And . . ."

"And?"

Roxy blew a sigh. "Earlier today I put the statue in your refrigerator."

He stared at her, anger dissipating like air from a balloon. "What?"

"I had a couple of free hours, so I moved it. Nobody's going to look here."

Flynn opened the office door and went out into the kitchen. Roxy followed him over to the vaultlike door of the walk-in cooler. He yanked on the door handle, and they went inside. Behind a hanging slab of beef at the back of the cooler stood a giant naked man.

Without a word, Flynn left the cooler and closed the door. He put his hands on his hips and looked at the floor. "I must be crazy."

She tried to smile. "You always had a crazy side. It was one of your best qualities. That, and you let me be on top."

"I let you be on top only long enough to catch my breath." Flynn continued to glower at her. "What about the Cleary kid? What are you doing with him?"

"He's a volunteer."

"Has it occurred to you that he may not be a cop yet, but his dad is the chief of police?"

"Yeah, I know."

"And Sage. Don't forget about Sage."

"I'm not."

"What does any of this have to do with Kaylee Falcone getting killed?"

"I don't know."

They stood together for a moment with a lot more to talk about.

But Roxy said, "I think I should go toss Paxton's car. See if there's anything interesting in it. Do you think he valet parked?"

"You can't ransack people's cars in our parking lot. It'll gives us a bad reputation."

Zack Cleary skidded into view, catching his balance on the counter. "Hey," he said. "They're leaving."

Roxy grabbed her truck keys from her pocket. "Now? Already?"

"I accidentally spilled some espresso on him, so they're going."

"Damn," Flynn said. "Are we going to have to comp their dinner?"

"Just dessert," Zack reported. "The other waiter is taking care of it. They talked about all kinds of stuff. Somebody named Dorothy maybe changed her will."

"Good work, tiger." Roxy slapped his butt. "Let's go. We'll follow them and figure out who she is."

"Sounds good." The kid was already tugging off his bow tie.

"Wait a minute," Flynn said.

"We're just going to follow them. I want to know who the girl is."

"You can't just run off." Flynn raised his voice as she turned to go. "Roxy, damn you, I want this thing out of here! You aren't the only one with people to protect! Hey! Are you listening?"

❋ 24 ❋

In the dark, Roxy followed Henry Paxton's car in the Monster Truck.

At the first intersection, Zack said, "Who's the guy at the restaurant?"

"Which guy?"

"The cook."

"Chef."

"Yeah, the one you were talking to."

"Flynn? Hell, he's your cousin! Or something."

"Oh, yeah." Zack smacked his forehead. "I thought he looked familiar. One of Uncle Pat's." The kid stared off across the hood of the truck for a second, perhaps mentally trying to climb the branches of the family tree. "How do you know him? I mean, the two of you—I thought maybe . . ."

"Don't burn too many brain cells, kid. What do you want to know?"

"He's Sage's dad, right?"

There wasn't much traffic, but seeing the BMW pull in front of a beer truck, Roxy pointed. "See Paxton's taillights? Don't take your eyes off them. I gotta hang back, or he'll spot the truck."

"I get it. None of my business."

Paxton drove across the Highland Park Bridge, the last bridge on the Allegheny before leaving the city limits. Roxy slowed to let him get a long way ahead across the empty expanse of the bridge, but she lost sight of him at the end. "Damn!"

"That way." Zack pointed.

Roxy floored the accelerator and was relieved to spot the back of the BMW as it hung a right off the exit ramp and went up on the highway. She followed. Paxton traveled two exits and then got off the highway and drove up into a wooded suburb where a lot of doctors and executives built grand houses. Trouble was, the roads curved and swooped among the trees, and Roxy began to fear she'd lose him for good. Or get spotted in his rearview mirror. Her truck was hard to miss. She drove cautiously and peered through the windshield. Trees obscured the moonlight, and the hilly terrain made it hard to see where she was going. But Paxton's taillights flashed ahead, and she blew a sigh of frustration.

"They're gonna notice my truck," she said, "if I get too close."

"Nah, don't worry. Everybody out here drives big-ass gas guzzlers. You fit right in."

"I hate the suburbs."

"Wait." Zack spun around in the passenger seat. "There he went. Turned into that driveway back there. Turn around when you can. We can go back and hide behind that big clump of weeds."

The clump of weeds turned out to be an elaborate landscaping display of rare grasses mixed with fall perennials. A scarecrow wearing a Steelers jersey stood in the middle of the bed, holding a pitchfork in one hand, a football in the other. Roxy pulled behind it, cut the Monster Truck's engine, and rolled down her window to listen.

"I used to have a girlfriend up here." Zack spoke softly in the sudden quiet. "Her dad was some bigwig at a company downtown. He gave her a car for her birthday."

"Where are we? Whose house is that?"

Roxy watched Paxton's BMW sitting in the driveway, engine still running. The occupants of the car were probably talking. Maybe kissing. A little spurt of heat flamed up in her chest. Jealousy? Or something else? "How do we find out who lives in that house? Maybe I should check if there's mail in the mailbox." She laced her fingers through the door handle.

"Don't bother." Zack had his cell phone in his hand, and his thumbs rapidly tapped on the keys. "I can do a reverse search online. That is, if I can get cell phone reception here. Hang on a sec."

Clever kid, Roxy thought. She strained to listen, but couldn't hear anything in the night air except the soft burble of Paxton's car.

"Bingo." Zack held the screen so Roxy could see it. "Somebody named Hyde, Q. And his wife Sandra."

Roxy stared at the little screen. "No kidding."

"If I knew his first name, I could Google for more information."

"Quentin. Quentin Hyde is Julius's brother."

"Wow." More tapping.

A car door slammed, and Roxy instinctively crouched in her seat. The woman who walked away from Paxton's car was really young. She didn't seem too steady on her feet, either. Roxy watched her climb the brick stairs at the front of the house, both hands gripping a heavy black railing. Her blond hair hung down around her shoulders, and the wraparound thing she wore on her shoulders trailed on the stairs behind her. She was either stoned or drunk.

Paxton made no effort to get out of the car to help her, which made Roxy's temper flare. He sat and watched as the girl went into the house. Then he put his car in reverse and pulled out of the driveway.

Zack said, "Quentin's wife is Sandra Hyde. Says here she's forty-seven and belongs to AA."

"That girl who had dinner with Paxton. She wasn't forty-seven, was she?"

"No way. She was about my age."

"But she's living at the Hyde house. Maybe a daughter?"

Zack remained glued to the small screen of his phone. "Says here, Quentin and Sandra have four children. Two girls—Adrienne and Arden."

"Arden?" Roxy remembered Sage's conversation at breakfast with Flynn. She was going to meet someone named Arden. At the time, Roxy assumed Arden was a last name.

"Damn," she whispered as the random facts fell into place.

"What's wrong?"

Roxy pulled out her own cell phone and dialed Loretta's house.

Without greeting, Loretta said, "It's after eleven. I'm asleep."

"Sorry, Lo. Not everybody goes to bed before the news. Is Sage at home?"

"I've had a long day. Of course Sage is here." Loretta sounded groggy. "I talked to her an hour ago when she was getting into bed."

"I'm sorry to ask this," Roxy said, unable to keep the anxiety out of her voice. "Will you go check now? Make sure she's really there?"

"Why?"

"Please, Lo."

Loretta sighed, but Roxy could hear background noise and knew her aunt was already out in the hallway and scuffing in Sage's direction.

A moment later, Loretta said, "She's here. Asleep in bed."

"Are the doors locked?"

"You know they are! Roxy, what's the matter?"

"Nothing." Roxy let out a long, pent-up breath. "Just me being paranoid. Sorry. I'll be in touch."

"Not before seven a.m. The last thing I need is something waking me up besides night sweats. Good night."

Roxy snapped her phone shut. It was a comfort to hear Loretta talking tough.

Roxy wasn't sure what she knew. But Sage talking with a Hyde daughter about the statue felt very wrong. And what the hell was Paxton up to?

Zack said, "Should we be following the car?"

Roxy started the engine. "I think I know where he's going."

Anyway, Roxy had somewhere else she needed to be.

She dropped Zack at his car. As he climbed out of the truck, she fleetingly thought maybe planning his torture and death for getting her daughter pregnant was not the best use of her time anymore. The kid had potential. Not a lot, Roxy decided, but a little.

She took his parking space and walked across the street to her house. Police tape barred her from going inside, and for once she decided to obey. Looking at Kaylee's blood on the staircase? Not again.

She went next door and let Rooney out of Adasha's fenced yard. The dog panted with the delight of seeing her again and ran circles around her.

Roxy gave the dog a thump on his flank, and he eagerly followed her back to the truck. They got into the vehicle, and Roxy started the engine, but sat thinking for a minute. About Kaylee Falcone and how maybe she'd been a silly, shallow girl, but she had a right to her dreams and her life as much as any rich bastard.

Sitting there, Roxy felt her blood pressure rising and decided it was definitely time to pay a call on somebody who could let her in on a few Hyde family secrets. Time to see Trey Hyde.

Fifteen minutes later, Roxy leaned her finger on the button beside Trey's loft door and left it there. She listened to the buzz for a full minute and a half until Trey finally unfastened the lock and opened the door.

He stood there in his underwear and socks, looking as bleary-eyed as any man who'd ever spent twenty-four hours being grilled by police. He scratched the back of his head. "You woke me up. I thought it was the cops coming back."

"You should be happy it's me instead." Roxy brushed past him into the apartment. The place looked as if it had been ransacked. Pillows and papers all over the floor, along with the contents of his refrigerator and the kitchen cupboards spread out on the countertop. "You need a phone number for the Merry Maids?"

"The police were here. They looked through all my stuff."

"Did they find anything interesting?"

"I don't know."

Roxy turned around and put her hand on Trey's chest. "Trey, baby, we need to talk."

"You mean now? Tonight?"

She pinched his nipple until his face woke up, and then she turned and walked into the kitchen.

Trey let the door slam and trailed after her. "The police are probably watching me."

"They definitely are. A couple of detectives are in the lobby, and there's a car with two more guys out on the street."

He rubbed his nipple. "How did you sneak past them?"

"I didn't. I waved as I went by."

Trey began to figure out a few things and he started to panic. "I didn't tell them a word about you, Roxy. Honest to God, I didn't say a thing. They don't know about you and me."

"They do now. I told them that myself." Roxy pretended to be calm. "They sure left a mess in here, didn't they? Do you have anything to drink?"

All the cabinet drawers hung open, and Roxy banged each one closed as she headed for the refrigerator. When she opened the fridge to scavenge, all that remained were some maraschino cherries and a liter of Dr Pepper. In the freezer she found seven unopened boxes of prepackaged Salisbury steak dinners from Jenny Craig and a bottle of Grey Goose. She grabbed the vodka.

Then, from a block near the stove, she pulled a very big knife.

Trey caught his balance on the island, and his eyes widened. "What's the matter, Roxy?"

Roxy pointed the knife directly at Trey's face. "It's time for you to do something good for me, Trey. And I'm not talking about sex. Did you hear about Kaylee?"

"Kaylee?"

"Is there some kind of echo in here?" She raised her voice, and he winced. "Or was my question too hard for you to understand? Did you hear about Kaylee Falcone? She's dead."

"I heard. I mean—they told me. Somebody killed her today."

Roxy cut around the island, moving fast toward him, knife in one hand, the bottle in the other. "Somebody shot her. In my house, Trey. Killed her on my staircase. I'm going to need a bucket of soapy water and a very big brush to clean up her blood."

"I'm sorry, Roxy. Really sorry." Trey backed up hastily. "I could pay for a cleaning service. Would that help?"

"A cleaning service would take care of the mess in my house, all right, but what about how I feel? Is there somebody you could pay to fix that, too?" She bullied him into the bedroom, watching him stumble over the pillows, his shoes.

"I'm sorry you feel so bad, Roxy. If there was something I could do—"

"There is. You're going to sit down on the bed and tell me everything you told the police. But first? Get out your little leather friends."

"My what?"

"Your restraints."

Trey gulped uncertainly, and his hands fumbled on the bedside table. On the second try, he managed to open it. "I swear I didn't tell the police about you, Roxy. Not a word."

"Not the velvet restraints, Trey. The leather ones."

"What?"

"Put the leather around your left wrist and loop it over the bedpost," she ordered. "Then give me your right hand. Hurry up."

She twisted open the bottle and took a tiny sip of the syrupy thick vodka.

Watching her, Trey's expression went from worry to sexual anticipation, then fear, very quickly. In a matter of moments, he was sitting on the bed with his arms outstretched, wrists secured to opposite bedposts with the thin leather cords he once bragged about buying in Amsterdam. Now, though, the look on his face wasn't nearly as pleased as when he'd told her about the sex shop he'd visited. His breathing came in shallow gasps. His boxer shorts were printed with little sea horses.

He said, "Do we have a safe word tonight?"

"No safe words, Trey. Because this is no game."

"Just put down the knife, okay? The knife makes me nervous."

"I like the knife. I want to see how sharp it is. I also want to know about the night Julius died," Roxy commanded. "I want to know everything you saw and did."

Trey swallowed hard and tried to summon some courage. "I'm not comfortable with this scenario."

"This isn't a scenario, Trey. It's real life. Do you want me to stuff a sock in your mouth? So I can carve my initials in your arms without listening to you scream, maybe?" She laid the knife blade on his goose-pimpled skin. Then she held the bottle above his mouth. Uncertainly, Trey lifted his chin to accept a sip, and she poured the thick vodka into his open mouth. He swallowed twice, choked, and then the alcohol sprayed. Roxy stopped pouring.

He flinched as if she might hit him with the bottle. "I didn't kill him, Roxy, I swear."

"Who did?"

"I don't know, I really don't!"

"Don't lie to me, Trey. Not while I've got this Boy Scout knife in my hand. What happened to Julius?"

"All I know is that we talked. I wanted—I asked him for money for the new treasure hunt. For the Spanish ship that went down in the

Caribbean. But he didn't want to float me anymore. He said I should talk to Quentin."

"Fast-forward. You already told me this stuff. Who else did you see that night?"

"I need to go to the bathroom."

"Do you think I care? Who else did you see, damn it?"

"You. Those morons in the kitchen."

"The Delaneys. And the demolition guys?"

"Ouch! That's sharp! Yes, them, and Quentin and Kaylee and—"

"Wait, who? Quentin?"

"My brother Quentin, yes."

"He was there? At the house the night Julius died?"

"I told you that before."

"The hell you did."

"I told somebody. And Paxton was at the house, too."

"Paxton? Henry Paxton?" Roxy paused, thinking. "When did you think you might mention all this to me?"

"It was none of my business! Whatever Quentin and Julius talked about, it had nothing to do with me."

"What about Paxton?"

"Huh?"

The favorite word of all the men in my life. "Was Paxton there to see Julius?"

"Yeah, yeah, he was there. Look, Roxy, I left Julius that night. I didn't stick around to ask any questions. Honest, I'm telling the truth. I didn't kill him."

"What did you have going with Kaylee?"

"What do you mean?"

"You and Kaylee were scamming somebody, right? The night Julius died, she came bawling in here and you told her you needed to be careful. What was that about?"

"Nothing."

Roxy upended the bottle and poured it over Trey's head. He cried out, choked, and shook his hair. "Okay, okay! We were seeing each other a little. You know—on the side. We didn't want Julius to find out. She was passing a few things to me—for cash I could use for my expeditions."

She tossed the knife onto the bed, abruptly conscious of what she'd been doing. The bottle slipped from her fingers and hit the floor with a crash. Liquid splashed. Glass broke in chunks.

Where had she heard that sound before?

Pop, of course. He'd used bottles as weapons. Blunt force. Or sometimes breaking the glass and brandishing the shards. Mama screaming. Pleading. Offering herself.

Trey snuffled up his tears.

Roxy put her hands to her head to keep it from exploding. To shut out the past. Focus on the now. There had practically been a party at the Hyde house that night. Quentin and Kaylee. And Paxton, too.

She turned away.

"Are you leaving?"

In the doorway, Roxy turned and looked back at Trey, a pathetic rich guy who wore boxer shorts with little animals, for crying out loud, and had to ask his mommy for money to play at being a grown-up. He made Roxy feel sick.

But not as sick as she made herself feel.

"I'm finished with you, Trey."

"You're not leaving me like this, are you? I can't get loose by myself."

They heard the doorbell buzz.

Roxy said, "That's probably the police. Be glad they showed up, Trey. Except now they're going to want to know what we talked about."

"Nothing," he promised. "I won't tell them anything."

"You sure?"

"Yes, yes. Just untie me first. Don't let them find me like this, Roxy."

Roxy said, "I let you keep your underwear, right?"

"Roxy! Please. Come back here!"

She left Trey on the bed and opened the door to the two detectives. "Hi, fellas."

She went down the stairs this time, and out to her truck, where Rooney waited. He woke up and licked her hand when she climbed into the driver's seat. She sat thinking about how close she'd come to really hurting Trey Hyde.

❄ 25 ❄

Arden's cell phone rang as she pawed through the last of her pill bottles on her bedspread. She almost didn't answer. There was nobody she wanted to talk to. Certainly not Henry, who had been so pleasant at the beginning, so nice saying she was beautiful and desirable when he surely must have remembered a clumsy little virgin who babbled too much.

But she picked up the phone and the worst happened.

Tiki said, "Arden, little lamb, we're here at the airport."

"We?"

"Yes, my uncle and I. We're waiting for the gentleman from Interpol to meet us. Then we're flying to Pittsburgh. We're coming to see you."

"Now?"

"No time like the present. What's your address, my sweet? I neglected to ask you earlier."

"But Tiki—"

"You're doing the right thing, Arden. You'll be the talk of the museum world. You'll have your pick of jobs! I can't wait to see your statue."

If she didn't have the statue, Interpol would arrest her. And the Greek Ministry of Antiquities would humiliate her family.

Tiki kept talking, and Arden thought about her best option. Taking all her pills at once, that was it. All her pills and the last of her cocaine. She'd have one glorious party, just herself and Malibu Barbie. If only she could remember how to do it without vomiting it all up before she floated away.

"Arden?" Tiki said. "Arden?"

❧ 26 ❧

At seven in the morning, Roxy woke on the cracked leather sofa in her office. Her entire body felt stiff and cold, and her right arm was numb from being curled up for a pillow. But Rooney was licking her face, and she could hear her cell phone ringing, so she was alive. She opened the phone and croaked a hello.

"Mom," Sage said in her ear. "I've got to leave for school in, like, thirty seconds. Where are you? In jail?"

Roxy had sat up, but fell back against the seat when the stiff muscles of her back protested. "How many of your friends start conversations with their parents like that?"

"None of them," Sage replied, and she laughed, sounding relieved.

"I'm glad you called. I needed to hear your voice."

"For?"

"I just did. Look, I'm sorry I missed you last night. I wanted to check in."

"Loretta told me everything. And Zack said you're okay. But I was worried, though."

"Thanks. I mean, sorry." Roxy listened to Sage with her eyes closed.

"At least you didn't get on the TV news. When Kiryn's father won that prize at the university, it was cool that he was on TV. But when Randy's stepmom got arrested for insurance fraud, the perp walk was like, totally humiliating for Randy. Everybody saw it. Somebody even put it on YouTube. I would've hated you on YouTube."

"Bullet dodged, then."

"Yeah, I guess." Then Sage took a breath and said, "Did you know that girl? The one who got killed?"

"A little, yeah. She was okay. Not smart, but she had a future."

"Mom." Sage suddenly sounded like she was eight years old again. "Could it have been you? Shot by some crazy person in your house?"

"No," Roxy said firmly. "I wasn't the target. Somebody went specifically looking for Kaylee. It had nothing to do with me, Sage. So don't worry, okay?"

"Okay, good. That's a relief." Sage covered the phone and spoke to someone else, then came back. "I gotta go, Mom. Kiryn's here, and we're going to walk to school. Love you."

"I love you, too," Roxy said. But Sage had already hung up.

She hung up. Before Roxy had a chance to find out if she'd met with Arden Hyde yesterday. Had Arden posed as an art dealer? And how had she found Sage?

Roxy cursed herself for being so fuddled this early in the morning. She tried dialing again, but Sage's phone went directly to voice mail.

"Damn!"

To herself, she said, "Maybe I'll be a better grandmother. I'm sure a lousy mother."

She checked her watch. Adasha would be getting off her shift about now. And she'd want to go for a run. But Roxy didn't want to talk to Adasha this morning. Not after what she'd done to Trey. And a run would probably kill her.

For no particular reason except maybe her inner homing pigeon kicking in, Roxy got in the truck and drove over enough potholes to get to the back door of Rizza's restaurant. A garbage truck roared past her, revealing there, in the thin morning light, Flynn unloading boxes from the back of his pickup. Judging by his cargo, he'd been to the market already. He had a couple layers of sweatshirts on to ward off the chill air, and a battered baseball cap backward on his head. A takeout cup of coffee sat steaming on the tailgate of the truck.

He acknowledged her arrival with a nod, but hefted a couple of cases of vegetables and carried them through the open door of the restaurant.

Roxy got out of her vehicle and made a beeline for his coffee. She stole a couple of slurps while he stowed his vegetables. The coffee tasted like heaven.

When Flynn came outside again, he took his coffee back. After a long swallow, he leaned against the tailgate, one ankle crossed over the other. "Where's Zack?"

"I put him into his own car a few hours ago."

"He went home?"

"I assume so." Trying not to look too hopeful, she said, "That's one good cup of coffee."

"Go buy your own. Primo's on Penn Avenue. The only reason I inquire about the kid is that last I heard, you were planning Zack's accidental death."

"Are you asking if I gave him a blow job?"

Flynn met her eye. "Did you?"

"Look," Roxy said. "I see you getting all interested in Sage, and that's nice, I guess, considering you were halfway around the world playing with guns while I was paying for her shoes and the braces on her teeth, not to mention sitting through the same Christmas pageant every year. Go for it. She's a good kid, and you're going to like her. But you being her dad doesn't give you the right to tell me how to live my life."

As if she hadn't spoken, Flynn said, "Did you fuck your daughter's boyfriend, Roxy?"

"No."

"Okay," he said. "I know you're screwed up, but at least you're not stupid when it comes to Sage."

"What about you? Are you nominating yourself for Father of the Year? While you're with Marla Krantz?"

Flynn tensed for a fight. "Okay, I'm with Marla now. What of it?"

It took all of Roxy's self-control to ask the question calmly. "Is she still shooting up?"

"She goes to the methadone clinic. It seems to work for her."

"What about you?"

Evenly, Flynn said, "I'm clean. Have been for two years."

His military tours in Afghanistan had been both good for Flynn and the worst thing he could have done to himself. He'd grown up. Learned to stand for something. But he'd made a teenage habit worse, and then traveled to some of the world's biggest drug destinations for a binge that lasted years. Now he'd come home after some mysterious but clearly life-changing event. The restaurant job showed he'd learned to take responsibility.

But his love affair with heroin rendered him untrustworthy, as far as Roxy was concerned. Probably forever.

She said, "Is Marla doing it for you? I mean, is she helping you stay off the drugs? Or is she going to screw with your head? Because staying clean is hard enough without your girlfriend—"

"Don't worry about Marla."

"Okay." She shrugged. "I hope the sex is worth it."

Flynn laughed. "It's not Marla I'm staying clean for."

"Who, then?"

"Don't play dumb," he said. "Sage."

"Oh. Well. Good. That's good."

Flynn handed over his coffee cup and let Roxy finish the last couple of swallows. It was still hot, and the caffeine warmed her blood. She found herself suddenly not knowing what to say.

Flynn said, "You don't need to worry about me. I'm not looking for some kind of sappy reunion, doing the family thing with you and Sage."

"Good thing."

"I mean, I know you better than most, Roxy. You've got a bad history, too. History that's really screwed with your head. It makes you do the stuff you shouldn't do. It makes you less than attractive, let's put it that way."

"So?"

"So I know all about being screwed up." He took off his baseball cap and dropped it onto the tailgate. "Maybe I ruined my life, but at least I'm trying to stay clean now. I'm giving myself a second shot. For Sage. And for myself."

"How's it feel so far?"

Another bitter laugh as he glanced around the alley at the Dumpster and the garbage and the back of his truck that smelled like chickens. "Shitty, as a matter of fact."

"But you're giving me advice?"

He shook his head. "Nothing like that. Just wishing you luck, I guess."

She threw the cup into the empty Dumpster. "Okay, fine."

It felt like a truce, standing there in the morning sunlight, facing each other after a lot of years of wondering and second-guessing and thinking about what could have happened differently. It wasn't any kind of resolution. But a truce was okay.

Flynn reached out and knocked her shoulder gently—just friends.

But it turned into something else. Roxy intended to give him a soldierly pat on the back, too, but suddenly her hand was sliding up his shoulder blade, and she was turning into his solid frame. A heartbeat later, they were wrapped in a hug.

He felt harder than he had so many years ago. And leaner. But of course that could have been the heroin. His shaved scalp prickled as she slid her fingers up the back of his head. He let one exploratory hand slide down her hip, but then she felt it curl around her butt to pull her closer against himself. And then his mouth found hers, and they weren't just hugging, but kissing.

A warning clanged in her head. A word bubbled up in her throat—*no, no, no*—but she fought it down. It felt weird to be with him again and good and wrong, but right. And then weird again.

An instant later, they sprang apart like the guilty teenagers they used to be.

"Uh."

"Yeah."

"Huh?"

"Right."

"I gotta get some sleep before the shift starts. See you later." Flynn turned around and nearly walked into a telephone pole. He dodged just in time, and left in a hurry.

Roxy scrambled into her truck and slammed the door, glad nobody could see her face. Except Rooney, who was panting just as hard as she was.

What the hell had just happened?

She started the truck and drove out of the alley, not sure where she was going, but going anyway.

When she could think straight again, she ran through the various people she could ask for more information about Kaylee and Julius, and she suddenly remembered Valdeccio, the Hyde chauffeur. Roxy checked her watch. In another hour, any self-respecting resident of her old neighborhood would be coming home from morning mass to make breakfast.

Or they'd be assembling in one other place.

She parked at the back door of the St. Dom's bingo hall and saw the haze of cigarette smoke already wafting out the open door. Leaving Rooney in the truck, she went inside to the clatter of the numbers tumbling in the cage and the patter of Archie Marone, who'd been calling the bingo numbers for as long as Roxy could remember.

Sister Margaret Ann sat upright in a chair by the door, sound asleep with her hands folded on her lap. Roxy remembered Sister Meg as the nun who terrorized kids to give pennies for lepers. She'd probably been the cause of more nightmares than any other human being in the city.

Spread out in rows of tables, neighborhood early birds guarded their bingo cards, good luck charms, and arrays of neon Bingo Daubers. They listened attentively to Archie, scanning their cards and marking off the numbers he called. The moratorium on smoking must have been lifted, because the whole hall stunk of cigarettes.

Hanging around the back of the room were the designated drivers—all family members waiting for the game to end so they could drive home Nonna or Aunt Pixie or Uncle Toots for lunch.

Among the waiting drivers, Roxy located Louis Valdeccio, leaning against the wall and passing time by drinking coffee and listlessly leafing through the morning edition of the newspaper. His mother was a bingo fanatic. Lucky guess that he'd be the one to take her home after the game.

"Louie, right?" Roxy said. "Valentino's uncle?"

Valdeccio crumpled the paper when he caught sight of Roxy standing in front of him. Unlike his nephew, the salon owner, Valdeccio had shaggy hair and a big gut cinched by a belt that looked as if it might give out any second. His breath smelled of cigarettes. But his face lit up at the sight of Roxy's chest. He didn't bother looking up from there. "Yeah, who's asking?"

"I'm Roxy Abruzzo. Carmine's niece."

Now and then, Roxy made good use of her family connection. It worked this time. Valdeccio straightened up like she'd mentioned the Pope or Frank Sinatra. He squinted into her face, maybe looking for a family resemblance. "Yeah?"

"Got a minute?"

"For Carmine, I got as long as it takes."

Sister Margaret Ann woke up, put one finger to her lips. "*Shh!*"

Roxy jerked her head toward the door. "Let's go outside."

Valdeccio tossed the remains of his coffee in a trash can and followed. In the alley, Roxy said, "I hear you worked for Julius Hyde."

"For ten years, yeah." He frowned, trying to figure out how his employment record might interest Carmine Abruzzo. "Why?"

"You were there the night he died?"

"I left a little while before he got shot. I told the police the whole story."

"The whole story?"

Disconcerted, he peered at her. "Look, why you asking me about that?"

Roxy shrugged. "You know. Carmine likes to stay informed."

"He knows about me?" Valdeccio perked up. "I heard he's sick. Maybe he needs a driver?"

"You never know. Tell me about what happened to Julius."

Valdeccio was with her then, trying to impress. Sucking in his gut and puffing out his chest, he said, "Yeah, I talked to Mr. Hyde a half hour before he died. We bitched about the homeless guy digging through the trash again. I chased him off, but he always came back, and that was annoying."

"Is that who killed Julius?"

Head shake. "I doubt it. Somebody else must've done it. I figure—well, it doesn't matter."

"No, tell me. What do you think happened?"

"I can't be sure. But there was always something going on in the family—you know, about money. Mr. Hyde told me about his mother's will getting changed. That he'd made a deal with somebody to make adjustments. That's what he called it—adjustments."

"How'd he do that?"

He lit a cigarette with a big Zippo lighter, maybe buying himself enough time to formulate the right answer. "I'm not sure. I heard him on the phone a few times when I was driving him around. He liked to bitch, but he didn't tell me everything."

"But you could piece things together?"

"Yeah, okay." He blew a cloud of cigarette smoke. "Sounded to me like he was paying off somebody to make adjustments in his mother's affairs."

"A lawyer, you mean?"

"Who else?"

"Without his mother knowing?"

"She was in a coma. How's she supposed to know anything?"

Roxy tried to get her brain around what she was hearing. "He paid a lawyer to change her will while she was in the coma. For a lot of money?"

He spread his hands in the gesture of I'm empty. "I got the impression they didn't want to use money. It was a trade. Mr. Hyde was giving away a statue. At least, that's what I think—"

"Wait. A statue?"

"Yeah, he promised the guy he'd give him something real valuable, but not cash that could be traced or anything."

"Did you tell this to the cops?"

Valdeccio smiled. "Hey, is it their business? I was loyal to the family, you know? I thought maybe one of the brothers might hire me—Quentin or Trey. But they cut me loose yesterday. Said they don't need me anymore. So do I owe them any loyalty now?"

"Depends on how you look at it," Roxy murmured, still thinking about Hyde lawyers. And being paid with a statue that hadn't been on the property, maybe, when Julius expected to give it away.

"Say, I didn't mean I couldn't be loyal to the family." Valdeccio looked anxious. "I can keep my mouth shut. Ask anybody. I never said a word about Mr. Hyde or his business. You tell Carmine if he needs somebody, I'm his man."

"I'll put in a good word."

She turned and walked away. Had Julius intended to give the statue to somebody the night he died?

"Call me," Valdeccio said after her. "Tell Carmine I'm in the book."

She waved and climbed into her truck. She grabbed the steering wheel with both hands to stop their trembling. She knew who'd killed Julius. And probably Kaylee, too.

❄ 27 ❄

Henry played a around of golf in the morning because his regular foursome had a standing 8 a.m. tee time. He won seventy-five dollars, which meant he had to buy the beer and burgers in the clubhouse afterward. Lunch was a pleasant, joshing meal with a rehash of the morning's shots. After shaking hands with everyone, he picked a lollipop from the bowl on the bar and strolled out to the parking lot.

Back at Hilltop, he found a roll of duct tape in the barn and an X-acto knife in the garage, which saved him from having to buy them new in a store with video cameras. He pulled a length of nylon rope from a peg on the garage wall, and then he put all his supplies in the trunk of his car. He drove into the city listening to jazz on a public radio station.

In Pittsburgh, he congratulated himself for getting lost only once before locating the car rental agency. He left his own car in a student parking lot and walked in the sunshine several blocks to rent an anonymous white cargo van. He drove it back to the parking lot to collect his supplies from the trunk of his car.

At the appointed time, he drove to meet Arden at her father's house. Obediently, she had Samson on a leash.

"Be nice to him," was all Arden had to say. She wore sunglasses, but Henry had a feeling she was crying. Either that, or she'd had so much cocaine that her nasal passages were shot.

By the end of the school day, Henry was parked along a city street watching a parade of schoolgirls in plaid skirts and kneesocks. It was impossible to pick out one from the crowd, so he followed the students for a couple of blocks, pulled ahead, and parked. Then he snapped a leash on Samson and took the dog for a walk.

He dropped a package in a trash can on the corner, then crossed the street.

Within half a minute, Sage Abruzzo found him, because who could miss a giant black and white Great Dane?

"Hey!" she called, dashing across the street to them. "Is that Samson?"

Henry smiled, friendly but not effusive. "It is. How did you know?"

Sage had been walking with a friend, another tall girl who hugged a book to her chest and hung back while Sage cuddled the dog's head. Samson was happy to see her. His tail whipped as he playfully accepted Sage's attention.

All according to plan. Henry wasn't too worried about his own appearance. He'd dressed himself in jeans and a gray Steelers sweatshirt with a ball cap over his hair. With sunglasses and ordinary sneakers, he looked like a thousand other men in a neighborhood full of grad students, college professors, and hospital employees. Besides, who was going to notice him? All attention was on the dog.

Sage was on one knee, hugging Samson. She tipped her face up to Henry. "We met Arden yesterday. She had Samson with her. Are you her husband, or something?"

Henry smiled, not too friendly. "Or something. I'm taking the dog back to her now."

Sage gave the dog one last pat. "Okay. Tell her Sage says hi."

"Will do."

Henry gave Samson's leash a tug and turned away. He walked a few paces before wheeling around again. He called, "Are you Sage Abruzzo?"

Both girls turned.

Sage said, "Yeah, that's me."

"Arden mentioned you at lunch today. She has some information for you."

Sage headed back in Henry's direction. "Oh? What is it?"

He could see the other girl had places to go. She murmured something to Sage, leaning the opposite way with some urgency.

Henry said, "I'm headed over to Arden's office now. Want to walk with me?"

The other girl spoke again. Sage said something over her shoulder and waved good-bye. The other girl didn't hesitate and walked away, which saved Henry the business of getting rid of her.

Sage came loping back to Henry. "Miracle of miracles, we don't have basketball practice today. So I have time to see Arden."

"Great," Henry said. "This way. If you don't mind Samson taking a detour now and then. When he really decides he wants to go somewhere, I have to agree."

Sage laughed easily. "He's a nice dog."

Sage looked a lot like her mother—tall and shapely, but athletic. She had a purposeful, confident stride, but her backpack was heavy, which was a lucky break.

Sage began to make conversation, but Henry wasn't listening. For a moment, he feared the diversionary part of his plan had failed.

But suddenly from behind them came a bang. Then a string of explosions—*pop! Pop! Pop-pop-pop! Pop-pop!*

On instinct, they both turned around. Smoke was billowing out of the trash can two blocks back. Some girls who had lingered nearer the school scattered like frightened birds. One dashed out into the street, causing a car to shriek to a stop. Another girl had started to run, but fell headlong on the sidewalk. Other kids saw her fall, and the screaming began.

Samson hid behind Henry's legs, whimpering.

"Oh my God," Sage said.

Henry took her elbow. "Stay back."

"What's happening?"

"Were those gunshots?"

"Oh, my God!" Her voice went higher, louder.

"Did you see what happened?"

"No— We should call the police!"

"I didn't see what happened. Did you? Look, those girls are already dialing."

"OhmyGod, ohmyGod—"

"Take it easy," Henry said. He let the dog wrap his leash around Sage. "You're okay. We should go, find someplace safe."

She turned to him, big eyes wide. "Maybe we can help."

"We didn't see what happened. We'll only contribute to the chaos. The police will be here any minute."

Chaos was breaking out for real. He couldn't have choreographed it better. Children crying, people running in all directions. The firecrackers were quiet now, but trash in the can had caught fire, and smoke frothed out into the air. Sage was babbling.

He steered her gently into the front seat of the cargo van.

He had time to put Samson in the back. He walked around the vehicle and got into the driver's seat. He closed the door and pressed the lock button. Sage was struggling out of her backpack, off balance and still babbling and distracted. He pulled the set of handcuffs from his pocket and clapped one steel cuff down on her slender wrist, the other around the bar beside the parking brake. He was quick. He had practiced. Sage whipped her face around to him, her mouth opening in surprise.

He had a handkerchief ready. A clean one. He wasn't a barbarian. It went into her mouth.

Her other hand was entangled in the straps of her backpack, so he made a clumsy business of grabbing it and wrestling with her.

By then, Sage had figured out she was in trouble.

Unfortunately, she didn't react as he'd assumed.

She began to scream behind the handkerchief. She thrashed her arm. And kicked. Her legs were too long to get much momentum, but she was strong. And determined. In seconds, she was curled on her back, kicking fiercely at the windshield with her heavy shoes. She arched her back and flung her body hard against the handcuffs. As he duct-taped her wrists together, she began to bang her head on the passenger window. The dog gave a muffled bark.

The cargo van had smoked windows, though. That was some reassurance. Nobody would be paying attention—not with the scene going on around the trash can.

And Henry was prepared. He slapped her only once across the face. The blow startled her long enough for him to use the nylon rope to lasso her legs. Seconds later he used more duct tape—already cut in lengths and waiting on the dashboard—to subdue her.

The last piece of duct tape went across her mouth.

In less than a minute, Henry was driving the van with Sage Abruzzo somewhat contained on the seat beside him. The dog quieted. He drove sensibly and passed the arriving police cars going the opposite direction. In the rearview mirror, nobody pointed at the white cargo van. Nobody had noticed their departure.

Also in the rearview mirror, Henry was surprised to discover his face was bleeding. Somehow, he'd sustained a scratch down his cheek. The blood welled up in the wound. He touched it, and his fingers came away smeared.

He took another moment to assess himself further. His heartbeat had already returned to normal. He had a bruise on the underside of his forearm, probably from a kick. There was a slight ringing in his ears. Otherwise, he felt fine. Elated, perhaps.

He glanced over to check on her. Sage glared at him from above the duct tape. She had tears on her face, but not from fear.

She was partially crouched on the floor, out of sight of passing traffic, with both elbows on the seat to hold her balance. She looked a little like an animal preparing to attack, but he knew she couldn't break the handcuffs. Her breath came in harsh bursts through her nose. The tape across her mouth was badly applied. He reached to smooth it properly, but she reared away from him, making a guttural noise in her throat. She had already figured out how not to choke on his handkerchief.

On the seat, a little electronic tune played inside Sage's backpack. Probably her cell phone.

"We'll get that later," Henry said to her.

Sage's phone rang several times. Either she had a lot of friends or her mother was already missing her.

As evening approached, Henry parked the van in the far corner of a suburban big box store's lot. An anonymous sort of place where a plain van wouldn't get much notice.

"Don't touch anything," he said to Sage in a conversational tone.

There seemed little point in adding a further threat.

He got out of the vehicle and stepped away from it to make the phone call. He kept watch on Sage through the open door. Her furious glare stayed fastened on him the whole time.

Henry used the first of several cell phones he'd purchased for the day's purpose. Roxy Abruzzo picked up on the second ring.

Henry said, "Miss Abruzzo?"

She said, "I've been hoping you'd call. How'd you get my number?"

"It's printed on the side of your truck."

Her laugh was easy. "You're pretty clever, Paxton. Can we get together?"

"You have something to discuss? So do I."

"Oh, yeah? What's up?"

"You first," he said genially.

"You heard about Kaylee Falcone, I suppose?"

"Yes, unfortunately. Poor girl."

"I just talked to a friend of mine with the police. The ballistics reports are back. Kaylee Falcone was shot with the same gun that killed Julius. With .45-caliber bullets, from a revolver. Maybe an older model like a Colt Peacemaker."

"Oh?"

"And funny thing. Trey Hyde mentioned to me that some relative of his collected older guns at their estate. Hilltop, I think he called it. Isn't that where you live?"

"I sincerely hope you haven't discussed this train of thought with the police."

"Not yet," she said.

"That's a relief," Henry replied. "Because I have something of yours, and I'd hate for something terrible to happen to her."

Roxy was silent.

Henry waited for her to grasp the situation. "Do you believe me?"

Roxy finally said, "She wouldn't be that stupid."

"She wasn't stupid at all. It was a bit of a trick, you see. And you'll be very proud of her. She fought like an Amazon."

"I don't believe you," Roxy said, her voice harsh.

"No? I'll call you back."

Henry disconnected the call and returned to the minivan. He leaned in, pulled Sage's backpack onto the driver's seat, and rummaged around inside until he came up with her cell phone. He dialed her mother's number.

Roxy picked up immediately. "Sage?"

"It's me," Henry said. "And here's what I'd like you to do, Roxy."

❋ 28 ❋

Roxy closed her cell phone and forced herself to breathe. She was standing out in the yard beside her truck. Inside, out of earshot, Bug Duffy was still sitting on the leather couch in her office. He watched her through the window, so Roxy hastily rearranged her face to resemble something like calm. In a minute's time, she pulled herself together sufficiently to go back inside.

"Sorry." She closed the door and pocketed her phone. "Business."

"Must be funny business," Bug said. "You look white as a sheet."

"Bad lighting. It's the only thing standing between me and a career as a supermodel." She sat down at her desk before her knees gave out. "What were we talking about?"

"The Delaney brothers."

"Right. They've disappeared?"

"For the moment. But they'll turn up again. They're definitely bad pennies."

"Any idea where they are?"

Bug squinted at her. "You sure you're okay?"

Roxy took a long, slow breath to keep herself from screaming. Sage was gone. Sage had been kidnapped. By Henry Paxton. Who'd killed two people already. She was sure of it. But to tell Bug now meant Sage's certain death.

"I'm fine." She looked at her watch, trying to do the math Henry Paxton had given her.

Bug said, "Do you have an appointment?"

She forced her voice to be steady. "I've got things to do. But I don't want to rush you. You guys need to catch whoever killed Kaylee."

"And Julius Hyde."

"Him, too."

"Okay." Bug got to his feet and reached for his cane. "I think we're done for now. If you hear anything or think of anything else, call me, right?"

"Right."

They went outside into the yard, where a city tow truck was winching Kaylee Falcone's car up onto the flatbed. Watching, Roxy thought her heart was going to explode. She said good-bye to Bug, but a minute later she couldn't remember what she'd said.

Sage was with Henry Paxton. He said he'd kill her if Roxy brought the police.

Roxy stumbled back into her office. She sat down on her swivel chair and put her head between her knees. She tried to think. Her brain felt like a red light spinning on top of a fire truck.

A minute later, Nooch shuffled into the office. "I wish the police would stop coming around here. They make me nervous. Whatcha doin'?"

Roxy sat up. "I need your help."

Nooch was eating a sandwich with the wrapping still half on it. Mouth full, he said, "I'm supposed to take Nonna to the doctor this afternoon."

"She may have to go alone."

"That's okay by me. You should hear her coughing. Someday she is going to cough up a lung, and it's going to lay there on the floor of the grocery story until somebody comes along and sweeps it up."

Roxy got up and checked the window. Bug was leaving, followed by the tow truck. Roxy grabbed her keys. "Let's go."

Rooney jumped into the truck with them.

At the restaurant, the prep staff was boiling bones and chopping vegetables while listening to the Rolling Stones. Flynn must have decided to sleep through until the dinner service, because he didn't appear while Roxy and Nooch pulled the statue out of the refrigerator and chained it to a handcart. Nobody asked any questions as they wheeled the statue out the back door and winched it onto the truck. Within a few minutes, they had it lashed securely and climbed back into the truck.

Roxy turned to Nooch. "Okay, listen. I'm going to drop you off at Loretta's house for a couple of hours."

Nooch was startled. "Huh? Why?"

"I need to do something on my own."

"Why can't I come?"

"Because I have to go alone. It's important."

Nooch looked curiously into her face. "What's going on?"

"I can't tell you. Believe me, I wish I could. But, look, I might need your help later. I want you to stay by the phone, okay? I'm going to call, one way or another."

"One way or another?"

"Never mind. Just don't let me down."

He looked wounded. "Have I ever let you down?"

Roxy couldn't help smiling. She patted his shoulder. "No, I guess you haven't. I need you to keep Rooney for me, too, okay? I can't take him with me tonight. Watch TV until Loretta gets home."

"He doesn't like me," Nooch said. "Loretta doesn't, either."

"Just don't put your feet on her furniture, and maybe she'll feed you dinner when she gets home."

"Okay. Rox? Is this about my hearing?"

His probation hearing. It was scheduled for tomorrow. Roxy slammed her hand against the steering wheel.

"What's wrong?"

"Nothing. I—I'll take care of that, too."

"I know you will," Nooch said, trusting her.

Making her feel like a heel.

When they reached Loretta's house, Nooch went happily inside. Rooney stood on the porch for a second, casting a puzzled look at Roxy. He'd be more help than Nooch in a crisis, but Henry had specifically told Roxy not to bring her dog. Or the police. Or anybody else who didn't want to get killed. With regret, she drove away.

An hour later, her cell phone rang.

In her ear, Henry Paxton said, "Are you ready?"

"Yes. Where do you want me?"

He gave her an address and hung up.

❊ 29 ❊

It was nighttime by the time Roxy reached the deserted steel mill. Years ago, it would have been the lifeblood of the neighborhood, but tonight even the nearby traffic had thinned out. She drove down a deserted industrial block to the entrance of the mill.

Across the street sat Bradshaw's—a bar that had once catered to steelworkers who stopped for boilermakers after their shift. Now it attracted a rough crowd. Neon signs glowed in windows that hadn't been washed in years. A couple of tough-looking patrons hung outside the front door, smoking. Nobody waved at Roxy.

A substantial chain-link fence—probably twenty feet high and topped with razor wire—surrounded the old steel mill. But, as promised, the rear gate was unlocked. Someone had snapped the chain with bolt cutters. Roxy had to get out of the truck to open it, then drove through and went back to close the gate again. Slowly, she drove around to the back of the main building, over the old railroad tracks used to haul steel long ago.

The grit of many years of abandonment crunched under her tires. In the distance, she could make out the shapes of the powerhouse and other, low-roofed outbuildings.

Out back behind the mill, it was very dark and the loading docks were empty. When she climbed down from the driver's seat, Roxy could smell the river close by. A cold breeze hissed in the bushes that grew up the fence. Two long concrete ramps slanted down to the docks where raw materials had once come by barge up the river.

Across the river, a locomotive hurtled by, pulling a long train of coal cars northward toward power plants that still burned coal. Closer on the water, the lights of a small craft motored up the river in the direction of the lock and dam. When the train had passed, the night was quiet. Only the thin strains of jukebox music from Bradshaw's broke the stillness.

Roxy put the prybar on the floor of the front seat where she could grab it in a heartbeat, then locked the truck and left it. She vaulted onto the concrete ramp and walked up to the loading dock. One of the four big garage doors stood open. She went under it and into the long, yawning space of the old mill. The place was dark, mostly in shadow. The equipment and machinery had long since been removed. The blast furnace had been disassembled and probably shipped to Korea. Long ago, someone had carefully swept up the giant factory, perhaps hoping it would some-day open again and put a thousand men back to work.

But before her tonight, the cold building stood empty. It ran longer than several football fields, with not a single electrical light to illuminate the space. High above, the roof opened to the sky.

With a nearly silent flutter of wings, a flock of bats suddenly whirred across the open air and disappeared into darkness.

About fifty feet ahead, a gleaming white cargo van sat in the middle of the concrete floor. On top of it was a small torpedo-shaped luggage container.

"Paxton?" Roxy called. Her voice echoed back at her, sending a shiver up the back of her neck.

No answer.

She began walking cautiously toward the van. One door hung open. Then, with a sudden burst of hope, she quickened her pace—then sprinted toward the vehicle.

"Sage!"

But the van was empty. Roxy caught her balance on the door and choked back the lump in her throat. The smell of gasoline was strong around the vehicle. It had been gassed up for a trip, she guessed. Maybe he'd spilled some of the fuel down the side of the van, too.

A long way down the floor, a dark figure suddenly moved out of shadow and into Roxy's peripheral view. She spun sideways.

"Paxton," she said, her voice carrying easily. "Where's my daughter?"

Henry was leading a large dog on a leash. A Great Dane with ludicrous black and white spots. The dog pranced happily alongside Henry, as if on parade at Madison Square Garden.

"Hello, Roxy." Henry sounded pleasant. "Thanks for coming. You followed all my rules?"

"I'm alone."

"And the Achilles?"

She shook her head. "First I want to see my daughter."

"She's fine. Trust me."

Roxy let that absurd remark hang in the cold air as Henry walked closer with the Great Dane.

She said, "I didn't take you for a dog person."

"He's not mine," Henry assured her. "I was going to return him to his rightful owner this evening and reap my reward, but things seem to have gotten out of hand. Maybe I'll just turn him loose on a highway and hope he has the brains to get himself home. Dogs can do that, right?"

He stopped about ten feet away. The Great Dane strained forward on his leash to sniff Roxy. His tail was high and wagging. His tongue hung out, giving his face a goofy smile.

Roxy must have tightened her hands into fists, because Henry said, "Now, now. Do I have to show you this?"

He lifted the edge of his sweatshirt to show the butt of a handgun. The revolver was tucked into his belt.

Roxy forced herself to relax her hands. "Where's my daughter?"

"You'll see her in good time. First we have business to transact."

"Forget that. I know what you're capable of, Paxton. So I want to see Sage, or you won't get the statue."

He shook his head, smiling a little. "It doesn't work that way, I'm afraid."

"Okay, then, where's your crew?"

"My crew?"

"You can't move this thing by yourself. It's very heavy. It probably weighs at least a ton. You'll need help."

"I very much doubt that."

Roxy shrugged. "See for yourself. It's outside."

Henry considered her information for a moment, as if finally realizing she might be speaking the truth. Then he said, "Let's take a look, shall we?"

Roxy led the way, listening to Henry and the dog behind her. The dog leaped around on the ramp, happy to be outside. When they reached the back of the truck, Roxy tugged aside one edge of the tarp to show the large sandaled foot of the statue.

"See? He's seven feet tall, made of solid marble. The two of us couldn't get him into your van if we worked all night."

Henry began to frown. He reached up and put one hand on the statue's foot. He gave it a shove, but the dead weight didn't budge. "How did you get it up there?"

"The winch." She pointed. "Plus I had help. I can winch it down to the ground, but after that, we're on our own."

Henry contemplated the problem. Finally, he said, "You planned this, didn't you?"

"I did what you told me to do. I can't help it if you're unprepared."

"I'm not leaving without the Achilles."

"And I'm not leaving without my daughter."

"So," Henry said at last, "what do you suggest?"

"We need help. If you don't have a weightlifter on speed dial, I could call the guy who works for me."

Music from the bar across the street wailed while Henry considered her proposition. "Can he keep his mouth shut?"

"He's trustworthy."

Henry made his decision. "Okay, call him. But the same rules apply."

The amiable dog came over and nuzzled Roxy's hand. She patted his neck without thinking. But she shook her head. "I'm not going to help you, Paxton. Not until you show me Sage. I want to know she's all right."

"She's fine."

"No. I'll make a trade with you now. Show me Sage, and I'll get you some muscle."

Henry walked away from the truck to think. The big dog resisted going with him—he wanted to stay with Roxy—but Henry yanked the leash. The dog dug his forepaws into the gravel. Henry stopped short, his arm pulled tight. He let fly a curse and dropped the leash. Startled to find himself free, the dog shook his entire body as if shaking off bathwater and then galumphed around in a circle.

Roxy ignored the dog and trained her gaze on Henry. "I'll keep my side of this bargain, Paxton. You can have the statue. It's brought me nothing but bad luck since I first put my hands on it. But I want Sage. I want to see her now, and then I'll call my guy to help load."

Henry said, "If you think you can double-cross me, you'd better think again. I've got years of strategizing under my belt, you know."

Through gritted teeth, Roxy said, "I believe you. I don't care about the statue now. Just give me my kid."

Henry shrugged. "Okay. This way."

He led her back into the cavernous mill, and they walked past the cargo van, across the vast floor. The place was very cold—somehow colder than outside. The air of abandonment made Roxy's teeth chatter. She clamped her jaw tight, though, determined not to let Henry guess how truly terrified she was.

Henry led the way to the farthest corner of the building, where some office space had been created with corrugated walls and heavy glass windows. Someone had tried to smash one window, but it hadn't shattered. A starburst of cracks emanated from a center. When Roxy looked closer, she saw it was a bullet hole in the glass.

Henry pushed the unlocked door open and stopped. "Watch your step. There's some junk on the floor."

It was very dark. Underfoot, Roxy accidentally kicked a clutter of scattered textbooks, open pages fluttering. Pencils and a torn notebook lay in a circle, as if Sage's backpack had been upended and shaken out. The sight of it brought a hot rush up from Roxy's heart.

They were in some kind of supervisor's office with a set of iron spiral stairs that led upward. Henry went over to the stairs, bowed slightly, and said, "After you."

Roxy grabbed the hand railing and started up. She itched to kick Henry's head. Maybe knock him to the floor below. Maybe she could overpower him, she thought. She longed to beat the shit out of him.

But there was Sage still to consider. Roxy felt her way up the stairs, straining to see in the darkness.

On the second floor she found herself in a kind of viewing room with a huge plate-glass window that overlooked the mill floor.

She glanced around the small space. "Where is she?"

Henry pointed. "Bathroom."

Roxy darted forward, pushing her way through a narrow door. On the floor, huddled in darkness, lay a lumpy shape.

"Sage," Roxy whispered, and she flung herself down next to her daughter.

Sage struggled up, and the gleam in her eyes was fierce. She made an awful noise in her throat, and Roxy reached to remove the tape from her mouth.

But Sage yanked her face away and shook her head, tears springing to her eyes. The tape had been partially torn from her cheek already, and Roxy could see her skin had torn with it.

"Oh, baby." Roxy cupped Sage's cheek. "Are you okay? Did he hurt you?"

Sage nodded fiercely, then shook her head, then tried to laugh. But she began to choke, too, and Roxy calmed her with hands on her shoulders. "It's okay," she soothed. "Don't try to talk. We'll be out of here in a minute, I promise."

Sage nodded, but her gaze left Roxy's face to look over her shoulder, and her eyes hardened.

Still on her knees on the cold concrete, Roxy turned to Henry. "Honest to God, Paxton, if you've hurt her, I'm going to kill you dead."

He smiled. "No need for that. You can see she's perfectly fine."

"I'm taking her out of here now."

"Let's wait until—"

"No, we're going now."

"Make your call first. Do you have your phone?"

Roxy whipped her phone from her jeans and punched Loretta's number.

Henry said, "Put it on speaker, so we can all hear what you're saying."

Holding Sage upright with one arm, Roxy put the phone to her ear with the other hand. She prayed Nooch would answer.

It was Loretta who picked up right away.

"Lo," Roxy said, "I need to speak to Nooch."

"He's eating me out of house and home!" Loretta cried. "The sooner you get him out of here, the less chance I'll kill him."

"I need to talk to him right away, Loretta. It's important."

"All right, all right. But you owe me for an entire pan of stuffed shells."

Nooch's voice came next. Amiable, as always. "Hi, Rox."

"I need you to borrow Loretta's car."

"Huh?"

"Tell Loretta you need to borrow her car," Roxy said curtly. She kept her eyes on Henry's face as she spoke. She gave the rest of her orders directly, listing Henry's rules. "Do you understand, Nooch?"

"Yeah," he said, but he still sounded confused. "You want me to come tonight?"

"Right now," Roxy said. "Right away."

Henry put his hand on the handle of the gun in his belt. "Hang up."

Roxy obeyed, praying that Nooch had got the message straight. She pocketed her phone and helped Sage to her feet.

Henry didn't protest. But he didn't make any move to assist, either. Roxy hoisted Sage upright before she realized the teenager's ankles were taped together. Her hands were cuffed behind her back, too. It was a struggle for Sage to move at all—she could hardly shuffle her feet—but she was determined.

Roxy could feel her daughter shuddering with cold, too, so she buffed her arms and roughly rubbed her back as they stumbled toward the spiral stairs. Roxy went first, essentially dragging Sage downward.

On the main floor of the mill, the Great Dane came loping out of the darkness, delighted to see Sage. He jumped up on her, and all of them nearly fell to the concrete floor. Roxy shoved the clumsy dog away and headed for the cargo van, half dragging Sage with her.

When they reached the van, Sage was breathing heavily through her nose. Frightened by how labored her daughter sounded, Roxy sat her down in the open door and tried to loosen the tape around her mouth. Sage cried out, but held still so Roxy could continue. Roxy winced each time a tiny bit of tape came free. But for Sage, the pain must have been intense. Tears rolled down her cheek and she kept her eyes squeezed tightly shut, but she didn't protest.

Behind them, Henry said, "How long will it take for your associate to arrive?"

"Fifteen minutes," Roxy guessed. "Maybe half an hour."

"And you guarantee he won't be bringing the police?"

She shook her head. "You heard everything. He's on probation, see. If he gets caught committing any kind of crime, he'll go to jail. I'm trying to keep him out of trouble. We don't want the cops involved."

"Convenient for me," Henry remarked. "What's he on probation for?"

"Assault. But it was a long time ago."

Roxy had worked half of the tape free and then slipped her finger into Sage's mouth. Out came a sodden hunk of cloth. Sage sucked air gratefully and leaned against the open door of the van as if exhausted. She pulled a grimace at the stench of gasoline still hanging around the vehicle.

A heavy quilted blanket lay on the floor of the van—the kind of blanket movers used to wrap furniture. Roxy grabbed it and bundled it around Sage as best she could manage. Then she set to work on freeing Sage's ankles.

Sage's voice was barely a croak. "Good news, Mom."

Roxy's heart nearly overflowed. Trust Sage to find the silver lining in the middle of a kidnapping. "Oh, yeah? What's that?"

"I got my period."

Roxy's first reaction, oddly enough, was disappointment. Then, seeing the relief in Sage's battered face, she hugged her daughter.

"That's enough of that," Henry said. "She's comfortable enough for the moment. Let's you and me start to get the Achilles off your truck. I want to get out of here."

Roxy hardened her heart and stood back from Sage. "In a rush all of a sudden?"

"Things haven't exactly gone according to plan," Henry conceded.

"Ever since you killed Kaylee, you mean?"

Henry didn't answer, but he narrowed his eyes. Sage sat very still, listening.

Henry jerked his head. "Let's go, Roxy."

She hated leaving Sage behind. But she obeyed and walked with Henry back to the loading dock.

Out of Sage's earshot, Roxy said, "I assume you killed Kaylee because you figured out she saw you shoot Julius."

Henry laughed. "She tried to blackmail me. Did she tell you that? I don't know why she bothered. There was a good chance she might actually have inherited this property. It's going to be quite valuable someday soon."

"So I've heard. What made you pull the trigger on Julius? You have some kind of disagreement?"

"He was backing out on a promise," Henry admitted, after only a heartbeat of hesitation. "We presumed his mother was in her final coma, so I revised her will one last time—in his favor so he could whisk his girl-friend off on a midlife crisis that even Hugh Hefner would envy. You don't need to hear the legal details. I was supposed to receive the Achilles in payment for my services. Imagine my dismay when I went to collect and Julius had chickened out and changed his mind."

"And the statue was gone," Roxy said.

"Exactly. He backed out on our deal, and I was left hanging to take the blame for tampering with my client's legal affairs. I couldn't let him ruin my career. And I must admit, I lost my temper."

"Did the Delaneys see you shoot him?"

"How did you guess?"

"I knew they were lying when they said Julius hired them to frighten Kaylee. And why would they make up such a stupid lie? Unless you were standing right there, holding a gun on them?"

"They weren't very imaginative, I admit."

"And you paid them to keep your secret?"

"Yes. Who knew I was buying a television from Walmart and feeding a snake?"

Roxy stopped at the top of the ramp. She tried to imagine the confrontation between Julius and Henry at the mansion. Julius had seemed upset. He probably knew he was going to argue with Henry. And when Henry came along to discuss the financial matters, Julius had to break the bad news that their self-serving plot was off. The fact that Roxy had stolen the statue at exactly the wrong moment had triggered Henry's reaction.

"And to think I had sex with you," Roxy said.

"An unexpected bonus for me," Henry replied.

"You're in some trouble now, Paxton. And I'm not talking about premature ejaculation."

He let the insult pass. "Things are unraveling a bit, aren't they? Fortunately, I have a place to go to in the Caribbean."

"You think you can ship the statue there?"

"No, no. I have a place to store it for a while first. Eventually, I'll make arrangements to sell the statue. I do have some connections."

"You mean Arden Hyde?"

Henry laughed. "Heavens, no. Arden can barely tie her own shoes. I had hoped to pin some blame on her, but I've run out of time, haven't I?"

"The police are going to figure out where the gun came from."

"I'll be out of town before that happens. And I've saved up a perfectly respectable nest egg, so I can live comfortably until the time is right to put the statue on the market. Shall we?"

Roxy went down the ramp to the truck. With Paxton watching, she unstrapped the handcart and unhooked the winch. The chain rattled down with a noise that echoed back at them from the high walls of the abandoned mill.

Henry said, "I'm almost sorry things had to end this way between us, Roxy."

She continued to ready her equipment. "Oh, yeah?"

"I suppose it's a cliché to say we could have made some beautiful Caribbean music together. I like you. And I'll admit I'm attracted to you, too."

"Despite the chip on my shoulder?"

He smiled. "That's part of your charm, I suppose."

She glanced at him. "There's still time, you know."

His face registered surprise. "Time to make a little whoopee? With your daughter watching?"

"My truck's right here. There's plenty of room inside. And you owe me. I'll give you a chance to prove you're not such a rotten lover after all."

Amused, he said, "I'm tempted. I'd like to see you on your knees right now, right here. I'd like to ram myself down your throat, then come all over your face. With her watching. Forget the truck. What's in it? Some kind of weapon? You think you can overpower me before I could shoot you?"

She shrugged. "It was worth a try."

Henry laughed. "You're one tough cookie, Roxy."

"Too bad you never met my father."

"Oh?"

"But he's in jail now, probably for good."

"What did he do?"

Roxy turned around and leaned her shoulders against the truck. "He killed my mother."

Henry's interest sharpened. "How did that happen?"

The time seemed right, so Roxy said, "He beat her up for years. No matter what she did to try to please him, something always made him mad." Roxy felt surprisingly calm. "They weren't married. She was one of his girlfriends, but she always hoped he'd marry her. She was the kind of misguided woman who loves her man no matter how bad he treats her. Eventually, he killed her. I happened to see it, as a matter of fact."

Henry didn't respond. But she had his attention now, for sure. By now, the story hardly seemed real to Roxy. She had managed to block all the details out of her mind, stripped the horror down to the bare facts.

Roxy said, "I liked him. Probably loved him in a screwed-up kind of way. I know my mother loved him—maybe worshipped him, even when he made her feel worthless. So I've been with tough guys all my life, Paxton.

Men who think they can get away with anything. Men like him, and like Julius Hyde. Most of them don't scare me, because nobody else can measure up to him when it comes to evil."

"You're saying you're not afraid of me, either."

"That's right."

"That's okay," Henry said. "I only need you to respect my position a little longer. See that container on top of the van?"

He pointed toward the luggage holder on the roof of the vehicle.

Roxy felt a heavy lump grow in her gut. In the open door of the cargo van, she could also see Sage helplessly trapped. "Yeah, I see it."

"I packed it with some rags soaked in gasoline, and a small gas tank. Not too big, but enough, I think, to destroy the van and anything in it." He pulled a cell phone from his pocket. "I've rigged it with this phone. A detonator is easy to put together, did you know? The directions are online."

"Don't do it," Roxy said.

"I won't. If you continue to cooperate. I know you're a clever girl. But put all those plans to trick me out of your head, all right?"

"Okay, I promise. Just don't hurt my daughter."

At last they heard a vehicle approach on the rutted street outside the fence. A door slammed, and someone opened the gate. A moment later, a car pulled around the side of the building.

Roxy suppressed a groan.

Loretta climbed out of the driver's side of her Cadillac. Nooch emerged from the passenger seat, making excuses immediately.

He said, "I told her not to come. I said you'd be mad. But I couldn't stop her. It's not my fault."

Loretta marched around the hood of the car, preceded by her bosom. She wore a pair of jeans, high-heeled boots, and a figure-flattering sweater—casual clothes, but hardly suitable for heavy lifting. "What's going on here? Roxy, are you up to something you shouldn't be? And who's this?"

"I'm sorry," Roxy said to Henry. "She's hard to control sometimes."

Loretta stopped short before them. "You look respectable. I was afraid she was meeting some kind of criminal out here." With one look at Henry, her demeanor softened from lawyer to matchmaker. "Hello, I'm Loretta Radziewicz."

"Henry Paxton." He mustered a smile, too, shaking her hand politely. "How do you do?"

"I'm delighted to meet a colleague of Roxy's. Have you known her long?"

"Long enough," Roxy said. "Look, Loretta, we've got some business to attend to. It won't take much time, so if you'll just wait in the car while we—"

"I can help. I'm able-bodied. Just because I'm a middle-aged woman with— Oh, I should have closed my door, I suppose."

From Loretta's car burst Rooney, fast as a bullet and growling like a demon on speed.

"Rooney!" Roxy called, and the dog came to her at once. To Henry, Roxy said, "He'll obey, I swear."

"Okay," Henry said. "Just remember I've got my phone right here." He patted his pocket.

Although Nooch missed the subtleties of the situation, Loretta's sharp gaze traveled from Roxy's face to Henry, and then bounced from the truck to the cargo van inside the mill. But she said nothing. She curled her fingers around Rooney's collar.

With her heart in her throat, Roxy said, "Nooch, give us a hand."

She climbed up into the bed of the truck and guided the chain around the wrapped statue. With Nooch's grunting help, she secured the load and set about running the winch. To Henry, she said, "Just put your hand up and guide it on the way down. Don't let it bang into the truck, okay? I can't afford the body work. And you don't want any damage to your property."

Nooch clambered down and helped Henry. Together, they hefted the statue onto the handcart. Henry grunted with the effort. Roxy unraveled a length of twine and wrapped it around the statue to steady the load.

"It'll take all of us to guide the cart up the ramp," she said.

"Let's go." Henry sounded jaunty.

The cart bumped over the gravel, causing the statue to sway danger-ously. But they wrestled it back into place, panting against the extreme weight. By joint force, they made the turn to start up the ramp. Nooch pulled, Henry pushed. Roxy steadied the load from one side, balancing the weight with a firm grip on the upraised arm of the statue.

Loretta let go of Rooney and jumped up to steady the other side. "What in the world is this?"

The tarp slipped at that moment, giving her a glimpse of uncircum-cised penis. The churchgoing Catholic lady in her reared back with a shriek.

Her cry brought the Great Dane out of the brush where he'd been dig-ging. The big dog leaped up onto the ramp and dashed in their direction just as they reached the halfway point of the ramp. He jumped up on Loretta, knocking her into the statue.

"Hey," Nooch cried out. He lost his grip on the handcart's handle.

Henry braced himself against the sudden lurch of the statue. "Do something, you stupid slut."

Nooch turned. He forgot about the handcart and swung his fist at Henry's face.

"No!" Roxy cried. "Nooch, don't!"

But it was too late. The statue began to slide. Henry went down as if he'd been hit with a sledgehammer.

And Rooney suddenly launched himself onto the ramp. Snarling, he made straight for Samson. The larger dog yelped, tucked his tail, and dodged behind Henry to escape Rooney's snapping jaws.

Henry tried to get up, but lost his footing and catapulted over the Great Dane. Rooney pounced. Henry, tangled between the two dogs, cursed.

Roxy shoved her shoulder against the statue, and it righted itself. Then the cart's tires got some traction. The handcart began to slip backward down the ramp toward the river. Roxy made a lunge for the handle, but she wasn't fast enough. The cart gained momentum and hurtled downward—a ton of marble zooming down the ramp toward the rushing waters of the Allegheny.

Loretta made a last-ditch effort to catch it. She hurried down the ramp. But the statue was faster. It plunged down the last few yards of the ramp and was suddenly airborne—flying through the air, turning end over end over the glittering water like a championship diver.

For an instant, it seemed to hang suspended in the air. Roxy held her breath. But then gravity took over, and the statue hit the water with a gargantuan splash. It floated for the briefest of moments. But gradually the weight of the marble was too much. Slowly, Achilles disappeared into the river. The dark water closed over it, and the priceless statue was gone.

Roxy took no moment to mourn. She threw herself down into the dog-fight.

Henry cursed. Rooney snarled. The Great Dane yelped with terror.

Roxy shouted for Nooch, but at the same time, she wrestled Henry Paxton's arm against the concrete and tried to grab the cell phone from his pants pocket.

"Roxy!" Loretta cried, scandalized. "What on earth are you doing!"

If the chaos weren't already enough, a gunshot suddenly split the air.

Roxy found the cell phone. She yanked it from Henry's pocket and hurled it with all her strength toward the river. It arced high into the dark sky and disappeared with a distant splash.

"Police!" a voice shouted.

There was more shouting after that, and a crowd of men waving guns and issuing orders. Trouble was, the dogfight continued. Both dogs rolled in the dust, over and over, Rooney snarling and biting, the Great Dane howling. Flashlights made the fight even more of an uproar.

In the hubbub, Henry Paxton rolled clear and got to his feet. He jumped from the ramp and started running.

The lead police officer turned to Roxy. With his weapon in one hand, he pulled her to her feet. "You okay?"

It was Flynn. The men surrounding him were not cops at all, Roxy realized, but the guys from the restaurant. Carl. Dougie. Even Ray. They were dressed in their black work clothes, which made them look like a SWAT team.

"Loretta called me," he said. "Said you needed help but didn't want the police."

"Go," she said. And pointed. "Sage is in that cargo van. It's rigged with explosives. She's hurt. Go get her. Please, Flynn, make sure she's safe."

Flynn didn't hesitate. He didn't even wait for Roxy to finish telling him to be careful. He turned and ran into the steel mill. Roxy had to trust him.

Roxy took off after Henry. Without a car, he couldn't get far.

She ran. He had a block's head start. Roxy ran past Bradshaw's, and a couple of guys came out onto the street.

"What's up?"

Roxy didn't answer, because she was gaining on Henry.

She ran him down and tackled him like a freight train. It was very satisfying to smash his face into a pothole. For Kaylee. For Julius. For Sage.

In an instant, she was surrounded by men from Bradshaw's, all ready to help. One sat on Henry's legs. Another punched him in the head when he tried to get up.

She'd call for the police in a minute. First she thought she'd like to break his nose and maybe a couple of teeth before he went to jail. The guys around her didn't hold her back.

❧ 30 ❧

On a cold but brilliantly sunny afternoon in November, Fair Weather Village held an open house to celebrate its new reflection garden. The weather was so bitter, however, that all the residents of the nursing home remained indoors to eat their coconut cake from the comfort of their wheelchairs.

Except for Dorothy Richardson-Hyde.

To attend the garden's dedication, Dorothy lay in a wheeled hospital bed among the trees, wrapped in blankets. In a coma.

Roxy Abruzzo and her daughter Sage sat on the stone bench beside the motionless bed, admiring the centerpiece of the garden— —seven feet of marble statue of a Greek gentleman who had a perfect physique and a noble, distant look in his eye. The statue stood among some newly planted bushes and a pretty reflecting pool. In the spring, flowers would bloom around his feet, and songbirds would probably poop on his magnificent shoulders.

"He doesn't look as if he minded his bath in the river," Roxy said. Thinking about the arduous job of locating the statue and carefully salvaging him from the river, she said a silent thank-you to Flynn and his father. They'd risked very cold temperatures and high waters to pull the treasure from his temporary resting place. Only a few nicks in the marble hinted at the statue's short sojourn in the Allegheny. And the public had been none the wiser that the priceless antiquity even existed, let alone spent a few weeks soaking in the water.

"The river might have done him some good," Sage agreed. "He looks cleaner. But how long do you think it will take these old folks to get upset and put a loincloth on him? To cover up his shocking parts?"

"I don't know." Roxy put her face up to absorb some of the meager autumn sunlight. "From the talk at the cake cutting, some of those old biddies are still frisky. They might like to leave him the way he is."

Sage slung her arm affectionately around Roxy's shoulders. "Do you mind too much, Mom? Giving up this statue?"

"No, I don't mind. I've been broke before. Giving up the statue doesn't feel much different."

"Okay, thanks." Sage smiled. "I got to thinking about all the stuff Arden said about important art going back to the country of origin. All her talk about heritage and museums and unscrupulous collectors made me worry that—well, it's a tough decision. So Mrs. Hyde should make the choice about what happens to Achilles."

"If she wakes up."

"Yeah, there's that to consider."

They both turned to study the slack face of Dorothy Hyde. She looked peaceful. Except for a little wrinkle between her eyebrows that Roxy hadn't noticed earlier. The rest of her lay very still, wrapped like a mummy in a swaddle of warm blankets.

"If she doesn't wake up," Roxy said, "I can always come back and get him, right?"

"Mom!"

Roxy grinned and patted her daughter's leg. "What about your friend Arden? What happened to her?"

"Sad, huh? Her overdose? But I hear she's gone into rehab with her mother. That might be a good thing."

"Too bad her mother is getting divorced. The newspapers say Quentin Hyde is cutting her loose so he can marry his brother's widow."

"Monica, yes," Sage said. "I read in the newspaper they're going to Beijing for their honeymoon."

"Or to invest in cell phone towers in China. Maybe I should buy some stock in that company. It'll help pay Nooch's legal bill for a couple more years."

"Sorry his probation hearing didn't go well."

"He didn't seem to mind. He'll keep working for me."

The door to the nursing home's party room opened, and Flynn came out into the sunlight. On a Sunday afternoon, he had the day off and looked relaxed. Even a little attractive in an old-high-school-flame kinda way. He sauntered across the patio, balancing two plates of coconut cake in one hand, and Roxy wondered if it was the cake that was so appealing or maybe the way Flynn's jeans clung to his hips.

He passed a piece of cake to Sage and kept the second.

He glanced down at Dorothy Hyde. "Think the old lady might wake up and want some cake?"

"Give it to me instead," Roxy said.

But at that moment Rooney burst out from under some shrubbery and ran across the garden, intent on a rabbit that skipped ahead of him. The bunny seemed to be teasing rather than running for its life. Sage must have thought the dog might catch the rabbit, though, because she handed her cake to Roxy and took off running after the dog.

Roxy watched her run—a perfect girl with a bright future ahead of her. Without a bun in the oven.

Roxy said, "I've made some mistakes in my life, but one of the best things that's ever happened to me is Sage. I've never thanked you for that, have I? For giving her to me?"

"I don't remember any thanking, no." Flynn sat down on the bench beside her. "A lot of screaming and cursing, but no thanks. Not even for letting you be on top now and then."

"Admit it. You thought me on top meant I wouldn't get pregnant."

"Lesson learned." Darkly, Flynn added, "I hope Zack knows better."

"Thanks for pitching in on her school fees, too. I appreciate it."

"No problem."

It felt a little odd to be sitting there, talking calmly to Patrick Flynn after so many years. Oddly comfortable, yet with a tingle of uncertainty, too. He wasn't like her father, Roxy reminded herself. Or Uncle Carmine. No, Flynn had almost become the kind of man a sensible woman might be glad to have around.

Too bad Roxy wasn't sensible.

She said, "I appreciate the other thing you did, to help get Sage safe."

"It's the kind of thing I do best—mayhem with guns."

"It's not the only thing you do well."

He glanced down at her, brows raised. "What are you saying?"

"You can cook. You make a decent cup of coffee. You've grown up into somebody I don't mind associating with my daughter."

"What about associating with you?"

"Forget it. You've got a girlfriend. And I keep myself busy."

"Yeah, I know. Too busy. You're working for Carmine, I hear. And God knows what else you're up to. Probably stealing more statues."

Sage returned with Rooney in tow, her face flushed and happy. She grabbed her plate and began to eat cake. "What are you talking about? Stealing this statue all over again?"

Flynn laughed. "I think that's exactly what she's thinking about!"

Beside them on her bed, Dorothy Hyde popped one eye open. In a clear voice, she said, "Over my dead body."